TOUCH OF FIRE

Quinn stuck his hand under my nose, his thumb and forefinger pressed so closely together I could barely see daylight between them. "See that there, S'rena?" he said in a bitter tone. "That's how much family feeling I got from these folks." As his hand descended, he grabbed my wrist cruelly, bringing tears to my eyes. "You think tears in those pretty eyes are going to get you anything?" He paused. "You don't know about the gold, do you?"

"Gold? What gold?"

"Time's running out," he said. "Just how many things am I supposed to believe you don't know about?"

"I know all about you," I cried.

He smiled. "Oh, not quite all," he murmured. His approach was so slow, his smile so lazy, that I had no hint of his intention until he reached out and pulled me close.

I'd been warned many times of the weakness of the spirit in the body's thrall; alarmed, I struggled to heed a warning I had never thought would apply to me . . . but it was too late. The heat of his lips persuaded a willing response to their urgent demand as I allowed my aroused senses to whirl my remaining misgivings into oblivion. . . .

JOYCE C. WARE

DARKNESS AT MORNING STAR

ZEBRA BOOKS
KENSINGTON PUBLISHING CORP.

To Joanie, Rosie and the members
of the Connecticut Chapter of RWA:
old friends, new friends, valued friends all,
in appreciation for their advice, support
and the good times shared.

ZEBRA BOOKS

are published by

Kensington Publishing Corp.
475 Park Avenue South
New York, NY 10016

First printing: October, 1992

Printed in the United States of America

ONE

Would I have responded to Belle's letter differently if her loving words had given me any reason to suspect what might follow? I've often wondered about that. My dear friend Malcolm Wilcox had often prodded me, in that gentle way of his, to reach for the sunlight. Had he mentioned the shadows my reaching arms might cast? I can't recall now that he did, but it doesn't really matter; life was quick enough to reveal them to me.

The morning the letter arrived I was being fitted for my wedding dress. It was a hand-me-down from Mother Rogg as all my dresses had been. Plenty of wear left in 'em, she used to say, and there was; but for my wedding I had hoped . . .

"Stand straight, Serena," she commanded. The words emerged from around the pins she held between her lips as a faintly comical "Stan state, Seena," but there was no mistaking the testiness of her tone. "A body'd think I was fitting you for a shroud. I'll never get this ruffle on right if you keep slumping like that."

As if I cared. The ruffle, a cheap bit of yellowed trim scissored from a neighbor's cast-off parlor curtains, would serve only to extend a skirt of unseemly shortness to a length that would seem merely skimpy. Nevertheless, in response to her impatient nudge, I obediently resumed my slow revolution on the low wooden stool that wobbled uncertainly on the braided rug whose wool strips, cut from worn-beyond-repair clothing, had crisscrossed through my hands on many a dark winter evening. *Waste not, want not, Serena.*

Do I sound ungrateful? I shouldn't and I'm not. Wilma and Howard Rogg were not my real parents, and although I addressed them as Mother and Father, they didn't pretend to be anything other than what they were: caretakers of an orphan child. They were dutiful guardians, exacting employers, and although rarely kind, never cruel. In short, we had a contract, the Roggs and I, and love had no place in it.

Mother Rogg shoved the last pin home with a heartfelt "There!" She lumbered to her feet, her breathing labored, and pressed a fisted hand to her back as she moved two steps back to look up at me critically. Plump fingers darted out to pluck at the amply cut, fussily trimmed bodice in which my modestly rounded bosom was lost. I curved in my shoulders protectively. She sighed.

"There you go slumping again. It's a good thing Ernest values a good character above good looks. I swear you look more like a ghost every day."

It was true. I would not be a glowing bride. The silver-blond hair I was secretly proud of was not enough to compensate for my pallor and the increasing prominence of my collar bones, but then Ernest Rogg was not the kind of man to kindle a glow in a girl's cheeks.

Father Rogg was a pharmacist. He owned his own shop and served the medical needs of the population, both human and animal, for many miles around. He was modestly prosperous—which is to say he had no debts to speak of—and his reliable, conscientious and devout nephew, Ernest, was both his assistant and hopeful heir-to-be. I have no doubt the parents of the other girls my age thought I'd landed on my feet a lot smarter than I deserved; I was equally sure their daughters harbored nary a pang of envy.

"A couple of inches taken in on each side should about do it," Mother Rogg mused, "but you'll have to come down off the stool. I can't reach way up to you from here, you know."

I jumped down, overturning the stool in the process. Ever since attaining my present height of five feet, six inches, I had been made to feel as if I had somehow done so deliberately, in order to discomfit the diminutive Roggs. I complained of it once to Malcolm Wilcox when, after completing the daily tidying of his house, I stayed on, as I often did, for tea. Without comment, except for the smile in his faded blue eyes and a twitch of his white moustache, he lent me his copy of *Gulliver's Travels* and suggested I read the section about Lilliput. As he intended, the misadventures, at once comic and frustrating, of a human of normal size among a population of very little people persuaded me to take my own plight less seriously. Oh, how I missed that dear, wise man!

"Did you hear me, Serena? You can get yourself out of my dress now, but be careful!"

The warning was unnecessary. What with the pins and all, it was like trying to make my way out of a blackberry thicket. When I said as much to Mother Rogg, she agreed that it was, and, with a rare smile, began to help, but a loud knock on the front door cut her efforts short.

"My stars and body! Who on earth . . . ?" She pulled her apron over her head and tidied disarrayed hair with quick little, darting plucks of her fingertips. "Serena! Close the parlor door behind me so you

7

can't be seen . . . it could be Ernest, you know."

Heaven forbid that Ernest should see his intended in her pinned-up frumpy wedding dress before their nuptial day! I stood, huddled, in the airless gloom, my mood as dark as the parlor's uninviting horse-hair-stuffed suite. Pristine as the day it was bought, I couldn't imagine anyone choosing the drab gun-metal-colored mohair with which it was uphol-stered. I preferred to think it was either the only fabric available, or the only kind the Roggs could afford at the time. I never asked, for fear of learning otherwise.

I stared at the motes of dust dancing in the narrow shafts of sunlight beaming through the parlor's stained, pin-holed shades, pairing and parting in a glittering gavotte animated by errant wafts of air. Lord knows my origins were as humble as that drifting dust; was it so wrong to wish for a brief flashing dance of my own?

Self-pity ill becomes you, I told myself sternly. *Ernest will be a good provider; you will have security, and one day you will have children to love and to love you in return.* I knew, deep down inside, that romance couldn't hold a candle to that kind of enduring love, but oh, what a lovely flame it must make!

I sighed deeply, and the pins marking the tucks to be taken in the bodice of the wedding dress pricked me into renewing my efforts to extricate myself before Mother Rogg returned. When she did, she seemed oddly distracted, and I turned away, hoping to ease the dress off before she took frowning notice of my lack of progress.

"It was Abner Quarles, Serena. He brought a letter."

I turned, unsurprised by the wonderment in her voice. Everyone the Roggs knew lived right here in Jericho, New York. The mail Mr. Quarles usually

8

brought were bills to do with the pharmacy, delivered monthly from Albany and New York City, with religious periodicals arriving twice a month for Mother Rogg and *Frank Leslie's Illustrated Newspaper* every week for Father Rogg, because, he claimed, of his professional need to keep abreast of the burgeoning trade in patent remedies it advertised. But letters? Never.

"It's for you," she added bemusedly, turning the envelope end over end as if to discover a different, less surprising addressee.

For me? The only person I knew who had ever left town for longer than it took to shed a tear at a wedding or a funeral was Malcolm Wilcox, and he was dead. I looked at Mother Rogg expectantly as she continued to revolve the long oblong in her hands.

"It's from that orphanage. What business could they have with you after all these years?"

What business indeed, I thought resentfully. I thrust out my hand, causing the pins in my bodice to prick the tender-skinned swell of my breasts as if to chastise me for my impatience. "Mother Rogg?"

She surrendered the envelope reluctantly, the transfer fanning the illuminated dust into a frenzy. I inserted the tip of my pinky into the corner of the flap.

"The dress first, missy!"

I swallowed hard, stifling the protest that clamored in my head, and stood, wordlessly obedient, as Mother Rogg slowly peeled the dress from my arms and body and just as slowly folded it, all the while darting glances at the letter now in my hands. Pretending unawareness of her curiosity, I heaped the musty fabric into her arms and waited until she had left the parlor before allowing my impatient finger entry into the mysterious missive.

Folded inside the outer envelope was another,

9

creased and stained, which had already been opened. It bore a Kansas postmark and was addressed to the agency that had arranged for my placing-out. A note was pinned to it. *To whom it may concern,* it began in an awkwardly formed yet strangely familiar hand. *Nine years ago, while wards of your institution, I and my twin sister, Serena Garraty. . . .*

The words blurred before my eyes. *Belle. The letter was from Belle.* My hands trembled as I eagerly unfolded the pages; the note, which had probably originally been folded around them, fluttered to the floor. The letter was dated March 6th, my—*our*—twenty-first birthday, a month and a half ago.

> *Dearest Reenie, I surely hope, if this letter reaches you, it finds you in good health. I have never forgotten the sadness of the day we parted at the Randall's Island Orphanage in New York. Hardly before I knew what was happening, I was aboard the westbound train the Children's Aid Society had assigned us. Before the week was out I found myself standing on a station platform in Kansas, where I was the first chosen from a whole lot of others. . . .*

I smiled. Even as a child, Belle had been vain. It must have meant a lot to her to be the first chosen.

> *I was taken by Mr. Ross Cooper to the Morning Star Ranch to be a companion for his ailing wife, Charlotte. She and Mr. Cooper have now passed on; but Morning Star is still my home, and I want you to come and share this wonderful place with me. I didn't write before, because if you were adopted—I never was, but the Coopers always treated me like one of their own—I don't reckon you had much of a*

say about your destiny before you reached your majority. . . .

Adopted or not, I hadn't had much of a say either before or after my twenty-first birthday about my destiny, if that was what marriage to Ernest Rogg constituted. *Destiny.* Something foreordained by the stars. What was that Turkish word Malcolm Wilcox fancied? *Kismet,* that was it. Could Ernest be my—be *anyone's*—kismet? If it weren't so sad, I might have laughed.

Please say you'll come, my own dearest twin, if only for a visit. We have so much to catch up on and share. I don't even know if your poor leg ever healed properly! Whatever you decide, telegraph me at the address below. That way I'll at least know if you are still alive.

It was signed, "Your lonely, ever-loving sister, Belle."

At the bottom, after the address, a few additional lines were scrawled; *Remember that song of Mama's about the pretty little horses? Bazz says you can have a little spotted Indian horse of your very own to ride across the prairie!*

The postscript, clearly a dashed-off afterthought, touched me deeply. Imagine Belle remembering the lullaby Mama used to sing! And who, I wondered, promising me a pony of my own, was Bazz? I traced my finger under the address: Morning Star Ranch, Ellsworth, Kansas. *Kansas.* It might as well be the moon. I would never know who Bazz was; never see Belle again . . . unless. . . .

I hastily slipped back into my cambric wrapper, determined to test the waters with Mother Rogg before my resolve wavered. I found her in the kitchen, preparing potatoes for the midday meal. Her head was bent, and I marvelled as always at the pinwheeled precision of the tightly braided salt-and-pepper plaits that encircled it. Malcolm Wilcox, who did not admire her hidebound ways, wondered if a match set to the end of it would send her off into a sparking cartwheel like the fireworks on the Fourth of July. "Everyone is entitled to a little excitement, don't you think, Serena?" The memory of his irreverence made me smile.

Mother Rogg turned. Her face was carefully expressionless; but she couldn't quell the glitter of curiosity in her lashless dark eyes, and I could have sworn that just before she spoke, her little button nose twitched with it. "I guess your letter brought good news. I haven't seen you smile like that in a month of Sundays."

"It's from my sister," I said. "My twin sister, Sybelle. I haven't seen her in . . . let's see if we were eleven when she left, it must be nine years, going on ten." *Ten years.* Why, that's almost half my life, I realized with a pang. "She's living out in Kansas on a ranch called Morning Star and she wants me to visit, and please, mayn't I?"

The words rushed out like a torrent through a downspout. Mother Rogg's mouth turned in on itself; her doughy cheeks puffed with indignation.

"My stars! Have you taken leave of your senses? Your wedding in two months' time and all there is to do? And where you think the money would be coming from—"

"There's the money I earned cleaning at Mr. Wilcox's—"

"More lollygagging than cleaning if you ask me! Besides, that's your dowry. Promised to Ernest. Better spent on furnishings to last you a lifetime than a visit to Kansas that'd be over before you could take a deep

12

breath. No, put it out of your mind, Serena. Now you know where your sister's at, you can write to her," she continued in a bright, brisk tone. "Why, you can have a regular correspondence, exchange photographs and the like."

"Yes, ma'am," I replied dully, knowing it wasn't the same at all. Belle and I had been apart so long, I felt I hardly knew her anymore. After she had joined me in the orphanage where my father had placed me two years earlier, we failed to develop that close bond, born of intuitively shared joys and apprehensions, experienced by other indentical twins I had known.

I could not recall if we had enjoyed that special affinity before our separation—my memory of those hungry, fearful, helpless years is mercifully blurred—but I knew that neither words penned on paper nor likenesses captured by a camera could reinvoke it if we had. No, I had to see her, to smile into blue eyes set aslant like mine, touch those similarly blue-veined, white-skinned arms and stroke the mirror-image silver hair, which, last time seen, had been confined in a single, long braid. I recalled its brushy tip bouncing at her waist as she walked away from my infirmary bed and, as I tearfully thought at the time, out of my life forever. As I reread Belle's letter, tears again filled my eyes. *Oh, Belle! There must be a way! I can't give up . . . not yet, anyway. . . .*

Just then, I heard through the open window Father Rogg's heavy, uneven steps on the front porch. Injured by a runaway carriage many years before, his twisted left leg increasingly protested the burden of his bulky body. By noon more often than not, his mood was testy and his temper short. It would do me no good to present my case to this judge.

13

"Mother Rogg, is Ernest's dinner ready to take to him yet?"

She looked at me in surprise. Such eager willingness was uncharacteristic of me. For the last year, it had been Father Rogg's custom to stay at home after the midday meal rather than return to the pharmacy, which left Ernest in sole charge until closing time. To compensate for the added duties and responsibility thrust upon him, it had been agreed between them that I would deliver a proper dinner to him every working day, which I dutifully did, whatever the weather or temperature. It was an agreement I hotly resented, for as Malcolm Wilcox had shrewdly observed when I expressed my indignation to him, since the added responsibility served to strengthen Ernest's position, the covered dishes I brought him were merely icing on an already provided cake.

I hastily packed a basket with the towel-wrapped dishes and, avoiding Father Rogg's frowning entrance into the kitchen by a hair, made my escape down the back steps and out the rear gate to Maple Street. The unfurling new leaves of the well-grown trees that gave the street its name twinkled greenly in the late-April sunlight. The Mossbachers' front walk, two doors down from the corner of Main Street, was edged with daffodils coaxed into early bloom by the unseasonably warm weather of the past week. I paused to admire their cheery golden trumpets, wondering as I did so if there were daffodils at the Morning Star Ranch in Kansas.

Kansas. My mind fair boggled at the thought of that wild vastness. Could a person like me feel at home on those high, wild, windswept plains so unlike the verdant farmland ringing this quiet, pretty town? Did Belle?

"Home," Malcolm Wilcox used to say, "is as much a state of mind as a place," which was why, perhaps, I

14

had felt more at home in his house—where we spent more time talking and reading together than I did cleaning—than anyplace else I had ever been.

"Where you off to with that basket, Little Red Riding Hood?"

I looked up, startled, to see Mrs. Mossbacher sweeping her front walk clear of fallen maple wings. Tall, gaunt and knobby-boned as an aged horse, with a long, wide-nostriled nose to match, her ready smile swept all such unkind comparisons away.

I returned her smile. "It's Ernest's dinner, Mrs. Mossbacher. To make up for the extra hours he's been working, you know."

She looked at me consideringly. "Do you think there's a chance of that weedy intended of yours fattening up some before your wedding day? I swear, it'll be like embracing a bag of antlers, Serena."

"He's a good Christian man, Mrs. Mossbacher," I protested weakly.

She gave a loud, eloquent sniff. "Fussing about how good everyone *else* ought to be doesn't add up to Christian goodness in my book, Serena . . . but I'll admit that when it comes to reckoning up vice and virtue most people in this town have doubts about my arithmetic."

"Maybe so," I conceded, "but as for me, I think the sum of your parts is something to be reckoned with."

"Hah!" she snorted. "I guess I'll take that as a compliment, Serena."

"That's how it was meant, ma'am." I ducked my head in a goodbye nod. "I'd better be going along now. Ernest'll be fretting for his dinner."

Mrs. Mossbacher's comment to that was conveyed wordlessly by the vigorous resumption of her sweeping. The rhythmic pump of her meaty forearms sent the maple wings swirling over my head, and as I rounded the corner onto Main Street I could still hear the brisk skritch-skratch of her broom on the herring-boned brick.

The Rogg Pharmacy was well situated, flanked as it was by Harold Cannon's hardware store on one side and Abe Seligmann's dry goods on the other. A farmer could hitch up after milking, come into town to pick up barbed wire, bag balm and sewing notions for the missus, and be home before noon.

On either side of the pharmacy entrance long, narrow windows framed enormous glass apothecary jars, one filled with a clear red liquid, the other blue, that shone like a maharajah's jewels when illuminated by the midday sun. Even in summer, with the green-and-white-striped awnings cranked down to provide welcome shade, a luminous fire seemed to glow in their depths. Father Rogg was very proud of his windows: no dust, no cobweb wisps, not even a marring fingerprint was tolerated. I could not count the times I had polished and repolished those plate glass expanses to suit him.

As I pushed open the door, the bell above it announced my overdue arrival. Ernest stood behind the counter polishing his spectacles. His neat white coat was as immaculate as always; the combed strands of his thinning hair lay across his domed pate as precisely as rows in a corn field. His head snapped up.

"Considering the hour, I don't know if it's dinner or supper you've brought me."

"I'm sorry, Ernest," I said, placing the basket on the counter. "I've had a busy morning," I added as I offered my cheek for his damp kiss.

"And do you suppose I've been idle, Serena?" he demanded, his polished jaws jiggling with indignation. "It's been one thing after another all

16

morning, ending with Jake Grimes insisting on showing me the boils the remedy I prescribed had failed to cure. Enough to take a man's appetite clean away."

"It's chicken potpie today, Ernest. Your favorite."

I lifted a dish from the basket and unwrapped the insulating napkin to release the tantalizing aroma of flaky-crusted chicken in a well-seasoned, creamy sauce. Ernest's tongue darted wetly around his lips. For a man as slim as he was—I don't know that I would have gone so far as to call him weedy, as Mrs. Mossbacher had—his appetite was awe-inspiring.

"Shall I set it out in the back room for you?" I offered. "I thought today I'd join you."

Ernest coiled a protective arm around the fragrant dish. "I really doubt there's enough for two—"

"Oh, I've already eaten, Ernest," I untruthfully assured him. "I just thought, with our wedding day so close . . . it's not that I don't value Mother and Father Rogg's counsel, for of course I do, but there are a few things only we can decide. . . ."

I lowered my lashes with maidenly modesty. Ernest bustled to the front door, pulled the heavy shade and, after consulting his pocket watch, revolved the tin hands attached to the clock inscribed upon the window covering. "It's half-past one, Serena; to accommodate you," he announced importantly, "I'll not reopen 'til two."

Heaven only knows what he thought I had in mind, but my heart sank at the thought of his reaction at having sacrificed a half-hour of trade to discuss the possibility of a visit he was sure to think idiotic. I waited to speak until he had finished his dinner and was chasing a last crumb of crust through the remaining gravy.

"A visit to Kansas?" he exploded. "With all there is to do in the few weeks left before our wedding? Abe

Seligmann tells me you haven't been in to order the bed linens even though the brass bed you wanted arrived from Albany a month ago! Whatever can you be thinking of?"

"I thought maybe we could go there on our wedding trip, Ernest. Everyone goes to Niagra Falls . . . maybe it would be interesting to do something different."

"Different? Well, Kansas would certainly be different all right! A dusty, flat wasteland instead of a renowned natural wonder? Sleeping in louse-ridden railroad way stations when we already have reservations at the grandest hotel in the Falls area? No thank you very much!"

"Sybelle is my twin sister, Ernest. She's my only kin! I haven't seen her for ten years . . . *ten years.* . . ." In the face of Ernest's implacability, my voice trailed off in whispery despair. I might have had better luck wresting a bone from a bulldog than understanding from Ernest.

He flicked crumbs from the corners of his set mouth, then slapped his napkin down on the deal table. "You've managed to survive the last ten years without seeing your sister; when you're Mrs. Ernest Rogg, there'll be more than enough to keep you busy and contented for the next ten."

I dropped my gaze to my folded hands in my lap. Busy, yes, but contented? Resigned was more like it. All at once I felt something hot and white begin to burn in my chest. Something more than resignation; bigger than resentment. Anger, that's what it was. Anger undiluted by guilt or harnessed by common sense; anger so strong I tossed the dishes, tableware and napkin higgledy-piggledy into the basket and scraped back my chair until it screeched in protest.

"I've taken up enough of your valuable time, Ernest," I said with a desperately achieved evenness.

"There's no more to be said on the matter."

"That's my good girl!" Although his tone was lightly placatory, I didn't have to see his face to be assured of the self-satisfied smirk on his lips.

As I walked toward the door, he called after me. "Pull up the shade on your way out, will you, Serena? And stop in to see Abe about the bed linens before you go home. Time's a wasting, you know!"

His "good girl" was I? Instead of turning left into the dry goods store, I marched across the avenue and down toward the railway station. *We'd see about that!*

My impulsive errand, once embarked upon, became a duty. That it was self-assigned did not in the slightest soften the grim determination with which I pursued it.

I spent the rest of that fateful afternoon interviewing the stationmaster and doing certain investigations at the town's modest library. In due course, the deep pockets of my skirt received for concealment three slim borrowed volumes and a packet of timetables with notations of railway fares, the amount of which made me feel quite faint. By the time I returned to the house on Maple Street, lavender shadows had invaded the dooryard, but Mother Rogg's annoyance about my "gallivanting" was soon assuaged thanks to an embroidered version of my visit with Ernest. She, too, pronounced me a good girl, and I went to bed that evening feeling more wicked than I ever had in my life.

How quickly I acquired a taste for wickedness! Over the next few days I stealthily assembled the clothes and few belongings that according to the old journals I had borrowed from the library, would equip me for life in Kansas. Day-to-day living may have become easier since the time of those early overland accounts, but progress could not eliminate

19

altogether the hardships described. I regretted leaving my few bits of finery behind, but a prairie ranch ravaged by cyclones and blizzards was no place for furbelows: the wool mittens and scarf set Mother Rogg had knitted me for Christmas was more worthy of a place in my portmanteau than my Sunday-go-to-meeting lace collar and fancy clocked stockings.

The day before my departure, I slipped my bag into a burlap sack and out of the house before the Roggs were astir. Later, I loaded it into an express wagon—rented for a nickel from the Candler boy down the street—along with Ernest's dinner, which I delivered on my way to the station. Ernest, busy with a customer when I arrived, noticed neither the wagon nor the burlap sack, and none of the acquaintances I chanced to pass remarked upon it. By the time I consigned my portmanteau to the incurious stationmaster's care and returned the wagon to its youthful owner, I decided that a successful life of crime, if one were bold enough, would not be nearly as difficult as I had once imagined.

That night I lay awake, pinching myself when I felt my eyelids droop, until the snores from the adjoining room settled into the rhythmic rumbling of deep sleep. I donned the costume I had chosen for my journey, then slipped downstairs into the small room off the parlor which was used, in lieu of adequate space at the pharmacy, as an office. Once, when I had asked for part of the weekly wage Malcolm Wilcox paid me for cleaning his house, Father Rogg had marched me in, opened the wide drawer of his huge oak desk and showed me the flat tin box in which my wages were deposited. "For your dowry, Serena. You came with nothing, but you will have this to take with you."

I was aware the Roggs had every right to keep my wages as partial payment for my room and board, and except for an occasional frippery denied, I never felt deprived. Indeed, after returning home, stimulated, from a day spent with Malcolm Wilcox, it seemed to me I owed him far more for the privilege of his company than I received for my housekeeping chores. For the hours spent at his bedside during his last weeks reading aloud passages from Shakespeare and Chaucer, I refused to accept anything. Be that as it may, when I opened the tin box and began to count out the bills stacked inside, I had to keep reminding myself that I had *earned* them: twenty-five cents a day, three days a week for four years and three months. *Count your pennies and the dollars will take care of themselves. A penny saved is a penny earned. . . .*

Mother Rogg's oft-quoted proverbs marched through my head as I flicked the bills through my fingers. Twenty-five . . . fifty . . . one hundred . . . *one hundred and sixty-five dollars!* I could hardly believe it. Did I dare? Did I really dare? I swallowed hard, patted the bills into a neat bundle and secured it with a length of stout string. *Better me than Ernest Rogg.*

Before returning the box to its accustomed place in the back of the desk drawer, I placed in it the note I had written earlier, expressing gratitude for the shelter Mother and Father Rogg had provided and regret for abusing their trust. As I eased open the back door, Mother Rogg's sleek black-and-white cat slipped through, pausing briefly for a purring arch against my ankle.

"Goodbye, Sugar," I whispered. He would, I realized sadly, be the only member of this family I would miss, and not even him very much. I stepped out on the porch. The morning light had not yet begun its pearly advance above the horizon. A cardinal called tentatively from the quince bush, pink-budded now, grown from a cutting given me by Mrs. Mossbacher. I would never see it in bloom again. But there would be prairie flowers blooming in Kansas, and who was to say the songs of the birds they sheltered would fall less sweetly on my ear?

I set my chin resolutely, patted my bill-stuffed, needleworked bag and set off down the path. Above me I glimpsed the morning star, bright symbol of my journey's end, and as I latched the gate behind me, Mother Rogg's high-pitched voice echoed in my head. *The Lord helps those who help themselves, Serena*—my footsteps quickened—*and don't you ever forget it!*

TWO

The Albany train was late. I took advantage of the delay to send off my wire to Belle, looking nervously back over my shoulder toward the street as the operator tapped out the words I had composed during the night. At length, I heard with relief the approaching chug of the engine. The only caring witness to my steam-wreathed departure was the stationmaster's mournful-eyed hound, who, grateful for a rare petting, relinquished my company reluctantly.

My memory of the next few days is a muddle of excitement and misery. From a girl cautioned never to exchange glances, much less words, with strangers of the opposite sex, necessity soon transformed me to a bold young miss forced to seek advice and services from men of all classes and colors. Indeed, it was a spit-and-polished young Negro porter in Chicago who kindly pointed out what I should have had sense enough to realize on my own.

Faced with a one-night layover and confused by the profusion of hotel advertisements posted in the vast, noisy, smoke-filled station, I turned to the first uniformed, official-looking person I saw, trotting alongside his loaded baggage cart to a side entrance where he raised a long chocolate-colored finger to point out a hotel he considered suitable for a lady traveling alone in modest circumstances. His eyes widened as I rummaged among the dwindling bills in my purse for a coin with which to thank him.

"Lordy, miss! You gon' lose that for *sho*, 'less you hide it. They's sharp eyes allus lookin' for easy takin's."

The journey from Chicago to Leavenworth, and from there on the Kansas and Pacific Line to Ellsworth, bore him out. Both trains were crowded with immigrants lured by the promise of cheap farmland, and coins I could ill afford to lose were twice extracted from my purse during the hectic rush to the railway restaurants for the twenty-minute meal stops alotted. I had, thank heaven, pinned what remained of the paper money to my camisole.

The train's hard, wooden coach benches seemed designed more for punishment than ease. The loose-fitting windows offered little protection against the soot and cinders, and the clangor of the train's progress over rough roadbeds was augmented by the wailing of the immigrant families' children. The frightened eyes of those poor little dispossessed strangers reminded me that this must have been the route—perhaps the very coach!—that Sybelle, too, had taken. The thought put my own discomforts in perspective. Calmer of mind, I allowed my head to sink upon the pillowy shoulder of the immensely large woman who, close-braced against me, was already asleep.

I was awakened, and in truth all but thrown to the dusty floor, by the jarring thud of the stop at Abilene, my next to last. This time I did not bother to join the stampede into the restaurant: my heightening excitement and the bawling of the poor creatures bound east for slaughter from the nearby cattleyards combined to rob me of my appetite. I did, however, employ the time to seek out the washroom where, in

24

relative privacy, I washed my face and hands, tidied my hair, adjusted my bonnet and brushed off my sadly disheveled, button-trimmed tan serge suit as best I could.

Heaving and steaming like some great prehistoric beast, the train paused at Ellsworth just long enough to allow for an exchange of passengers before resuming its lumbering way west with a snort of steam and scream of whistled rage. One of the disembarked passengers, a salesman by the sample case he carried, strode off toward the hotel; another, an older woman dressed in widow's weeds, was borne off with hugs and kisses by a wagon load of kinfolk of assorted ages. Was it a long-awaited visit, I wondered, or had she been pressed to spend her sunset years with her children and grandchildren? Would she be happy? *Would I?*

I waited with my bag on the platform, not knowing what to expect; not even knowing, since I didn't know if my wire had arrived, if I was expected. The town, what I could see of it, was dispiritingly bleak. Dust swirled in the wake of buggies and wagons, horses and cattle; the awnings, even the leaves of the few scraggly trees, were caked with it. I sighed. My eyes darted from side to side hoping to catch a gleam of silver hair.

I stepped back into the shade, and as I did so a voice rasped behind me, "You be Miss Garraty? Miss S'rena Garraty?"

I whirled, startled, to find a bent, wizened little man peering up at me from under the brim of what must have been the dirtiest, most misshapen hat in creation.

"Them eyes is the same," he muttered. "You must be her."

I stared down at him, not sure whether to be indignant or amused.

"The name's Cobby, ma'am. Cobby Hawley. I'm

here to take you to Morning Star. That yourn?" he inquired, aiming a stubby finger at my bag.

"Yes, Mr. Hawley."

He grunted and picked up the bag. "Cobby'll do."

As I was soon to learn, Cobby Hawley's few words to me that afternoon were for him a positive torrent of communication. I trailed after him to a wagon loaded with sacks and boxes and kegs of every size and description. Two horses drowsed in the traces, but no silver-haired girl smiled down at me from the narrow, high plank seat.

I tried to hide my disappointment from this grizzled stranger. "My sister didn't come with you, then?" I asked.

Cobby wedged my bulging bag in the remaining corner.

"No room," he said, as he slung a worn canvas over the pile of supplies. "Comin' in, mebbe, but not goin' back." His inflection made it clear that anyone with a brain in her head should have been able to figure that out on her own. I didn't care. "No room" was better than "hadn't a mind to."

He finished tying down the canvas, then gave me a hand up and waited impassively for me to settle myself down next to him on a seat just wide enough, I now realized, to accommodate two. He then plucked a corncob pipe from the pocket of his fringed, greasy leather shirt, clamped it upside down between his teeth and urged the horses into a smart trot with a slap of the reins across their broad backs.

The damper having been put on further idle conversation, I contented myself for the next hour or so by observing the surroundings. Once we were beyond the town and the dust cloud which hung above it like a miasma, the first thing that struck me was the size of the sky. I'd never seen a sky so big, so wide, so blue. Could this vast azure dome be the same sky that skulked behind trees and peeked over the hills back East?

The wagon dipped sharply down into a gully, at the bottom of which sheltered a stand of tall, rough-barked trees. I smiled at the sight of their arching limbs, thick-clustered with large, trembly green leaves, but as we gained the other side I looked back, puzzled, suddenly realizing that back East there would have been a stream purling through a dip like that; here there was only the shadow of a watercourse traced in sand.

"Mr. Hawley . . . Cobby? Where's the water?"

His eyes slid toward me, scrinched almost shut, and slid back. He pulled his corncob pipe, reluctantly, from his mouth. "Comes and goes." Back popped the pipe, as if to plug a leak.

The horses trotted on, the wagon rattling behind them like a barrel of tin cans tied to their tails, but I was hardly aware of fatigue or hunger or the sun beating down on my head. The town of Ellsworth had long since dropped out of sight. The prairie now stretched out around us in all directions, not flat, as I had been led to believe, but in great waves of grassy earth, an inland ocean whose crests, foamed with yellow and lavender flowers, undulated to the horizon.

I threw back my head and took a deep breath. The air was redolent with a clean, spicy aroma reminiscent of the wormwood in Mrs. Mossbacher's herb garden. Could those gray shrubs, whose spiky branches occasionally fell victim to the revolving wheels, be the sagebrush I had read about? As I leaned out and down to pluck off a tip, I felt bony fingers clutch at my arm.

"I'd like to deliver you in one piece, if you don't mind." Cobby Hawley's tone was as fierce as his grip.

Startled, I pulled myself back up and folded my

27

hands in my lap. "I'm sorry if I alarmed you. You see, I've only read about the prairies, and the early settlers . . . well, most of them weren't very complimentary, although considering the hardships and illness and loss they suffered, I guess that's not too surprising . . . ," I hesitated. My companion offered no comment. "What I'm trying to say is, I had no idea it was so . . . so . . ." I flung my arms wide, momentarily at a loss for words. *"Beautiful!"*

Cobby looked at me sideways again, harder and longer this time. "Suits some," he mumbled around his pipestem.

Which meant it suited *him*, I decided. I wondered whom it didn't.

Groups of slow-moving cattle had begun to dot the landscape, strange, rough-looking creatures unlike any I was familiar with from the prosperous dairy farms back East. Strange, too, were the barbed-wire-wound posts fencing the prairie equivalent of pasture land, one small stretch of which seemed as big as the entire town of Jericho. I couldn't imagine what kind of wood could produce those smooth-skinned, square-cut, honey-colored lengths.

The wagon slowed as Cobby turned off the main traveled road, and a closer look at the posts that marked the turn revealed the reason for my puzzlement.

I pointed to one in amazement. *"Stone* posts?"

The track we were now on led along the edge of a low declivity at the bottom of which were clumped the same rough-barked trees I had seen earlier. Cobby jerked his head in their direction and removed the pipe from his mouth. "No trees, 'cept for them cottonwoods. Rot out in a season. Plenty of stone, though."

The descending sun, slanting in from the west,

blinded me as the wagon mounted a long, slow grade crisscrossed with cattle and game trails. I shaded my eyes with my hand, and as we topped the rise I could see far ahead a spine of rock arching sinuously out of the prairie's green skin like the coil of a huge serpent. Set to one side, farther than the upthrust rock's shadow could be thrown, was an impressive structure built of the same stone as the posts I had remarked upon earlier. It glowed like wild honey in the late-afternoon light.

Cobby shifted beside me. "That be Morning Star."

I had envisioned a simple, weathered farmhouse with chickens scratching and clucking in the front yard. This looked worthy of peacocks. "It's a wonderful name, isn't it!" I said. "There must be a romantic story to go with it."

I looked over at Cobby expectantly, but his frown told me that by now I should have known better. He clamped his yellowed teeth tighter than ever around the well-grooved stem of his pipe. We rode the rest of the way in silence.

The wagon rolled to a halt in front of a horseshoe-shaped dooryard. Arrived at through miles of flowing prairie grasses, the contrast was unsettling: massive, rough-hewn, stone pillars marched sentry-like around its perimeter as if to contain the huge purple trusses of the lilacs exploding in astonishing profusion behind them. Flanking the entrance to the house and reaching almost to the roofline was a taller, stouter pair with curiously slitted caps that gave them the look of helmeted warriors. But before I had time to wonder what menace they had been intended to guard against, the wide, iron-bound wooden door opened, and a young woman, her hair a wealth of red-gold ringlets, ran out to greet me.

"Reenie!" she cried, holding up her arms to me.

29

"Welcome to Morning Star!"

I slid down off the wagon seat, heedless of barked shins and snagged petticoats. "Oh, Belle," I whispered as I embraced her. "I missed you so." She smelled sweetly of powder and rosewater, and suddenly conscious of my travel-weary self, I backed away, holding her hands in mine. "Oh, my goodness, let me look at you."

She had changed. Not only was her hair ringleted and its blondness more strawberry than silver, but the rounded voluptuousness of her figure made me self-consciously aware of my slimness. I still looked like a girl; Belle was a woman.

To my surprise the envy in my thoughts was expressed in her voice as she brushed her fingers across my cheek. "Your skin is still like porcelain, Reenie. The Kansas sun and wind has taken a right fearful toll of mine."

It was true, I realized regretfully. The fine-grained complexion we had shared had coarsened, and the lines radiating from the corners of her eyes unfairly aged her; but she had roses in her cheeks and a pleasing golden glow.

"I'd trade my porcelain for your bloom of health, Belle."

Belle laughed and hooked her arm through mine. "Health is for horses, Reenie. It's all right for a lady to be healthy, but she shouldn't ever look it."

I was astonished. "But Mother Rogg always said—"

"Your Mother Rogg don't live in Kansas, I take it?"

I burst out laughing. "Heavens, no! Nothing like it!"

"Well, then! You see, out here a woman can be one of three things: if she's lucky and has her wits about her, she can live like a lady. That's what I intend to go on doing."

"What are the other two choices?"

"Hardly choices, Reenie, just what most females end up as: workhorse or whore."

I didn't know what to say; I wasn't used to such plain speech from a woman or prepared for the hardness in Belle's voice. At that moment, however, Belle beckoned to a stolid, dark woman who had appeared seemingly from nowhere and instructed her to take my bag inside.

"I reckon you'd like to wash up a bit, darling," Belle suggested tactfully, as she ushered me into a large entrance hall hung with musty tapestries. It had the look of the English manor houses Malcolm Wilcox had carefully detailed in the sketchbook he always took on his travels, and which I never tired of looking at with him. I had no way of knowing if these hangings, too, were genuinely old, but the dust looked the accumulation of decades, if not centuries. The baronial effect was disturbed, however, by boxes piled here and there along the stone walls and the large, dirty Indian rug lying askew on the floor.

"Come on down when it suits you, Reenie, and we'll have a late tea. Supper'll be late, too, I'm afraid. I expected Bazz back by now, but this way we can have a nice long gossip, just the two of us, so shoo! Off with you! Sooner unpacked, sooner down."

I leaned forward to dart a grateful kiss on her cheek before turning to follow the woman who waited passively at the foot of a flight of broad stairs, my bag clutched in her brown hand. I turned back to Belle. "What's her name?" I asked in a whisper.

Belle shrugged. "I haven't a notion. We call her Rita. Sometimes she answers to it; sometimes she doesn't. She comes and goes, never staying long enough for it to matter very much."

I wondered at her acceptance of what must have been an unsatisfactory situation, but, given my lack of experience with household servants—servants of any kind, for that matter—I dismissed it from my mind. There were too many other, much more interesting, things to engage my curiosity.

The woman deposited my bag beside my bed and departed wordlessly, her dark eyes as opaque and expressionless as pebbles. Had she understood my request for water? Should she have helped me unpack? I shortly discovered, however, that a pitcher of water was standing, covered, on a washstand I had not at first noticed, and the putting-away of the contents of my portmanteau hardly required assistance. I arranged my cherished books, left to me by Malcolm Wilcox, along the bureau top under its mirror; in front of them I set out my modest assortment of grooming tools.

As for my clothing, although the wrappers I had chosen to bring with me were suitable for the overland covered-wagon travel I had read about, they were hardly up to the standards of either Morning Star or, judging by the pretty yellow, flowered-sprigged dress in which she had greeted me, Belle's. When I lifted them out, my choices seemed even more dispiriting than I remembered: gray cambric and a faded blue-and-white calico. The least drab was a two-piece brown-and-white-striped cotton sateen I had trimmed myself with a collarette of Irish embroidery. Fortunately, the other pair of shoes I had brought were also brown, rather new, of a nice quality of kid.

I folded the gray and the blue into a bureau drawer—they were hardly worth hanging in the narrow, white-painted wardrobe—and laid the brown-and-white on the bed, whose brass bedstead was in need of polishing. Guiltily, I traced the tarnished curves with my finger.

Would Ernest ever find someone willing to share the brass bed he had bought for us? Probably, I decided. There would always be a girl grateful for a nest of her own, no matter how grudging its feathering. Wishing the poor thing well, I sighed and turned to the washstand to perform the ablutions neglected for so long. The cool water was wonderfully refreshing, and the crisp pungency of the lavender water I had impulsively purchased at a pharmacy near my Chicago hotel was, I assured myself, worth every penny of its shocking cost.

Revived, I changed into my last clean set of undergarments and walked toward the two large windows commanding a wide view to the east. I would enjoy being wakened by the morning sun, and I wondered what bird songs would greet me at its rise.

I turned, braced my arms against the wide stone sill, and regarded the spacious, high-ceilinged room with mounting pleasure. The furnishings were simple but well-built, and I was especially grateful for the large lamp, more than adequate to read by, on the bedside table. A bright, boldly patterned Indian rug—much cleaner than the one in the hall downstairs—lay on unpolished wooden floorboards; another, more finely woven, served as a counterpane. Tomorrow, after doing my laundry, I would fling both windows wide to clear the room of a lingering mustiness, polish my bedstead until it gleamed, and then, with Belle's permission, cut a bouquet of those extraordinary dooryard lilacs to grace my bureau.

I sighed contentedly and turned again, my breath fogging the cooling glass. Daylight was almost gone now; a slivered moon had begun its ascent. It suited me, this landscape: I was not a religious person, at least not to the pious degree Ernest had expected of me, but here on this sky-arched prairie, as clean and pure as the biblical land of Zion, I sensed the presence of God. My life thus far had been a pilgrimage of sorts, and I felt I had at last come home.

*   *   *

I found Belle seated in a large alcove of the spacious parlor that opened directly off the front hall. Crude wooden furniture and Indian rugs waged a stylistic war with Victorian upholstered pieces, and through the crowded battlefield wound paths edged with discarded newspapers and periodicals. Except for the dust that lay undisturbed over all, it looked like a room that was either just being moved into or out of.

"Reenie! Join me here in front of the fire. Cool nights are the rule here, well into June."

She had changed into a spring green, bow-trimmed costume which suited her sun-mellowed coloring well. Her glossy curls reflected the firelight. A silver tray, whose tarnish accentuated its elaborate chasing, sat on a low bench in front of the small sofa on which she sat. Instead of a teapot, however, it held a slender decanter and two small glasses, crystal from the look of them.

"I thought, seein' how late it's got, sherry might suit you better'n tea."

I sat down beside her, plucking out the folds of my skirt as I searched for something to say. *Would sherry suit me?* I hadn't any idea if it would or not, never having been allowed anything alcoholic. Even our communion wine had been grape juice. *Lips that touch liquor will never touch mine*, Ernest used to say. . . .

"Why, I think that might be very nice, Belle. But only a very little bit, please."

Belle slanted an amused look at me as she poured the amber liquid. I'm sure she guessed my lack of experience. She handed me a glass and then smilingly raised hers. "Together again, Reenie!"

"Never to part," I rejoined. I took a cautious sip. I returned my sister's smile as the sherry's creamy mellowness trailed warmly down my throat. "Now then, Belle, tell me everything! After Mr. Ross

34

Cooper brought you here to Morning Star, *then* what?"

Charlotte Cooper had lingered on for four years, Belle told me. "She suffered so near the end, poor thing." Afterward, she helped with the general household chores, taking over as housekeeper when "that snappy old thing" left Morning Star six months later.

"But you were only fifteen, Belle! How on earth could you be expected to cope with a big house like this by yourself?"

"There was only Ross—Mr. Cooper—and Basil." She laughed. "Men aren't very fussy when it comes to housekeeping, Reenie, and there are always Indian women passing through looking for work."

"Is Basil the Bazz you wrote me about?"

"Did I? I'd forgotten—"

"As an afterthought. Something about a pony . . . ?"

Belle's brow furrowed. "A pony? I can't imagine—" She shook her head. "Maybe Bazz will remember. He's been away on business, but I expect him back tonight."

Whoever this Bazz or Basil was, I wondered why he would be able to explain something Belle had written to me. It was all very puzzling. I looked at Belle expectantly.

"Basil is Lottie and Ross Cooper's son," she explained, correctly interpreting my expression. "We grew up together. Bazz is two years older'n me—than *us*," she corrected smilingly. "We're like brother and sister."

I felt a sharp pang of envy as I thought of the years wasted; the years in which the bond that should have been ours was established with somebody else.

"You'll like Bazz, Reenie . . . he reads a lot, just like you always did. He's a musician."

A musician running a cattle ranch? It seemed to me as unlikely a mix as the furnishings.

35

Belle sensed my skepticism. "No, really, that's his piano there, under that cloth." She gave a bitter little laugh. "Lordy, what a storm *that* provoked!"

"When does he have time to practice, Belle? I would think running a ranch as big as Morning Star would take all a man's time and then some."

Belle's smile faded. "It does. Cobby Hawley was Ross's foreman, so for the time being he's in charge—until Quinn takes over."

"Quinn?"

The córners of Belle's mouth pulled down, and the soft light in her wide-spaced blue eyes took on a steely glitter; but before she could speak, a brisk tattoo of footsteps approached us rapidly across the stone-flagged entrance hall.

As Belle turned away from the fire toward the door, her glossy, ringleted head became itself a leaping flame in the shadowy room.

"It's just what we feared, Belle," said an angry male voice from the doorway. "That bastard breed's got us over a barrel and—"

"Bazz!" Belle leaped up, her hands fluttering protestingly. "Mind your tongue! Whatever must Serena think!"

A tall, slim man traced the path to the fireplace with the easy grace of youth. He kissed the cheek Belle presented, but his eyes—they were very pale, but whether blue or gray I could not tell—were fixed on me. A slow smile revealed the gleam of white, even teeth.

"Serena! Can it really be you? Belle's chattered on so about you I feel I know you already!"

He reached out a long, slim hand. Automatically, I extended mine, which he first warmly grasped and then, to my utter surprise, lightly pressed to his lips. A lock of hair the color of tarnished copper fell forward to softly brush my knuckles. It was a gesture I might have thought pretentious; instead, given the

36

warmth of the smile that accompanied it, I found it . . . charming. I had never met a charming man before. Ernest had pronounced charm untrustworthy in a woman and unmanly in a man. As I stared up into those elusively colored eyes—sensing nothing either alarming or effeminate—I noticed a glimmer of quiet amusement. I felt his hand gently detach itself from mine. I colored hotly. I hadn't meant to cling: he must think me a very simple miss indeed.

"Do you really have a pony for me?" I blurted.

Belle and Basil burst out laughing. My hands flew to my mouth. I sounded like a spoiled child! What on earth had gotten into me?

"No more sherry for *you*, sister dear," Belle said with mock sternness as she poured a glass of the amber liquid for Basil.

"Oh, dear, I *am* sorry," I said.

"You needn't be," Basil said. "I find you just as delightful now as I'm sure I will in the morning when I introduce you to Bingo. She's a sweet little creature. A true little Indian pony, too."

"Not one of Quinn's Appaloosas, Bazz!" Belle cried. "He won't take kindly to that."

Basil frowned. "If I worried about everything Quinn didn't take kindly to, I'd never do anything at all, would I? But no, it's not one of Quinn's. Cobby knew of this one. Belonged to the youngest Flagler girl. After she died, her parents couldn't bear seeing the animal around the place."

"Please. Who is Quinn?"

Belle and Basil looked at one another. "She'll have to know sooner or later," Basil said quietly.

Belle sighed. "Quinn is Bazz's half-brother. His father sired him on his way back from the California goldfields. Took a fancy to a woman he met somewhere along the way, and after Bazz's mother took to her bed he'd . . . well, every so often he'd . . ."

Basil took up Belle's faltering tale. "What your sister's finding hard to say is that whenever the lust built up in Paw, he'd go back to his whore. She was half-Comanche, which makes Quinn not only a bastard but a breed as well."

Basil fell silent and stared broodingly into the crackling fire. I looked up at Belle, trying not to show the shock I felt. She stood with her hands folded tightly together. Anxious lines creased the space between her brows. Obviously not all of the story had been told.

"Bazz's grandfather owned a big ranch just to the north and east of here," she began. "His mother was an only child, so after her parents died, the two holdings were joined. When *she* died, Ross brought Quinn to Morning Star to live—Lottie wouldn't hear of it while she was alive, not after—"

Basil waved an impatient hand. "That's not important now, Belle. What *is* important is that Quinn and my father were at each other's throats from the moment he arrived here, and within two years Quinn lit out for Nebraska, where he was taken on by a big spread owned by an English syndicate. I guess they found some good in him," he conceded grudgingly, "because four years later he was made line boss, then top screw. The word that got back to Paw about Quinn didn't make him like him any better, but he couldn't resist throwing Quinn up to me all the time, either. 'That Quinn's sure a chip off the old block,' he used to say."

"And of course the more he said it," Belle added, "the more Bazz resisted doing what was expected." She tossed her head toward the piano. "The piano's arrival was the last straw."

"'You oughta be out brandin' calves 'stead a'playin' them fool scales,'" Basil quoted in an exaggerated drawl.

"Well," I ventured, "I suppose from a rancher's

point of view it's understandable that—"

"Ranching is one thing, justice is another," Basil broke in. He gripped the arms of his chair and leaned forward. "If you can't 'understand' that—"

"Easy, Bazz, easy," Belle whispered. "You see, Reenie, a month after their row, Ross died as a result of a ridin' accident, but in the meantime he'd changed his will. Knowing Ross, he likely would have changed it back again once he cooled off, but his new will left Morning Star to Quinn."

I was stunned. "All of it?"

"All of it," Basil answered in a tightly controlled voice. "Even the holdings my mother inherited from my grandfather. Quinn has to pay me what the court has determined the Wohlfort land is worth, but . . ." He shrugged.

"But the judge, besides being a rancher himself, spent many an evening playin' cards and drinkin' with Ross," Belle amplified, "so you can imagine how fair his opinion was. It's purely a scandal, if you ask me," she added heatedly.

"Isn't there someone . . . somewhere you can appeal?"

Basil grinned, but there was no mirth in it. "Out here, Serena, all the judges are either ranchers or lawyers whose fees are paid by ranchers." He threw up his long hands. "Quinn has given us no choice but to leave Morning Star as soon as he has the funds to satisfy my claim and my father's bequest to your sister."

"It's not much, Reenie," Belle said, "but I'm grateful Ross thought to leave me anything. I'm young and healthy, I can make do; but Morning Star is Bazz's home."

Home. The word echoed mockingly through my head. I watched as Belle perched on the arm of Basil's chair and rested her head on his, an unconscious gesture born of long familiarity. I ducked my head, willing away the sudden sting of tears. They, at least, had each other; as for me, the promise of the home Belle's letter had tantalizingly offered had vanished like the smoke from the bridges I had so blithely burned behind me. Not that I wished to return; Malcolm Wilcox had long since been laid to rest in Jericho; my mother was dead and buried I knew not where, and my father had chosen to give me away. The bitter truth was I had no one back East to love and nowhere else to go. . . .

Except for the fire, the large room was dark now, the long, curved-top windows framing the fast-advancing night. A long, sobbing wail broke the stillness, followed closely by another in a higher key. I sprang to my feet, heart pounding. *What on earth!*

Basil chuckled. "Nothing to be alarmed about, Serena. It's just the coyotes' nightly serenade. On moonlit nights you can see them sitting out there on the rise, muzzles pointing toward the sky, sounding as if their wild little hearts were breaking." He rose and stretched. "I'm starving, Belle, what's for dinner?"

"I put a stew on to simmer earlier, and I bullied Rita into making that corn flatbread you like so well. I thought it might be a treat for Reenie, too—"

All of sudden I began to cry.

"Lord love us, Reenie, whatever is the matter?"

"I thought that Morning Star . . . I thought that we . . ." I wiped my streaming eyes with the handkerchief Basil silently offered and took a deep breath. "I ran away, Belle. I have no place else to go."

"Good heavens, darling, did you think I was going to let you go now that I've found you? We've loads of time yet . . . we'll work something out." She took my hand in hers and patted it. "Why, we're family, aren't we, Bazz?"

"The only one I've got now," Basil agreed.

As I followed them and the savory aroma of Belle's

40

stew out to the kitchen, I couldn't help wondering why it was necessary for them to leave Morning Star. The house was very large, large enough to comfortably accommodate even persons who were not on the best of terms. Regardless of legal entitlements, how could anyone deprive a brother of his lifelong home? What a selfish, heartless man Quinn Cooper must be. I did not like him, I decided. I did not like him at all.

THREE

I awoke the next morning to a room flooded with sunlight. I sat up in bed and stretched, luxuriating in the uncommon novelty of sleeping until mid-morning. I could remember it happening only once before, during my first winter with the Roggs when I suffered a weakening bout of dysentery. It had been a grudgingly granted favor lest I develop a taste for slothful ways.

I stretched again, feeling wonderfully refreshed. I had awakened briefly during the night from a dream, but the memory of it—I vaguely recalled climbing up and down an improbable number of staircases—had already largely eluded me. Only the tip-tapping sound of dream-slippered footsteps teasingly remained. Had the nighttime excursions of resident mice been thus transmogrified? More likely squirrels, I decided, recalling their rackety invasions of the Roggs' attic. Either possibility would be better than the twitchy-nosed, red-eyed rats I had occasionally seen scuttling along the cobwebby timbers above the laundry tubs in the orphanage's cellar. How Belle hated that dank, dark cellar! I smiled wryly to myself, recalling how, more often than not, I somehow ended up doing her laundry chores as well as my own.

My recollection of those long-ago days, however, proved no match for the present bright reality of the Kansas sunshine streaming across the floor, warming both the wide boards and my bare toes as I scampered to the washstand. Once dressed, I wandered down into the kitchen, which I found as disordered this morning as the rest of this puzzlingly unkempt household. The top of the vast wooden table that dominated the center of the room was littered with a bewildering variety of pots, jars, strainers and funnels, and dried herbs hung in bunches, together with strings of red peppers, from crude iron hooks screwed into the stout beams crossing the ceiling.

My breakfast consisted of cornmeal flatbread left from the previous evening's meal slathered with preserves of an unfamiliar but tasty sort. There was no milk. Rita, silent, stolid, seeming more a copper-sheathed statue than a living person, received my request uncomprehendingly, and resumed her preparation of something that smelled of beans and spices.

I reached beyond her to pour a cup of coffee from the pot set at the back of the blackened range and cleared a place on the crowded table top for my plate. It was there, perched on a high stool, that Belle found me.

"I was beginning to think you'd decided to dream the day away, Reenie." She kissed my cheek. "You're lookin' mighty perky this mornin'."

"Do I? I certainly feel so." Taking a last sip of the bitter, gritty coffee, I shuddered. "I wouldn't mind tea instead of coffee with my breakfast, though—if you have any, that is."

Belle laughed. "China or India, take your pick. But if you're plannin' on bein' a real westerner, you'd better get yourself a liking for coffee brewed to a rancher's taste."

Any plans I might have had in that regard would seem to have already been dashed, I thought, but I smiled brightly, determined to put the best face on things.

"Bazz and I decided that today, your first full day at Morning Star, is yours to plan as you wish. We can go to the corral and meet your pony . . . but maybe you'd rather explore the house or stay in your room and read; you always were such a reader, Reenie. . . ." Her trailing, offhand tone was accompanied by a rapid downward sweep of her lashes that alerted me: Belle had not lost her teasing ways.

I grinned, calling her mild bluff. "I'll save my reading for a rainy day; today is for riding!" My smile brightened further, then dimmed as I looked down at my gray, schoolmarmish garb. "This dress and a blue one like it and the brown stripe I wore last night . . . it's all I have, Belle."

"Never you mind about that," she countered briskly. "I put out some riding clothes of mine in your room, so you just scoot up and change and meet me at the front door. I got a few things to tend to here."

I whirled toward the door, then hesitated, torn between excitement and guilt. "I shouldn't take you away from your duties—"

"Fiddlesticks! I was just stirrin' up a batch of healing salve for the stock; it can wait."

"Are you sure?"

Belle turned to face me; her chin assumed a defiant tilt. "No one tells me what to do or when to do it, Reenie. It can wait."

How many times in childhood had we faced each other in this fashion? Her pugnacity used to unsettle me, but for now at least, I found its familiarity endearing. As instructed, I scooted.

*　　　*　　　*

I didn't walk down to meet Belle; I strode. They say clothes make the man, and from the minute I slipped on her soft leather riding skirt, boots and wide-brimmed, fawn-colored felt hat, I felt a different person altogether. Belle clapped her hands at the sight of me.

"You look a proper cowgirl. Almost," she amended, her blue eyes narrowing. She tapped the hat a little forward and down on the silver hair I had braided into a single sleek plait, and pulled her loaned belt two unused notches tighter, sighing enviously as she did so.

She opened the door and waved me out into the brightest, bluest day one could imagine. The tops of the prairie grasses bowed in deference to the urgent wind that rattlingly propelled the metal blades of a tall windmill churning beside an old wooden trough a couple of hundred yards to the west of the dooryard, its mossy squatness in striking contrast to the massive formality of the stone-pillared portico in which we stood. Beyond it stretched the prairie, featureless except for the battalions of wire-bound stone posts that marched, lockstepped, to the horizon. There were no other structures in sight.

"It was the first thing Ross Cooper built when he bought this land," Belle said, when I voiced my curiosity about the trough. "Lottie used to nag him about getting rid of it, but he'd just laugh and say it was good for a man to be reminded of his beginnings."

A swirling updraft scudded up the stone facade behind us, trailing in its wake the fragrance of the lilacs flanking the wide doorstep. I was about to ask Belle's permission to cut some of the voluptuous purple trusses for my room, when something—an after-scent of cloying, almost rank sweetness hinting of decay—stilled the question even as my lips parted.

"Is this where you grow your herbs?" I asked instead.

She nodded happily. "It was Lottie Cooper's idea to plant them here when she saw how tall and thick the grasses grew behind the pillars Ross had erected on this spot. She told me the roots had spread so far and deep it took a team of oxen to pull them out! In the spring, just about the time the morning star first shows in the sky, my herbs start greenin' up, earlier than anywhere else I know of. There's not a garden like it anywhere in Kansas," Belle declared, "nor an herbal book the match of Lottie's. It was brought over from Austria, handed down through generations of her mother's people. She added receipts of her own once she got familiar with the plants out here; I did, too, after she died."

I could tell Belle was proud of her contributions. "What accounts for it?" I asked. "This . . . lushness, I mean."

Peonies planted beyond the lilacs thrust up flower stems as stout as walking canes topped with crab-apple-sized buds eagerly seeking the light. Their leaves, darker and thicker than any I had ever seen back East, were massed so densely they seemed more a carapace than a canopy.

Belle shrugged. "The pillars protect them some from the wind, and I reckon they draw up water from the same source as the trough—that prob'ly accounts for the roots reachin' down so far. And manure, of course." She grinned at me. "Lots of that on a ranch, Reenie."

She put her hands on her hips and surveyed the crowded beds with satisfaction. "The poppies'll be coming along soon, all white and purple, then the foxglove and monkshood, and near the pillars, briony and nightshade." She pointed toward the arc of stones. "They're climbers, you see, and the

46

nightshade's purple flowers and red berries look real pretty against that pale honey color. And, oh, Reenie, wait'll you see the Jimsonweed! It throws out these great big trumpet-shaped white flowers. . . ." Belle's eyes shone. "Why, I reckon they'd turn the angel Gabriel green as pea soup with envy! Course, this is the best time of year: everything always grows lickety-split through June, but come the hot weather in July and the garden droops along with the rest of us."

I found it difficult to share Belle's enthusiasm. Mrs. Mossbacher's garden had enjoyed similar advantages, thanks to her living next door to a dairy farm, but I could never recall it ever producing anything—I stared at a huge peony bud groping blindly, mindlessly toward the light—quite so . . . so out of the ordinary.

Belle's mention of manure prompted my next question. "There must be barns and stables and quarters for the hands, Belle, but *where?*" I searched the wide landscape in vain from under my wide hat brim.

Belle linked her arm companionably through mine and led me out of the courtyard down a wide, dusty path ribbed by the passage of many wagon and buggy wheels.

"That was all part of Ross Cooper's plan, Reenie. He wanted the grand stone mansion he built for his bride to grab up all the attention of the visitors to Morning Star, so he tucked the working part of the ranch out of sight. Actually, you can see it from above if you think to look, all hunkered down around Beacon Rock. That's the rocky spine you see first thing when you top the rise. The early settlers looked for it like sailors do a lighthouse, to mark the trail west to the mountains. Bazz calls it Rattle Rock, 'cause of it lookin' so much like a snake."

47

Seeing my look of alarm, Belle patted my arm reassuringly. "Rattlesnakes are part of living here, darlin'. There're worse things than that back where we come from. Lots worse," she added, as if to herself, her soft mouth twisting in a sudden grimace.

But before I had time to reflect on her bitterness, it had passed.

"Oh, yes," she continued matter-of-factly, "we have snakes, and blizzards, and cyclones, too. In fact, accordin' to Bazz, his grandpa Wohlfort refused to let his precious little Lottie marry Ross until he dug her a cyclone cellar."

I wondered at Belle's sneering tone. "A cyclone must be a terrible thing," I said.

"I reckon so. I saw one once, great black thing whirlin' like a top off on the horizon . . . I remember how still it was, the air so hot and heavy the birds could hardly fly it seemed, and the sky a queer greeny gray. . . ." Belle's voice hushed, and her eyes, remembering, looked unseeingly beyond me. "But it was way far away," she resumed briskly, her walking pace picking up with her speech. "So far's I've heard no cyclone ever came near to touchin' down at Morning Star. If it did"—she turned and pointed up in the direction from which we had come—"why, we'd just scoot down into Lottie's cellar. See that door set low off the north side of the house, slanting out in the shadows?"

Squinting, I nodded.

"Stays lovely and cool down there all summer, lined with stone the way it is. We use it to store my elixirs, as well as preserves and root vegetables."

"Do you grow vegetables in the dooryard garden, too?"

Belle laughed. "Rita takes care of the table food. Carrots, onions . . . she even keeps chickens. Lord knows where she gets 'em, but I can always tell when

48

Rita's back when I hear chickens clucking in the pen between her vegetable patch and her shack. Hard to see it from here, but it's above us, beyond the cellar entrance, overlooking the corrals. . . ."

She shook her head and placed her fisted hands on the rounded swell of her hips. "Listen to me, going on and on about such dull old things—wouldn't you rather go meet Bingo?"

Without waiting for my eager nod of assent, Belle strode ahead, her heels sending up little puffs of dust. The path continued curving down, its verges clothed thickly with short- and tall-stemmed grasses boasting what to my eastern eyes seemed an astonishing variety of color and texture, the whole starred with blue and yellow florets dancing to the tempo of the tireless breeze.

Near the great twisting spine of rock, shrubs grew. For the most part they were unfamiliar sorts, but the unfurling reddish leaves of a scrubby patch had an oak-like look about them, and from their midst there presently issued a melodious fluting whistle that made my heart leap up.

"Just a meadowlark," Belle said in answer to my hushed inquiry. I found it hard to comprehend how such a glorious song could be so carelessly dismissed. "Common as cottontails," she added, as a young rabbit, disturbed by our passage, zigzagged wildly across our path, its huge, moist eyes fixed with terror.

"Have you mice here, too?" I asked, thinking of the pitter-pattering in my dream.

Belle laughed. "Oh, Lordy, yes! I swear they come in regiments sometimes."

As we rounded Beacon Rock, low wooden buildings, a large barn and fenced enclosures came into view, and I was able to differentiate the pulsing sound I had been aware of for some few minutes as loud rough-voiced exchanges puncutated by shouts

49

of laughter and a barrage of whinnies arising from a group of handsome, oddly marked horses protesting their confinement. Cobby Hawley sat hunched on the top rail of the nearest corral, a corncob pipe protruding upside down from pursed lips, aloof from the half-dozen or so rangy, scruffy men lounging on either side of him. A change in the tone of their banter and a shuffling rearrangement of postures alerted him to our presence.

"'Bout time." He squinted at Belle. "Bring the salve?"

"First things first, Cobby. My sister just arrived, you know. I'll have it for you soon enough."

I was about to apologize for being the cause for the delay, when Belle, sensing my intent, jabbed me fiercely, stopping the words on my lips.

"I've brought Serena to meet her pony." It was a statement, not a request, and the implicit demand, accepted as unremarkable, discomfited me, perhaps because if I had dared such an attitude with anyone while living with the Roggs, I would have been given very short shrift indeed. Despite her present predicament, Belle was obviously used to having her way at Morning Star; I wondered why.

Cobby leaned back to rap one of the men on the head. "Jed, go bring out Bingo for the young lady."

The man he addressed as Jed rubbed his head where Cobby's sharp knuckles had landed, and made a pass at slapping the dust off his filthy clothes with his hat. He nodded at me politely enough, but his hot-eyed glance at Belle and his deliberate closeness as he eased behind her made me uneasy, as did the low, snickering exchange among the other hands as they whisperingly compared, behind grimy hands, Belle and me.

Belle ignored them; following her lead, I remarked to Cobby I'd never seen horses like the ones wheeling

50

restlessly around the corral. "They don't seem very . . . manageable."

"Them's Quinn's Appaloosas. Indian breed. These here're young and full o' ginger. Good horses," he said with an emphatic nod. "They's only half-broke, o'course," he added, sliding sideways to dodge a well-muscled spotted rump and a set of energetically lifted heels.

Jed appeared from the barn leading a neat little brown-and-white-splotched mare. Her ears were pricked forward, and intelligent dark eyes peered out at us through a long forelock. Her tail almost swept the ground. I thought she was the dearest little horse I'd ever seen. Cobby took the reins from Jed and led her close to me.

"Let her sniff you," he instructed. "A horse is like a dog and a cat that way. They like to know who they're dealin' with."

Bingo stretched her neat head out toward my outstretched palm and whiffed at it with flaring pink nostrils. After a moment she tossed her head and whickered softly.

I was thrilled; I turned to my sister. "Did you see that, Belle? I do believe she likes me!"

Belle smiled at me indulgently. "I do believe you're right, Reenie. Help her on, will you, Cobby? I don't know that she's ever ridden—"

"I have," I broke in. "But not very much," I admitted, "and usually bareback. Never in a saddle like this." I eyed the boxed stirrups and horned protuberance on the pommel nervously.

"Not much different from the kind Buffalo Bill uses, Reenie, isn't that right, Cobby?"

Cobby's reply was a snort, whether of agreement or scorn, I wasn't quite sure.

"It'll be like riding in a rocking chair, darlin'," Belle added encouragingly. "Up with you!"

51

A moment later, thanks to Cobby's vigorous boost, I was in the saddle; a few minutes after that I was circling inside one of the smaller, empty corrals under his critical scrutiny.

"She's been been trained good and treated better, so settle easy . . . don't go haulin' on them reins, missy! . . . *thass* right, *thass* right . . . give'er her head, she'll take you where you oughta go . . ."

"How about where I *want* to go, Cobby?" I called back over my shoulder as we circled, trotting now, past him. "Don't I have any choice about that?"

"Ain't many choices on the prairie. Hers'll be better'n yours."

I had progressed to a lovely slow canter, even nicer than the rocking chair Belle had promised, when Bazz came riding up on a tall, prancing chestnut as elegant as the man astride him. *How wonderful they look*, I thought.

"Reenie's taken to riding like a duck to water, Bazz," Belle announced.

"Well, Serena?"

I pulled up Bingo in front of him. "How can I ever thank you? She's . . . she's absolutely perfect!"

"Your smile is my reward, Serena." Basil bowed forward and swept his Stetson off his head in a manner befitting a cavalier's plumed hat.

Cobby snorted. A plain man himself, he obviously had little tolerance for fancy phrases and gestures. As for myself, Basil's fine eyes regarding me—yes, I could see now that they were gray, pale and clear as spring water—and the sweet curve of his wide mouth suddenly brought to mind a line from the prologue to Chaucer's *Canterbury Tales*, one of the last things, a favorite, that I had read to Malcolm Wilcox. *He was a verray parfait gentil knight. . . .*

Basil winked at me before addressing Cobby. "Would you approve," he began solemnly, "of my

52

asking Miss Garraty to ride out with me to Chalk Pond this afternoon?"

Cobby looked astounded, the pipe almost dropping from his mouth. "Not for me to say," he blurted. When he belatedly realized Basil had been asking his opinion not of the invitation but my ability, he darted an angry look at him. "She'll do," he muttered.

Cobby stumped off, ignoring the thanks I called after him.

"I guess Cobby doesn't much care to have his leg pulled, Basil," I remonstrated gently.

He frowned. "Cobby has a skin as thin as cobwebs, always has. It never seems to stop him from saying what *he* thinks. Sour little toad. He came with my mother from her parents' ranch; you'd think that—" He stopped short. "The fact is, Cobby doesn't like me, Serena, no more than my father did. There's nothing I can do to change that, but sometimes . . ." He shrugged.

Sometimes he wanted to hit back. I knew that feeling, but the method Basil had employed seemed . . . oh, not quite worthy of a perfect gentle knight.

My misgiving, if that's what it was, was a tiny passing cloud on an otherwise perfect day. Basil somehow assembled a simple picnic lunch, and the setting at Chalk Pond more than made up for the meal's shortcomings. Cradled in a bowl of low hills about three miles to the northeast, the pond, ringed by willows, was fed by springs uncovered during the quarrying of a long-depleted bed of limestone. At the end where we sat it looked to be quite shallow, three feet or less, and so clear the pond's inhabitants could be viewed as if in an aquarium. Stands of blue flag, planted there by his mother, Basil said, unfurled straplike leaves among the slenderer grasses. At the other end, cattails crowded against a wooden platform, like youths impatiently waiting their turn to dive. Judging by the darker color, this was the deepest part. A dozen or so feet, according to Basil.

"Seemed more like a hundred the day Quinn tried to drown me," he added offhandedly.

I stared at him, aghast. "You can't mean that."

But he did. His father, Basil said, had brought Quinn for a visit, contrary to the expressed wishes of Basil's mother. One very hot day, Basil had begged to go wading at the pond.

"I was very good at wearing my mother down," he admitted wryly, "but she didn't feel up to taking me—as I said, it was very hot—and since I didn't know how to swim, she refused to let me go by myself. So Quinn offered to take me. We hadn't seen much of him; he preferred spending his time with Paw and Cobby—he was fifteen, almost a man in my nine-year-old eyes—but they were busy that afternoon with something that bored him, at least that's what he said.

"It seemed harmless enough," Basil said. "After we left, Mama went to her room for a nap, but she couldn't settle down. Her unease grew until finally she ran down to the barn. My father said he was too busy to go, so she asked him to hitch up the buggy for her. He refused."

I was shocked. "Good heavens, Basil, how could he?"

"He thought she was hysterical. He was right, she was; she had reason to be. In the end, Cobby took her, and when they got to the pond they saw me struggling at the deep end, trying to keep my head above the water. I was exhausted. Sometimes I still dream about Quinn's hand clutching at my ankle. The way Mama told it, his head and shoulders broke

54

above the water just as I disappeared. She screamed at him—oh, how she screamed, Cobby said. 'Leave him be, you breed bastard! Leave my boy be,' and she lashed out at him with the buggy whip, and he yelled and dove back under to yank me down again.''

"Oh, Basil!"

"Quinn denies it, of course. Anyway, she ran out on the dock, sprawled out full length, reached down and pulled me up by my hair. No sooner was my face above water than Quinn came lunging up next to me and pushed me up and out onto the platform. Do you know what he said to my mother then? 'You damn near killed him, you silly cow.'''

"But certainly your father—"

"My father couldn't decide what to think, but he sent Quinn away; and when he brought him back to Morning Star after my mother died, the two of them were so much at odds over every little thing, I assumed Paw couldn't help but think that Mama's version of the 'accident' was the right one after all. I guess I was wrong.''

"There's no way you can know that for sure, Basil. If I were you, I'd think whatever put my mind at rest.''

"And I think it's time you called me Bazz,'' he said.

We were seated side by side on a blanket he had untied from behind his saddle. The horses contentedly grazed a few yards away on the tender spring grasses. He looked at me. "You're not much like your sister, are you?"

I self-consciously patted my wind-disordered hair, very much aware of his intent regard, unable to read the expression in his quick-silver eyes. "I'm thinner, and my hair's straighter and paler than hers now, but—"

"I don't mean physically, Serena, I mean inside, in

55

your heart. You're so much more . . . *accepting* of life.''

"Belle is wonderful!" I protested fiercely. "She's so lively and spunky and—"

He placed a long finger across my lips. His eyes invited me to drown in their pale depths; his smile was as sweet as honey.

"Oh, Bazz . . ."

"Bazz is very hungry," he murmured.

I took a quivering breath and leaned toward him—even Ernest would have guessed my expectation—then colored hotly as a packet of sandwiches was flourished beneath my nose.

"You shouldn't tease," I whispered.

"It's hard not to, when you're so adorably teasable."

"Cobby's not the least adorable, yet you teased him."

Basil stared at me, then gave a shout of laughter. "And Belle's not the only spunky one. Here, have a sandwich."

We passed the rest of the afternoon in an amiably foolish fashion, making faces at ourselves in the clear, still water; feeding crumbs to the little olive-backed, orange-sided killifish that rose pout-mouthed to our bait; tracing fantastic beasts, child-like, in the puffy flat-bottomed, fair-weather clouds; attempting to capture frogs that escaped in soaring, plopping leaps to hang daringly, green on green, on grasses reaching up from decades of wind-blown silt layered below.

That was the first of many excursions to the pond, always on Bingo, sometimes with Basil, occasionally in a festive threesome, Belle and the food arriving in a buggy, but mostly, contentedly, alone. There was so much to see: crowds of dragonflies, hovering on splendid gauzy wings, dispersed in a rainbowed burst of color by the splashing arrival of mallards and pintails, their murmurous quacks expressing smug delight at having spied this blue dot of watery repose in the vast expanse of prairie. Bullfrog tadpoles prospered to enormous size, and once, surprised by me while stalking one, a stripy length of snake slipped in silently from the stony verge to cut flamboyant scallops across the placid surface.

For Basil and Belle and me, the days drifted by, unremarked, like bits of thistledown. If there was any urgency to prepare to leave Morning Star, I was unaware of it. After the first week, Quinn Cooper was rarely mentioned, much less discussed. Meals were haphazard—more often than not, the kitchen was taken up with Belle's herbal preparations—and I found myself beginning to view the unkemptness of the great house, except for my own room, which out of habit I kept in order, with a more tolerant forgiving eye.

In any event, Rita was hopelessly unequal to unsupervised tasks, and Bazz spent most of his time at his piano. Once, when I complained mildly to Belle, she reminded me sharply of the hours she spent helping me alter clothes of hers to fit me. Chastened, I abandoned any further attempts to organize the household and decided instead to adopt Belle and Bazz's attitude of allowing tomorrow to take care of itself. Having done so, my enjoyment of our carefree life together was unfettered: I had gained a family if not a home, and of the two, family was far dearer.

The reverse was true down at the working center of the ranch. There, the ripening of spring increased the urgency of chores to be done, and Cobby's gruff commands could be heard at all hours. The hands were seldom seen lounging along the fences these mid-May days—except for Jed, who always managed to wangle himself into Belle's vicinity—and when their eyes strayed toward me as I came and went on Bingo, Cobby soon set them straight. Once, he suggested I groom Bingo out of sight of the men.

"Seein' you like that, missy, strokin' her and whisperin' in her ear . . . it gives 'em notions."

I could tell from the way he ducked his head and twisted his hat in his hands that speaking to me like that had cost him a dollar's worth of embarrassment. But I realized, too, that in his own crabbed way he'd come to like me, so although it was sometimes inconvenient to respect his advice, his wish to protect me touched me more than I dared let on to him.

Taken all in all, very little marred a succession of idyllic days. True, the dooryard peonies' blood-red blooms, shoulder-high when fully grown, exuded a ripe meaty odor that to avoid I took to entering and leaving the house through the kitchen. At night I continued to skitter up and down staircases that existed nowhere else but my dreams, but repetition made my sleep-time journeys more boring than bothersome, although it sometimes crossed my mind to wonder why I had seen no evidence of the legions of mice that evoked them.

Our peace was shattered one morning in late May. I had ridden out on the prairie shortly after daybreak, as had become my custom. There had been a cloudburst in the hours before dawn, and the price paid for that morning's concert of bird song was a generous spattering of mud: on Bingo, on the saddle leathers, and on the boots whose extended loan by Belle had evolved into ownership by me, a transfer confirmed by her teasing aside to Bazz at supper one evening that I probably even wore them to bed.

Exhilarated by the spicy, fresh-washed scent of the prairie, I stayed out much longer than usual. It was

58

nearing noon by the time I left Bingo, sponged and curried, dozing in the corral, and as I bent over inside the barn door to scrape clots of mud from my boots, a lusty thwack on my bottom sent me sprawling. As I lay there, outraged, in the straw—I assumed one of the hands, Jed most likely, had taken the liberty Cobby had warned me about—I heard from above me an unfamiliar deep-voiced drawl.

"Laws-a-mercy, Belle, and here I've been thinkin' you always landed on your feet."

I pulled myself up, with no help from the stranger who stood, arms akimbo, watching me. A well-worn, dust-streaked black hat, pulled low, hid his eyes; his cheeks were dark with unshaven stubble, and a stalk of prairie grass dangled from the corner of a mouth curved in a careless smile. He obviously found my predicament entertaining. I set my hat straight, tossed my braid over my shoulder and stared up at him, too angry to speak.

Six feet or more to begin with, his hard, whip-thin figure made him seem even taller. He returned my stare. His eyes, seen closer than I found comfortable, were as dark as jet. Unlike that lifeless stone, however, something danced in their depths, a cruel mischief that slowly ebbed as he realized he had made a mistake. I waited him out, relishing his confusion. Somehow, I doubted a man like this would admit to it.

"Hell, you ain't Belle!" he accused.

I was right; he hadn't. "I'm her twin sister, Serena, here on a visit."

He plucked the straw from his mouth, then pushed up the brim of his hat, revealing dark eyebrows arching almost to the line of untanned skin that rimmed his broad forehead. "My God, you mean there's a matched set of you? Not really matched, Belle's brass and you're silver, but *two* of you? My,

59

oh, my, think of Paw missin' out on that." He shook his head from side to side in exaggerated surprise, presenting in profile as he did so a broken-ridged nose and a jaw line as sharp as an axe blade.

"Too bad you won't be stayin' long," he added. More than a comment, it was a pronouncement, delivered in a tone as uncompromising as the glare of the midday sun.

I fear I gaped. *This lord-of-the-manor air . . . he can't be, he can't possibly be. . . .* "You don't look at all like Bazz," I muttered, more to myself than to this overbearing stranger.

He grinned hugely. In his black eyes little lights began to dance again. "I surely don't, S'rena." He stuck out a calloused, very brown hand. "Howdy, I'm the bastard brother, Quinn."

FOUR

"Cobby around?" Quinn Cooper continued. "I got me a wagon to unload and—"

He broke off as a slim figure appeared behind him out of the shadows, his footsteps as soft as feathers.

"God*dam* but I hate being stole up on . . . who'n hell are you?" Quinn demanded.

The boy started, as a deer might at the approach of a predator.

"His name is Sharo," I said. "Cobby hired him on a couple of weeks ago. He needed a good hand with your horses." I placed a quiet emphasis, deliberately, on "your." "The other men you left him with . . ." I shrugged dismissively.

Quinn's black eyes slanted toward me, then away again. He knew I was right. "Couldn't afford no—" But he had hardly started before he stopped, grunted, and clamped his mouth tight shut. I fancied I could read his mind: *Explain myself to a woman? Not very damn likely!* He turned to Sharo. "You good with horses, like the lady says?"

The lad's dark eyes dropped under his scrutiny. "Cobby thinks so."

"I ain't askin' what Cobby thinks, boy, I'm askin' you."

The eyes came up. "Yes."

Quinn nodded. "All right, then," he said, sensing as I did the confidence implied by the terse answer. "Say, what blood are you?" he added conversationally.

Sharo tensed as he wrestled with the question, trying to figure what right this hard man had to ask it.

"Quanah Parker's my uncle," Quinn offered. "Sort of." This mysterious comment, delivered with a smile and obviously meant to be encouraging, had the opposite effect.

"I'm not Comanche! My father Pawnee."

Quinn Cooper grunted. "Pawnee, huh?" He edged a dried ball of manure out of the straw with the toe of his boot and sent it flying. "Cobby should've known better."

The manure thumped dully against the side of his heavily laden wagon. The handsome black Appaloosa tethered to the rear of the wagon bed shied and threw up its head, and from inside, from under a filthy blanket, something whimpered.

A puppy, I thought. A frightened puppy.

"How could you leave a creature smothered out there in the sun like that!" I turned away in disgust. "Sharo? Bring some water!" I commanded.

As I strode toward the wagon a small thin hand groped up out of the enshrouding blanket, followed by a big-eyed, hollow-cheeked, very dirty, coppery-skinned face. It was a girl, not a puppy; a very young girl, from the look of her. Scrawny shoulders hunched as she peered at us fearfully over the splintered edge of the wagon bed, and as I neared her, she whimpered again and shrank back.

"Sharo?" I called back over my shoulder, "hurry with that water!" I whirled on Quinn. *"How could you!"*

As Sharo approached with a brimming bucket, I saw his eyes narrow as they registered the girl's presence. His footsteps slowed. Quinn grabbed the bucket from his hand.

"Keep your thieving Pawnee hands off her! She's mine, and I intend to keep it that way." He gestured toward the horse with his head. "Tend to my 'Paloosa; I'll see to this one."

Quinn waited until Sharo, realizing delay was not to the girl's advantage, reluctantly led the horse away. He then lifted the bucket into the wagon bed, groped around inside and shortly came up with a wooden ladle. The girl snatched it from his hand, and as she thirstily drank, Quinn leaned close and spoke low to her in words I was unable to understand but which the girl, as indicated by her nods, did. Oddly, she did not seem to be frightened of him, but sometimes, as I well knew, a familiar unpleasantness is preferred to the unknown.

"Serena?"

I turned, seeking the source of the voice. It was Bazz, hailing me from the path down from the house. I ran to meet him.

"We were worried about you. Belle had visions of Bingo stumbling into a prairie dog burrow and . . ." His words trailed off as he took in the scene. "My God, is that—"

"It's your brother, Bazz. He's come back, and he has this poor little Indian girl in tow and . . ." I paused to take a deep breath. "Oh, Bazz, he's everything you ever hinted at and more. The thought of him having Morning Star. . . ." I shook my head, too distressed to continue.

Bazz patted my shoulder. He started toward the wagon. "Well, Quinn. Didn't expect you to turn up this soon."

Quinn spat in the dust, just missing Bazz's toe. "Bad pennies have a way of turnin' up, Bazz. Sometimes sooner; sometimes later. I guess I plumb forgot to ask which'd suit you better."

"Were you able to accomplish your . . . business?" Bazz's jaw twitched from the effort of maintaining a calm demeanor.

"Some . . . mostly, I guess," Quinn replied with maddening, deliberate vagueness. "Plenty of time to get to that. Right now I have a little human business to attend to." He turned, snugged the blanket around the girl's shoulders and hoisted her out of the wagon. "Upsy-daisy, Spotted Fawn."

His cheery tone contrasted shockingly with the appearance of the girl he set down on the dusty ground. She was barefoot; her hair was matted with dirt, and as she scuttled past us in the direction Quinn pointed out to her, the ragged blanket slipped from her torn dress, exposing a spine crisscrossed with inflamed welts. I gasped.

"Unusual cargo, even for you, Quinn," Bazz said. His expression was unreadable as he intently monitored the girl's progress up toward the low stone building Quinn had commandeered for his temporary quarters after the reading of his father's will. Something smouldered in the pale depths of his eyes, but whatever it was—horror? disgust?—I knew he was unlikely to reveal it in Quinn's presence.

Quinn had walked up beside us. He was watching Bazz. His dark eyes went suddenly dead, as if an iron shutter had slammed down. "Won her in a poker game," he volunteered, his offhand tone at odds with the tension I sensed building beneath the surface. "Soap and water and a slathering of that salve of Belle's'll soon put her to rights."

"And then?" Bazz said.

"I don't rightly catch your meaning, Bazz."

"What will become of her, after she's 'put to rights'—"

"Or near as can be," Quinn amended with a careless smile.

"For God's sake, man!" Bazz exploded. "You don't

mean to keep her in your quarters, do you? Why, she's only a child!"

"Older'n she looks. Older'n those two you and Belle brought. Old *enough*." His eyes, as he stared into Bazz's, now held an unmistakable challenge.

This time, Bazz was unable to control a grimace of distaste. He turned his back on Quinn. "Serena? You coming?"

I felt torn; I wanted to leave, but the girl . . .

"She needs a woman," I blurted.

Quinn stood staring after Bazz. He blinked and slid his dark eyes toward me. "Hmm-mmm?"

"The girl—Fawn, did you call her?—she needs a woman—"

"I can manage."

"But—"

His eyes narrowed to slits; his mouth thinned to a knife edge. "Spotted Fawn's mine, bought and paid for. I don't much care for folks interferin' with my property, and that means you, that brassy-haired sister of yours and that highfalutin' half-brother of mine." He ticked us off on square-tipped fingers. "Is that plain enough for you, S'rena?"

Shocked into speechlessness by his callousness, I turned to hurry after Basil. As I did so, I noticed Sharo out of the corner of my eye, standing in the shadows just inside the barn door. I could not see his face, but the fists dangling clenched by his sides betrayed his emotion concerning the scene he had witnessed. They seemed to symbolize the helpless rage Bazz and I, too, had felt, and I resolved I would do whatever I could to help delay the occupation of Morning Star by its unworthy inheritor.

Belle's reaction to the news of Quinn's unexpected arrival was . . . well, not odd exactly, but not quite, if I had thought about it beforehand, what I would have expected.

She stiffened. Her lips drew back from her white teeth, and her long exhale was almost a hiss. "That means we don't have much time."

"I think he was deliberately baiting Bazz," I said. "I doubt he has your money yet, not all of it anyway . . . isn't that how it seemed to you, Bazz?"

Bazz didn't answer. I looked from one to the other. He and Belle were staring at each other in a way that completely excluded me; I felt like an urchin pressing her nose against a bakery shop window.

"Bazz?"

He looked at me blankly.

"Do you think Quinn's ready to settle your claims?"

"Oh. No, not quite. Shrewd of you to catch that, Serena," he added. "Quinn's a sly one."

So was Ernest, I thought. Not like Quinn Cooper, of course, but . . . sly is sly.

"I'll help you pack, Belle," I offered. "If we do a little bit each day . . ."

My earnest words faltered as Belle turned her head, very slowly, to look at me. Her eyes were as cold as pond ice, her expression sneering.

"Always the good girl, aren't you?" Her tone made me wince. "Helpful. Loyal. True. . . ."

All at once her lips began to tremble; the ice in her eyes melted into tears. She reached out for my hands and clutched them to her breast. "Oh, Reenie, here I am taking my worries out on you, as always. Say you'll forgive me?"

I did, of course. For reasons I had never quite understood, life had always been harder for Belle than for me. The track I followed ran relatively smooth and straight, and even though its destination was rarely of my choosing, I could usually anticipate and prepare for the effort it took to maintain a steady course. But Belle, whose ambitions swelled higher than mine, always seemed to seek out a rougher roadbed, which ended more often than not on abandoned sidings.

Once, when called in to answer for the robbing of pennies from some of the other orphans' meager hordes, Belle, afraid of being denied a place on the orphan train as a result of a series of such misdemeanors, had tried to place the blame on me. The director was not fooled. "It's not Serena's way," he had calmly stated. And indeed, until my escape to Morning Star, it never had been. I had always circled risk with the wariness of a starving cat offered food by strangers, and although I had proved myself equal to the challenge of my adventurous flight, I doubted I could ever match Belle's strength of purpose, misguided though it might sometimes be.

Despite the hostility expressed so openly between the brothers that afternoon, Quinn Cooper joined us unannounced, well-scrubbed and freshly shaved, for supper. Belle looked unsurprised, and greeted my whispered expression of indignation with a shrug. "Just like him," she whispered back. To my astonishment, her smiling welcome seemed utterly sincere. Knowing what she really thought of him, I wondered sourly if she would have smiled as sweetly if she had heard him refer to her as brassy-haired.

If Quinn's tidied appearance was intended to disarm us, any such effect was quickly soured. As I stood by my chair at the trestle-legged table set in front of one of the wide curved-top windows, I watched him thread his way through the parlor. His dark eyes flicked left and right at the piles of periodicals and other accumulations. "I swear, Belle," he drawled as he drew our chairs in under us, "I've seen wildcat dens cleaner'n this house."

"I can't quarrel with that, Quinn, your acquaintance with cathouses being a whole lot wider than mine."

I ducked my head to hide my amusement. Belle had flicked him on the raw for sure. But he let it pass, and his next remark was in praise of the beans.

"Best I've et in many a day. My guess is Rita ain't took off yet."

"Rita likes to cook. It's about all she *does* like, far as I can tell. She's so tight with words her joints squeak."

Quinn whooped. "That's a good one, Belle; I'll have to 'member that. You always did have a smart way with words, but how come your sister here talks prettier than you?"

Belle's eyes narrowed. "How do you mean, prettier?"

"Educated. Like brother Bazz-eel here," he added, pronouncing the name with exaggerated emphasis. "You been to college, too, S'rena?"

"I'm an orphan, like Belle; how would I ever get to college?"

"You stayed with rich folks back East, then?"

I laughed. "No, they weren't rich, and no, they weren't educated . . . not the way you mean, anyway."

They continued to look questioningly at me, Bazz and Belle as well as Quinn. "If you must know, it was a man I cleaned house for. Malcolm Wilcox. He was a college professor at Cornell University . . . retired by the time I met him. He traveled a great deal, to England and France and Italy, and he could describe the places he'd been and the people he met so you could almost feel you'd been there yourself. . . ." Remembering, the room faded away. "He used to read to me while I worked . . . he had the most wonderful library—why, it was like having a private college of my own!"

Belle leaned forward. "I guess he had more'n a few

pennies to rub together, to buy all those books and do all that traveling."

"I suppose so, Belle."

"And from the sound of it, you didn't get much cleaning done."

I ducked my head; Belle sounded uncomfortably like Mother Rogg.

"Sooo," she continued, "he must have liked you, Reenie. Quite a lot's my guess."

"Well, yes, I guess he did."

Belle's eyes twinkled at me from under her lashes. "So how come you never got to be Mrs.—what was his name?"

"He was my *friend*," I protested hotly. "Malcolm wasn't a well man—"

Belle pounced triumphantly. "Malcolm, was he?"

I stared at her. "For heaven's sake, Belle, he was old enough to be my *grand*father!"

Quinn laughed. "That never would've gave your sister a lick of pause, would it, Belle?"

He had hitched his chair back on its rear legs. His black leather, silver-buttoned vest fell open over a white linen shirt made whiter by contrast. Almost as white as his strong, even teeth. One tanned thumb was hitched in his belt; the other combed back a lock of the thick, dark glossy hair that fell shaggily over his ears and splayed out like a dark fringe across his collar. I was not deceived by his lazy sprawl. Bazz, seated across from him, was as neat and contained as a well-schooled thoroughbred under saddle, but I sensed that sufficiently prodded, Quinn would rear up with a wild stallion's fury.

I ignored his comment, and in an effort to stop the sharp retort I was sure Belle's lips were forming, I added, "In any event, I was already promised."

"Already *promised?*" To judge from the way Belle's blue eyes all but popped, my diversion was hugely successful.

"To Mother and Father Rogg's nephew, Ernest. He's a pharmacist, like Father Rogg. I know what you're going to say, Belle," I added hastily, before she could, "but Ernest's not a very . . . *easy* sort of person, and he talks like . . . like a Sunday school teacher. So when I got your letter . . . well, suddenly I had two choices," I said lightly, deciding my hours of soul-searching need not concern them. "I could either spend the rest of my life with Ernest or with Belle at Morning Star."

"You were thinking to live here at Morning Star?" Quinn asked curiously.

I had his full attention, and it threw me on the defensive. "At first I did. I guess I misread Belle's letter. . . ." I looked at Belle, hoping she would back me up, or maybe that she would contradict me—I wasn't quite sure which—but her eyes skated away. All at once, looking at her and at Bazz sitting tensely beside her, I realized they had written the letter together. Not that it mattered, but it accounted for the odd combination of graceful phrasing with an occasional awkwardness, and the scrawled postscript Belle hadn't remembered.

"Anyway," I continued with forced lightness, "I thought the name so beautiful I just couldn't resist—"

A bark of laughter interrupted my justification. "Morning Star, beautiful?"

I nodded, perplexed by Quinn's amusement.

"I guess nobody thought to tell you."

"Tell me what?" I searched my sister's face. Her eyes were downcast; her fingers aimlessly traced the engraving on her napkin ring's silver oval. Whatever it was, she wasn't happy about it. Neither was Bazz.

"For God's sake, Quinn," he muttered, "let it be. Leave the girl her illusions."

"For God's sake, Bazz," Quinn mimicked, "'pears to me S'rena's got stomach enough for the truth of it.

70

It ain't every gal who'd bounce a pillar of the church for those stone pillars Paw ordered quarried for Morning Star."

"But I didn't know about the pillars before—"

"'Pears to me," Quinn repeated, casting a dark look in my direction, "if she came out here with more on her mind than a pretty-soundin' place name, she'd better know the truth of it afore she digs herself in any deeper."

Quinn leaned back in his chair, which creakingly protested his sudden shift in weight. He pulled a black cheroot out of his vest pocket, struck a match on the underside of his chair, set the end of the cigar alight and took a long pull. A moment later his lips puffed forth a circle of blue smoke which floated lazily up to the shadowed ceiling along with our mesmerized gazes.

After carelessly tapping the ash onto the floor, he turned his attention back to me. His face had cleared; the lights in his eyes began to dance again, flooding me with apprehension.

"Did that professor feller have much to tell you about Indians, S'rena?"

I shook my head.

"Interestin' folk, the Indians. 'Course they ain't really Indian, but you must of known that. They're a whole lot of different people: some're peaceable; some—like my mother's people, the Comanche—get riled up easy. And they all got religion. Not your Ernest's kind; but it suits the life they know best, and every tribe's got ceremonies dependin' on their particular kind of living: plantin', huntin', war, death. . . . Now, you'd think, wouldn't you, S'rena, that the plantin' ceremonies'd be the tamest of 'em all, and maybe some is, but the Pawnee . . . well, the Pawnee was some different, and the *Skidi* Pawnee even more."

He paused to take another long draw on his

cheroot. "Just for a little while here, let's us pretend I'm that professor feller, S'rena. So tell me, when do you s'pose is the most *anxious* time of year for farmers?"

I eyed him warily; his bland tone didn't fool me. "I only know about the dairy farms back East, but spring, I guess. Planting time."

"Same thing here. Plantin' the corn; hoping for warm weather and enough rain to make a crop big enough to take 'em through the long winters. Those Indians could've worried themselves sick about the soil being warm enough and wet enough and fer-tile enough. But they had a special sun god—Tirawa, they called him—who fathered a child on Mother Earth, a daughter you can see in the eastern sky each spring, just before dawn.

"The morning star! I remember seeing it the morning I left Jericho . . . did I tell you, Belle? It seemed like a heavenly omen."

Quinn grinned. "Mid-April that woulda been?"

I nodded.

"Pretty lady, our Miss Morning Star, shinin' so bright by her lone; but like a lot of pretty ladies she purely likes to be indulged before grantin' her favors, and those Pawnees, that Skidi branch anyways, took it in their heads that what she liked best was blood . . . 'specially the blood of a girl as pretty as herself, not yet touched by any man."

I looked at Bazz in horror. He turned his eyes away, a mute confirmation of the truth of what Quinn was telling me. "Are you telling me these people sacrificed their own children?"

Quinn shrugged. "Sometimes, but mostly they captured one from some other tribe. From what I heard she'd be placed in the charge of the Wolf Priest and kept in a mud-plastered lodge set apart from the rest of the village and bathed and oiled and fatted up like a suckling pig for a Christmas feast, thinking

72

these sweet rituals was to make her fit to be the bride of a Pawnee chieftain's son."

According to Quinn, as spring warmed the prairie, so did the attentions of the old squaws to the girl. They bathed her hair and skin with special herbs and dressed her in soft, white doeskin decorated with porcupine quillwork.

"Well, you can imagine how thrilled she musta been! In her own tribe, she'd been just another no-account girl-child; here, those Skidi priests were treating her like a reg'lar princess!" He paused to blow another smoke ring.

"When do you suppose she suspected they had something other'n a royal wedding in mind? Maybe when the warriors began to build a scaffold. Maybe when they led her from lodge to lodge to beg for wood to fill the pit dug beneath it. For sure the night she was dressed in black, save for a feathered headdress, and led through the village to the scaffold where she was tied, stripped naked of her finery, and left to wait for a dawn she must've known was her last. . . ."

And when the morning star broke over the edge of the world that morning, an iron-tipped arrow was shot into the maiden's heart, which was cut out of her body and burned to purify the farming implements.

Quinn grinned after telling us that. "As tools, they prob'ly weren't worth a whole helluva lot, so I guess they figgered they needed all the help they could get. They flung the rest of her, hacked bones and all, into the burning pit to roast some before spreading the whole mess out over the newly planted corn and beans." He shook his head wonderingly. "Some kind of religion, eh, S'rena?"

Belle threw down her napkin, screeched back her chair and left without a word. Her silver napkin ring rolled clatteringly across the table. I slowly worked her discarded napkin through it, collecting myself as I did so. I had not come all this way to be routed by a sadistic bully.

"Why are you telling me this?" I asked as calmly as I could manage. "What possible purpose—"

He broke in. "Because although the Skidis mostly lived up north in Nebraska, along the Loup River, a group of 'em moved down here, hopin' to escape Comanche raids. They sheltered down near Beacon Rock, and they held their ceremony here, right on the ground this house is built on."

"That makes no sense," I scoffed. "If your father named his ranch Morning Star, he must have known this ground was . . . was . . ."

"Soaked in blood? He did. You see, Paw's parents were killed by Pawnees, back in the thirties that must've been, isn't that so, Bazz?"

Bazz shook his head, unable to speak. I suspected he himself had been acquainted with only the bare outline of the hideous story Quinn had recounted with such relish.

"His folks put him down in their cyclone cellar. Nothin' near as fancy as the one here, of course. It wasn't nothin' but a pit dug in the floor of their sod house and covered with planks. When the Indians came, his paw threw a rag rug across the planks, and he wasn't found. But he never forgot huddlin' there in the damp and the dark and hearing what was going on above him. Anyway, buildin' this house where he did, on Pawnee sacred ground, was his way of thumbing his nose at them. The girls the Pawnee stole was mostly Comanche, like my maw . . . like Spotted Fawn." He paused and frowned. "There's been a passel of poor girls lost at Morning Star, S'rena."

"But the land is still beautiful . . . and the name is, too, in spite of your effort to make it repellent to me."

Quinn shrugged. "Don't matter to me one way or t'other, seein's how you won't be here long enough for it to matter to you."

He ground his cheroot out on his plate, got up from his chair and bowed to me elaborately. "Tell Belle I sure 'preciated her hospitality. I better go collect Spotted Fawn from the kitchen. She musta had enough to eat by now, and it's way past her bedtime."

Was I meant to infer something from his parting remark? I held my tongue, choosing not to think so. After Quinn left, Bazz pushed back from the table, his excuses meaningless formalities muttered barely loud enough for me to hear. I could hardly blame him. I followed slowly in his swiftly retreating footsteps; then, feeling stifled by the stale, smoke-fogged air, I paused at the front door, opened it, and stepped out on the wide stone doorstep. My breath plumed in the clear, cold air, and above me the moon glittered like a skin of ice pried from a bucket. As I pulled my shawl tight around me, my eye caught movement flickering between the pillars. It was Quinn's spare figure, silvered by moonlight, striding down the path to his quarters with Spotted Fawn trotting behind him like a cowed spaniel.

Quinn's words about collecting Fawn from the kitchen returned to me: was this sadly mistreated child being "fatted up" for a ceremony of his own devising? After soap and water and Belle's salve had done their work, would she, too, be anointed with fragrant oils and robed in soft white doeskin? Another Comanche girl's innocence betrayed?

I turned abruptly. The fringes of my shawl brushed the petals of the peonies, releasing a gagging scent of carrionlike sweetness. The gigantic blossoms, their redness black in the absence of sunlight, lolled like severed heads from stems that despite their stoutness, were no longer able to hold them aloft.

Severed heads? I shrank back, repelled by the ghastly image that sprang unbidden to my mind, and yet . . . *Why had nothing short of a team of oxen been able to rid this place of its tenaciously rooted weeds?* The garden planted in their stead was nourished by manure, Belle had told me—*Lots of that on a ranch, Reenie*—but no one had fed those weeds. . . . How far and how deep, I wondered, had the blood of those cruelly sacrificed maidens seeped?

It hardly bore thinking about. My hand tightened on the door knob, but my gaze strayed back to the peonies in dreadful fascination, as if to a fatal accident. *If I snapped off one of these obscene blossoms, would the torn stem's sap run clear?*

I shuddered and turned away. Would I ever again be able to think of Morning Star as beautiful?

FIVE

I woke very early the next morning, my muscles cramped with cold. I threw back the covers and dashed to the window, intending only to close it before returning to my bed's downy shelter, but the chill stillness of the great stone house overwhelmed me. *Silent as the grave . . . cold as a tomb. . . .* I hugged myself, shivering, as the morbid phrases trooped unbidden through my mind. *Sleep is but a little death. . . .*

A return to bed seemed no longer in the least appealing, and a pale wash of gray on the horizon diluted the nighttime gloom sufficiently to allow me to move with assurance from window to washstand. The water's icy splash raised goosebumps on my arms, and I hastily crossed to the wardrobe to don my riding clothes, ignoring the rim of dust clinging to the edge of my skirt and the mud smeared across the toes of my boots. My shirtwaist was fresh, but the heavy, oily sweater I pulled on over it hid its cheery gingham checks. My dreary reflection in the mirror mounted above the bureau confirmed my fearful expectation; should I lose my way today on the prairie, I doubted anyone could distinguish me from the dry earth, grasses and limestone outcrops that could become my final resting place.

That's quite enough of *that,* I told myself, my mouth twisting in wry rejection of the dismal scene I had painted. I tiptoed out on the landing. Except for the sighing groan of roof rafters adjusting to the easing of the night's windless chill, the silence was absolute. I crept down the stairs, willing them not to creak under my booted feet, and into the kitchen, where the pots and dishes from last evening's supper clustered unwashed on every available horizontal surface not already taken up by Belle's herbal preparations. Grimacing distastefully, I picked up a blackened pot, intending to clean it, but hastily discarded the notion as the pungent odor of the clotted remains of the beans Quinn had so enjoyed rose thickly to clog my nostrils and rile my stomach.

What a sorry excuse for a household! The big pot of inky coffee standing neglected on a back grate was as cold as the huge black range itself, which would take ages to fire up hot enough for cooking. Actually, I was more relieved than disappointed about the coffee—I had yet to acquire a taste for the acid, oily brew—and just as I despaired of finding anything edible, my eye fell on a basket containing a couple of thick slices of Rita's cornmeal bread leftover from supper. Left uncovered, the edges had curled and dried. It would be like eating coarse sawdust. But my gently gurgling stomach persuaded me to slide them into one of the sacks Belle used for storing her herbs, to which I added a thick mug from the unmatched assortment wedged higgledy-piggledy on a greasy shelf. Dry bread and water may not have been the menu I would have chosen, but something was better than nothing.

As I let myself out the kitchen door, a glowing slice of orange inched over the horizon, warming the gray sky to blue. My spirits heightened along with the color; even my breakfast fare seemed less crude: for centuries, peasant folk all over the world had thrived on bread and water; who was I to expect, or deserve, better?

Bingo whickered softly as I led her out of her stall, one of the few animals allowed valuable barn space. I had Cobby to thank for that, unconvinced as he was of my ability to whistle her up on my own. Being thought incapable, I reflected, sometimes had its uses, a shocking concession that tempted me to throw myself astride Bingo bareback, Indian style, although I knew my seat was still too uncertain for the rough terrain. Caution prevailed, reinforced perhaps by my earlier vision of my dun-colored form sprawled unnoticed among the prairie grasses; besides, the saddle horn made a handy hook for my breakfast sack.

As we made our way out of the sheltering basin in which the ranch buildings clustered, a soft southern breeze lifted the tendrils of hair that had escaped from the single silver braid trailing down my back. The sleepy twitterings of birds waking to the wonder of the morning swelled into a chorus of warbles and trills, causing Bingo's ears to prick interestedly. Heedless of her bulky presence, wings flashed from bush to bush beneath her very nose, to which the steady little creature's only response was an occasional "whuff" of astonishment.

By the time we reached the pond the breeze had freshened, sending ripples chasing across the surface as if unseen fingers were tracing silver patterns on its watery skin. I settled down at the base of a willow springing plumelike out of the uneven bowl in which the pond nestled. Bingo grazed, untethered, no more than an arm's length away, faithful as any dog. She turned her head to watch my progress with my cup to the pond and back, then, assured of my safe return—or so I imagined—resumed her grazing.

The cornbread tasted good, the water even better. I sighed contentedly, and began idly to braid Bingo's long brown-and-white tail. Thanks to Belle, I had a clean place to lay my head and honest food to fill my stomach, and even though our future after Morning Star was uncertain, I trusted we would somehow provide for one another. Loyalty and trust: without it, life was like a world without color; with it, one needed little else—nothing, in fact, and yet . . .

What about love? I loved Belle of course, but when it came to the kind of love a woman feels for a man, and he for her . . . I shook my head. I had no idea of it; none at all. How could I be disappointed by not having something I couldn't even define? I shouldn't be, I told myself, but oh, how I yearned. . . . "Yes, I do, Bingo," I whispered. *I do, I do.* . . .

At the sound of her name, Bingo turned and pushed her soft pink-and-white muzzle against my forehead, knocking my hat off and sending it rolling down toward the pond, where it lodged in a patch of young cattails. She pulled her lips back from her big, yellow teeth as if amused by her prank, then yawned hugely, her jaws twisting in a comical fashion.

I laughed, and continued braiding her tail. Enjoying the day, my mind wandering, I began to hum; gradually the hum became a long-forgotten song. *Hush-you bye, don't you cry,* I began falteringly, tracing slowly back through dimly remembered years, pushing aside the clouding veils, *go to sleepy little baby.* . . . I closed my eyes, Bingo's coarse tail hairs twisting and twining automatically between my fingers as the words of the song coiled smoothly up out of my memory like pearls on a waxed string: *when you wake you shall have all the pretty little horses—blacks and bays, dapples and grays.* . . .

Mama's song. The one lovely memory from that cold, smoky, dark flat wedged into a narrow lot amid

80

the Bowery's saloons, the drunken shouts of their reeling patrons often drowning out her high, sweet voice. *Again, Mama, lull-me-bye again. . . .* I laid my tear-wet cheek against Bingo's warm haunch. "All the pretty little horses. . . ."

Poor Mama. I recalled the day she was taken away, after the coughing that had racked her frail body had stopped. "Good riddance," I remembered my father muttering as I clung, whimpering, to her waxy arm, wondering why she was so still. Is that what he thought when he left me, pale and sickly in comparison to Belle's bloom, at the orphanage? I had regained my health by the time Belle joined me there after Papa died, and since we were again identical as two peas in a pod, she delighted in playing jokes based on our twinness. My meek nature was no match for her daring inventiveness, but I was so glad to have her with me again I never begrudged the laughter that was usually at my expense.

Bingo's tail slipped from my fingers, the braid painstakingly accomplished slowly unwinding as I sat back on my heels, remembering. The truth was that no matter how much alike we looked or how giddily she sometimes played, Belle's occasionally childish ways had little to do with childhood. She never spoke much about those two years we were apart, but I suspected the poor health that delivered me from the care of a father more often drunk than not had, in fact, been my good fortune.

I ate the last of the bread and scattered the crumbs from the sack into the pond where, one by one, they were sucked in by little fish that flashed up in swarms from darker, deeper waters, competing greedily for my unexpected offering. Suddenly I heard a horse snort. I looked up to see Quinn Cooper hunkered down on the ledge above me. The reins of the tall black horse looming behind him trailed loosely down over his shoulder. His intent dark-eyed gaze made my throat constrict with alarm.

"Makes you feel sort of like God, don't it?"

I stared at him uncomprehendingly. "I beg your pardon?"

He grinned. "Them fish," he said, waving his hat in their direction. They riffled the surface in their panic; the few crumbs remaining on the surface slowly sank, to be snatched by fish more daring than the others. "They've prob'ly been swimmin' around down there hopin' something tasty'd come their way, and all of a sudden, down it comes, kinda like rain after a rain dance."

"Well, I don't know about *that*," I said, surprised by his fanciful speculation. "It was meant as a treat. But it turned out to be more a hand-to-hand, or rather fin-to-fin combat."

He laughed, and eased his way down the bank to sit beside me. "That's how life is, S'rena. A body never can tell how a good deed's gonna be took. One thing for sure, gratitude's usually in short supply."

I smiled in wry agreement. His brown eyes, meeting mine, held a golden flicker in their chocolate depths; last night that dancing light had seemed more like a spark struck from cold steel.

"Was that you I heard singin'?"

I felt the color rise in my cheeks. "It wasn't meant to be shared."

He shoved his hat back off his forehead, tugged at a thick, dark lock and frowned in elaborate puzzlement. "No way I could know that, was there? There we was, just amblin' along, when we hear this little bird callin' out for the pretty horses, so Bucket pricked up his ears and came right along, never mind about where I might have had in mind to go."

"*Bucket?* Why on earth would anyone give such an unlovely name to a beautiful animal like that!"

Quinn pulled his hat flat back on his head. "You sure rile easy, S'rena," he drawled.

I hadn't expected an answer, so I figured that was the end of it. I was wrong.

"I had my reasons," he continued, "three in fact." He clamped one pinky finger around the other. "He was the buckingest colt you ever saw . . ."

He transferred the hooked pinky to his ring finger, which sported, I noticed for the first time, an impressive dome of gold. "It was my Paw's," he said, seeing my interest. "Called it a token of what'd be mine some day if I kept my wits about me." He grinned, leaving me no wiser than before—deliberately, I'm sure—and resumed his counting.

"His hindquarters looked like a bucket of white paint'd been splashed on 'em . . ." He paused, snatched at his middle finger, waggled it at me and mouthed the word three.

I started to tell him I was perfectly able to count, caught myself just in time, and contented myself with the purse-lipped look of reproof I used to earn from Mother Rogg for behavior she considered impertinent. I seldom was; I suspected Quinn Cooper was seldom otherwise.

"And sometimes," he continued with a cocky grin, "when you're in a hurry or a hard place, you want a name that'll carry a piece." Without warning, he cupped his hands around his mouth. "Bucket!" he roared. "Bucka-Bucka-Bucket!"

Startled, the big horse snorted and plunged above us on the ledge, then peered down at Quinn anxiously, ears twitching, long forelegs splayed, his hooves dislodging pellets of earth which released choking puffs of dry dust as they crumbled down upon us. My heart pounded in my chest. Unsure of the horse's intention, I drew my legs under me, preparing to spring to my feet; Bingo, who had been drowsing nearby, shied away with an indignant snort.

"Back now, Bucket," Quinn called mildly. "Back

it up, *thassa* boy." Reassured by his master's return to sanity, Bucket moved back from the edge and began to graze; Bingo maintained her wary distance.

I stared at Quinn. "Why do you do things like that?"

He stared back, then rose to his feet in a flash of grace, one minute cross-legged beside me, the next, standing above me, arms akimbo. "Like what?"

I shaded my eyes with my hand. I disliked having to look up at him; I disliked his intent to intimidate me even more. "Deliberately pushing people off center. You did it last night at dinner, all those stories about Morning Star, and now here, with me, using your horse as an unwilling accomplice."

He scuffed the toe of his boot against mine. "Those stories are true, S'rena."

"So, I'm sure, are your reasons for choosing to name your horse Bucket." I pulled my foot away from his. "That's not the point: it's not *what* you say; it's how you say it. Scaring people half to death. There's no need for it."

He folded his arms and looked down at me, his outward calm belied by the muscles tensing beneath the faded blue cloth stretched tight across his lean, hard thighs. "Sometimes," he began softly, "keepin' a person off center is the best way to stay on top of things. When I let the best of Paw's men go—"

"Why would you do a thing like that?" I blurted.

He smiled thinly. "Top hands; top wages." His words, clipped and hard, warned me not to pursue what was clearly a sore subject. "As I was sayin', those I got is either green as spring peas or saddle bums. 'Cept for Cobby, of course—and maybe that breed, Sharo," he conceded grudgingly. "The way I see it, if they always knew what to expect from me, good or bad, they'd either slack off or leave." He shrugged. "Actually, since everyone always expects the worst of me, I've never had much success confusing folks with evidence of my good character.''

"Like the time Basil almost drowned here?"

Deploring the tremor in my voice as I challenged him, I stood up and began edging away, eyeing him warily. I needn't have worried; he winced as if slapped.

"I should've known there was more to you than just pretty tunes and tears," he muttered, "being Belle's twin and all. She been bending your ear? Cobby's the only one who knows all there is to tell on it, and he's not much of a talker."

"Cobby?"

"Cobby and me, we built that dock up at the deep end of the pond the summer Paw brought me here to Morning Star. Cobby can't swim, and when he saw me and the good times I had blowing and diving like a whale in a fishbowl, he figured maybe I could show Bazz how it's done, working up, gradual like, to the deep part.

"It ain't much of a dock, slapped together with green wood and horseshoe nails, but Cobby reckoned Bazz'd be more venturesome if he knew there was something more'n cattails to grab on to." He paused. "You swim, S'rena?"

I hesitated, wondering what possible difference it made, then shook my head. "I never had the opportunity."

He scratched his earlobe thoughtfully, then grabbed my arm and led me to a spot, only a few feet to the right, that put me in a direct line with the mossy platform.

I might neither like nor trust Quinn Cooper, but there was no denying the unnerving effect of his physical presence. I had never known anyone so . . . so thoroughly masculine. Not blatantly so, not arrogantly—although there was more than a hint of arrogance about him—but assuredly. He fair took my breath away. I pulled my arm away as if from

85

a burning brand.

He looked at me in astonishment; then, as I glared back defiantly, amusement caused his eyes to crinkle at the corners. "Hell's fire, girl," he hooted, "didya think I was fixing to throw you in?"

Until then I hadn't, but I was determined not to let my expression reveal the stab of alarm that made my mouth go suddenly dry.

"Now lookahere," he commanded, pointing dead ahead. "Think of yourself starting off from here, water hardly up to your belly button, then paddling out and pushing yourself off the bottom. You see how it'd be? Paddling and pushing, up and out, up and out, until a time comes when you find yourself reaching down with your toes and finding nothin' there? Well, it's some scary at first, and needs a lot of encouragement. That's how the trouble started. By the time it ended, there wasn't nothing I could say or do to turn it back to the way it really was."

I found Quinn's earnestly delivered confidence unsettling; was it possible he was telling the truth? "You admit you coaxed him out beyond his depth."

"Well, course I did! How else was I supposed to get the little critter out there? I don't hold with throwin' younguns in and trustin' in the Lord to hold 'em up. His mama, though, she wasn't about to give me any room on it—those lawyers got a name for it, but I can't rightly bring it to mind."

"Benefit of the doubt?" I supplied.

"There you go," he drawled, saluting me with one finger. "You see, Cobby worried some about Bazz and his maw. He purely admired Bazz's mama, Cobby did. By the time I met her, her black hair had turned gray, and what with her squinched little face and bright shoe-button eyes, she sort of put me in mind of a mouse; but Cobby, who'd known her all her life and came with her to Morning Star, says she was the prettiest little thing he ever saw. I guess Paw thought so, too, seein' as how he did everything but lasso the moon to win her; but she had . . . notions, I guess you'd call 'em, and Paw didn't hold much with that sort of thing, unless they were his own, of course. After a while he tired of Lottie's notions, then Lottie herself.

"Accordin' to Cobby, she began lookin' to Bazz for comfort a mother oughtn't rightly expect from a son. She got him to thinkin' the sun rose and set on him, which left him, accordin' to Cobby, with about as much gumption as a suck-egg dog."

"But how could Cobby possibly have expected you to change that? You couldn't have been much more than a boy yourself."

"Well, sure, I was only fifteen, but Cobby didn't expect much; he just thought maybe I could give the kid a shove in the right direction. What the hell, S'rena, no one had ever took me serious before. It was s'posed to be a surprise for his folks, but I sure put the saddle on the wrong horse. . . .

"Bazz did right well at first, paddlin' around happy as a little puppy dog. Then, like I told you, I tried taking him from this shallow end to the deep."

"He says you tried to drown him."

Quinn's eyes narrowed at my blunt words. "The hell I did. What I was *trying* was to get him to duck his head. You can't never feel at home in water if you're fightin' the whole time to keep it dry. First the face, then the head, then down like a pollywog. That's how my maw learned me, and it was right about then *his* maw hove into sight, screeching like a kettle on the boil, her horse so spooked he dang near turned the buggy and himself over on top of her. Cobby said she exploded outta that buggy, leavin' him to peg along after her fast he could on those bandy legs of his.

"I knew we was in trouble soon's I saw her. . . ." Remembering, he shook his head. His eyes drifted beyond me, and it seemed as if he wasn't telling the story of that day so much as trying to understand, fifteen years after the fact, why it had all gone wrong. either that, or he was a very accomplished liar.

"Soon as Bazz caught sight of her. he started blubberin' like a baby in a beehive. So there they both was"—Quinn threw out his arms and let them fall helplessly to his sides—"her screamin' and him thrashin' 'til he got tuckered and started to sink. *Scared?* Why, his eyes near popped, and when he opened his mouth to yell the water just poured down his gullet like a flash flood down a gopher hole.

"After that I was too busy trying to keep him up to pay much attention to his maw. That's when she loosed the buggy whip on me." He pantomimed the flourish, ending in a convincing imitation of the crack of braided leather. "Boy howdy, it stung some. That's when I let go of Bazz. By the time he finally got hauled up, her pullin', me pushin', he was sloshin' like a water bag."

"Is that when you called the poor woman a silly cow?"

"Did I?" Quinn grinned at me. "Coulda been worse."

I looked back at him thoughtfully. He hadn't denied it. I wondered what else was true; not much, I suspected.

His grin faded. "She damn near killed him."

"If it happened the way you're telling me, why did you leave Morning Star?"

He looked at me scornfully. "Because Lottie Cooper saw what suited her, Bazz was so shook he took what his maw said for gospel, never mind what me or Cobby had to say about it, and Paw was lookin' to get shed of me. Had been for some weeks."

"Why was that?"

The light in his eyes vanished as abruptly as a snuffed flame on a candle. "None of your business."

"And yet he gave you Morning Star," I continued, as if to myself. "I wonder that nobody challenged it, but I suppose that's not my business, either."

I could tell he didn't like my tone. "You're right about the last part, lady; about the first, my brother and your sister plumb wore themselves out tryin'."

"Why wouldn't they? It's his mother's family's land; Belle spent half of her life here. But I'm beginning to understand why she didn't write me earlier. If your father was anything like you, I probably wouldn't have been any more welcome at Morning Star when he was alive than I am now by you." I compressed my lips, willing them not to tremble with the anger I felt. "How could you turn your own brother out to make his way among strangers? To live in your father's house yourself—? It's . . . it's . . . *unconscionable!*

Quinn snorted. He stuck his hand under my nose, his thumb and forefinger pressed so closely together I could barely see daylight between them. "See that there, S'rena? That's how much family feelin' *I* got from these folks!"

His eyes flashed fire. He pulled the brim of his hat low, and when he next spoke, his voice was as cool as long-extinguished ashes. "He'll do just fine, ol' Bazz will. He'll have enough to build a parlor around that fancy pi-yanner of his and then some. As for Belle's de-pri-vation of sisterly companionship, Cobby says no one ever heard tell of you 'til before you showed up.

"Course her time was pretty well taken up with Paw," he added in a tone calculated to offend. "After his will was read and she learned she'd be getting hardly enough to dust a fiddle, well, she was powerful flummoxed. All that sweet-talking and tail-swaying for nothing." His grin slowly faded. "At least my maw was an honest whore," he drawled, looking at me speculatively through narrowed eyes.

"I haven't figured out yet what kind you are."

I slapped him. I hadn't meant to, not wanting to give him the satisfaction, and as my hand descended, he grabbed my wrist cruelly, bringing tears to my eyes.

"You think tears in those pretty eyes are going to get you anything Belle's bold looks couldn't?" He laughed harshly, abruptly loosing my wrist as if he found the feel of it abhorrent. The marks his strong fingers left on my white skin bloomed fiery red. "Quite a pair, you two. One of you heads, the other tails"—I colored at his lewd implication—"but the same coin when all's said and done."

The last was said in a mutter, almost as if he were reassuring himself of a conclusion already reached. I started to speak, then thought better of it. If Quinn Cooper wanted to see Belle and me in black-and-white terms, no words of mine would change that, and I had no reason to care one way or the other.

He returned my silent stare, his lean figure, clothed in dark leathers, an exclamation mark against the sky-reflecting pond and its soft fringe of spring green grasses. A hard man. Capable of tenderness, no doubt, but only as a convenience, a cloak to be donned and discarded at will. The inner light I had sometimes seen dancing in his dark eyes was, I now suspected, fueled by animal spirits devoid of human compassion. He turned, preparing to climb back up the bank to his horse.

"Where were you when your father had his accident?" I demanded.

"Here. At Morning Star," he answered shortly. I could tell the question was not to his liking.

"But where exactly? Surely that's no secret; you must have been asked at the time."

He turned back toward me, eyes narrowing as he perceived the intention of my interrogation. "No one had to ask me; I was ready enough to say. I was with him, cuttin' out cows the outfit I was with was looking to buy. You thinkin' maybe I spooked the bull that made his horse rear and throw him? Or just kind of calfed around 'til he lost enough blood? That's what Bazz likes to think." His face hardened, deepening the grooves that led from his nose to the downturned corners of his mouth. "I couldn't save Paw; no one could. But it's easier for Bazz to think I let Paw die, maybe helped it happen, than admit he cheated himself."

"Cheated himself? By preferring music to running cattle?"

My scornful attitude amused him. "Running cattle's what you do on a ranch, S'rena. Bazz knew Paw: he knew what store he set on this land and his cattle; knew he wasn't a tolerant sort of fellow." Quinn shrugged. "Bazz took his chances same as me when I left."

"The fact remains he was disinherited of the only home he ever knew."

"Hell, S'rena, that's not the burr under ol' Bazz's saddle. He don't give a hoot for Morning Star; what riles him is the gold."

"Gold? What gold?"

Quinn greeted my bemused expression with a broad grin. "You think I don't know what's going on up to the house? I seen them candles twinkling past the windows late at night and those puffy little pouches under Belle's eyes the next morning. Time's runnin' out, and they haven't found it yet, have they?"

"I haven't the least idea what you're talking about! The only gold I've seen or heard of here is that ring on your finger."

Quinn raised his eyebrows in exaggerated surprise, then burst out laughing. "How long you been here, S'rena, five, maybe six weeks? Just how many things am I s'posed to believe no one's told you?"

"I know all about you!" I cried.

He smiled. "Oh, not quite all," he murmured. His approach was so slow, his smile so lazy, I had no hint of his intention until he reached out and pulled me close. There was no tenderness in the dark eyes that searched mine, but he smelled warmly of horseflesh and leather overlaid with a subtle spiciness of his own. Inhaling it—how could I not?—I felt . . . breathless.

Mother Rogg had often warned of the weakness of the spirit in the body's thrall; alarmed, I struggled to heed an admonition I had never thought would apply to me, but it was already too late.

The abrasive passage of his unshaven cheek over mine seemed a caress, no matter its roughness; the heat of his lips persuaded a willing response to their urgent demand. Dimly perceiving I would never have experienced a kiss remotely like this if I had married Ernest, I allowed my aroused senses to whirl my remaining misgivings into oblivion.

SIX

I wish I could say I tried to free myself from Quinn's embrace, but in all honesty I cannot. Not only did he end it, but he scrambled up the bank without so much as a by-your-leave, pausing at the top only long enough to brush his hands against his Levi's, giving me shamed cause to wonder whether he was freeing them of dirt or the lingerings of my touch. *Did he think me easy?* It was a humiliating thought.

Chastened, I retrieved my hat and breakfast sack, mounted Bingo and started back. Despite myself, I stole a glance over my shoulder. He was still there, watching after me. Seated on his horse, shoulders hunched, arms folded back like dark wings, hands clutched atop the saddle horn, Quinn seemed a predator, more hawk than man. Or perhaps, considering his easy, sometimes playful manner, a cat was a more apt comparison: soft paws releasing cruel claws when least expected.

I urged Bingo to a faster pace, shivering as a bank of dark clouds fast advancing from the west devoured the sun. As we topped a rise affording a view across the working heart of the ranch to the great stone house beyond, its shadowed bulk seemed more fortress than residence, guardian of long-ago dark events and of secrets I was only beginning to suspect.

After relinquishing Bingo to Sharo, who had become almost as fond of her as I, I trudged up the path to the house. As I approached, my earlier dour impression was reinforced by two dark shapes huddled side by side behind the pillars, sheltering there from the wind gusting ahead of the clouds. Shrouded, ominous, they put me in mind of the Furies, those Roman daughters of night and darkness Malcolm Wilcox had once described to me. They had haunted my dreams for days afterwards, always threatening, sometimes wearing faces of haunting familiarity.

As I uneasily watched, one of the shadows, slighter than its companion, rose swiftly to glide away like a twist of smoke. I was almost sure it was Spotted Fawn. The other, bulkier, figure—it was Rita, I realized—turned to enter the house.

A moment later the door opened again, and Basil stepped out between the pillars; another moment, and the sun beamed forth once more, transforming his auburn hair into a bright copper helmet. Catching sight of me, he waved; I could see the welcoming gleam of his smile from where I stood below him on the path, and the relief that swept over me was so great I fair stunned him with the intensity of my greeting.

He laughed, fending me off as one would an eager puppy, but the laughter did not quite reach his gray eyes. Although his smooth-skinned face had yet to acquire the grooves that made his half-brother seem older than the six years that separated them, something had served to make Bazz wary of expressing emotion; something that now caused him to shift restively under my intent scrutiny.

Why did some fathers insist that the twig must emulate the tree? Did it spring from a monstrous sort of pride? Denied eternal life, had Ross Cooper's next best hope been a reverential facsimile of himself by his sons? Poor Bazz! Seen at best as counterfeit by his father, his legitimate and greater family claim to the ranch had been ignored, bypassed in favor of Quinn, the bastard tarred by his father's brutal brush.

"Belle tells me you were out early again this morning," Bazz said. "Sometimes it's hard to believe you two are really twins!"

"Well, Belle doesn't have Bingo to go exploring on."

Bazz grinned. "If Belle had Pegasus to ride she'd be no more likely to go exploring, Serena. She finds the prairies dull."

"Dull! But things are happening there all the time! I noticed three new varieties of wildflowers on my way to the pond this morning—"

I broke off in confusion, knowing the pond was a sensitive subject for Bazz and not wishing to mention my encounter with Quinn, but I needn't have worried.

"The only plants that interest your sister are those she uses in her concoctions, and she grows most of those herself."

"That may be so, but I wager she knows at least as much about them as Ernest, and he's a trained pharmacist!"

"Ernest?"

"Ernest Rogg. The man I mentioned last night . . . the man I was to marry."

Basil nodded. "Ah, yes. The pious apothecary. I, for one, am very pleased you didn't."

I glanced up at him under my lashes. Did I dare infer a more than friendly interest in me? Might he truly become my perfect gentle knight? Would I be the one to erase that shadow in his eyes?

He smiled and bent attentively toward me as if guessing my wonderings. But as his intent smile persisted, I sensed a hollow politeness animating it.

95

Quinn's sneering drawl came uneasily to mind: *You think I don't know what's going on up to the house?* That candlelight he'd seen late at night, the scurryings in my dreams that I had ascribed to mice, could that have been Belle and Bazz, the one visiting the other? *Shh, we don't want Reenie to hear. . . .* Having grown up together, almost like brother and sister, it was natural they might feel diffident, ashamed even, about revealing the . . . mature turn their childhood affection had taken.

"You're right of course about Belle and her herbs," he said, "but unlike your observations of the prairie flowers, her motives are very practical. That healing salve of hers, for example: she has buyers waiting on every ranch for miles around for every bit of it she whips up. She keeps a good store of it on hand in the cellar, and another batch is always in the making."

"That's not what she told Cobby!"

"Morning Star doesn't pay for it," he said tersely. "Come, Serena, no need to frown," he added in a lighter tone. "Cobby's so afraid of running out he always has a couple of extra jars tucked away someplace, and Belle knows it."

I accepted Basil's gentle reproof without comment. Faced with the possibility of real privation, it was no wonder Belle felt hard-pressed to store up every penny she could. I resolved not to pass judgment so quickly in the future. "What will you do about your piano, Bazz?" Surprised by my sudden change of subject, his eyes narrowed warily. "When you—we—leave Morning Star," I amplified, realizing my thinking had run ahead of his.

"I hope to take it with me. If I leave it here, it'd be just like Quinn to chop it up for kindling some cold night."

"You're forgetting summer's coming on, Bazz. There can't be enough cold nights in the months ahead to drive even him to such a measure, and surely we'll be settled someplace by fall."

He shot a curiously speculative glance at me. "No matter when we leave we have to make it through the spring first. I don't know how much truth there is in those awful stories Quinn told with such relish last night; but it's a fact Morning Star's always had trouble keeping Indian help here during this time of year, and since my mother died, we've had no other kind up at the house." He nodded toward the dense vegetation in the stone-edged beds. "It's the garden, I think. Being creatures of the prairie, they can't understand why it grows like it does."

Nor did I. No matter what Belle had to say about its sheltered location and the care taken with its feeding and watering, I couldn't dispel the uneasiness I felt whenever I saw it. I recalled her boast about how early it greened up—unnaturally early for these parts. Mid-April, she'd said. Which was, I knew, the time of the vernal equinox, when a bloody sacrifice, made upon the rising of the morning star, had fed and watered the crops once grown here with the blood, flesh and shattered bones of innocent children.

". . . as the days grow longer," Bazz was saying, "they do less and less around the house; instead they shuffle out here to sit and stare for hours at a time. Sometimes, you can hear them chanting." He grimaced. "Enough to make your skin crawl.

"Then one fine morning we come down to find they've gone." He shrugged and kicked at a pebble. "It doesn't usually matter—there are always women coming through looking for work—but this year only Rita came back. There's no knowing how long she'll stay, and what with the packing and all. . . ." He smiled wearily.

"No garden, no matter how peculiar, is about to scare *me* off," I assured him in words pluckier than I felt. "I may not be as strong as Rita, but I'm a good worker. Even Mother Rogg granted me that much, and she wasn't an easy woman with praise—except for the good Lord, of course, and sometimes I felt even He had to earn it." I placed my hand on his arm. "We'll manage, Bazz."

He patted my hand awkwardly. "Yes," he muttered. "Yes, I'm sure we will."

The sun beat hotly down on our heads. It must be nearing noon, I realized. "Is Belle in the kitchen? This morning it looked as if she'd been spirited away spang in the middle of her herbal preparations."

He sighed. "The kitchen always looks like that. Drives anyone trying to actually cook there loco. Her door was closed when I came down, Serena. I don't think she's up yet."

"Not *up* yet?" I exclaimed. Then, recalling the candlelit nocturnal activity Quinn had reported and my subsequent interpretation of it, I felt heat rise in my cheeks. I withdrew my hand from Basil's arm. "If you'll excuse me, I think I'll go see if she's all right."

"Don't be surprised if she takes on some," Bazz called after me. "Belle's not at her best in the morning."

I resented his knowing this. How much else did he know about my sister? Things that I did not? Cheated by circumstance of the life we might have had together, I determined to do all I could to make up for the time we had lost.

There was no answer to my gentle rap on Belle's door. I turned the knob and peered inside. The curtains were still drawn. "Belle? Belle, are you awake?"

A rustling of the bed clothes was my answer, followed by a low moan.

"Belle?"

"Out, out, *out!* Rita, I swear to God I'll put a knife to your greasy scalp—"

"Belle, it's me, Reenie."

"Reenie? Ohmigod, it's still dark . . ."

Belle's voice, still thick with sleep, trailed off into a mumbled slur of words I was just as glad I couldn't distinguish. As Bazz had predicted, she was not at her best. The air was close, smelling of stale perfume overlaid with an odor I could not at first distinguish until, upon opening the curtains, I noticed a sherry bottle on the floor, almost hidden by the folds of a lavishly embroidered coverlet which lay in tumbled disarray across the high, wide bed.

"What the hell, Reenie!"

Belle rose upon one elbow, a protesting hand shading her eyes. A lacy cap covered her head; her face, deprived of her hair's softening frame, had no defense against the pitiless midday light.

"It's almost noon, Belle. I must talk to you."

She groaned. "Give me a minute. I have to use the chamber pot and then rinse out my poor mouth. Tastes like Custer's army charged through it on the way to Little Big Horn."

I nodded, and perched on the bed.

She looked at me pointedly. "If you don't mind, Reenie? I'll let you know when I'm ready."

Stung by her edged tone, I hastily retreated; when she invited me back in—it seemed hours later, but in fact was probably no more than fifteen minutes—she was a different person.

"Darling, I *am* sorry!" She smiled contritely and hugged me. She smelled of lavender, and the room, its windows now flung wide, had been swept clean of stale night air by the sun-freshened prairie breeze.

"Bazz warned you might be a bit cross."

Belle, who had turned to a handsome mahogany pier mirror to arrange with expert little tweaks of her fingers the strawberry-blond curls cascading across her white shoulders, looked back at me smilingly.

"Cross as an old bear is more like it. Many's the time I've growled at him when he's brought me my morning coffee."

"Would you like some now, Belle? You must be starving!"

She waved a dismissive hand as she crossed to her wardrobe to study its contents, her enviably rounded figure in enticing contrast to her demure white batiste chemise and drawers. "My poor stomach's still having a hoedown with last night's chili, Reenie. I had to get up twice in the middle of the night, and finally searched out the sherry to help put me back to sleep. I hope my pitter-pattering about didn't bother you none." She sighed. "Truth to tell, I haven't slept well since Quinn came, and probably won't until he leaves."

So it was insomnia, not assignations, that accounted for those nocturnal candlelit excursions. "You should have wakened me, Belle; no reason you should suffer alone."

"Nonsense!" she said briskly, presenting me with the sleeve of a pretty yellow dimity dress to button for her. "No reason for you to suffer, too."

"It's Quinn Cooper I came to talk to you about. I met him—that is to say, our paths crossed—out at the pond this morning. He said some things . . . and, oh, Belle he hinted at worse. . . ."

Belle went very still. She turned away from me abruptly and began making her bed. As she tugged the coverlet into place I could see her hands shaking.

"Oh, Belle!" I blurted. "I'm sorry if I—"

"It's all right, Reenie!" Her voice was tight and muffled. She swallowed hard, folded her betraying hands together and sat down at the foot of the bed. She inhaled deeply, her eyelids drifting shut; when she looked at me again there was purpose in her blue eyes. "I'm all right now," she said, beckoning me to sit down beside her. "Knowing Quinn, I can imagine the bees he set loose in your bonnet."

I nodded, too miserable to speak.

"About me and his paw?"

"It's not so much what he said as what he implied. I thought you ought to know so you could stop it from going further."

"Me? Stop Quinn?" Belle laughed. "Not hardly damn likely! Besides, it's true. You're prob'ly the only one in these parts didn't already know. I hoped to spare you that, but Quinn . . . well, he's never been known to spare anybody anything."

"Are you saying you and Ross Cooper were . . . *lovers?*" The novelty of speaking of a relationship of this kind almost overtook my shock. "But . . . he was *married!*"

Belle reached out to pat my hand. "Reenie, Reenie, what an innocent you are! Ross Cooper wasn't the kind of man to content himself with one woman, especially not a skin-and-bones little sparrow like Lottie, gone to seed hardly before she finished bloomin'. He had himself a breed fancy woman— Quinn's maw—before he got married, and kept up with her after, too. Then I came along. Lookin' fresh as a prairie rose. He figured me bought and paid for, in a manner of speakin', and he just couldn't keep his hands off the merchandise."

"He was supposed to *protect* you, not bed with you!"

"Protection was the farthest thing from that man's mind, from the very beginning. At first I was just s'posed to tend to Lottie. She wasn't bedridden yet, and I helped her with the herbs. I liked that . . . still do. But later, when she wasn't fussin' over Bazz, she was forever lyin' herself down and callin' for me to either open or close the curtains in her room, tidy her bed linens, or fetch wet rags for her headaches, wrung

101

out and placed just so. Up and down, up and down, the whole livelong day.

"Ross left me alone the first three years—just getting shed of Lottie's complaints contented him well enough. Then, the year I turned fourteen, Ross looked hard at me one day, and that was that."

I was appalled, as much by her matter-of-fact tone as the fact of a grown married man—a father!—turning a defenseless fourteen-year-old into his . . . whore. I had hated Quinn for saying it; I hated his being right even more.

"Was there no one you could turn to? The wives of other ranchers? A preacher, maybe? Wasn't there *anyone* ready to shame him?"

"Lordy, Reenie, these ranches out here are like little kingdoms: no one tells a king what to do, preachers least of all. The other women had troubles of their own: most of 'em got married off to men they hardly knew when they wasn't much older'n me, and when they saw me in town dressed in the finery Ross bought me, they was more jealous than anything else. Ashamed? Why, struttin' through Ellsworth with a young thing like me on his arm, the other men watchin' all hot-eyed, he did all but crow like a damn rooster."

"Yet you and Basil are friends . . . how can that be?"

Belle shrugged. "Bazz figured out soon enough that if it wasn't me, it'd be someone else—you've heard that old saying, the devil you know is better'n a stranger? Besides, I took his paw's mind off *him*, and—" Belle stopped abruptly. "No point in goin' on and on about it; it's enough to say Bazz and I came to an understanding."

"Nothing more? I mean, you and Bazz never . . . ?"

"No, Reenie, Bazz and I never." She solemnly crossed her heart with one finger. "Ross would have killed him. Besides, I'm not his type. Now *you,* on the other hand. . . ."

"*Me?* But we're identical twins! How could I be his type if you're not?"

Belle tilted her head to one side; a faintly mocking smile played on her lips. "So we are," she murmured. "I had almost forgotten." The look in her eyes was unfathomable. She reached and coiled a lock of my hair around her finger; released it, fell straight as an arrow. "Not a twist or bend in it," she whispered.

"But you see, I know Bazzy," she continued briskly, "and I can tell he's got a soft spot for you." She got to her feet. "I've got to do something about the herbs I left on the kitchen table last night . . . I could use an extra hand, Reenie."

I wasn't quite ready to let her go. "What about Quinn, Belle?"

"What about him?" she asked flatly.

"Well, you certainly aren't friends with him."

"Quinn doesn't have any friends."

I thought of Cobby—he was Quinn's friend, or did Quinn just think he was? "Why did he leave here, Belle, that first time? I know about Bazz and the trouble at the pond—Quinn told me his version this morning—but there was something else. He refused to say what it was, and I wondered—"

"Did somethin' happen with you and him this morning, Reenie?" Her expression hardened; she fixed me with narrowed, knowing eyes. "That smiling swagger of his got to you, huh? And now you're wondering if maybe Bazz and me judge him too hard?"

Her sneering tone unsettled me—or was it the grain of truth in what she said?

"I'll tell you why he left. He tried to rape me, that's why! He sniffed out what was between me and his paw first time he saw us together, and if I was comin' around to the bull, he saw no reason why the bull calf couldn't have some, too." She laughed. "I can guess why he don't want you to know: no girl likes learnin' she's second best."

I dropped my gaze, not knowing what to say.

"Shocked you some, have I? Well, let me tell you, Reenie, life on a ranch don't allow for much nicey talk. Girls like us, no one to look out for us, we're kinda like furniture, used 'til we wear out. If we're pretty and smart enough to do what's expected, maybe we get polished up and allowed to sit in the parlor, but we're still property. I was Ross Cooper's property; Quinn took me for common."

She laughed, but there wasn't any amusement in it. "Ross would've sooner forgave Quinn drowning Bazz than putting his spurs to me, so soon's I threatened to tell, he took off. He smartened up some in the six years before he came back, but all you got to do is look at that scrawny little breed he's got in tow to know he's still mean as a snake. You keep shy of him, Reenie, hear?"

I was relieved when Quinn didn't put in an appearance at supper that evening, and over a second cup of coffee, I asked Bazz about his music. His response was immediate, his pleasure at being queried disarming. He had been tracing the paths of traditional songs from east to west, he told me, recording the changes in the melodies and the new lyrics written to express new experiences and circumstances.

"You mean like that old English song, *Greensleeves?* The choirmaster at my church back in Jericho told us the same tune was used for a Christmas hymn written after the Civil War."

"Exactly! And that old ballad, *Barbara Allen* . . . why, practically every state and territory has its own version of that one. And take our own *Yankee Doodle,* did you know that's been claimed by every nation in Europe?"

I could tell from Belle's bored expression as we chatted she did not share our interest, but she perked up when Basil began to play.

"Do you happen to know this one, Serena?" The verse was unfamiliar, but as he launched into the jaunty refrain of *Who's Gonna Shoe Your Pretty Little Feet?*, I clapped my hands with delight.

Basil sang in a clear, strong tenor voice, and he welcomed my soprano harmony with a smile of encouragement. We were well pleased with ourselves, and as I watched his hands gracefully coaxing melodic chords from his fine piano, the thought of them touching me, caressing me—*he has a soft spot for you, Reenie*— made me feel suddenly warm.

Thinking that a religious song might cool my blood, I asked Basil if he knew *Amazing Grace*.

"One of my favorites," he said, "with lyrics as sweet and true as your pretty voice. Will you sing it for us?"

Flattered, I did, my confidence growing with each succeeding verse. By the third, I was in full voice, and the words, in the past sung so often they had all but lost their meaning, brought tears to my eyes.

> *Thro' many dangers, toils and snares,*
> *I have already come;*
> *'Tis grace hath brought me safe thus far,*
> *And grace will lead me home.*

The notes died away into silence broken only by the crackling of the fire on the hearth.

"I swear, S'rena, that was pretty enough to tempt the devil himself into churchgoing."

It was Quinn's voice, drawling in from the doorway.

"Speaking of the devil . . . ," Belle rejoined tartly.

"Mind if I join you?" Quinn asked, ignoring her

taunt. He ambled in without waiting for an answer. "Fawn and me was out takin' a stroll in the moonlight when we heard you playin' and singin' in here. Sounded real nice and homey."

"Fawn was welcome to come, too," Bazz said quietly.

Quinn grinned and sprawled down across from Belle, stretching his long legs across to rest his booted heels on a stack of periodicals. "Oh, I reckoned on that, Bazz, so I sent her home."

Basil's fingers struck a series of discordant notes before they clenched, knuckles whitening. I looked from one to the other, baffled by the challenge I sensed lurking in Quinn's innocuous reply.

"Right cozy in here, folks," he continued blandly. "Any coffee left?"

"Coffee, but no cups," Belle snapped.

"Well, then, I'll just use yours, Belle—unless you got some loathsome disease I ought to know about."

"I wouldn't tell you if I had," she muttered.

He winked at me. "Just one big happy family, eh, S'rena? And, hey, Bazz, speaking of families, how 'bout *Clementine*? You should know that one; Paw sang it often enough. A real rouser, *Clementine*. 'In a cavern, in a canyon . . .'" His voice was deep, loud and off-key, but he waved his cup in happy disregard of his vocal shortcomings; and before long Bazz had taken up the tempo, and the rest of us joined in to sing of sandals made from herring boxes only to be lost, along with the poor maid who wore them, in the raging brine. It was, as Quinn had said, a rouser.

"Would you favor us with that song I heard you singing this mornin', S'rena?"

"You mean the one Bucket heard," I teased, forgetting Belle's warning. He raised his cup at me and grinned.

Sensing a private joke, Bazz frowned. "Would I know it, Serena?"

106

"It's called *All the Pretty Little Horses . . .* it's a lullabye."

He shook his head regretfully. "I don't think—"

"Our mama used to sing it: 'Hush-you-bye, don't you cry, go to sleepy little baby.' . . . Remember, Belle?"

I strained to see her blue eyes in the gloom, willing her to recall, but she raised her hand to shade them, a fluttering gesture, almost like a bird taking wing in fright. It was almost as if she were trying to shut me out.

"When you wake, you shall have all the pretty little horses . . ." Her voice, when it came, was wavering, her pitch uncertain. "Blacks and bays . . . dapples and grays . . ."

"Coach and six-a little horses," we finished together.

"Hell's roarings, Belle," Quinn said, "you sing almost as bad as you keep house."

Belle burst into tears. Basil crashed out a mighty chord, then slammed a fisted hand into the palm of the other. "Damn you, Quinn!"

Quinn raised his eyebrows and spread his arms wide, whether in apology or protest I was unable to tell. Probably the latter, given his stunning lack of sensitivity to the feelings of others.

"I swear I never have known folks to get so riled by the truth. Maybe I speak a little plain sometimes, not havin' a store of fancy words like yours in my poke, but truth's truth, no matter how its wrapped."

"How do you expect me to keep a proper house, or even want to, when we're waitin' on your eviction notice?" Belle cried. "Can't get decent help, and the ones we get are more trouble'n they're worth."

"No one worth her salt wants to work for you, Belle. Those two women that stood by Lottie Ross long as she lived got hired on at the Flagler spread. Cobby heard 'em say they could take her notions

107

better'n your airs."

Belle sprang to her feet. She began to pace, pausing to glare down at Quinn, her fingers working agitatedly as if yearning to close around the strong column of his weathered, tan neck. "Airs, huh? The truth you're so all-fired fond of is that those ugly old crows couldn't stand bein' told what to do by an orphan girl like me. You think I didn't hear 'em squawkin' to each other about how I was no better than I should be? Course I heard! I was meant to hear, not only that but a whole lot worse."

"Speaking of orphans," Quinn said, blandly ignoring her indignant outburst, "whatever happened to those two you and Basil signed up for, even though you had no right?"

I looked at Belle, startled. Neither she nor Bazz had mentioned anything to me about bringing orphans to Morning Star.

Belle drew herself up. "We had every right. Every human right, that is. I know what it's like to be without a home, and neither of them was going to get one in a hurry. Wispy little dark things they were, hardly looking strong enough to earn their keep. They needed us; we needed them. Why should some silly rules stand in the way?"

"What happened to them, Belle?" Quinn's voice had quieted, but there was no softness in it. Was Belle now to be censured for doing her Christian duty?

"All I know is they showed their heels before they hardly got settled in," Belle said, resentment clipping her words short. "The first one, Ada, couldn't do enough for us when she started out here that spring, but she soon changed: expected everything on a silver platter; flat out *refused* to help in the garden with everything shootin' up like Jack's beanpole. By early June, less than three months after we took her in, she was gone, along with Lottie's fancy silver combs. The next one, same story, except

108

Tessie ran off with a saddle bum that came and left fast as a dose of salts."

"Yeah, seem to remember hearing something about that. Funny thing about that feller, he showed up at the Bar Five a few months later. Alone."

Belle shrugged. "Pro'bly ditched her after the novelty wore off, and with those scrawny girls I reckon that didn't take long. We never saw or heard of them again, and good riddance. You got any more questions, St. Peter'll have to answer them for you."

Quinn's eyes glinted. "St. Peter, huh? You got reason to think they're hangin' around his gates, Belle?"

This pointless cat and mouse game had gone on quite long enough, I decided. "If the girls arrived in the spring, maybe they heard those stories about Morning Star," I broke in. "I saw Rita and Spotted Fawn squatting out behind the pillars this morning, staring at Belle's garden as if they were under a spell . . . or casting one. Bazz tells me this happens every year at this time. It's no wonder the house-keeping suffers," I added pointedly.

"Fawn told me Rita was mighty upset about some plants that just came in bloom," Quinn offered. "Look more like purple snakes' heads than flowers, she says."

Belle heaved an exasperated sigh. "That'll be the foxglove. It's one of the best of the healing herbs. Those fool Injun women see whatever suits 'em."

I thought of the monstrous peony blossoms, as darkly red as newly coagulated blood, and shuddered.

"Spirits walkin' on your grave, S'rena?" Quinn taunted. "That's what those squaws see heavin' up outta that blood-soaked earth. You call 'em healing herbs, Belle, but what *they* see is the avenging spirits of tortured innocents."

Belle's hand splayed up across her throat; Bazz,

109

who had moved behind us to the fireplace, kicked viciously at a smouldering log, sending sparks buzzing up into the huge, dark chimney like a swarm of angry bees. I stared at Quinn, aghast.

Assured of his audience, he chuckled softly. "I reckon we'll soon be seeing Rita's heels, too."

SEVEN

I awoke during the night from the dream that had plagued me since my arrival at Morning Star, the one in which something, distantly beckoning, lures me up and down staircases of improbable length and number. But the soft footfalls passing outside my door were real, and although as light as the fall of feathers, they were surely more deliberate than the scurryings of mice or squirrels. Was it Belle, attempting to walk her insomnia into submission?

I slipped out of bed and cracked open the door. Candle held high in one hand, my sister, cloaked head to toe in white, stood at the end of the corridor, but she was not alone. Her other hand clutched the arm of a man, robed and slippered, who bent solicitously toward her; there was no mistaking the glossy cap of pale auburn hair reflecting the candle's flickering light.

Concerned, I opened my mouth to call out, then hesitated, wondering if the confiding tilt of Basil's head wasn't more suggestive of a rendezvous than an emergency. I eased my door shut and leaned back against it. Had Belle, reluctant to admit the truth, misled me about their relationship? If so, I could hardly blame her: they may have grown up thinking themselves as brother and sister, but judging from their posture as they stood there, eyes intent on one another, Belle's white nightdress could as well have been a wedding gown. I returned to bed, where I slept fitfully until dawn released me from my uneasy ruminations.

I followed the mouth-watering aroma of bacon to the kitchen, where Basil, perched on a stool drawn up to the kitchen table, was eating breakfast. The table had been cleared of Belle's herbal paraphernalia, and Rita silently offered me a plate of bacon and biscuits with white gravy, acknowledging my surprised thanks with an unsmiling nod. A moment later, when the steaming cup she brought me proved to be tea, not coffee, I humbly revised my assessment of the dark, stolid woman: I had no idea she was even aware of my preference, much less willing to accommodate it.

"It's a perfect June day, Serena," Bazz declared. "What do you say we go on a wildflower hunt? If we pack a lunch, we can take our own sweet time searching out the places I used to go with my mama. I swear, she was better than a book: she not only knew where everything grew, but when they were most likely to be in bloom—not just the season, mind you, but the very week. It varied from year to year, of course, depending on the weather during the preceding winter, but she always took that into account. You were right about Belle knowing a lot about her herbs, but Lottie Wohlfort was her teacher!"

I was struck, not only by the loving pride in his voice, but his reference to his mother by her maiden name. Somehow, I doubted it was a conscious choice. But, although Bazz's eagerness was infectious, in light of the rendezvous I had inadvertently seen last night, I resisted immediate agreement. "Belle won't mind not being included?"

"Good Lord, why should she?" Bazz replied, his eyebrows describing an arc of astonishment. "Besides, it was her . . . that is, if we stay here, she'll find all kinds of boring tasks for us to do."

It was her idea? Is that what he had started to say? Although it hardly mattered who initiated it, I felt a pang of disappointment. "You tempt me, Bazz. I've never dared play hooky before."

Bazz smiled. "Better late than never, Serena." He unwound his long legs from the stool and pushed it back against the wall under the hanging bunches of dried herbs, whose gray-green, shriveled leaves released a pungent aroma as he brushed against them. "Tell you what, if you'll help Rita with our lunch, I'll break the news to Belle that her slaves are rebelling, then go down and saddle up the horses. I'll be looking for you there in, oh, about an hour—and remember to bring your hat! A bright, windless morning like this one can be a scorcher by midday."

His solicitousness touched me. I couldn't imagine Quinn Cooper ever caring about the effect of the sun on a woman's complexion. I couldn't imagine him caring if she fainted dead away from the heat; he'd probably just sling her over his horse's rump and tip her into the pond or the horse trough, whichever was handiest.

We spent a grand day together, Bazz and I. He looked a proper rancher in his clean Levi's, blue shirt, red-checked neckerchief and pale gray Stetson: too neat for a cowpoke; not slicked up enough to be mistaken for a greenhorn. His tall chestnut horse, Dancer, was a well-mannered animal, responding handily to the nudgings of his master's heels, and his elaborately tooled boots, judging from their mellow

113

sheen, were a source of considerable pride. When I said as much, Bazz nodded.

"These boots and Dancer were both given me by my mama."

"But I thought you were only a boy when she died," I said.

He nodded. "Sixteen. But Mama had her dreams. She put aside enough to pay for my schooling and buy me a good horse and custom-made pair of boots when I came home to take my place at Morning Star. She had a lawyer in town open an account in my name in case there was ever any question about it." He laughed bitterly. "Paw was of the opinion I should have earned it all by the sweat of my brow. He figured if an occupation didn't put a man in the way of breaking his bones, it couldn't be real work. Never occurred to him book work could be every bit as hard as cowpunching or bronc busting."

"Harder!" I exclaimed. "Any fool can chase a cow."

Basil grinned down at me, amused by my indignation. "I wouldn't go *that* far, Serena. It's different work, a lot of it muscle work maybe, but it's not easy. Quinn happens to be good at it; I'm not."

"But it's not *fair!*"

"No, it's not," he agreed. His mouth thinned. "But Paw never gave a damn about fairness; his opinion was all that ever mattered."

Bazz took his chances same as me.... But he hadn't, really; the deck was stacked against him from the beginning.

We rode on in silence, our thoughts accompanied by the soft plop of the horses' hooves and the jingle of their bridle fittings. To me it seemed shameful for a land as wide and pure as this to be sullied by man's injustices. Just then, I noticed a break in the rolling grassy vastness. Bazz moved Dancer ahead and turned

114

down a sudden steep, stony track, similar to the ledge above the pond but longer and twistier. At the bottom, a thicket of shrubs enveloped them. I urged a reluctant Bingo in after them, and when we emerged on the other side into an open sandy clearing, Bazz had already dismounted in the shade of a huge cottonwood tree. Behind it, half-hidden in the dense undergrowth, I glimpsed the edge of a long, low roof. Below it, sagging on its hinges, a plank door yawned wide.

"Look, Bazz! There's a little old house back there . . . did Indians live here?" I began threading my way through the interwoven branches.

"Watch out, Serena! There's apt to be rattlers in there! I didn't mean to alarm you," he said in a calmer voice as he arrived by my side. "That's a line rider's shack," he explained. "They're not used much, but every ranch's got a few of them tucked away to shelter riders—any riders—caught by a storm. In the summer, rattlers find 'em a handy place to wait until it's cool enough to hunt. They don't much like being disturbed."

I drew cautiously closer. There were no windows, and the only furnishings were a couple of crude stools, a stable and a rusty stove. The table legs appeared to be cuffed with tin cans.

"They're supposed to keep rats from climbing up to eat food left on the table," Bazz said. "Delightful life, eh? Snow and rain and dust storms outside, rats and snakes inside, with nothing to do during the long nights but read the cans by the light of a stove so full of holes it gives off more smoke than heat."

It was a bleak picture Bazz painted, and his brooding expression suggested that for him that delapidated shack represented everything he hated about ranching: physical hardship, isolation, brutishness. He took my hand, and I willingly followed him back to the clearing.

"What does 'reading the cans' mean, Bazz?"

"It's a sort of cowboy contest, Serena. Every fellow that's ever worked on a ranch sooner or later memorizes the words on the labels of the cans used in every kitchen and cook wagon. They recite 'em for entertainment. There's no set number of contestants: there can be two or twenty-two. Five cents' penalty for each mistake in punctuation; ten cents' for a wrong word."

"Good heavens! I never heard of such a thing."

Bazz grinned up at me as he spread out the blanket he had tied behind his saddle. "No, I reckon not."

A pretty little streamlet sparkled close by, hardly more than a foot or so wide. It was spring-fed, he told me, soon lost in the thicket we had come through, but deep enough here for the horses to plunge their muzzles in for a refreshing drink.

"And," he added, removing his boots, "for us to cool our feet while we cool our tea."

I gratefully followed his lead, first wedging the jar of tea under the deeply undercut edge of the stream, then sitting back beside him to enjoy the gentle rush of water through my dabbling toes.

"Forget-me-not," Bazz suddenly said. "Not me, silly," he added in response to my startled look. "Those little blue flowers over there, where the shade is deepest."

I followed his pointing finger, hardly believing I was seeing here, in this dry land, the same dainty, sky-blue, yellow-eyed florets so familiar from wet places back East.

"This is the only spot I know of where it grows hereabouts," he said. "Mama used to say a woman traveling west with her family might have stopped here one day to rest in the shade, maybe wash off the dust in the stream, and left some seeds brought from

116

home as a sort of thank-you token. My mama had lots of stories like that: some she heard; some she made up herself, like this one."

"It's a lovely story," I said. "I'm sorry I didn't have a chance to know her."

He eyed me speculatively. "It's hard to imagine two females looking less alike," he said. "Mother's hair was black and shiny as coal; yours is like moonlight." He gently splashed water on my ankles with his toes. "Your skin is pale, too," he mused. "Much paler than Mama's . . . paler than Belle's, too."

Was that meant as a compliment? I couldn't tell.

"Belle used to be as pale as I, and of course her hair was the same shade, too."

Bazz smiled wryly. "Belle heard Paw say he favored red hair and curls on a woman. She went out of her way to please him; it wasn't easy for her, sometimes. *Never* was, for me."

Was that what had formed the bond between them, I wondered? Two anxious children at the mercy of a hard taskmaster? Poor Belle. Mother Rogg may have shown me little tenderness, but she had unfailingly protected me. Too much, I had sometimes thought, but now. . . .

I felt a sudden surge of anger. "Those women who worked for your mother?" I blurted. "Surely Quinn can't be right about them not wanting to stay on with Belle. Why, she's the dearest girl in the world!"

Bazz lifted his feet out of the stream and waggled them in the air to dry. "Well, let's just say they didn't see eye to eye. Mama was folks, you see, and they never got over thinking of Belle as a stranger come to take their place. At the end, that's what she did, you know. She tended my mama as if she were her own. Up all hours with her, brewing the special herbal elixirs she craved." He pulled on his socks. "Besides,

117

as you heard tell last night, hardly anyone chooses to stay at Morning Star any longer than obligated—not even that long sometimes. Look at those ungrateful urchins Belle and I tried to help.''

"You know, Bazz, maybe the Morning Star legend had nothing to do with those girls running off. Maybe the first one decided town life would be more to her liking than working out here on the prairie; maybe the second one, if she was ditched like Belle thinks, joined her later. Were they really as scrawny as Belle says? Judging from Morning Star, I imagine the ranches out here generally have a lot more single young men than girls . . . mightn't a bunch of lonely cowboys think them pretty, seeing them all dressed up in saloon finery?''

"Pretty? Maybe, dressed up like you say.'' He reached over for his boots, then sat back, remembering. "They had little foxy faces and black, black hair. . . .'' A funny little smile came and went, his voice so soft I could hardly hear him. "Like that little breed Quinn's got,'' he said, tugging on his boots. "Without the bruises,'' he amended.

"Really? They weren't twins, though, like Belle and me?''

Basil grinned, crouched down, dipped his fingers in the stream and flipped water in my face. "There's no one in the whole wide world like you and Belle, Miss Garraty,'' he said. "C'mon, up with you, I'm starving!''

Fortified by a lunch of bacon and generously buttered biscuits leftover from breakfast and washed down with cool tea, we mounted up and resumed our wildflower hunt. By the time we surrendered to the heat of the afternoon sun, we had found a stand of evening primroses—white instead of the yellow variety I was familiar with—prairie phlox, great tangles of roses and a bush of morning glory, whose

118

long flaring trumpets had already twisted shut, as if too delicate to withstand the full light of day. This seeming fragility, Basil advised me, did not extend to the root system.

"Once," he told me laughing, "when Mama found a particularly handsome specimen—not far from here, if I remember correctly—she decided she must have it for her garden. So she brought first me, then Cobby, to have a go at it. It wasn't until between us we'd dug a hole as big as a cookstove, with no end to the taproot in sight, that she finally abandoned the idea."

Suppose they had succeeded in transplating it in the Morning Star garden. I shuddered as an image of roots swollen as thick as tree trunks invaded my mind. Roots burrowing deep, seeking and leaching out the ghastly sustenance provided there.

". . . and later, the sunflowers come into bloom," Basil was saying, unaware of my dark preoccupation. "They're my favorites." He paused. "Mama thought them too common."

The note of guilty regret in his voice saddened me. Surely there was no call for a son, no matter how devoted, to share all his mother's likes and dislikes. I had grown fond of Basil, we had many similar interests and—thanks to Malcolm Wilcox's patient tutoring—a common language in which to discuss them, but I feared he was the kind of man who would find all women wanting in comparison to his mother. On the other hand, if I were as unlike her as he had said, maybe I could chance the competition. . . .

"I like sunflowers, too," I said, defying Lottie's sainted image. "I shall be sorry to miss them."

"Oh, but you won't. The land between the Missouri and the mountains is populated by battalions—no, whole *armies* of sunflowers. Actually,

119

come July, there's no escaping them."

I wondered if any had been planted in the garden at Morning Star. I did not ask: the thought of those yellow-rayed faces, grown in that cursed place to gigantic size, their cyclopean heads seeking the sun in slow revolution, as mindless and pitiless as praying mantes, repelled me. *Armies of them. . . .*

Bazz looked down at me, concern in his gray eyes. "You look suddenly pale, Serena—are you feeling the heat?"

I smiled weakly, reluctant to admit I was suffering more from my fevered imagination than the heat of the day.

Wordlessly, Bazz turned his mount toward home; gratefully, I followed his lead, a decision approved, judging from their eagerly quickened pace, by Bingo and Dancer, too.

Heat of another kind greeted our return. A dust-raising brawl in the corral near the barn, egged on by the cowhands lounging along the rail and shouting encouragement, turned out to be between Quinn and Sharo, Cobby's protégé, although that was hardly a term Cobby himself would use, even if he knew the word.

Jed, seeing my arrival, detached himself from the others and slouched over to take Bingo. "Sharo's got his hands full, miss," he said. I didn't care for his leering smile. "Started as a dust-up, but looks to me as if Quinn's plannin' on cleanin' the kid's plow."

"What on *earth*—"

I hadn't meant my exclamation as a question, but Jed chose to take it that way. "S'all over that little breed filly. Seems the kid took exception to Cooper's rights to her. I coulda tol' him the boss'd help him chew gravel, talkin' outta turn like that."

"Why didn't you?" I demanded.

His leer widened. "Not as much fun in it."

Knowing he was trying to spark a little fun out of me, too, I counted to ten before speaking. "Since you kindly volunteered to put Bingo away, see you cool her off well first."

His expression was a caricature of dismay: not only had I called his bluff, but I had deprived him of seeing how the fight turned out. Satisfied, I turned back to see Cobby stumping into the corral on his stubby legs, laying into the two flailing men as if he had four arms instead of two.

"Awright! That's enough of that, now. You, there, you stiffs," he called, addressing the onlookers along the fence, "git back to work! Show's over." He shooed a limping Sharo out of the enclosure. The boy's face was bloodied, his clothes dust-caked and torn. "A washing-up'd improve you some," Cobby called after him, his tone kindlier than his words.

"You can turn Dancer into the pen now, Bazz," Cobby said, "seein' we finally got these human critters drove out of it."

Bazz led Dancer by Quinn without so much as a glance in his direction, distaste evident in the set of his mouth.

"He's of the girl's blood, Quinn," I heard Cobby say to him as they approached. "Half-blood least-wise."

Quinn dismissed Cobby's argument with a downward slash of his newly raw-knuckled hand. Then, seeing me, he grinned; seeing the swagger in his walk, my already heated blood boiled.

"You're almost twice Sharo's age and weight," I said. "Do you call that a fair match?"

He wiped the blood from his cut lip. "Riled again, eh, S'rena? The kid held his own well enough, but if you're that all-fired concerned about him, why'n't

121

you go play nursie? I've already got someone to look after me."

This last was said deliberately loud enough for Sharo to hear. He spun around, lunged for Quinn, stumbled, and as Cobby came trotting up to calm him, I could see angry tears tracking through the blood and dust on the boy's face.

Quinn, ignoring them, retrieved his hat from the post where he'd left it, brushed it off, set it on his head and strolled on by with that smooth, hip-hitching gait of his toward his quarters—and Spotted Fawn— as if he hadn't a care in the world.

Bazz walked up beside me. "I swear, Serena, Dancer's more of a gentleman than Quinn."

Having spent most of the day in the company of his well-mannered horse, I was inclined to agree.

"Cobby said Sharo and Fawn are of half-blood," I said. "Does that mean they're related in some way, like you and Quinn?"

He frowned. "It means they're mongrels, half-white, half-Indian. Breeds, we call 'em. Not even their own people will take them in. What's worse is that the Indian half of these is Pawnee. Paw wouldn't have tolerated Pawnees at Morning Star, and I advise you to have nothing to do with this one," he said, inclining his head toward the injured lad. He put his arm around my shoulders. "Come along, Serena, you're still a little pale. My fault for keeping you out in the hot sun so long."

Knowing what it's like to have no home and no one to call your own, I resisted Basil's well-meant solicitude. "I'm always a little pale, Bazz," I said. I smiled as I gently detached myself. "You go on up to the house. I'll join you later after I've seen to Sharo."

"But Serena—"

"You know how women are, Bazz; we can't resist

tending wounded creatures. Kittens, puppies, people—you said yourself how good Belle was with your mother; well, we're two of a kind!"

Unwilling to assist, Bazz departed alone, his shoulders stiffening with disapproval as I, persisting in my obdurate intent to play—how had Quinn put it?—"nursie," asked one of the men to bring a pail of clean water to the barn. Cobby supplied strips of sheeting and a jar of Belle's salve, and together we ministered to Sharo's injuries, which were more painful—bruises, really—than serious.

"Bazz 'pears to have taken to you some," Cobby offered as he wrapped a bandage around Sharo's salve-slathered knee. He seemed surprised.

"You think me too plain?" I inquired.

"Plain? *You?*" His astonishment that I could think such a thing both pleased and confounded me. I was quite sure Belle didn't suit his taste in womenfolk.

"Well, he keeps saying how pale I am. . . ."

"Ladylike, I calls it," Cobby said. "Not like some," he muttered, bending down to tear the bandaging strip down the middle with his teeth. "He usually favors the little dark ones, like his maw," he added, securing the bandage with the ties he had made. "Pretty as a kitten, she was."

"How long is it now, Cobby?" I asked as I gently washed the dirt from Sharo's cut, bruised face. "Since she died, I mean."

"I know what you meant," Cobby said gruffly. "Six years. No need for it, either. The sickness was mostly in her head if you ask me. Ross never understood that, never tried to, and that made it worse."

"Then, I guess it was lucky Belle was here to care for her."

Cobby grunted. "Yep, passed away six years ago

123

this month, she did. The bad things usually happen here in June. Startin' with haulin' up those fool stone pillars year after the house was built. That pair with the slits? The way Ross fussed with his compass gettin' 'em set just right, never sayin' why, drove us all loco. One feller busted his leg, another dern near broke his head, but it had to be done that day, Ross said. Like I say, June ain't a good time at Morning Star. Wasn't no diff'rent for poor Lottie." He smoothed salve on Sharo's face, his calloused fingers as gentle as feathers. "There you go, young feller," he said briskly. "From now on, you be mindin' your own business."

"I thank you, Cobby, and you, too, Miss Serena, but Spotted Fawn is of my blood. I would be less than a man if I turn away."

A grimace of pain twisted Sharo's mouth as he pulled himself to his feet, but his dark gaze remained steadfast. Although I admired his pure, young heart, I couldn't help but regret the disillusionments awaiting him.

Cobby squinted up at him, then pulled his pipe from his pocket and studied it thoughtfully. "If that's how you see it," he said at length, "I reckon I'll put your name on that jar of salve."

Sharo, holding himself proudly erect despite his twisted knee, nodded. "I'll go see to Bingo now."

"But Jed already—" I broke off. Sharo's expression told of his reservations about Jed's reliability more than any words could have done, and more diplomatically, too.

"Thank you, Sharo, I'd appreciate that."

"He's a good 'un, breed or not," Cobby said as we watched him cross to the barn. "The hands, none of 'em'd have him for a bunkie, but he's welcome enough."

"All things considered," I said dryly.

124

He eyed me shrewdly, nodded, and thrust his stained empty pipe in his mouth.

"Then, why can't Quinn Cooper—"

Out came the pipe. "Quinn's got a lot of his paw in 'im. Ramrod proud. Ross tried to take the bucks outta him first time he come. Couldn't, and made up his mind he couldn't be rode. I told Ross to give 'im more rope, but then that trouble with Bazz almost drownin' come up. . . ." He inspected his pipe. "Lottie never could stand havin' him around."

"Quinn's a half-blood, too, isn't he . . . like Sharo and Fawn?"

"Quinn's only a quarter-blood. Accordin' to Ross, his maw was half-Comanche. Fierce people, the Comanche. But it wasn't his bein' a breed bothered Lottie; it was Ross bein' his paw."

"Where did Quinn go?"

"Up Nebraska way. Big limey outfit up there hired him on. Made line boss 'fore he was twenty, then top screw. Pro'bly be foreman one day if he'd stayed."

"Why didn't he, Cobby? He could have sent someone else down to Morning Star for the cattle."

Cobby shifted uncomfortably. "Not for me to say, miss. He come back a sight more bridle-wise, but I saw that same look in his eyes . . . that wantin' look. Never said nothin'—plays a lone hand, Quinn does—but I could tell."

Proud, fierce and covetous. A dangerous combination. "Was Ross Cooper's death an accident, Cobby?"

His gnarled fingers clenched. "Lordy, Miss Serena, why'd you wanta ask me sumpin' like that? It happened in June's all I know."

"Does that mean you think there's a curse on Morning Star, like Quinn says?"

Cobby stepped back from me; the look in his eyes was troubled, almost haunted. "Don't matter if I do or don't. Morning Star . . . well, I'm snubbed to it permanent. Come this time of year, I jest keep lookin' over my shoulder." He pointed his pipestem at me like an accusing finger. "If you keep shovin' off your range like you done with me just now, you'd best do the same."

EIGHT

We didn't see Quinn at supper that night or for two nights thereafter. Basil figured he was licking his wounds; Belle's comment to that, delivered in a righteous tone that made us laugh, was if there were any justice in this world, he'd probably poisoned himself. When he reappeared the third evening, there didn't seem to be a mark on him.

"Been using my salve, have you?" Belle said after looking him over.

Quinn looked at her from under the brim of his black hat and grinned. "No need, Belle. Fawn got ways of her own."

"Oh, I reckon she has," Belle said, a sly smile curving her lips. "Don't seem to have improved your manners none, though."

"How's that, Belle?"

"A gentleman takes his hat off in the company of ladies."

"Well, as you've kindly pointed out to me before, I'm no gentleman, and sorry to say I've got my doubts about the rest of what you said, but . . ." He swept his black hat off with a flourish, loosing a thick lock of dark hair upon his tanned forehead. "Evening, ladies and gentleman." His mocking grin lit up the dim room. "Got any of that fancy wine of yours?"

He sat down and waited expectantly, but soon realized none of us were about to jump to do his bidding. "Want I should go up and see if you still got any hid under your bed, Belle?" He started to get up. "No trouble—"

"Damn you, Quinn! Everything's a joke to you."

His grin faded. "Not everything, Belle. Not everything by a long sight."

Basil thrust him a small tumbler half-full of sherry. "If you want a wineglass, I'm afraid you'll have to supply your own."

"You mean there's special kinds?" I couldn't tell if he was serious. "This'll do just fine." He raised the glass to his lips and downed it in a single gulp. "Right tasty. Not like whiskey, of course, but I can see why the ladies like it."

I could sense Bazz bristling.

"Back East, men like it, too," I said.

"Back East, S'rena, men are *s'posed* to like a lot of things the ladies like. The ones that don't . . . well, why do you suppose all those wagon trains keep headin' west?"

"For the same reason Paw did," Bazz broke in. "To get what the lady he liked best expected of him. Not much difference that I can see."

"You got a point, little brother, except the way Cobby tells it, your maw would've married Paw anyway. It was your grandpa who had the expectations. Cobby says Paw never did like bein' tied to another man's saddle horn, and once he broke free . . . well, he wasn't about to be tied down permanent by no ribbons and lace. Your poor little mama got herself caught between 'em."

I assumed, although it surprised me, that Quinn's mention of Lottie Cooper was meant to be sympathetic; Bazz inferred no such thing.

"You called her a silly cow!"

"She damn near got you drowned, and I got the blame fer it!" Quinn rose to his feet, rigid with anger.

Bazz's head bobbed and weaved like a snake about to strike.

"Dear Lord!" I cried. "It's been twelve years!"

Quinn blinked, and slowly relaxed; Bazz raked a trembling hand through his auburn hair, then plunged his hands in his pockets and turned his back. His ragged breathing rasped in the ensuing silence.

"What I came for," Quinn said at length, "was to say I expect to settle your claims in two weeks, and when I do, you'd better be ready to clear out." The weather-etched lines on his face seemed grooved in stone; his tone brooked no argument.

Belle lunged toward him, her small fists raised. "Two weeks?" Her voice was shrill with agitation. "How do you expect us to be ready in two weeks? There's no one to help us pack, not enough boxes to pack in and nothing to haul them out of here in if we had 'em."

Quinn laughed, fending her off as easily as a wolfhound would an overwrought terrier. "You've had months to get ready, Belle. Maybe if you got yourself up before noon and Basil spent less time lollygagging on the prairie with S'rena, you two wouldn't be in this predicament."

He settled back down in the chair and folded his arms across his chest. "Plenty of time to bunk the girl on the road, Bazz," he drawled. "Considering how Paw got outfoxed by one of 'em, though, it beats me how you'll ride herd on the pair. Maybe you could find a nice house in town somewhere, a place you could play your pi-yanner every night. Girls like these are always in demand. Why, I reckon their rent'd pay *your* rent. . . . What d'ya think?"

129

"I think you're a foul-mouthed son-of-a—"

"Don't say it, Bazz!" Quinn pushed himself out of the chair again. "It's you and me got differences. My maw's got nothing to do with it."

"She bred you!"

"Not all by herself, she didn't!"

The two men glared at one another through narrowing eyes. Fearing Bazz would fare no better than Sharo if it came to a fight, I tried to think of a way to calm the swell of hostility, but it was Belle, brooding nearby in distracted silence, who finally broke the impasse.

"No one ever outfoxed Ross Cooper," she said. "In the end he always won. *Always.*"

In my first weeks at Morning Star, unprepared for the coarseness I detected in Belle, I would have been stunned by the bitterness that lent her words their grating edge. But now, knowing of the sexual intimacies she had been forced to accept from the man she thought her benefactor, I admired her resilience. What other choice had she in this isolated, accursed place? Better coarse than cowed! Quinn's salacious insinuations served only to reinforce my loyalty.

Belle slipped her arm through Basil's; I crossed to his other side. Faced now with three pairs of hostile eyes, Quinn frowned, not quite sure what to make of it. Seeing him thrown off balance was a pleasing novelty, but I had no sooner registered it before his expression cleared.

"It's the gold, isn't it?" His mouth curved in a wicked smile. "Not ready to leave, huh? Well, I reckon not. Not 'til you finish scrabbling around fer it in the night like rats after cheese." His frown returned, blacker than before. "As God is my witness," he thundered, a finger thrusting skyward, "if you try leavin' here with Paw's gold in your

130

poke—*my* gold!—I'll hound you to the gates of hell itself!"

Quinn's departure left us standing silently agape. Belle was the first to recover. She took my hands in hers; her eyes sought mine imploringly.

"That gold Quinn was ranting about," she said, "we need your help."

Bazz turned white. "For God's sake, Belle!"

Belle shushed him. "You heard him, Bazzy, we have only two more weeks. We need all the help we can get."

"You know I'll do whatever I can," I said, "but if this mysterious gold really is Quinn's. . . ."

Belle's eyes glinted with familiar mischief. " 'Finders, keepers,' Reenie, remember?"

My heart sank. Belle's habit of blithely appropriating whatever caught her fancy had often gotten us into trouble at the orphanage. Unable to identify the true culprit—Belle never accepted blame; I refused to assign it—the director meted out identical punishments. I never denied the obligations of our relationship then, nor would I now. No matter the rights or wrongs of it, Belle, my twin, was about to be evicted from her home; Quinn was a hard-hearted stranger.

I took a deep breath. "Tell me about the gold."

It was a story that in one guise or another had been often told. Ross Cooper, Bazz told me, had come west with his parents, seeking escape from their hardscrabble Vermont farm to the wide grassy prairie. But they were farmers, not ranchers; the unfamiliar demands of dry-land farming soon drained their hopes and energy, and by the time of their cruel death

131

in an Indian raid their limited resources had been exhausted.

Left alone and penniless, the nine-year-old boy drifted from one to another of the modest holdings of neighboring farmers who had survived the attack. None of them were more than marginally successful, and although Ross was willing to work hard for his keep, he was neither old nor strong enough to really earn it. The humiliating need to depend on the kindness of strangers kept him on the move. He formed no ties or loyalties, determining at an early age to acquire by his own efforts whatever would bring him the independence he craved.

Although hardly more than twenty when he hired on at the Wohlfort ranch, Ross Cooper was by then a seasoned hand. His arrival there was not by chance: the ranch's prosperity was a popular topic of envious conversation among the territory's floating population of cattle stiffs, most of whom, Ross suspected, resented the demanding standards he saw as opportunity. His capacity for hard work together with an unerring eye for a promising colt or bull calf soon recommended him to Emil Wohlfort; his bold good looks attracted his boss's pretty daughter even sooner. Neither of them, Bazz said, were aware then of the raw ambition fueling his high spirits.

Old Man Wohlfort, once he got wind of the liaison, promptly threw Ross off his spread with nothing more than he came with. No penniless cowhand, no matter how good a worker, was good enough for his cherished little Lottie, and he'd seen too many carefully bred heifers covered by scrub bulls to take any chances.

Equipped with no more than a tired horse, a second-hand saddle and a bedroll, the angry young man wasted no time brooding; instead, using his resentment to hammer out a new purpose for his energies, he headed west to the California gold fields to seek his fortune.

"Three years later," Bazz said, "he triumphantly returned with a starter herd of travel-weary stock bought cheaply from wagon trains arriving in Denver from the East, and a set of plans for a grand stone house drawn by a British architect lured by gold fever and down on his luck."

"I wouldn't have thought a herd of worn-out cattle would be much to be triumphant about."

"That's what they were when he *bought* them, Serena. But Paw was a spinner: he took his own sweet time driving them back through the free grass growing on the prairie and arrived here with a herd to be proud of."

"What do you mean, 'spinner'?" I asked.

"That's a bronc that leaps and whirls backward, Reenie," Belle broke in. "You see, whatever Ross did was usually contrary to most folks' thinkin', and in those days the wagons rattling on through to California never gave a thought to the good grass crushed beneath their wheels."

"Green gold, Paw called it," Bazz said. "It's different now, of course, what with the California gold fields all but played out and cattle on the move everywhere you look. Back then, land was cheap, so Paw bought up what my grandpa hadn't gotten 'round to. There wasn't any fencing in those days, so with the herds just grazing where they'd a mind to anyway, I guess Grandpa figured he already had enough land in his name. Soon as Paw had the deeds recorded, he began building this house."

Having explored by then to the limits of the Morning Star holdings, I asked the question that had several times occurred to me. "But why here? Why not overlooking the pond, or down in the southwest quarter below that sheltering slope?"

133

"I'm afraid Quinn was right about that, Serena. Paw built here deliberately, out of . . . oh, I guess you could call it defiance. Defiance of the Pawnees who slaughtered his parents, and of Emil Wohlfort's refusal to 'sacrifice' his precious only daughter to a cowpuncher. Paw didn't have much of a sense of humor, but maybe he thought of it as a sort of double-barrelled joke."

A gruesome sort of joke, I thought. "He told you this?"

Bazz laughed. "Oh, no. Paw hardly ever told me anything. Demanded a lot, but I don't know that we ever had what you might call a conversation. When he felt like talking, it was Belle he chose for listening."

"He loved to yarn about the building of Morning Star," Belle said. "The barn and bunkhouse and corrals, they were the easy part; even this house didn't cause much excitement, though it was a sight grander than anything else in the territory at the time, but those pillars!" She giggled. "The pair with the slits? After they got 'em hauled up into place the first time, Ross came 'round, lined 'em up with a compass, got madder'n hell, and had 'em pulled right back down. I forget how many haulings-up and pullings-down it took to get them set right."

Something nudged at my mind, but whatever it was, was overwhelmed by the thought of the cost of what Basil and Belle had described.

"Surely one herd of grass-fattened cows couldn't have paid for all this," I said. "Is this where the gold comes in?"

Bazz and Belle looked at one another. "There were rumors of it all along," Bazz said.

"Some were rumors and some not," Belle added. "The word spread like a prairie fire how Ross'd paid for the land and the buildin' of this house and all:

134

he'd struck gold in Californy, a lot of it. What the *rumors* were, is that a lot more gold was hid, here on Morning Star—and still is."

I raised my eyebrows. "Really, Belle—"

"It *had* to be, Reenie!" she exclaimed. "It's the only way Ross coulda kept Morning Star going in such high style through good times and bad." Her head bobbed vigorously as if to physically drive her point home. "It was only when he died things took such a turn for the worse. Quinn doesn't know where the gold is any more'n we do: the only way he can pay us off is by layin' off hands and sellin' stock. But you mark my words," she said, her voice rising, "the minute we leave he's going to start tearin' this place apart!"

"But how can you be sure it's hidden here, on Morning Star? It could be anywhere—it's a big state, Belle; there must be a lot of banks with vaults in Kansas."

"Not in a bank, Serena," Bazz said. "Paw didn't trust banks. But the thought of us looking under every bush and searching every gully here at Morning Star would have tickled him."

"No, it's here!" Belle insisted. "Didn't he tell me that himself, Bazz?"

"He was drunk," Bazz returned flatly.

"All the more reason to think it the truth." She turned to me. "Once, when we'd had a little . . . misunderstanding, he asked me where my heart was, and then he said, 'Is it hidden in stone, like my gold?'"

Bazz and I exchanged a look.

Belle sighed with exasperation. "Don't you see? Not under a stone or beside a stone: *in* stone! You look around here with that in mind, Reenie, and you'll soon see how many queer jigs and jags and thick places this house has with no reason for 'em. And just this past winter, at a shindig over to the

135

Faulhaber spread, didn't one of those old codgers tell about building the bunkhouse, and the way the doorsill had to be fit in just so, like a lid on a box? Those were his very words, 'like a lid on a box.'"

Belle's eyes sparkled; her face shone with animation. "Remember those jigsaw puzzles at the orphanage, Reenie? You always found the hard pieces. Besides," she added, looking at me slyly through her lashes, "it'll be a whole lot easier searching in daylight."

I laughed. "You roamed through my dreams, you know, and Quinn saw your candles one night. He thought you were—" I broke off, embarrassed.

"Lovers? Like I told you, just friends, Reenie. Bazz is fair game for fair lady," she added airily, glancing encouragingly from one to the other of us.

"First things first," I said gently. I had no wish to hurt Bazz's feelings, but neither did I wish to make any sort of commitment before I had a clearer idea of what his feelings for me really were. I recalled the hot, demanding pressure of Quinn's mouth on mine and the unsettling eagerness of my response. In comparison, Bazz's courtship—assuming Belle's interpretation of his kind attentions to me was correct—seemed . . . unenthusiastic.

"Was this house completed before your parents were married, Bazz?"

"Oh, yes. Grandfather Wohlfort insisted on it being more than just an impressive set of plans on paper before he would give his blessing. The only thing added later was the storm cellar. Grandfather insisted on that, too."

"What about the trough and that rickety windmill? They're so much meaner than this house."

"Those came first, to water the cows that became the foundation of that first Morning Star herd. The usual run of range cattle were longhorns driven up

136

from Texas, gaunt at best and damn near as wild as the buffalo they supplanted. The ones he brought in were Durham stock. He liked to hear the windmill spinning in the wind, and he always cleaned that slimy old trough himself. He used to say it did a man good to be reminded of his beginnings."

Detecting a sneer in Bazz's voice, I thought of the boy he had described, wandering from place to place, given the lowest, meanest jobs, doing what it took to stay alive. "There's nothing wrong with a little humility," I said quietly.

"Humility?" Belle gave a hoarse shout of laughter. "Remember how he gloated 'bout the bargains in cattle he got from those gold-crazed farmers, Bazz? Why, there wasn't a humble bone in Ross Cooper's body! How d'ya think Quinn came by the strut of his? Like tom turkeys, the pair of 'em."

"Tom*cats*," Bazz muttered.

"That, too," Belle agreed.

"The Wohlfort holdings came later?" I asked.

"Yes," Bazz said, "after my grandparents died of the cholera. Mama was expecting me when they took sick, and Paw refused to let her visit them. She never saw them alive again. They left everything to my mama, and Paw bought up most of the land from her over the years. Never paid her what it was worth, of course."

"Wasn't there anyone to give her advice? No trusted family friend? Other relatives?"

Bazz shook his head. "It never occurred to her she needed any advice. The garden preoccupied her: nothing had ever grown for her like that before. In those years before she took to her bed, when she wasn't digging and planting and harvesting her herbs, she was stirring and bottling or drying and sewing them into sacks. First Mama, now Belle. Between the two of 'em the kitchen's hardly ever had

137

an inch to spare for anything as uninteresting as food preparation.''

Belle frowned. "If we don't find the gold, you'll be glad enough of the money the herbs will bring when we leave here.''

"I was only teasing, Belle,'' he said with a placatory smile before turning back to me. "To finish what I was saying, Serena, Quinn's settling with me now for what's left of the Wohlfort spread.''

"Is *he* paying what it's worth?''

Bazz shrugged. "He's paying only what it's worth to him to get rid of me.''

"But surely there must have been other buyers for good grazing land like this!''

Bazz spread his hands wide. "My dear girl, the acres Mama left to me are virtually surrounded by Morning Star. Over the years, seeing the price of comparable acreage rise, Paw put off buying the best of Mama's holdings until last, knowing damn well no one else would buy it without access. As a result, the more valuable it became as grazing land, the less, because of its situation, it was worth to an outsider. A vulture couldn't have stripped her cleaner.''

"Reenie, I don't see these questions taking us anywhere.'' Belle's tone was testy.

"Just one more,'' I said meekly. "The plans that British architect drew, do you know where they are?''

"Whatever do you want them for?''

"Maybe they'll tell us something about those jigs and jags you mentioned.''

"Lordy, Reenie, I swear we've pushed and pulled at nearly every block of stone there is.''

"Nearly isn't every, Belle.''

"She has a point,'' Bazz said. "For instance, we could have pushed on the wrong side, or on the top instead of the bottom.''

"Could they be in his desk?'' I asked, pointing to

138

the huge fumed oak structure that dominated the wall on the other side of the room.

"Quinn and the lawyers cleaned *that* out first thing after the reading of the will," Belle said. "I swear, Bazz, wasn't it a treat to see Quinn's face when he come across that stack of bills Ross hadn't paid?" They exchanged amused glances. "The only other place I can think of that hasn't already been looked through is that big old rawhide Mexican trunk up in his bedroom."

"Then, let's go up and look in it now," I said.

Belle and Bazz looked at one another.

"Is there a reason we shouldn't?" It was my turn to be testy. It seemed a little late in the day to turn squeamish.

"Ross kept what he called souvenirs in that trunk," Belle said. "Some are . . . well, a mite unusual."

"Like?"

"Like . . . oh, Lordy, Bazz!"

"Like Pawnee scalps, Serena," Bazz said.

An acid flux rose in my throat. "You can't be serious."

"That's what he said, Reenie," Belle added. "Called them his 'hate tokens.'"

"Are you telling me Ross Cooper actually scalped—"

"Oh, no, not Paw himself!" Bazz said. "He bought them years and years ago off some Indians—Sioux, Comanche, I don't remember exactly. Old enemies of the Pawnee is all I know, and there were a lot of those."

Even if true, I wondered how bad they could be, refusing to be daunted by the very unpleasant picture that invaded my mind. "Those plans might save us a lot of time," I said, firmly quashing a sudden impulse to deny further involvement. "Which room was his?"

"I haven't been in it since Ross was laid out," Belle said, her eyes wide with dismay.

"I'll go, Belle," I said. "Just tell me which it is."

The lantern's steady glow chased back the shadows. The room, third floor, first door on the right, was very large and austerely furnished. The bed's feather tick had been removed; across the rope lattice that had supported it lay a soft draping of deerskins, so pale they were almost white. It looked like a catafalque for a warrior chief.

There were rifles stacked on racks on the walls; a lariat and a braided buggy whip hung from stout pegs. Beside a plain, unvarnished washstand stood a rush-seated chair, so straight-backed and shallow-seated as to discourage any thought of relaxation. There were no curtains at the deep-silled windows, no rugs on the boot-scuffed floors. It seemed a chamber more suited to a monk than a rancher fond of high living. Whatever time my poor sister had been forced to spend with the man had not, I was convinced, been spent here.

I raised the lantern to see a long, coffinlike container opposite the bed. *Could that be where Ross Cooper had been laid out?* Fighting back my impulse to flee, I knelt in front of the battered trunk. The stained lid flopped back to reveal the long leather tube Bazz had earlier described. It took only a moment to confirm the nature of its contents; having done so, I exhaled, startling myself with the hiss of my escaping breath, unaware I had been holding it so tightly.

I closed the lid on whatever else the trunk contained. Considering the sad lack of familial affection at Morning Star, it was quite possible the

140

scalps Bazz spoke of existed only as something darkly hinted at to discourage trespass, like a gate posted with signs warning passersby to beware of the dog chained behind it. Whatever else Ross Cooper may have been, he was obviously a very private man, the kind of man who would take care to discourage invasion of his quarters whether or not there was a demonstrated need to do so. No wonder Lottie Cooper had turned to her son for solace.

Bazz withdrew the roll of plans from the tube, took them to the kitchen and chivvied a grumbling Belle into clearing a place on the herb-covered table big enough to accommodate the large sheets. The heavy paper was yellow and dog-eared, but the black-inked lines were as sharp and clear as the day they had been drawn. Bazz soon discovered a space behind the fireplace that neither he nor Belle had been aware of, and Belle excitedly pointed out several places where walls were indicated as thicker than comparable sections elsewhere. I wondered aloud about the storm cellar, which had been added after the house had been completed.

"I imagine it was planned on the spot when the men arrived to build it. There could be all kinds of hidey-holes down there with no one the wiser," I said, finding myself caught up in the game. "Why, your father could have made them himself, after the men stopped work for the day. Tomorrow why don't I—"

"I'll look after the cellar, Reenie," Belle broke in. "We use it as a root cellar and to store my bottled elixirs. No one will think twice about seeing me going in and out."

I had no sooner nodded agreement before Belle and Bazz began to argue about the stone bunkhouse

141

which Belle saw as a prime possibility.

"With hands going in and out all the time, it would have been too risky, Belle!"

"I reckon he had to get to it only a few times a year. . . ."

As they wrangled I looked idly through the sheets of plans. My attention was caught by a drawing of the mansion's stone facade, not as a plan, but as it would look when seen from above and off from one side, semicircle of pillars in place, long cast of shadows and all. As my eyes traced the sensitive lines and artful shadings I felt another nudge at my memory, stronger this time, yet I knew I had never been anyplace where I might have seen anything remotely like this. Perhaps I was merely bemused by the placement of a house so grandly formal in this frontier setting. How sad that a man talented enough to plan it had ended, broken and penniless, in a rough makeshift town a continent and ocean away from home!

"Do you suppose the gold might be under one of these pillars?" I mused aloud.

Bazz and Belle moved back beside me. "What do you think, Bazz?" she asked, aroused by this new possibility.

"I think, unless he had a team of horses and a tackle, he'd never be able budge one of those things; if he did, everyone would have known about it."

Belle and I looked at each other, her sheepish look no doubt mirroring mine.

"It's been a long day, girls. I say we go to bed and draw up a plan of attack in the morning," Bazz suggested.

Belle stretched and yawned. "I'll be along in a minute. If the weather holds, the poppy heads will soon be ready to harvest—maybe as soon as tomorrow. I have to prepare for it, just in case. You've seen them, of course," she said to me.

I shook my head.

"Lordy, Reenie, how could you have missed that cloud of white and purple? Come look, before they shatter!"

She tugged at my arm; I followed reluctantly. I loved poppies, but I doubted I would Morning Star's.

We stepped out on the terrace. The peonies, thank God, had passed, but the foxgloves' reptilian heads reared menacingly above the poppies Belle proudly indicated.

Their billowing blossoms, glistening like silk taffeta of an unearthly translucency, appeared to undulate in the windless night air. The gray-green stems were clothed thickly with hairs that looked stiff and sharp enough to draw blood. Here and there a swollen head, having shed the fancy dress of its petals, oozed a milky ichor.

I stepped back. "I'm sorry, Belle, I realize you're as dedicated to this garden as Lottie Cooper was, but I find the plants here . . . well, monstrous."

Belle turned stiffly to stare at me. I couldn't see her face clearly enough to read her mood, but when she finally spoke she seemed more defensive than angry.

"I reckon that's 'cause you been livin' back East where everythin' grows so puny."

That was neither true nor the point; but how could Belle be expected to know about the flowers in the East, coming out here directly from New York City?

"Lottie called them luxuriant," she continued. "She used to say, 'Belle, have you ever seen anything so luxuriant?' Well, let me tell you, my herbs're bigger and better than anythin' Lottie Cooper ever grew!"

Her tone conveyed a self-satisfaction that bewildered me. *How could she not see what I saw?*

"I think of them as my babies, Reenie," she

143

continued, wagging a finger in mock admonishment. "Don't you know better than to find fault with a woman's young'uns?"

I took refuge in silence. I tried to recall what Malcolm once quoted to boost my spirits after one of Mother Rogg's tongue lashings; something from Romeo and Juliet about roses smelling sweet no matter what they were called. Let Belle think of those wretched plants as her babies if she wished; to me they were and always would be monstrous.

NINE

The furtive searches we embarked upon the next morning soon disheartened me. Relieved of her nighttime prowls, Belle now arose at the same time as Bazz and I, torn between the need to harvest her herbs and her desire to search for the elusive gold. She was not at her best in the morning.

The house grew more and more disordered, and sometimes, as I walked the long corridors—seeking oddities in the stone structure; rapping for hollow places—the trapped, stagnant air seemed oddly misty, as if I were looking through fine gauze. Bazz ascribed it to the dim light, and indeed a succession of unsettled gray days had all but robbed the prairie of its color; Belle testily suggested a need for spectacles. Both explanations were reasonable enough, but neither satisfied me.

The entire responsibility for preparing meals and tending to household needs had settled on Rita. If she left, which Quinn had pronounced just a matter of time, one of us would be saddled with the job. There was little doubt in my mind who this would be. With this unappealing probability in mind, and with the intent to delay the inevitable, I remonstrated with Belle one morning for haranguing Rita about bringing in wood for the fireplace.

"Well, I beg your pardon! I'd forgotten what a little prig you are, Reenie!"

"Belle, I was only thinking—"

"You're always 'just thinking'! 'Just thinking' is what you do best, you and your precious Malcolm Wilcox. Maybe I don't talk as pretty as you; but I know what I'm about, and don't you ever forget it!"

I turned without speaking and retreated upstairs. I hadn't realized I'd talked that much about Malcolm; I certainly hadn't meant to throw up my acquaintance with him to her as a measure of my superiority.

I brooded in my room, feeling immensely sorry for myself until I reflected on the fact that this was the first quarrel we'd had since I arrived. Not even a quarrel actually, more a misunderstanding. All sisters have them, I told myself; besides, I already knew Belle really wasn't at her best in the morning.

Feeling considerably cheered, I walked from my room down the hall to the small room in the northwest corner. In temporary use as a storeroom for Bazz and Belle's half-filled packing boxes, it had been Bazz's nursery and opened across from the room that had once been his mother's. After Ross Cooper died, Bazz moved down there from his boyhood bedroom on the top floor opposite his father's. Might Quinn, once he had gained possession of Morning Star, take the dead rancher's austere sanctuary for himself? I pictured Fawn's graceful, dusky form cradled in the pale doeskins on that rope-latticed bed. . . .

Enough! I crossed to the front corner of the nursery-storeroom to inspect the unusually wide sill of the window there, only to find my disturbing thoughts made flesh in a compelling tableau taking place below on the path leading down to the working center of the ranch.

Quinn, easy-seated on his black Appaloosa, was

leaning toward Spotted Fawn. As I watched, the girl's sharp-chinned little face lifted up toward his, her finger pointing beyond him. He smoothed her dark head with his cupped hand and gently pushed her forward—down toward his quarters, I assumed— to be rewarded with a flashing smile before she dashed off, light-footed as the creature whose name she bore.

The subject of their exchange was clearly Sharo, who stood clench-fisted a few yards to one side, his stiff-legged departure blocked as Quinn wheeled his big stallion into the youth's path. Sharo ducked, as if to escape a blow, and as Quinn's face came into view, I saw his mouth working angrily. The horse continued to back and fill until, intimidation having lost its savor, Quinn allowed the boy escape. Plainly, his capacity for gentleness—if indeed that was what I had witnessed between him and Fawn—was limited.

I turned my attention back to the windowsill. It protruded into the room a good six inches or more than the other sills in the house, and on close inspection I saw that a long slab of stone of nearly identical coloration had somehow been affixed to it. I doubted if a knife blade could have been inserted in the joining.

Had a niche been chiseled within it? A hollow deep enough to conceal the bags or bars of gold our minds envisaged? The Ross Cooper I was beginning to understand might have found a certain humor in concealing his treasure in the room intended as a nursery. An occasional private visit of a father with his child was unlikely to be questioned, and even if removal of the gold was observed by young eyes, who would pay heed to the babblings of a toddler? Just as children see in their rooms at night the giants read to them about by day, so might it be assumed that gossip overheard about the long-rumored cache of gold had been transformed by a youthful imagination into glittering reality.

Bazz greeted the fevered workings of *my* imagination with an indulgent smile.

"I'm afraid the real reason for it is more prosaic than yours, Serena," Bazz said. "Apparently I was a venturesome infant, and when quite young I managed one brightly moonlit summer night to haul myself up on the sill to watch the 'doggies' gathered near the trough, where they had come to drink." He paused. "The window was open; the doggies I yearned to play with were coyotes."

Bazz laughed at my involuntary gasp. "That was Mama's reaction when she walked in to find me teetering on the edge. Paw refused to have bars installed. He said he wasn't about to have people accuse him of caging his boy like a wild animal . . . as if Paw ever cared what anyone thought," he added in a mutter. "But Mama kept after him about it until finally he had the blacksmith in Ellsworth forge an ornamental grille which was attached by long flanges to the wooden frame." He pointed out the holes, roughly filled, that I had failed to notice. "The sill was widened to support the bottom edge."

When I expressed curiosity about how the widening had been accomplished, Bazz told me the local sandstone was relatively soft and easily drilled when newly quarried. "I imagine Paw attached the slab with long bolts and then plugged the holes so my busy little fingers couldn't get at them."

We fell silent.

"Well, at least you know your father went to a lot of trouble to keep you safe," I said.

Basil raised a dark, slender eyebrow. "Dear Serena, always searching for a silver lining." He cupped his long hand to my head, reminding me of Quinn's caress of Fawn's. "Knowing how Mama must have taken on, I'm sure he only did it to secure a little peace."

"When was the grille taken down?" I asked as together we descended the stairs to the ground floor.

"I don't remember exactly. It was just before Quinn came that first time, so I guess I was nine. Paw didn't think it right, Mama going in and out of my room the way she did, so he made me move upstairs." He shook his head. "It was hard on her, Serena. Mama was a sensitive, impulsive woman. It was important for her to be able to share thoughts and events as they happened. Who else was there but me?"

"But, good heavens, Bazz, you were only a short flight of stairs away . . . surely they couldn't have been—"

"It was hard on her," he insisted. "As for the grille, after the nursery was dismantled it was put to good use in the storm cellar. Mama had the blacksmith add hinges and a lock so it could be mounted on the shelves where she kept her herbal mixtures. Far as I know, it's still there. Some of those elixirs . . . well, she didn't want anyone helping themselves."

Remembering Father Rogg's similar precautions at his pharmacy, I nodded. "Have you explored the space behind the fireplace yet?"

Bazz gave me a rueful smile. "Assuming there is one, I haven't yet figured out how to get into it. When I first saw that space drawn in on the plans, I wondered how Belle and I could have missed it, but for all we know it isn't there. Just because plans indicate something, doesn't mean it was built that way. Especially out here, where every man's got his own notions about what makes sense and doesn't. The masons, seeing no sensible use for a place like that, mightn't have bothered making it."

"But Bazz—"

He held up his hands. "I know what you're going to say. Faint heart never won fair fireplace."

I laughed. "Or words to that effect."

149

Bazz stepped off the bottom riser, and turned to look up at me. He took my hands in his and leaned to kiss my cheek. His lips were warm, his breath sweet. His mouth brushed down to lightly graze mine. "Or words to that effect," he murmured.

We trailed out to the kitchen to report our lack of success to Belle. Wreathed in steam, her sleeves rolled to the elbows, her face frowning as she stirred at the pots bubbling on the big black range, she might have been one of Macbeth's witches come for a visit from his Highland castle, except I doubted any of those formidable ladies had strawberry-blond hair. Pinned up in an untidy twist, her steam-dampened locks had escaped to fall lankly across her forehead. I idly wondered at their coarseness. I knew henna accounted for the color; could it also have caused Belle's fine hair to thicken?

He reaction to Bazz's theory promptly reclaimed my attention.

"Any lazy meddler fixin' to change Ross Cooper's precious plans sure woulda got the scriptures read to him in a hurry! You'd best keep on tryin', Bazz. How 'bout you, Reenie?"

I reported my lack of success. "You and Bazz had pretty well covered the upstairs already, Belle. I've run out of places to look."

"What about the bunkhouse?" She fanned away the steam around her head; her eyes were hard and bright.

I avoided her penetrating gaze. I was reluctant to admit that its proximity to Quinn's quarters had kept me away. "I used to ride Bingo every morning, but we've been so busy lately. . . ." I shrugged and smiled weakly. Prevarication didn't come easily to me.

"Then, you'd better start up again," Belle said sharply. "If Bazz and I started prospecting around down there, it might get Quinn to wondering."

She wiped her perspiring brow with her forearm. "I got my hands full enough with the herbs and searching the cyclone cellar without ridin' herd on you two! I'd plum forgot how deep that cellar went and how cold it is even in summer. Near turns my bones to icicles."

Her words alarmed me. "You shouldn't stay down there too long, Belle. A chill can turn into fever awfully fast." The memory of my mother's cold, still form powerfully invoked the sense of loss and loneliness I knew would never cease aching deep within me. "No amount of gold's worth your getting sick!" I blurted.

Belle regarded me through narrowed eyes; her hand slowed its stirring. "Lordy, if that isn't just like you, Reenie. Better poor and healthy, is that it? Don't you ever get tired of those Sunday school maxims of yours? If I was you, I'd give up tryin' to wheedle the natural cussedness out of folks."

Her choice of words didn't sit well. "I care about you, Belle. I wouldn't use an expression of my feelings to coax you—or anyone else—in or out of anything."

Bazz laughed. "Why, Belle does that all the time! Are you sure you two are twins?"

Belle and I looked at each other. "'Identical opposites,'" she whispered, quoting an orphanage matron who had more than once become exasperated out of patience with us. I can't recall which of us began to giggle first, and the succeeding exchange of do-you-remembers, tumbling one on top of the other, soon eased the awkwardness.

Belle was right, of course; I had dragged my feet long enough. Before Bazz told me about the local sandstone's peculiar qualities, my sister's speculations about sills fashioned like boxes seemed to me

151

more wishful thinking than a real possibility. Now that I knew otherwise, nothing justified further delay in carrying out my assignment to spy out the bunkhouse. Quinn was the one forcing our departure; why should I harbor qualms about deceiving him?

I was put to the test the next morning. As I started down the path toward the barn, I became aware of a continuous din issuing from a cloud of dust rising over the corrals. My ears soon distinguished the piercing squeals of frightened animals from the hoarser shouts of men, and as I rounded the corner the dust-hazed air assaulted my nostrils with the rank stench of burning hair and flesh. The corrals seemed too small, their rails too slight, to contain the milling cows and calves that bleated and bellowed within them.

In the midst of the wheeling, plunging confusion, mounted cowpunchers whirled ropes, sending the released loops flying with astounding accuracy toward the heads of terrified calves, whooping when a noose connected as intended, cursing explosively when it did not. Once roped, the bawling calf was hauled away from its protesting mother to the pen nearest me where, just outside its gate, a large fire blazed.

I watched in mounting dismay as calves, roped a second time, were unceremoniously slithered on their sides, their backs or their rumps to the fire's smouldering edge. There, after the rope was stripped away, the poor creature's head was twisted so as to keep its flailing body flat on the ground. A second man shoved one of the calf's hind legs forward with his booted foot, then pulled the other leg to the rear with both gloved hands. As the squealing victim lay helpless, its bulging eyes rolling wildly, a third cowboy applied to its hip a white-hot length of iron pulled from the fire, while a fourth nicked its ear with a knife.

The men, each with his neckerchief pulled tight across his nose, eyes narrowed against the smoke, were unrecognizable; the outlines of their hunkered bodies wavered specterlike in the columns of visible heat. One of them, responding to another's nudge, turned in my direction. There was no mistaking the corncob pipe clutched upside down between his teeth. Motioning another of the men to take his place, Cobby trudged over to where I was standing.

"Have to get Bingo yourself today, miss."

I nodded. "I can see you've got your hands full, Cobby. What's going on here?"

He gestured with his head toward the chaotic scene. "These be calves born on the range we brung in for brandin'. Fine Hereford stock," he said, pride animating his usually noncommittal tone. "Quinn knows what he's about."

One of the red-coated, white-faced little animals, just released, scrambled stiffly to its feet to wander off dazed in search of maternal consolation. His sturdy box-shaped body was a good bit scruffier than the pretty little Jerseys on the dairy farms I'd known back East, but when I said as much to Cobby, he snorted indignantly.

"The Crown Bar Five wouldn't be paying no twenty-five dollars a head for milk cows!"

"The Crown Bar Five?"

"That outfit Quinn worked for up Nebrasky way," Cobby said. "Driving them up there soon's the brandin's done."

"Will Quinn be going with you?"

"Will Quinn be goin' where, S'rena?"

The noise having muffled the sound of Quinn's approach, I started at the unexpected rumble of his deep voice directly behind me.

"To Nebraska," I said. "Cobby was telling me about taking these calves there, and I was just wondering—"

"Be back before you leave . . . you gonna miss me, S'rena?" He stood very close; his dark eyes smiled down into mine.

"Why, I'd sooner miss the devil!" I exclaimed.

He started to laugh, then broke off with an angry shout. "Hey, you! Jed! Take it easy with the little feller! If I ever see you haulin' one of my colts like that, you can jest haul yourself out of here."

Jed looked up, surprised, from the calf he had been dragging through a patch of glowing embers dislodged from the blazing logs. I could see smoke rising from a wide-singed swath of fur.

"Hell, Boss, a horse is a horse; this ain't nothin' but meat."

"And I'm telling you these are blooded stock you're treatin' like range mavericks. Here at Morning Star we have roundups not cow-hunts, and if you're too dumb to tell the difference . . . ahhh-hh-h, get on with it," he ended in a mutter of disgust. He wheeled toward me. One hand rested on the butt of the holstered gun slung low on his right hip, and from the look on his face, I feared for one heart-stopping moment he was going to take out his frustration on me.

"Mark what I say, S'rena," he said, addressing me tight-lipped with hardly a trace of his customary drawl, "once I'm clear of Bazz and that sister of yours and get back on my feet, you'll see a change here at Morning Star, starting with hands in the bunkhouse as good as the stock they'll be driving."

"Brave words," I taunted, "but regardless of how it changes, for good or ill, I won't be here to see it— much less care." That wasn't entirely true, of course, but I was too riled just then to worry about niceties. I'd grown to love the prairie, and I'd miss Cobby and

154

Bingo; but for me Morning Star had lost its sweet promise. It had become an unhappy place, unfit for the ordinary lives of ordinary people like me.

I thought of the morning star rising here, year after year, suffusing the spring horizon with its cold, deadly brightness. My anger emboldened me to sally forth on dangerous ground. "Tell me, Quinn Cooper, do you suppose your father really knew what he was about when he built his grand stone mansion on that accursed, bloody ground? Don't you suppose he lived to regret it?"

Quinn stared at me expressionlessly. Ashes and dust caked the lines of his face, lending it a severity more akin to gray Vermont granite than the golden Kansas sandstone. "I don't *suppose* nothing about any of it. What I *know* is I've heard more'n enough of your female foolishness. I got work to do."

It was near noon when Bingo and I arrived back at the barn. Bazz was waiting in its cool recesses; clearly he had something to tell me. Exhilarated by our wild gallop home across the prairie, I had lost my taste for conspiracy. I avoided his eyes and turned a deaf ear to his whispered words, and when we emerged out into the sunlit dust smelling of cattle and lathered horses and the honest sweat of the men astride them, I found it unaccountably, perversely, exciting.

I crossed to stand near the holding pen's gate just as Sharo released a bawling calf newly branded by Quinn. The youth and the man, so recently at odds, worked in surprising harmony, wasting neither words nor motions.

Bazz, who had reluctantly followed, paused beside me, one hand resting on my shoulder. "It's a bloody business," he said, his voice a rasp of distaste.

Quinn, overhearing him, rose to his feet, stretched, and strolled over to lean against the rails of the corral.

155

He pulled his sweat-stained kerchief from around his neck and slowly wiped the blood from his hands. The warm, healthy smell of him filled my nostrils; seeing them flare, Quinn boldly winked at me, but his words were for his half-brother.

"No dirty hands for you, eh, Bazz?"

"I hate it. Always have," Bazz said. "That's what Paw could never understand."

"Nothin' wrong with hating to hurt critters . . ."

Quinn paused, and as the two men eyed each other I sensed strong emotions churning beneath their clipped words. Basil's pale eyes dropped first.

". . . but that don't keep you from eatin' 'em, does it?" A slow smile curved Quinn's lips as he pushed himself off the rails and reached out to drag his soiled kerchief down Bazz's cheek. "There you go, little brother, bloodied without liftin' a finger."

It was a brutal gesture. At my gasp, Quinn turned to me, his eyes hot and intense. "Those English fellers up at the Crown Bar Five tell me that's what's done to a boy on his first fox hunt, 'cept they use the fox's lopped-off tail to do the honors. Blooding, they call it."

Bazz paled. "You bastard!" he hissed.

Quinn grinned. "You got that right."

Bazz urged me away as Sharo called for Quinn's assistance with a balky calf. But although the confrontation was over, I was inexplicably reluctant to leave. I could make no sense of it. I met Quinn's eyes in a long, searching glance. *Was it yearning I saw there?* I resisted Bazz's impatient tug at my arm.

Sharo called again. Quinn exhaled a long sighing breath, as if making a painful decision. "You're old enough to take care of yourself, S'rena . . . ," he said slowly. He turned toward Bazz; his head lowered bull-like, in primitive challenge. "But if I ever catch you sniffin' around Spotted Fawn, I swear I'll kill you."

He spun on his booted heel. I watched as he strode across the dusty, hard, hoof-pounded earth toward the fire and the cruel demands of the life he had chosen. My well-schooled sensibilities reproached my body's response to his lithe muscularity. No decent woman should be drawn to a man like that; besides, he had made his priorities quite clear.

I clutched Basil's arm and smiled up into his handsome, troubled face. He had been kindness itself ever since my arrival. Once the three of us were on the road, I told myself, three young, healthy, carefree Gypsies with Morning Star behind us and enough money to start us off . . . why, we could do anything we set our minds to!

And yet, as we trudged up the path to the big house, its honey-colored stone pearly in the blaze of the midday sun, it slowly came over me that at no time since I arrived two months ago had there been any talk, any happy speculation, any mention at all of where our travels might take us or what we hoped for our future. Our *shared* future, the promise of which had directed my every decision, animated my ever move, from the day I received Belle's letter.

I had kept it safe, that precious letter, as one might a fragment of bone of a miracle-performing saint of old, and although I could hardly any longer make out the faded writing on its creased, yellowed pages, I would cherish it always.

TEN

As Bazz and I approached the walk leading to the front entrance, a rank odor drifting like invisible smoke from Belle's garden slowed my steps. Deeply cut leaves as big as platters crowded the space where the poppies had so recently spread their crinkled cups. *How could anything grow that large so fast?* The heavy, bloom-laden stalks rearing above them, tip groping toward tip from either side of the path, threatened to burst the bounds of their stone-fenced beds. I had no wish to pass beneath their arch.

I swerved to the right, intending to enter through the kitchen. Basil tugged at my arm.

"Before you go in," he said, "there's something you should know." He hesitated.

"What is it, Bazz?" I prodded, sensing his reluctance. "As a matter of fact, I have something to tell you, too. You and Belle both. Good news, I think."

He looked at me questioningly.

"You first, " I said, giving him a gentle nudge.

"This morning I found the entrance to the space behind the fireplace."

"Good for you!"

He shook his head. "Pure dumb luck, I'm afraid. I pushed and I pulled at what I thought were joinings of the stone slabs until my fingers were numbed by the effort. Finally, I did what frustrated people usually do when faced with a situation like that: I kicked at it."

I blinked at him. "You don't mean—"

"Oh, but I do, Serena. The entire stone facing promptly gave way. It had been bolted together like the windowsill in the nursery, then mounted on a simple swivel device triggered by pressure at a particular spot on the bottom edge." He gave a self-conscious laugh. "If I hadn't lost my temper, I might never have gotten inside. It's very small, more a nook or cubbyhole than a closet."

He fell silent for so long I felt like kicking him. "For heaven's sake, Bazz, call it whatever you like; what did you find in it?"

"Nothing."

I stared at him.

"Nothing, that is, but a wooden chest so heavy I couldn't lift it. That's when I called Belle in from the kitchen. I dragged it out, she opened it, and when we saw the contents glittering in the lamplight—well, we were pretty excited. But when we hauled the chest out into better light we realized our golden hoard was nothing but iron pyrite." His look invited my commiseration.

"I'm sorry, Bazz," I said slowly, "but I don't know what iron py . . . py . . ."

"Pyrite," he repeated. "I keep forgetting how new you are to the West, Serena. It's also known as fool's gold. Pretty to look at, but as Belle said, 'worth no more'n tin pot with a hole in it.'"

I sighed. "Well, maybe my news will cheer her. Those calves Quinn is branding? He's selling them to that ranch in Nebraska he rode for before your father's . . . accident. He can't settle with you and Belle until he's paid for them, so as soon as the herd is ready to move, Quinn and Cobby will be leaving."

Bazz's eyes lighted up. "That means they'll be away at least a week. We'll have plenty of time to look wherever we want, whenever we want."

"Won't that depend on who's left behind?"

Bazz shrugged. "I don't think any of those drifters are much for carrying tales to the boss. Cobby's the only one with any loyalty to Quinn, and if he's going with him . . ." His words trailed off as his gaze drifted dreamily beyond me. "Do you suppose he'll take that little girl of his along?"

"Spotted Fawn? I should certainly hope not! From the look of her, she's not yet recovered from her last excursion with him."

"Maybe if you offered to look out for her . . ."

I smiled. "You have a kind heart, Bazz. I'll do that . . . not that I expect it'll do much good. Now! Shall we hunt up Belle?"

No sooner had I poked my nose inside the kitchen then Belle exploded.

"Did Bazz tell you what that father of his did? I swear if I'd of known about it then, I sure wouldn't have made his last years so blame easy. Bastard!"

"Good heavens, Belle! You make it sound as if he did it on purpose."

"Of *course* he did it on purpose," she said, rolling her eyes in exasperation. "Big joke! Haw-haw! Lordy, what a ninny you are sometimes, Reenie."

"Well, I'm sorry you think that, Belle," I said, blinking back sudden tears, fearing she'd think me even more of a ninny if she noticed them.

"Sorry never bought any bacon."

"Tell her, Serena," Bazz urged.

"Tell me what?" She held up her hand. "But don't if all's you got to say is you found more of that fool's gold in the bunkhouse sill."

"I won't tell you that, because I haven't looked yet,

160

but in a day or two we can look all we want: Quinn won't be here, and neither will Cobby."

Belle regarded me with a sceptical squint. "What's she talking about, Bazz?"

Bazz nodded to me, and I took her through the events of the morning. As I talked, Belle's squinty look relaxed; when I finished, she gave a little yip of delight. "You're a right smart little prospector," she said, her rosy mouth spread into a grin. "When the cats are away—"

"—the mice will play," Bazz and I chorused.

"And all of Morning Star," Belle added, spreading her arms wide, "will be our oyster."

"Except there aren't any oysters out here, Belle," I said, laughing.

"Try telling that to the Grand Hotel in Ellsworth. Why, I reckon the cans of 'em they sell during a year'd fill a wagon. And then there's prairie oysters, but considerin' the company you kept back East, I guess you never heard tell of those. I used to make 'em for Ross all the time, ain't that so, Bazz?"

Bazz nodded stiffly.

"Ross Cooper sure liked his whiskey, Reenie, sometimes a little too much, and that's when I'd stir up a prairie oyster to clear his head and settle his stomach. Mashed up canned tomatoes mixed up with a raw egg and a few bits of dried chilies."

"It doesn't sound very appealing," I said.

"Seems to me most things s'posed to be good for a body don't, like praying and minding your p's and q's and passing sweet-talking cowpokes by . . ." She winked at me.

"Oh, Belle," I said softly, slightly shocked by her boldness, but delighted to have her teasing me again.

"All right, troops, gather 'round," she commanded, all business again. "Now, here's what we're gonna do . . ."

161

It was like a game, I told myself, a big jolly game like the kind we used to play at the orphanage. But as Belle outlined her plan, her animated face reminded me anew that although for me just being here now with her and Basil—talking, laughing, *sharing*— was happiness enough, hers was linked to a future whose dimensions remained unknown to me.

The next day promised a repeat of the preceding two. The clear dawn sky soon became gauzed with the promise of unseasonable warmth, and the dirty disorder of a house whose dankness mystifyingly increased as the days warmed and lengthened, made me welcome any excuse to remain out of doors, even if it involved spying. *It's a game, nothing but a game,* I again assured myself, as I let myself quietly out the kitchen door.

Lost in thought, I had started down toward the corrals, when a loud halloo behind me claimed my attention. I turned, whipping my hand up to shade my eyes, for although the sun had not yet topped the roof, the mansion's stone bulk was surrounded by an aura whose brilliance jolted me with its intensity. I blinked my watering eyes and saw Bazz waving at me from between the massive slit-eyed pillars. He cupped his hands around his mouth.

". . . anything from town?" he called.

The aura grew brighter still. I steepened the angle of my shading hand. I had forgotten Bazz had volunteered to go into town to buy much-needed supplies. Cobby was too busy to be spared; the other hands too apt to bring things we didn't need and forget those that we did. *Anything from town? A few yards of sprigged muslin for a summer dress? Lavender toilet water?* Nothing Bazz should be asked to get for me. It could wait. I shook my head and turned away just as the sun's rim blazed above the slates, transforming the pillars into flaming swords.

In front of the corrals, a stout trail wagon was being loaded with bedding for the drive to Nebraska with the branded calves. A number of blackened pots and pans hung from a frame over which a stained canvas sheet had been slung, and a couple of the hands were lashing a water barrel into the box. As I drew closer I saw a faucet protruding through a roughly hacked hole. Judging from its well-worn edges, this wagon had seen its share of cattle drives.

Strong language issuing from the direction of the barn preceded Jed's arrival with a pair of round-barrelled bay mules. As he backed them into the traces, the discordant plonking of the iron utensils set in motion by their balky maneuvers caused the near mule's ears to twitch irritably.

"Hey, watch out for ol' Dan, there!" Cobby called, peering around from the back of the wagon. "When he twitches he kicks."

Sure enough, the next moment the mule lashed out sideways so fast I wouldn't have seen it had I blinked.

"Damn jughead," Jed muttered, "ain't even fit for crowbait." The mule accepted the rough hooking-up that followed with surprising placidity. "I'm a bronc buster, not no mule skinner," Jed shouted back over his shoulder in Cobby's direction.

"That a fact." Cobby seemed unimpressed. "Anyway, it won't be you bouncin' in the wagon."

"Oh, yeah?" Jed sneered. "Who's the lucky one?"

"Sharo."

Jed looked as surprised as I felt, having viewed Sharo and Quinn's openly expressed antagonism more than once. "So, am I goin' or stayin?"

"Not up to me. Quinn'll tell you himself what he's got in mind," Cobby said.

163

Jed's glance darted toward me. I didn't care for the way his tongue slid along his lips.

Cobby followed me into the barn. "Best stay up to the house while we're gone, Miss Serena."

"But Bingo—"

"Just turn her out into the fenced pasture with the other horses when you come back in today. I don't want you here," he said, jabbing his pipestem toward me, "an' I don't want him up to the house neither. If he bothers you, I want to hear about it."

It was on my lips to protest I wasn't about to play spy for anybody until I realized that was exactly what I had been doing for Belle and Bazz. "I won't come down," I promised. "Not alone anyway."

Cobby grunted, gave Bingo's round little tummy a couple of judicious jabs, then cinched her up tight. When we came out of the barn, Sharo had already taken his place on the wagon. As I prepared to mount Bingo, Quinn ambled across from his quarters, a bulging canvas sack slung over his shoulders and Spotted Fawn trotting at his heels. She was still very thin, and although her abrasions had largely healed, her skin still showed blotches of lavender and yellow discoloration.

My pity for Fawn vied with my anger with Quinn. Had she come out at his bidding for a public farewell? Whatever his purpose, I dropped Bingo's reins and strode over to offer my services as Bazz had suggested. Before I could reach them, however, Quinn had lifted the girl and his sack into the wagon along with extra clothes for the men, bedding and foodstuffs. Was Fawn just another provision for the trail? I wondered that he hadn't earmarked her along with the calves.

"I was going to offer to look after Spotted Fawn while you were gone, try to put some roses in her cheeks, but I can see I needn't bother."

164

"Fawn don't need the kind of roses you and Belle'd give her, and she sure don't need Bazz lookin' at her with or without 'em."

"Bazz looking at her is a sight better than what you're doing to her!" This time I didn't bother to lower my voice. The hands, hugely entertained by our exchange, sniggered.

Quinn glared at me, ordered the men into the bunkhouse to await his instruction, then clutched my arm and hauled me into the barn. Bingo, left outside, her reins trailing in the dust, whickered plaintively.

"Don't you know better than to pass your high-and-mighty judgment on what I do where the whole world can hear you? Damned if I know why you're so blamed set on thinking the worst of me, S'rena, but I'm telling you, from now on keep it private."

I looked down at the gloved hand clenched around my arm. "Telling me?"

He released my arm as if stung. "Asking you," he amended. His mouth was a grim line; his tone was belligerent. I judged him a man who would think it a weakness to plea innocent to murder even if he were. "Request noted," I said coldly. I turned to leave.

"It was . . . decent of you to want to look after Fawn." His reluctance to make this admission roughened his voice.

"The offer still holds."

He fell silent behind me. *Could he be having second thoughts?* At length, I felt his hands rest on my shoulders. The pressure he exerted was too slight to force me to face him, yet I did. The barn was dim, smelling sweetly of clean hay and warm horses. A narrow beam of light filtered down through a splintered plank of siding to glaze his dark hair with silver. He tucked his gloved forefinger under my chin and lifted my head to meet his dark, searching gaze.

165

"Maybe you aren't like Belle," he whispered. "Maybe—"

I closed my eyes, expecting his kiss. Wanting it . . .

"Quinn?" It was Cobby's voice. "The men're waitin' on you . . ."

His hands fell away, and he walked past me out into the sunlight.

Feeling empty and oddly bereft, I waited until I was sure the yard was empty before walking out to mount Bingo. The sun was very hot now. The harnessed mules stood square and solid, eyes half-closed, steady as time, and although I could not see her, I assumed Fawn still crouched in the wagon box, as patient as the mules, as afflicted as Sharo, who sat on the seat above her hunched in misery.

Neither Bingo nor I had the heart for a lengthy excursion that day. A hot, dry wind began to blow from the west, steady enough to dry my lips painfully but not strong enough to dispel a cloud of biting flies that caused Bingo to toss her head, distracting her attention from the gopher-hole-pocked terrain. The rattle of a snake, disturbed by our passage past the scruffy bush affording it shade, was the final straw. Our moods in disconsolate harmony, my pony and I turned back, topping the ridge above the corrals just as the train of riders, horses, bleating calves and creaking wagon set forth below on a long curving course that would take them well north of us.

Quinn headed up the party, his tall, black Appaloosa setting a pace slow enough for the others to follow without strain, steady enough to keep the calves close-herded. A cowpuncher, too shrouded in dust to put a name to, kept his horse moving back and forth along the line of calves; I could not tell if the whistle that floated up to me was for his own amusement or meant to distract his charges from their mothers left behind. Woody's blaze-faced bay moved up fast on the other side of the herd; Cobby brought up the drag on his agile little sorrel, clever enough to round up a wild, range-wintered bunch on her own, or so he claimed.

Trailing the herd was the chuck wagon, with Sharo's high-spirited gray mustang jittering unhappily at the end of the rope that secured him to it, unable to escape the flapping of the canvas cover fingered by the wind. The clank of the pots and pans carried up to my perch on Bingo. I sighed to think of Spotted Fawn jolting all this day and the next in that springless, airless, noisy box.

Upon entering the yard, I was bewildered by the scene that greeted me. Jed and Cookie and Smiley and all the rest had either mounted or were about to mount the handsomest of the horses in their respective strings. The astonishing part was not the smart look of the horses, however, but the men themselves. Spit and polish, every last one of them.

"Going to town, miss," Cookie said, with a nod of his head, politely pinching the brim of his Stetson between his fingers. "The old man tol' us not to come back 'til Sunday," he added. "We left everything shaped up."

Sunday? That was five days away. I knew it was customary for the hands to be given some time off after the spring roundup, but from what Cobby had said, I doubted this was what he thought Quinn had in mind. If the news had come from Jed, I might have been suspicious, but Cookie, an older man, had always seemed to me a reliable sort. *Five days.* Why, they wouldn't have a cent left among them, considering all the cards that could be played, whiskey drunk and women bought in five days.

I surveyed them anxiously. Anticipation gleamed in every eye. Smiley, a light rider, had infected his prancing piebald horse with his spirits; even Jed's big, raw-boned roan, as heavy as his rider's style of saddle-sitting, snorted impatiently. *What call had I to pass judgment?*

I forced a smile. "Easy come, easy go, eh, boys?"

The men relaxed and grinned. Jed sidled his roan up beside me. "I'll come back sooner if you like," he whispered insinuatingly. His words were oddly drawn out; his eyes unfocussed. "I already spoke with your sister up to the house . . . mebbe the three of us . . ."

Deprived of its usual scruffy growth, Jed's razor-nicked, blood-streaked chin proved to have little in common with the bold jawline popularized by illustrators of western tales. It was on the tip of my tongue to tell him he would have done better to visit the barber shop in town, but thought better of it. A tart reply would do little to chasten a man like Jed, especially if he had already begun his whiskey drinking in the bunkhouse, as I suspected. I decided instead to misinterpret his insulting offer.

"That's very thoughtful of you, but Mr. Basil Cooper will be looking out for my sister and me. There's no need to cut short your holiday on my account."

He glowered at me and moved his horse closer—I think it was my reference to "Mr. Basil Cooper" that particularly riled him—but by then the other men had begun to move out. Jed roughly wheeled and spurred on his roan. Soon, the eager, squeaky-voiced yips of the youngest among them swelled into a chorus of full-throated whoops as the pack of them galloped off, billows of dust rolling in their wake.

There was something both grand and sad about

the sight of them hightailing it aross the prairie, full of foolish expectations unlikely to be realized, sure to return broke and weary to start the cycle all over again. The cards would never get better, nor the whiskey, nor the women, but men in exile feed on dreams; it would have been cruel to remind them of truths that deep down inside, they already knew.

I turned Bingo out into the pasture, and as she trotted off to greet Bazz's Dancer with a friendly nudge of her soft muzzle, I envied her the built-in protection of her satin-smooth coat. Despite the shade provided by my hat's wide brim, my face felt tight and tender; the dust-hazed glare made my head throb, and the clean cool water I pumped up at the trough did little to ease my mouth's stale dryness.

I didn't walk so much as trudge up the incline to the big stone house. If I entered through the kitchen, I would have no excuse not to tell Belle about seeing Quinn leave for Nebraska and the men for a holiday in town, and she would press me to start my search.

Longing for the quiet of my room, I turned up the front path instead. The cool dankness I had deplored earlier now seemed inviting. As I approached the arc of stone that contained the garden's unnatural growth, my intent to look neither to the right nor left proved as impossible as avoiding thinking of something one is told not to. The deeply cut leaves I had first noticed that morning had grown another foot, almost to shoulder height, and thick veins now swelled above the dark green surface slicked with oozing sap. From below, coarse liver-red stalks thrust up clusters of seed pods whose purplish, fleshy spines writhed in the hot sun, as if a brood of bizarre deep-sea creatures, impaled there, had been flung up on a hostile shore. Their stench hit as hard as a closed fist.

I lurched, my breath coming in quick gasps, my vision blurring. A swimmy feeling overswept me as

169

the looming semicircle of stone shafts seemed to edge closer, closing the gap behind me, surrounding me. . . .

I took a deep breath and forced myself to close my eyes. When I opened them, the pillars had retreated to their accustomed places. Around the central pair I saw that vines, *pretty* vines, had begun to twine out of the rankness below: one was a morning glory, quite ordinary except for the intense blueness of its flowers; the other, delicately tendriled, with heart-shaped leaves and dainty greenish white flowers, must be the briony Belle had pointed out earlier along with the nightshade that clothed an adjacent pillar. Their unremarkableness cheered me immensely.

My room, thanks to its eastern exposure, was blessedly dim at that late-afternoon hour. I filled my washbasin with cool water and dipped my whole face in, rejoicing in its refreshment. I crossed idly to the window as I gently patted my sun-reddened skin dry. Before long, I reflected ruefully, my complexion would become as weather-roughened as Belle's.

I leaned against the cold stone of the sill and slowly shed my dusty riding clothes. The big house's long, dark shadow sprawled across the near landscape; beyond it, through the slanting light, now copper, now gold, a dust devil danced. *Or was it?*

I squinted, fancying I saw in the whirling, shifting shape the form of a horse and rider galloping headlong upon some urgent errand, but how could that be? Basil had taken a wagon to town; Morning Star was empty of riders. A neighbor, perhaps? I squinted again, harder, but saw only settling dust. It had been a whirlwind, nothing more. After all, how urgent could a neighbor's errand be that would take him to the east side of the house where there was no

170

door to admit him? I turned away with a sigh. Everything here, like the pioneers seeking a new life, looked to the west. Was I the only one who preferred to see the sun rising?

But the sun was not all that rose in the east. So did the morning star. And here, on this very site, upon the shining of its bright, cold light above the horizon, the cruel god Ross Cooper defied had ordained death.

ELEVEN

I opened my door the next morning on a profoundly silent corridor. Obviously no one else was astir. The kitchen, too, was empty. Had Rita taken advantage of the exodus of the hands to garner an extra hour or two of sleep for herself? Belle and Bazz had, so who was I to find fault?

I found half a loaf of bread in the larder, slathered a slice of it with preserves to disguise its staleness, and took it together with a cup of tea into the parlor, grateful for some quiet time for reflection. Nothing seemed to be working out quite as I had hoped, but the hard truth was that I could hold no one but myself responsible for those hopes. *Come share this wonderful place with me,* Belle had written, but she hadn't said anything about sharing it for a lifetime—in fact, she had been ready to settle for a visit if that was all my circumstances allowed.

I stared unseeingly into the dark fireplace, hardly conscious of the sour smell of the half-burnt logs, of the musty aftertaste of the bread or the tepidness of the tea. Perhaps a visit was all Belle had really expected or wanted. As I realized how flimsy the foundation of my castle of dreams was, tears stung my eyes. *Just a visit? After so many years?* I had no wish to lose again the sister twice torn from me in childhood, but what proof had I that Belle shared my longing? Or that Basil's mildy flirtatious attentions arose from anything more deeply felt than gentlemanly courtesy? Belle, Basil and Serena. A third wheel, as always. Useful, perhaps, as I had been to the Roggs, but not wanted; not *loved*.

But I was no longer a child, I reflected, and for too long now I'd been acting like one: eager to jump at Belle's bidding to earn her smiles, no questions asked. I set down my cup and raised my bowed head out of my wallow of self-pity. Quinn would be returning in a few days to pay Belle and Basil what was owed them and turn them out, and yet their plans remained undefined, as if waiting to be shaped by the finding of a cache of gold no one was really sure existed. I had stood by patiently, passively, long enough. It was time for answers.

I mounted the stairs resolutely and entered Belle's room without knocking, sensing I might fare better if I caught her unawares. The room was dim; the air close and heavy with perfume. To my surprise, I saw Belle standing at the window, dressed and motionless, as if intently viewing an absorbing scene through the lace curtains.

"Belle?" There was no answer; she remained turned away from me, rigidly erect and unhearing. *"Belle?"* This time my voice was, I confess, tinged with alarm.

"Go 'way, Reenie!"

The cross, sleepy, familiar voice seemed to come from behind me, but how could that be? Bewildered, I crossed to the figure at the window. Seen closer, it was a fully clothed dressmaker's dummy, and what I had thought were Belle's strawberry-blond ringlets were attached to a wig framing a featureless wire-mesh face. I whirled toward the rumpled bed. *What on earth. . . .*

The surprise of my unexpected entrance, which I had naively hoped might work to my advantage, was more than matched by my shock when Belle abruptly sat up, the gesture setting in motion the silvery fall of fine white-blond hair that brushed her bare shoulders. It was like looking into a mirror.

We stared at each other for a long moment. Belle recovered first; she beckoned me closer.

"I wanted us to leave here as real twins again, Reenie, so I decided to wear a wig until my hair was its own color again, just like yours. See?" Belle fanned her fingers up through the silken strands, which, when released, joined glimmeringly together again like a glide of water.

I blinked. "But *why*—"

"It was to be a surprise." She pouted prettily. "I always did like surprises, Reenie, remember? Not that we ever had many," she added in a resentful tone. "But now that you've found me out I won't have to wear that hot old wig anymore."

"Does that mean Bazz knows about it?"

Belle smiled. "Well, of course, silly. Fact is, he's the one got it for me. I gave him a lock of my hennaed hair for the matching, but when the wig arrived I could've sworn it'd been matched to a pull from a horse's tail. Have you ever seen anything so coarse and common-looking?"

It seemed to me an awfully elaborate surprise to little point; but Belle had spent many happy hours at the orphanage devising similar jokes, and I found myself as unable to decide now as then whether Belle was by nature a schemer or I a humorless prig.

I gave a mental shrug, laughed, and plumped down beside her. "Well, I did wonder what on earth

174

could have happened to it. I thought maybe it was something to do with the water out here—in fact, I've been inspecting my own hair with more than a little anxiety."

"And never a word about it! If that isn't just like you, Reenie. I swear, sometimes I think you're too good for this wicked old world."

I hugged her; the questions could wait.

When we descended arm in arm an hour later, we found Bazz pacing back and forth in front of the staircase. Hearing our footsteps, he said, without looking up, "Well, it's about time—"

His expostulation trailed off into astonished silence as he turned and beheld a pair of silver-haired young women. His eyes darted from one to the other. "Serena? Belle? Which is . . . who is . . . ?"

I laughed. "I surprised Belle out of her surprise for me, Bazz, but it looks as if you're more than making up for it!"

Once I had identified ourselves for him, Basil's eyes immediately sought Belle's. "Surprised? Yes, I guess you could say I'm surprised," he said flatly.

Belle fluttered her hands. "Well, Serena being so ladylike and all, I just never figured on her bustin' in unannounced, so instead of *leaving* Morning Star as lookalikes, we decided to start now. Course with the hands gone to town there's only old stone-faced Rita here to see us, and if she's surprised, how'll we ever tell?"

Belle turned to Bazz. "You should've seen her face when she saw me without the wig! Flummoxed, I'd call it—sorta the way you look now." She cocked her head at me. "Come to think of it, Reenie, you never did say what brought you barreling into my room like that." Her tone was offhand, but her blue eyes

175

were alive with curiosity.

I looked from one face to another. "It's not important right now," I said, alerted by Basil's frowning face. "Is something the matter, Bazz?"

"Rita's gone," he said.

Belle gaped at him. "Gone?"

"Cleared out. Skedaddled. Vamoosed," he amplified testily. "Another little surprise for you this morning, Sybelle Garraty."

Belle quickly recovered. "Not much of a one, Bazz. She was getting broodier and broodier, the way she always does this time of year. Did I tell you I caught her chanting in the dooryard yesterday?" Her lips tightened. "I put a stop to *that* in a hurry, I can tell you. Superstitious lot, those Injuns; I'm glad we're rid of her."

"I can't help thinking your garden had something to do with Rita's uneasiness," I ventured. "Like Bazz said last week, I imagine Indians, who live closer to nature than people like us, might think the growth there . . . unnatural."

"Oh, for pity's sake, Reenie! There's nothing 'unnatural' about big, healthy plants. I already told you they've always grown faster and larger here than anyplace else. If you ask me, it's just that my thumb is a heap sight greener than most, Injuns included."

"Yours and my mama's," Bazz murmured.

"Your mama's, too, of course," Belle added compliantly, but judging from the proud look on her face it was plain my sister thought she deserved most of the credit.

I forced a smile, then dropped the subject. Everyone needed something to be prideful about, I chided myself; who was I to pass judgment on Belle's horticultural accomplishments? Besides, hadn't Cobby praised her herbal salve? Kind words came hard to that wizened little man, and I'd seen for myself how effective it had been when applied to Sharo's cuts. If Belle was able to distill good from those dreadful plants of hers, her thumb was more than just green; it was downright miraculous.

"Well, with Rita gone, I guess we'll just have to divide up the chores between us, won't we? The horses have been turned out to pasture, so at least we don't have to worry about feeding the stock," I said briskly. "You have your herbal brews and salves to do, Belle, so I'll tend to the chickens and kitchen garden and the cooking, and Bazz can finish the packing. I don't imagine we can take much with us: I saw some half-filled boxes in the old nursery, so we'll need only a few more and some canvas covers to keep our things dry."

"If that isn't just like you, Reenie," Belle said. "Fussing about details when there's gold to be found."

Detecting a sneer in her tone, I could feel the color rise in my cheeks. "We can't eat gold, Belle, and if we don't find it, we'll need your herbal concoctions as a source of income—or so you keep telling us."

We glared at each other. "My word," Bazz drawled, "I can see it's going to become harder and harder to tell you two apart. Obviously neither of you gives a hoot about my opinion."

Our silver heads whirled toward him, identical frowns on our faces, belligerent words at the ready, only to be disarmed by his amused grin.

Belle laughed and clapped her hands. "Grantin' due respect to all you said, my dear sister," she said with elaborate courtesy, "*I* say let's make the most of having Morning Star all to ourselves: gold first; food, herbs and packing later! Bazz, you take Quinn's quarters."

Basil paled. "Oh, no! He'd kill me if he ever knew I'd been through his things—"

"For pity's sake, Bazz, it's the *building* needs lookin' at, not Quinn's things. Before he took it over for himself it was a storehouse, remember? All kinds of hidey-holes, I expect. 'Sides, he'd never have taken those precious calves of his to be sold if he'd already found the gold, and if he had, can you see him leavin' it lyin' around, easy pickings?"

"No, I guess not," he murmured, somewhat mollified.

"Course not!" She turned to me, all business. "I'll keep on searchin' the storm cellar; you do the bunkhouse. That's the least likely place, actually, 'cause there's always so much goin' on there, but that's where the hollow doorsill I was told about is, and Ross coulda got at it at night when the hands were sleepin'." She laughed. "They snore so loud I swear you could run a locomotive by without wakin' 'em! And if nothin' turns up today, tomorrow we can do the barn. Shouldn't take long, only the foundation is stone."

Bazz left, as if anxious to get his unwelcome assignment behind him as quickly as possible. I turned, then hesitated. Belle obviously expected me to hasten obediently in his footsteps, but despite the titillation inherent in a hunt for hidden treasure, I simply couldn't justify taking part in it myself. I used to look the other way when Sybelle pocketed a coin or a trinket found at the orphanage, able then to tolerate the sour note struck in my conscience by her triumphant chant of "finders, keepers," but this was a whole new dimension of discordancy.

I drew myself up. "I'm sorry, Belle, but I can't do it. If your benefactor *did* hide gold on Morning Star, then it rightfully belongs to Quinn. I can understand your loyal impulse to help a dear old friend get what you feel is his due, but for me to help . . . well, no matter how shabbily Bazz may have been treated by

178

his father, for me to help would be stealing, plain and simple."

"Benefactor? Ross Cooper my *benefactor?*" Belle's voice rose to a shriek. "I earned everything I ever got here the hardest kind of way! First I was nursemaid to that crazy wife of his, run ragged tending to her fool notions; later, no sooner had my first blood showed than he took me to bed, expecting me to be available whenever it pleased him, day or night." Belle's lips trembled. "Lottie was still alive then, Reenie, and sick as she was, she *knew.*" She laughed hoarsely. "Some kind of benefactor."

I stared at her, aghast. "I . . . I can't find words to express how sorry I am," I said at last in a low voice. "He had no right to ill-treat you so—and I hope God saw fit to punish him for it." I reached out to squeeze her shoulder. "But by law the gold belongs to Quinn," I persisted doggedly, trying not to allow the shock I felt affect the right of the matter as I saw it.

Belle heard me out expressionlessly, but her blue eyes flamed with anger. Before she spoke she took a deep controlling breath. "Ross may have left Morning Star to Quinn; but there was nothing in his will about any gold. Seems to me, once it leaves the ranch it's no longer part of it. Besides, Bazz says possession is nine-tenths of the law—why should we worry ourselves about Quinn's measley tenth? If the shoe was on *his* foot, do you think he'd waste any time worrying about us?"

"Probably not," I admitted, "but that's not the point—"

"Then, I'd sure like to know what in *hell* is!" Belle broke in heatedly. She threw up her hands to forestall an unwelcome explanation. "I really don't understand you, Reenie," she said with a sorrowful shake of her head, "but truth to tell, I never did. You never were much good at looking out for yourself; still aren't, far as I can tell." She eyed me speculatively. "Maybe it's because life's been easier for you than me."

"Easier for me?" I stared at her uncomprehendingly. "Who was sent off to the orphanage first? Papa chose *you* to stay with him, Belle, not me."

Belle gave a hoot of harsh laughter. "You mean all these years you thought he loved me best? Lord love us, Reenie, the only reason I got 'chose' is because you were too sickly to do the cookin' and cleanin', and too pale and skinny to keep him warm. Sometimes he even loaned me out to other men's beds to earn him a night of drinking." She fixed me with eyes as dark and dead as a prairie sinkhole. "I paid the price for your innocence, Reenie, and don't you ever forget it."

I turned away, feeling suddenly sick. My blind ignorance of such monstrous things reproached me; my priggish qualms about the gold seemed ridiculous in comparison.

Belle stepped up behind me; her hands lightly clasped my shoulders. "I never wanted you to know, Reenie," she whispered, "but maybe, knowing, you can understand why any feelings of Christian charity I might've had left from Mama's teachings just plum dried up."

I turned back and entered her embrace, my cheek against hers, her warm breath stirring the silver tendrils of my hair. *Bone of my bones, and flesh of my flesh.* "Oh, Belle . . . oh, my dear sister."

I closed my eyes and drew her closer. How she had suffered! Betrayed first by our father, and then by the man supposed to be her protector. And Quinn was no better, I mused, thinking of his abusive treatment of Spotted Fawn. She, too, was hardly more than a child . . . *like father, like son.*

Why on earth should I think I owed Quinn Cooper

fealty? He hadn't asked me here; he didn't want me here; I owed him nothing! And Belle was right: it was unlikely ethical considerations ever gave him pause —why should I insist on mincing observances of my own moral niceties?

I stepped back, then reached out and softly laid my palm against my sister's cheek. "We may not always see eye to eye, Belle, but we're the only family we've got. I'll see you through this as best I can."

TWELVE

The absence of the men from the bunkhouse should have made the searching of it an easy task, but I found its stillness profoundly disquieting. The disorder I found there—scattered clothing, unwashed metal cups, empty milk and bean tins—had the stale, fetid odor of abandonment. It was as if a deadly plague had overnight robbed the shabby building of its living inhabitants.

Dust whirled up by the corded edge of my skirt wavered in the air like a filmy curtain as I made a hasty survey of scarred, rough-planked walls studded with hooks and nails, tacked with yellowed poster pictures of scantily clothed women, and bearing the carved intitials, some crude, others elaborately curlicued, of a generation of cowhands. Belle was right: a cache of gold could not long have remained here undiscovered.

Eyes watering, I retreated outdoors. Hot as it was, the outside air was at least scoured by wind and sun, and I took a deep, reviving breath of it before turning my attention to the foundation. The large, flat slabs extended no more than a foot above the ground. I could see no seams in the individual stones, and they were too large to move without mechanical help, which couldn't have been managed without attracting attention. The only remaining possibility was the wide doorstep's curious boxlike sill that Belle had mentioned. On close inspection, the top of it did indeed seem to have been fitted like a lid, but my fingers proved too tender to pry it off.

Sucking their bruised tips, I set off toward the barn. I had a memory of a tool Sharo used to clean out the horses' hooves that would suit my purpose well. The corrals were empty, but in the distance I saw a group of horses grazing near a trough whose spillover had encouraged the growth of a wide, encircling swath of greenery. On the near edge of it stood Bingo, her tail swishing contentedly as she munched the tender shoots. I called her name. Her head came up, ears pricked, a succulent curl of grass trailing comically from her mouth. How I missed our prairie excursions! *Surely this task could wait. . . .* I hesitated on the path. No, I told myself, you gave your promise. I walked resolutely on; Bingo resumed her grazing.

The barn was as still as the bunkhouse, but although the mingled aromas of hay, straw and dried horse manure might never rival the fabled perfumes of Araby, to me they smelled far sweeter. Once my eyes had adjusted to the dimness of the interior, I spied the wooden box in which the tool I was looking for should be, and so it was: cleaned, oiled and ready for use at a moment's notice. No wonder Cobby gave Sharo such high marks. As I turned to leave, I heard mewing peeps issuing from one of the haylofts on either side of the high, wide door opening. Lower than the main loft, they allowed fodder to be easily reached and forked down by a single cowhand.

I mounted the short, stout ladder nailed to the loft's front and peered over the edge. There, nestled in a hollowed pile of fragrant hay, were four kittens: two blacks, an orange-and-white and a smoke gray, their eyes the chalky blue of the very young. Their mother was nowhere to be seen—off on a hunting trip, no doubt—and three of the kittens, their pink mouths opening wide in hisses of alarm, retreated prudently from my unfamiliar and alarming odor.

The gray, propelled by curiosity, approached me one reeling step at a time. It flattened when I reached out to touch its fuzzy little head, but a gentle stroking coaxed forth a tiny tenor purr. It was a sign of trust unusual for a barn cat, more accustomed to short shrift than affection from humans. "Too young to know better, aren't you?" I whispered.

I pulled myself up into the loft and settled back into a billow of hay. Once my motion had stilled, the kitten cautiously advanced to explore the edge of my skirt. I lifted it very gently onto my shirtwaisted bosom where, after a single startled mew, it soon curled, paws and tail neatly tucked up. "Hush-you bye, don't you cry," I softly crooned, "go to sleepy little baby . . ." The warm ball of dozing gray fluff felt as weightless as eiderdown against my breasts, but I found the sense of its closeness . . . its *aliveness* . . . uncommonly gratifying.

I wondered if I might adopt it. *No*, I told myself a second time that morning. We would be leaving soon, and it was too small, barely a handful, to be exposed to the rigors of an uncertain journey with as yet no known end in sight. I could look out for myself, but this little creature still had some growing up to do. I sighed, and gently nudged it back to its litter mates. The other kittens forgot me in the excitement of greeting their returning sibling. I smiled as they tumbled over one another, forgetful in the joy of the moment of the danger I might pose, still needful of their mother's watchful eye.

A sharp pang of longing pierced me. Would I ever have a baby of my own to watch over? Would I ever have a man of my own to caress me with a loving hand? I shivered, remembering Quinn's touch. Hardly loving, yet it had made me feel so alive! Those black eyes; that careless, flashing smile. I recalled that muscular thrust of leg as he walked . . . *strode* across the yard to dispute my championing of Sharo. A hard man, a man who gave no quarter to anyone who challenged his authority, a man who no doubt thought gentleness a weakness fit only for women-folk, if then. *Like father like son.* Why, then, did the thought of Quinn make my heartbeat quicken when Basil, a handsomer man, a better and finer man, did not?

Unthinkingly, I reached out and ran my fingers back against the lay of the gray kitten's fur. It hissed and swiped me with a paw whose claws left a smarting reminder that its trustfulness should not have been taken for granted. And yet, I knew that if my circumstances were different I still would have chosen to adopt it. I had never much cared for the placid, smug, domesticated cats I had known in childhood.

I idly continued watching the kittens: one of the blacks was a bully; the other one, bullied, vented its frustration on the orange-and-white; my venture-some gray, in blithe disregard of the litter's pecking order, took and gave offense in equal measure. *Peas of the same pod.* . . .

Before our reunion at Morning Star, it had never occurred to me that Belle and I were anything other than peas of the same pod. Oh, she had always been bolder, brasher than I; she hadn't cared, as I so fiercely had, whether the other children liked her, but still, in the ways that really mattered, hadn't we been more alike than not? More alike, certainly, than these kittens. Now, however, I sensed a dissembled intimacy in our conversations and a hint of obligation in her embraces.

I thought of what Belle had suffered. My foster parents may not have loved me, but they wouldn't have tolerated my innocence being traded for anything less than a wedding band. The terror and pain of forced submission to the physical demands of a depraved father, followed by a guardian's betrayal, was all but unimaginable to me.

My poor sister! Was it any wonder she was wary? Perhaps the twinship I saw as a bond, to be lovingly shared, seemed to Belle a cage whose reentry she now regretted, the more so having invited it herself. She was the venturesome gray of our litter; I had no right to order her priorities to suit my narrow notions of right and wrong, and when I tried, I had no one but myself to blame for her verbal scratches.

I sat up abruptly, scattering kittens in all directions. *Good heavens! Here I am, lolling in a hayloft, when I should be attending to the priority I had, for better or worse, agreed to share with Belle.*

As the kittens scampered back to their nest, their coats became touched with fleeting bright halos of illumination. I turned my head to find its source, and flinched from the searing brilliance of a narrow beam of light arrowing down through a knothole above, like the searching gaze of some huge pagan god. I descended to the barn floor, bemused by my extravagant metaphor. What did I know—or care—about the ways of pagan gods?

The tool I borrowed weighed heavily in my pocket as I crossed the dusty yard to the bunkhouse, but I sensed even before I used it to pry off the top of the sill that I would find nothing of interest. Indeed, the

186

hollowed stone contained nothing at all, not even the dried husks of insects, so tightly had it been fitted. True, the coating of dust on the bottom held a faint shimmer, which could possibly be a residue of gold long since removed, but even if so, this tantalizing hint provided no clue to its present whereabouts. If anything, it made it all the more likely that any gold secreted at Morning Star had been long since spent.

I made my way slowly back to the house to make my discouraging report. As I topped the rise and viewed the Morning Star manse against its rolling prairie setting, the cyclopean pillars flanking the entrance might have been the pagan gods I had fancifully evoked, eyes and all. Unlike the barn knothole, no light beamed dazzlingly through them, but if it did . . .

In my mind's eye I suddenly saw, with the clarity of a fine steel engraving, the rising sun's rays thusly focused, as dazzling as a faceted diamond. But the pillars were differently proportioned. There were more of them, too, some of which, unlike these, were topped with massive stone crosspieces. The picture was much too vivid to be a product of my imagination; it was a memory, but a memory of what?

I stood there as if rooted, staring at the pillars before me, willing my mind to bridge the gap between their reality and the vision in my mind. It must have been something Malcolm Wilcox had described to me, or something he showed me . . . something that had been niggling at the back of my mind, on and off, ever since I arrived. . . .

All at once it flooded back: the illustrated books Malcolm brought back from England after his last trip there and his account of a visit to the temple of great stones raised, some said, to the ancient Druid gods of Britain. . . .

Hadn't Bazz said the architect who designed Morning Star was English? He would have known about that prehistoric circle of stone. The name played hide-and-seek in my head. Stone circle . . . stone hemicircle . . . stone *henge* . . . that was it! *Stonehenge.* A circle of stones whose pillar-flanked altar—bloodied, some believed, by human sacrifice—was intended by ancient worshippers to mark the rising of the sun on the morning of the summer solstice.

I looked up at the six limestone pillars. A semicircle, not a circle, and the pierced pair framed the entrance of the great stone house instead of an altar heelstone, but the similarity of the concept was striking. It was just the sort of thing that would have appeared to the hard and unforgiving man Belle and Basil had described to me. Ross Cooper would have enjoyed the challenge of having those huge pillars cut and erected on this bloody ground, and relished even more what they represented: the revengeful defiling of a sacrificial site sacred to the tribe who had murdered his parents, coupled with an arrogant adaptation of the powerful symbolism of the summer solstice to his own ends.

Elsewhere, spring heralded the renewal of life; at Morning Star, Cobby had intimated, it more often than not ushered in a season of sickness and death. Was this the price exacted for the defiance of gods whose favors were bought by the blood of innocents? I shuddered. No wonder the usually plain-spoken little man had taken refuge in allusion: it was safer to avoid what could neither be understood nor defended.

I stared at the two blind-eyed monoliths, guardians of a secret revealed but once a year. I knew where the gold was now, or at least I would at the moment of sunrise the morning of the summer solstice.

Which one, I wondered, would point the way to where it lay hidden?

My discovery should have lent wings to my heels, but as I approached the kitchen entrance my footsteps dragged. Why should I be reluctant to share my discovery? Was it because Belle and Bazz might think me daft? Even if they did, wouldn't they be ready by now to clutch at anything offering a glimmer of promise? And yet, the more I thought of it, the more far-fetched my idea seemed. I pictured Basil's raised eyebrows and Belle's derisive smile as I spun a theory arrived at by linking a ray of sun through a knothole with an uncertain memory of ancient stones and pagan rituals.

My mouth went dry. Perhaps I had better take another look at the architect's drawings before saying anything, to make sure it was rooted more in fact than fancy. We had all but ignored the sheets depicting the facade, assuming its ornamentation had no relevance to our search for the gold's hiding place, but I remembered them as being quite detailed. Yes, I told myself, that was the only prudent thing to do.

Reassured by my decision, I pulled open the screen door and was immediately enveloped by the pungent aroma arising from herbs brewing in kettles boiling furiously on the big black range. Belle and Bazz, steam-wreathed, seemed like figures in a shadow play. Bazz was sitting slumped on Belle's high stool, his face pale and drawn, his skin scratched and bleeding. My sister was applying salve to his wounds none too tenderly, all the while muttering what were clearly angry reproaches.

"Good heavens, Bazz," I cried. "You look as if someone tied you up in a sack full of cats. Whatever happened?"

Belle looked up, startled. She frowned. "Well, it's

189

about time! I could've searched the bunkhouse three times over by now.''

"I just wanted to be sure I didn't overlook anything,'' I protested. Stung by her criticism, I saw no reason to mention my interlude with the kittens in the hayloft.

Belle paused in her ministrations. "And . . . ?''

I shook my head. "I looked everywhere, inside and out.''

"Damn!'' Belle applied a last swipe of salve to a long, deep scratch, still beaded with blood, on Bazz's neck. He winced.

"Bazz?''

He slanted a sullen look at me, then turned his head away.

"Please, Bazz,'' I persisted, "tell me what happened?''

"You guessed about right,'' Belle supplied, "'cept it wasn't a sackful of cats—all it took was one big old tom. He finished with Quinn's quarters sooner than he expected, so he decided to search the barn. To spare us the trouble, he said.'' Her voice had taken on the false brightness of a Sunday school teacher trying to compensate for the listlessness of her pupils. "One of those cussed barn cats didn't take kindly to his trespassin'.''

"I'm . . . I'm sorry, Bazz.'' I had been going to say I was surprised I hadn't seen him in the barn, but I had already piously claimed to have spent my time searching the bunkhouse. "Is there anything I can do?''

"If you're handy with a needle, you might sew up his shirt later.''

I looked closer. Bazz's head was still turned away from me, but I could see several long rents in the front of his bloodied shirt. "Of course,'' I said, wondering at the fury of the attack. The only cats I had seen in the barn were the kittens . . . but if they were nursing when Bazz came in and the mother thought he posed a threat to her babies. . . . *Yes, that could account for it.*

Belle ruffled Basil's auburn hair. "This young feller needs a nursemaid. Fact is, he needs something else even more, don't you, Bazz?"

Basil hunched lower to escape Belle's hand. She clasped his shoulders and gave a little shake. "C'mon, Bazzy, you can't 'spect me to ask her for you."

Already unsettled by Belle's rapid shifts in tone, this new, falsely playful one set my teeth on edge. "Ask me what?" I demanded.

I saw Belle give Bazz a surreptitious nudge. He sighed, drew himself up, and slowly turned his head. His gray eyes, dulled, expressionless, stared out at me above pale cheeks slashed with crimson. He looked dreadful. "Serena—" His voice broke; he swallowed, hard. "Serena, will you do me the honor of becoming . . ."

The words, run together, dropped off into a whisper.

I stared back at him. "I beg your pardon?"

"Speak up, Bazz!" Belle hissed.

He shut his eyes for a long moment. When he opened them, they were once again alert and focused. "Serena, will you . . . will you marry me?" This time, his voice gathered strength at the end.

Belle's beaming smile faltered as I stood there dumbly. I could feel hot tears welling in my eyes. Angry tears. I didn't trust myself to speak.

"Reenie? Cat got your tongue?"

I whirled on my sister. "I don't recall asking you to act as my matchmaker, Belle. Is that why you invited me to Morning Star? As a convenient mail-order bride for your chum?"

Belle's eyes went blank with shock. "Reenie, darling! I never—"

"Maybe, if he had asked on his own, with no prodding from you, I might have considered answering, but *this* ... this is demeaning. Even Ernest treated me with more respect." Defiance did not come easily to me. My mouth felt cottony; pulses of pain traveled up the taut cords on my neck into my skull. I drew a deep, shaky breath. "Now, if you'll excuse me, I'm going to my room. I've developed a frightful headache."

"You'll be coming down for supper?" Belle asked.

I paused in the doorway. "You'll have to do the best you can with whatever's in the larder," I said over my shoulder, guessing from her querulous tone she was more anxious about the meal than the loss of my companionship. "I would have prepared something earlier, but I knew you didn't want me to take the time."

There was no reply; I hadn't expected one. We all knew the truth of it: first things first, which in this case was Ross Cooper's cursed gold.

My room, thanks to its position on the eastern back side of the house, was dim and cool. When I closed the door behind me, I was on a private little planet of my own; my only connection with the everyday world were the wide windows, which offered breezy refreshment by the simple action of lifting up the sash. I leaned on the broad stone sill and inhaled the grassy fragrance of the sunbaked prairie. The tightness in the back of my neck eased, the pain seeming to flow out over the sill into the long shadows thrown by the eclipsing bulk of the great stone house. If only my heart and soul could be refreshed as simply!

I lay down upon the bed, drew over me a shawl I had left folded at its foot, and closed my eyes, hoping that drowsiness would overtake me. As I did so, a bird flew in the open window. Wings beating against the walls, beak opened wide in panic, it made a single erratic tour before arrowing out again into the sky's wide blueness. Startled into wakefulness, I stared after it, wondering if my stay here at Morning Star, measured against historic time, might not be fairly represented by that bird's sudden, unplanned detour from its life's expected course.

Sudden? How else describe my flight from marriage to a man I did not love and from foster parents who did not love me? *Unplanned?* Except for my arrival here—it seemed so long ago!—nothing had happened as expected. Bazz's awkward, reluctant proposal was only the latest in a series of unsettling surprises: There was the hardness I detected in Belle—less surprising now in light of her subsequent heartbreaking revelations; Quinn's explosive arrival and the relish with which he unfolded the bloody history of the ground on which this house had been built, transforming Morning Star from a place offering a new life of promise to one blighted by revenge and greed. And the garden. . . . No, I would not think of that. I would not allow myself to reflect upon those monstrous plants and Belle's baffling, prideful attachment to them.

You're forgetting the good things, I chided myself. *What about Belle's generosity? Dear Bingo and our carefree jaunts across the prairie? The love of music and books shared with Bazz? Our singing together has a warm and happy energy, heads together, closely harmonizing. . . .*

My troubled thoughts eased; my mind drifted pleasurably along the slow, eddying currents of recall. Wildflowers and morning bird song . . . distant thunderheads spreading like inkblots across the wide blue sky . . . the pond and its sheltering willow . . . *the pond where Quinn kissed me.* . . .

A rapping at my door roused me from a dream of whirlwinds. Bingo and I, retreating from a threatening scud of clouds, raced across the prairie, our course twisting tortuously to escape the dark, roaring corkscrews that appeared from nowhere to block our progress, now here, now there. . . .

Heart pounding, thinking at first I was hearing distant thunder, I sat up as the door quietly opened.

"Serena?" It was Bazz, carrying a tray. He entered hesitantly; his eyebrows had an anxious tilt. "I hope I haven't disturbed you. I've brought you something to eat . . . and an apology." His eyes flicked around the room, seeking a place to set the tray.

I removed books from the table by my bed. "You can put it here, Bazz." I considered scooting my legs over to give him room to perch beside me, but thought better of it. "And bring over the chair next to the bureau for yourself."

As he did so, I inspected the contents of the tray. Except for the cup of tea and tin of milk that accompanied it, my appetite was not tempted by the plate containing two slices of cold, greasy meat— hacked no doubt from the ham Rita had fed us for several nights before her disappearance—a portion of charred beans and half of the heel of the stale loaf I had eaten for breakfast.

"I'm not very hungry, Bazz, but I appreciate the thought."

"I'm afraid I'm not much of a cook," he said with a rueful smile as I edged the plate to one side and added milk to the tea.

I raised my eyebrows at him over the edge of the

teacup. Belle herself had mentioned his need of a nursemaid.

"But that's not why I asked you to marry me," he added.

"Then, why did you, Bazz? You don't love me."

My challenge caught him by surprise. He flushed and dropped his eyes. "My mother loved my father; it didn't bring *her* much happiness."

"I realize that, and I'm sorry, but—"

"A man ought to be married, Serena," he said.

"You're really not making much sense, Bazz," I said gently.

"Yes, I am," he protested. "I'm saying that love isn't everything. I'm saying that I . . . I like you better than any girl I know. . . ."

I suspected he knew too few to make that much of a recommendation. "You and Belle are very close," I pointed out.

"That's different," he said with a flat certainty that puzzled me. "We share . . . memories, not interests. You and I . . . we like the same books and poetry, we even know the same songs, and you must admit our voices blend well together." His eyes brightened. "Why, with a little practice, we could give concerts in the towns along our route! Most people like music, and Belle could use the opportunity to sell her elixirs to the audiences we'd attract. I could even write duets especially for us and—"

"We could do that without being married, Bazz."

He looked stricken. "I'm sure I'd grow to love you, Serena, you're so good and sweet."

How perverse the human heart was! I liked Bazz. I enjoyed his company, and he was a paragon of virtue compared to his renegade brother, and yet . . . and yet I had a sense of something missing, something hollow. I thought of the gray kitten's hiss and clawed reproof when I ruffled its fur. Did I perversely yearn for the excitement of loving against the grain? All I knew was that Quinn, against all reason, stirred my senses, and although I did not know what that signified, I was unwilling to settle for anything less.

I reached out to pat his hand. "There's no need to rush into anything, Bazz. I have no doubt there'll be a preacher in every town we pass through."

"Belle won't like it," he said in a tone of near desperation. "People will talk!"

"I'm not about to get married to please my sister, Bazz! People will probably take you for our brother, and if they don't, why should we care what strangers we're unlikely to ever see again might say about us?"

Bazz got up from his chair and walked over to the window. He stood there for a long moment, staring out in silence at the empty prairie. The sun had set; shadows had begun to darken the corners of my room. When he turned back, his face was indistinct in the gloom.

"So that's that, eh?" His low voice expressed resignation, but I noticed a slight relaxation in the set of his shoulders.

"It's for the best, Bazz, you'll see. And if we change our minds later . . ." I shrugged and lifted up the tray. I had drained the tea, but could eat no more than a few bites of the ham and bread.

He stepped forward to relieve me of it. "As you said, it shouldn't be hard to find a preacher happy to do the honors." He paused at the door.

"Can you manage it?" I called.

He glanced over his shoulder. "Are you referring to the door or your sister?" His tone was flat, almost bitter.

Oh dear. "Bazz, if it would make it easier . . . just tell Belle I decided to sleep on it."

"Thank you, Serena." He rested the tray on his

hip. "Who knows, maybe your dreams will bring you a change of mind."

He backed out smiling. As the door drifted shut behind him, I lay back with a relieved sigh. If my hunch about the stone pillars proved right, Belle would have more interesting things to think about tomorrow than marrying me off to Basil Cooper.

THIRTEEN

Up before dawn, my stomach protesting its emptiness, a search of the pantry revealed that if someone didn't set about replenishing the larder, there would soon be nothing to eat. Except for a hambone, some dried beef and a dozen or so cans of milk, the staples—beans and peas, sugar, coffee, cornmeal, flour—were all in short supply. Bazz was supposed to have gone to town for that very purpose; obviously other errands had taken precedence. I sighed. *Didn't anyone but me give a fig about food?* Cobby would have to set out with the wagon for town as soon as he returned from Nebraska, and if the men returned from their holiday first. . . .

But that was no concern of mine, I assured myself. My responsibility began and ended with the preparation of enough food for the next couple of days and to start us off on our journey. At least there was enough for that; the men would just have to catch themselves a cow.

By the time my bread dough was ready to set aside to rise, the big pot of soup I'd prepared earlier had begun to simmer. I gave the hambone, peas and chopped onion a last vigorous stir before putting on the lid and damping down the heat. I had already prepared a new batch of sourdough starter, collected eggs, watered and fed the hens, and pulled onions, beets and carrots from the kitchen garden.

These chores had been Rita's responsibility. To eyes accustomed to Father Rogg's precisely planted and hoed rows, her garden's dense litter of straw seemed pointlessly untidy, but I soon realized that on this dry, windswept prairie it served a practical purpose Belle would have done well to emulate.

"My herbs aren't like those common vegetables of Rita's," Belle had protested when I said as much, after running out to help her with the bucket of water she was lugging over from the old wooden trough. "They all got needs of their own." She pointed to the vine scrambling up one of the pillars. "That briony over there is a hardy critter, with a root reaching to just this side of China. I swear it'll outlive you and me. But the annuals, like these poppies here, need a little cosseting. Can't have 'em dryin' up before they make the seeds for next year's crop."

But someone else would be planting next year's crop, I realized as I recalled Belle's words. Unless, of course, she intended to take the seeds with her to another house, another garden. I wondered where that might be. I had no money at all, and Belle and Bazz had intimated that even after Quinn had settled with them we'd have to watch the pennies. How much could Belle's elixirs be expected to bring? Without the enthusiasm of my comrades to buoy my spirits, the fecklessness of our schemes overwhelmed me. Three homeless wanderers with only salves and songs to offer? *Dear God, what would become of us?*

My hands stilled on the beets I had been cleaning, their juice staining my fingers, and I stared unseeingly out the window until roused by a twitter of bird song heralding the approach of dawn. I had all but decided during the night that my theory about the solstice sunrise pointing the way to Ross Cooper's gold was fanciful rubbish, but suppose it wasn't? One look at the plans would tell me what I needed to know. If it did, wasn't it possible for someone else to come to the same conclusion? Someone like Quinn? Surely it wasn't my fault if he hadn't!

I continued to stand there, buffeted by indecision, no longer able to tell right from wrong; not even sure if there *was* a right and wrong. If the gold wasn't mentioned in Ross Cooper's will, that meant it belonged to whomever found it, didn't it? Belle's childhood chant sing-songed up out of my memory again. *Finders, keepers, Reenie!*

I sighed and slid the beets back in the basin of water with the carrots. I'd delayed long enough.

Turning up the lamp I had brought down with me, I crossed through the wide hall to the parlor. Disordered when I arrived three months ago, it was in chaos now. Bazz, bowing to Belle's demands, had produced trunks and boxes in a variety of sizes and conditions and set them down higgledy-piggledy where gaps in the piles of books and periodicals allowed. Just inside the doorway was a row of stoutly made wicker hampers, which upon inspection I found to be already half-full of jars and bottles containing Belle's herbal concoctions, each bearing a neatly hand-printed, gilt-bordered label: Morning Star Tonic . . . Belle's Balm . . . Heal All Ointment . . . White Poppy Compound. I was impressed; this was no ordinary home-grown enterprise.

As I closed the lid on the last hamper, I felt it wobble. Protruding from beneath it was Belle's herbal, its worn black covers securely tied lengthwise and crosswise with braided cord in preparation for our journey. I slid it into the capacious pocket of my apron, knowing how anxious she would be when she missed it.

The plans for the house still lay in disarray on the desk. I whisked away the dust with the skirt of my apron, and removed the pages detailing the facade to the dining table, where I secured their curling top edges under the base of my lamp. I turned up the wick to gain a brighter light. Moments later, the rosy glow of dawn began to pale the lamplight's dancing reflection in the broad window above the table.

The big stone mansion sat within a bowllike depression whose eastern rim rose higher and steeper than the one that bound it on the west, but as I watched the sun's first rays beaming across the high-ridged horizon I realized that from my room on the second floor its height was not nearly so apparent as it was from here.

I looked at the sketches of the facade. It was all there: the semicircle of pillars with the pair of eyed monoliths symmetrically flanking the wide front entrance and the Palladian window—Malcolm Wilcox had greatly admired Palladian windows—at the end of the corridor above. The effect was very grand. Yet the longer I looked, the more sure I became that in actuality the pillars were off-centered. I recalled Cobby telling me they were cut and erected after the house had been built, but the plans made it clear they had not been an afterthought. *Why, then, had they been placed off center. . . .*

Suddenly it all came clear. If the architect had never visited the site, he couldn't make exact calculations; his sketches could show only what was intended. By all accounts, Ross Cooper possessed a keen intelligence: supplied by the architect with instructions on how to figure the angles, and able to command enough manpower to both erect and shift the position of the pillars as required, I had no doubt

201

he was equal to the challenge. A man had to have a rough knowledge of a number of skills to succeed as a rancher, including the uses of a compass. The builders of Stonehenge had accomplished a more daunting task without one. I leafed again through the brittle papers, studying the diagrams marked with angles and degrees and sighting lines, trying to make sense of a note about "the obliquity of the ecliptic" which appeared to have something to do with the slow change in the tilt of the earth's axis over time.

At length, my eyes aching from the effort of tracing out the faded spidery writing, I straightened up, stretched, and blew out the lamp. The sun was well above the horizon now, a blazing orb of white in a cloudless sky. Today, the twentieth of June, would be just another hot day; tomorrow, at the dawning of the summer solstice, we'd soon know whether the golden promise of these yellowed drawings would be fulfilled. Even if Ross Cooper had failed, he had at the very least provided his bride's grand house with the most imposing entrance in the territory.

Belle walked into the kitchen just as I was taking cornmeal muffins out of the oven.

"Mm-mm-m, I swear nothin' smells as good as somethin' fresh-baked." She hugged me from behind, hitched herself up on her stool, and gave a tremendous yawn. "Bazz and me were up 'til all hours sortin' and packin'. Looks like you've been busy, too . . . guess your headache must've gone."

I wondered if that would be her only reference to our discord the night before. I decided to follow her lead.

"Slipped away in the night," I said, smiling. I cleared a space on the table in front of her and set down the muffin tin. "We have fresh eggs this morning; would you like one with your muffin?"

"I would!" Bazz called from the doorway. "Fried, over easy, if you please."

"Sunny-side up for me," Belle said.

Bazz lifted a corner of the cloth on the rising loaves I had set on the back of the stove. "Eggs, muffins, fresh bread . . . and isn't that pea soup I smell? You see, Belle? Now that you moved those messy concoctions of yours out of here some real home cooking can be done!"

Belle bridled. "You'll be glad enough for the money my concoctions will bring on the road."

"Pay him no mind, Belle," I said. "What I saw in the hampers looked very impressive. If I had any money, I'd buy some in a minute."

"No need for you to buy any, Reenie, no need at all." She began to laugh, great hearty peals which set us all off, although I hadn't the least idea what she found so funny.

I crossed to the cupboard for plates for their eggs. As I reached up, my apron caught on the drawer pull below. I heard something drop to the floor.

"Belle, look here! Isn't this that herbal journal of yours?" Bazz waved it aloft.

The color drained from Belle's face. "You had no right, Reenie." Her voice was flat; her mouth hardly moved. I'd never seen her so angry.

"I saw it under one of the hampers; it must have slipped off the top . . . I meant to give it to you as soon as I saw you . . . it's tied just the way you left it, see?" My beseeching words tumbled out in a disorderly rush. Too many words. I stopped abruptly. "I'm sorry," I whispered.

"You're always sorry." Her narrowed eyes slid past me. "Give it here, Bazz!"

Bazz loped around the table holding the book just

out of reach of her upstretched grasping hands. "Finders, keepers," he chanted. "Isn't that what you always say, Belle? She calls it her bible, Serena," he said in a loud aside to me. "Any prophecies or revelations we should know about? What do you say to a reading or two from the herbal gospel according to Saint Sybelle?"

The eggs had begun to sizzle. "Stop your teasing, Bazz," I said. Actually, baiting was more like it. "Give Belle her journal and me your plates."

The braided cord must have loosened during his horseplay, because presently a smaller book, finely bound in smooth red leather, fell to the floor. Belle lunged for it, but Bazz was too quick for her. He snatched it up and read aloud the ornate gilt lettering on the cover. *Charlotte Wohlfort. May her life always be as sweet as her scented herbs.*

Bazz ceased his cavorting and stood stiffly erect, both hands grasping the little red book. His mouth thinned to a red slash. "This was Mama's. Grandfather had it specially bound for her sixteenth birthday." He leafed through the pages. "The Wohlfort herbal," he muttered. "Lord knows how old some of these receipts are." He pressed it to his heart. "I looked for it after she—" His voice broke.

Belle's herbal, its pebbled black covers shoddy in comparison, lay forgotten on the table where he had tossed it. Her attention was riveted on Basil.

"Your mother wanted me to have it. You know she did, Bazz." She leaned forward, her hands gripping the edge of the table so hard her knuckles turned white. "All our notes are in it, hers and the ones I made when she was . . . before she died. *I can't work without it.*"

To my surprise, he turned to me. The oddest look overspread his face. He had never questioned Belle's authority in my presence before—could he be seeking

204

my forgiveness? My approval? I could not tell.

"Bazz, please," I whispered.

He waited a long moment before he nodded, as if satisfying some internal doubt, then silently relinquished the book to Belle's outstretched hand. Without a word she slipped it into the pocket of her skirt, buttoning the flap to secure it.

I slid the eggs out of the pan onto their plates. They ate in brooding silence, eyes downcast, each waiting for the other to make amends. It looked to be a long wait. I decided a change of subject was in order. The choice was easy.

"I know where the gold is," I announced.

They gaped at me. Bazz's fork clattered to his plate; Belle blinked, then frowned. "This is no time for jokes, Reenie."

I shook my head. "It's not a joke. I know where it is—that is, I'll know where to look for it tomorrow morning at sunrise."

Belle's eyes narrowed. "What in *hell* are you talk—"

"What's so special about tomorrow's sunrise, Serena?" Bazz cut in.

I twisted my fingers together tightly. *How could I make them understand?* "Come with me . . . I have something to show you."

I showed them the architect's sketches, told them about the arrangement of the great upright stones known as Stonehenge, and explained as best I could the significance of the sunrise on the morning of the summer solstice. The conclusion I had drawn did not impress them.

Belle giggled. "I think the prairie sun's scrambled your poor brains, Reenie."

"Why would Paw do such a damn fool thing?"

205

Bazz scoffed. "Mama told me she suspected he built this house not so much to please her as to outdo her father, and I guess he did that, all right. Grandfather and everyone else in the territory. If this were my house, I'd pull those pillars down."

"Even granting what you say," I said, "according to Cobby, although the pillars were cut and hauled up along with the blocks used to build the house, they weren't erected until the following June, months after the house was finished. He said the pair with the slits gave the most trouble because of your father fussing with his compass, ordering them skewed first this way, then that. 'Drove us all loco,' he said. Cobby could see no reason for it; but there must have been one, otherwise why go to all that trouble? And why wait for June to come around again?"

"Morning Star was just starting up," Bazz said. "There were a lot more important things to do!"

"But winter is the slack season on a ranch," I countered, "so why delay all that pulling and hauling until one of the busiest months of the year? Don't you see, Bazz? He had to wait for the summer solstice in order to place them properly!"

Bazz and Belle fell silent, still skeptical, but no longer scoffing.

"Let's go outside," I suggested. "Maybe your eyes will convince you."

The air, hardly stirred by a listless breeze, was stifling. Except in the garden Belle so lovingly tended, the earth had dried to a fine dust that puffed up from beneath our shoes as we walked. Unless it rained soon, I feared the prairie grasses would offer Quinn's cattle little nourishment during the long, hard prairie winter. We paused in the opening of the low stone wall that marked the perimeter of the

206

house lot and turned toward the facade. The blaze of the sun above it made me throw up my arm across my eyes. From here, the height of the eastern ridgeline as depicted in the architect's sketches impressed me anew. I wondered aloud how Ross Cooper had been able to supply so accurate an estimate.

"It's not so surprising considering how well my father knew it," Bazz said. "He must have ridden over that ridge a thousand times when he was range boss for my grandfather, good weather and bad." He shook his head. "It's a miserable occupation, but it teaches a man the lay of the land better'n any map I ever saw."

I lined myself up between the eyed pillars. As I suspected, they violated the symmetry of the mansion's classic design. The big front door should have been centered between them, but it wasn't. The shaft on the right had been set just enough off-center for its top to intersect the flanking right-hand side light of the Palladian window gracing the western end of the corridor above. A window of the same design had been similarly placed at the eastern end. Exactly opposite, in fact, if my theory was correct. *Ridgeline to window, window to window, window through eye. . . .*

"Let the blessed sunshine in . . ."

Startled, I tuned to look at Belle. She was staring up at the eyed pillars. "What did you say?"

"Remember that hymn old Maltby taught us at the orphanage, Reenie? Something about opening our hearts to let the sunshine in?"

I nodded, recalling a perky little song played with great chord-thumping enthusiasm by the Reverend Maltby's wife.

"I guess I've passed by these old stones a jillion times, but just now, lookin' up and studyin' on 'em like this, I remember Ross and me coming up to the

207

house from the corrals. Years ago it was, not long after I came to Morning Star, and I stopped, and I looked up at 'em and recited what I just did, and I asked him, 'Mr. Cooper'—he wasn't Ross to me yet— 'Mr. Cooper, does the sun ever shine through those holes?'

"Lord knows what put the idea in my head, but he whipped around and looked at me real fierce, then muttered something about everything having a season. Then, seein' me looking so ignorant, he began to laugh, and, oh, he just laughed to beat the Dutch. I never did know what he was talkin' about," she added resentfully.

I knew. Raised by churchy people like the Roggs, how could I not? "He was quoting from the Bible," I said. "I guess his folks must have been God-fearing people. As I recall, the passage reads, 'To every thing there is a season, and a time to every purpose under heaven.'" I looked at Bazz. "What do you think about my theory now?" I asked.

"*I* think," Bazz said, reaching out to squeeze my hand, "that the last laugh will be on Quinn."

Belle and Bazz exchanged satisfied smiles and started slowly back toward the house. I lingered, turning to look at the wide expanse of prairie stretching out beyond the old trough and windmill, dotted clear to the western horizon with posts cut and hauled over thirty years. My eyes soon tired of counting them: short posts set in rows along the ranch road; stout posts encircling holding pens; tall posts hung with gates; posts that served no easily recognizable purpose. Hundreds of them, all of them stone, their solid contours wavering wraithlike in the heat-shimmered air. My breath caught in my throat. *What if my theory proved as insubstantial?*

As I brooded thus, I became aware of a curious silence. It was almost as if the blanketing heat had

208

fashioned muffs for my ears. Then I realized that the screech of straining metal that had accompanied my every waking hour at Morning Star had stilled. The windmill, its blades at rest, seemed to sag beneath its rusty burden; the green-slimed surface of the wooden trough it served glistened with a sickly iridescence.

Perspiration dewed my brow; I could see it darkening the bodice of my dress. *All those stones. . . .* I closed my eyes to blot out the sight of them. If the sun's first rays failed to point the way tomorrow morning, we would have to admit defeat: we could not survive an unguided search for the gold in this scorching heat; with the return of Morning Star's hands in the offing, we could not postpone it.

No point in fretting about tomorrow, I scolded myself, not with all there was to do today. I started up the path behind Belle and Basil. The sun, almost at its zenith, blazed down mercilessly, without even a passing cloud to offer relief. Dead ahead rose the massive stone house, its soulless perfection accentuated by the shadowless light. Set in this vast, parched, treeless saucer of land, it seemed more tomb than shelter, its monstrous garden a funerary planting. No wonder Quinn chose to live elsewhere.

Ahead of me, Belle's and Bazz's silver and auburn heads bent close as they talked. Adjusting their plans to fit the exciting hypothesis I had offered, no doubt. I trotted up behind them.

"We can leave soon's we get help hitching up the wagon Quinn's lettin' us have," I heard Belle say.

Bazz grunted. "We're doing the bastard a favor by taking that old relic off his hands."

I was bewildered. "You mean we're leaving before Quinn returns from Nebraska?"

Belle whirled to face me. Her sweat-dampened silver hair hung lankly; droplets of perspiration tracked an uneven course down her dusty cheeks.

Knowing I must look much the same did little to improve my spirits.

"Quinn *knows* we've been lookin' for the gold; don't you 'spect he'd find a reason to poke through the wagon and our trunks lookin' for it?" She shook her head and sighed. "I swear, Reenie, for all your learnin', you sometimes got no more sense than a soda cracker."

"What makes you think he'd need a reason to look?" Bazz flung back over his shoulder. She turned back toward him, their voices too low for me to hear.

"What about the money he owes you," I persisted. "Don't you want it before you leave?"

"My lawyer's got instructions . . . that's the main reason I went to town."

No wonder we were so low on supplies! He'd been too busy with the lawyer to bother with getting them. I smothered my annoyance. "But, Bazz, I don't—"

"Trust us, Serena."

Bazz delivered his answer without looking at me. Plainly, he considered the details of his transactions with his brother and his lawyer none of my business. He was right about that, I suppose, but I couldn't help resenting his and Belle's airy disregard of my questions and their taking my trust for granted. Belle was my only blood relative, my sister, my twin, but Bazz and she enjoyed a closeness I could only envy. I had chosen to hitch my poor, tarnished star to their wagon; I would just have to accept the consequences of that choice with as much good grace as I could muster.

To this day I don't know how I managed to accomplish so much that afternoon. The house offered welcome relief from the heat, thanks to the thickness of its stone walls, but the coolness was only relative; hardly enough to account for the shivers that overtook me soon after I stepped inside. Perhaps it was the dankness, more pronounced than ever, or perhaps it was my state of mind. Whatever the cause, the tasks I energetically undertook kept my blood coursing warmly and unquiet thoughts at bay.

After packing my belongings, except for a nightdress and a handful of essentials, I turned out my room and bedding, heedless of the dust and feathers that whirled in my wake.

Belle barred access to her room. "I haven't had time to do my sortin' yet, Reenie, and I can tell you Bazz won't appreciate you pokin' through his things, either."

"But, Belle—"

"But, Belle," she mocked in a tone of honied sweetness. "Who're you tryin' to impress with all this spic and spanning, anyway? Quinn's the only one'll see it."

Hurt, I turned away wordlessly to seek more agreeable company downstairs, my broom bumping along the steps behind me.

I found Bazz in the parlor, tacking covers on the boxes of music and books he was taking with him. His piano had already been swathed in quilts; Belle's four hampers of herbs were stacked in the hall. Our clothing, bedrolls, food and water and cook pots had yet to be added.

"Is all this going to fit in one wagon?" I asked.

Bazz looked up at me. The tacks he held between his teeth confined his answer to a nod.

"Including the three of us?"

Bazz spit the tacks into his hand. "The wagon Quinn gave us may not be much good, but it's big enough for all this and then some. Besides, only Belle will be in the wagon. She'll be driving; you and I will be riding."

211

As I suspected, the plans had already been made. Seeing no need for further conversation about them, Bazz stuck the tacks back between his teeth and resumed his pounding.

I took out my frustration on the floor, ignoring Bazz's coughing protest as dust eddied up behind my ferociously yielded broom. Within an hour I had restored the big room to a semblance of order, but when I turned to share my satisfaction with Bazz I found myself alone. I trailed out into the kitchen to stir up the soup and bake the bread that had risen to a lovely plumpness through the morning. That done, I decided to set a proper table in the parlor in anticipation of the first decent meal in days.

I bustled back and forth to the kitchen, my quickened steps accompanied by a hum. *Spoons for the soup, forks for the vegetables.* I eyed the table critically. I'd forgotten napkins and a basket for the bread, and a bowl of flowers would be nice . . . surely there must be *something* suitable for cutting in Belle's garden. . . .

I recalled the new spurt of rank growth as we passed by that morning. Contrasted with the parched prairie wildings, I had found its undiminished vigor odious. On our return, after the wind had died, I could have sworn I heard a hushed leafy rustle as we passed, as if the plants were jostling for position. The thought of forcing my way through that jungled vegetation was abhorrent. I decided the improvement in the menu would have to make up for the lack of floral decoration.

I stepped back from the table and surveyed the room, pleased with the results of my afternoon's handiwork. *There now,* I congratulated myself, *even Quinn will have to admit I'm worth my keep.*

No sooner had the thought entered my head than I realized I would not be here when he returned. I slumped into one of the big wooden chairs, as drained of buoyancy as a punctured balloon. My fears returned to assail me. *Where would we go? What would we do?* I had not come all the way to Kansas for adventuring; I had come seeking a home. Not just any home: I could have married Ernest if that was the sum of my desires. I had traveled to Morning Star prepared to work hard to secure a place alongside my sister; I had arrived to find her not only dispossessed, but changed.

I loved Belle, I always would, but the cruelties she had suffered at the hands of men she trusted had scarred her; she trusted no one but herself now. I doubted she could understand my need for a purposeful life, much less wish to share it. Unwilling to curb the independence I had so newly secured for myself, I had for a time lost sight of that need, but now, on the very eve of departure, I realized it could not be denied.

Purpose. I thought of Sharo's quiet, sure handling of the horses, and of Cobby's way with the men, knowing when to let well enough alone, coming down hard only when the need for it was clear. A demanding life, but a satisfying one. Especially for the cocksure new master of Morning Star. Oh, yes, Quinn Cooper had purpose in abundance.

My gaze settled on Bazz's piano, shrouded in quilts to keep out the dust of the journey. Did he have ambition enough for a career in music? I had no knowledge of what might be required, but I suspected it took more than a clear tenor voice and a talent for writing pretty songs. If he lacked the will to resist my sister's demands, how could he cope with the world's? I didn't like Quinn—his coarseness and arrogance deeply offended me—but there was no denying his energy or the respect, even if sometimes grudging, paid him by the men in his employ. If

213

Bazz's kindness and charm had blinded me to his weaknesses, perhaps my ruffled feathers had prevented me from seeing any good in his roughneck brother.

I continued to sit, hands limp in my lap, only dimly aware as yet of the subtle shift in my perceptions, an all but imperceptible reordering. I stared unseeingly at the wall of closely joined stone. As my glance flitted along the course of the smaller, rougher stones framing the window above the table, the look of them nudged free the memory of a fieldstone wall built on a farm near the Roggs' house. The site lay on my route to school, and in good weather I had dawdled along that stretch, wondering why the builder chose this stone instead of that, glad it wasn't me doing the hard digging.

I remember thinking it queer that the trench was deeper than the wall was high, and once, in passing, I said as much. The man looked up at me and spat, just missing the dusty toes of my shoes, but his voice, when he spoke, was amiable enough. The first course had to sit below the frostline, he told me, otherwise nothing would stay put for long.

We became friends, the wall builder and I. He taught me about choosing stones; sometimes, he even allowed me to lay a few. *Two on one; one on two.* . . . It was orderly work, and on mornings when it was going particularly well I would pause to sit and watch, arms clasped around my legs, chin resting on my knees, losing myself in the satisfying rhythm of it. Those were the only days I was ever tardy at school.

I curled my fingers over my palms as the long-ago sting of the teacher's ruler came freshly to mind. I recalled Malcolm's later rephrasing of the wall builder's advice: *Dig deep and lay your foundation well, lest adversity nudge the stones laid on it awry.* My fingers relaxed. It had, after all, been a small price to pay.

I gazed out at the lengthening shadows, out to the eastern ridgeline, up to where the sun would rise the next morning, ushering in my day of reckoning. An overwhelming sense of loss gripped me. *What kind of life could be built upon a wagonful of elixirs and a rosewood piano?* Belle and I may have been paired in our mother's womb, but our paths since, separated in childhood and forked by bitter circumstance, had distanced us, stretching the bond of twinship to the breaking point. It was time to face the hard truth of it: she and Bazz would fare better without me.

My need for order and purpose would only hold them back. Here, at Morning Star, it could be put to good use. I had no quarrel with Quinn Cooper. I cared little for his roughshod ways, but he was a practical man: with Rita gone and Spotted Fawn too frail to take her place, I figured if I offered an honest day's work for a place to lay my head at night, I had a chance of striking a bargain with him—he'd be getting the best of it, after all.

I could move out of this mausoleum into Rita's vacated hut next to the vegetable garden. It was small and simple, hardly more than a lean-to, but the sagging porch, built of odds and ends of scavenged lumber, looked out over the barn and corrals. I would welcome that. Nothing like the sight of the ranch's busy comings and goings, early and late, to help keep loneliness at bay. . . .

The gold, my conscience squeaked. *You're forgetting the gold.*

I hadn't, of course; how could I? *A pot of gold at the end of a sunbeam.* The more I thought of it, the crazier it seemed, this elaborate riddle concocted in the gold fields by an architect down on his luck for a cowboy with a lucky strike. Had Ross Cooper intended what remained of his cache as spoils for whoever had the wit to find it? Even if Quinn inherited the right to the gold along with the ranch, how could he be expected to make the connections I had? What did Quinn know of druid stones and solstices? Besides, didn't I owe Belle and Bazz something in return for their kindness?

In the end, I compromised. I would make a separate peace tomorrow with my sister; another with Quinn when he returned. Let Belle and Bazz take the gold; if Quinn allowed me to stay and work at Morning Star, I would strive to prove myself worth my weight in it.

FOURTEEN

Belle took another piece of bread from the basket I passed to her, and sighed. "I swear, Reenie, that dress looks a whole lot better on you than it ever did on me."

I looked down at the pretty costume I had changed into for dinner. It was of fine white cambric figured in cornflower blue, with lacy ruffles at the wrist and neck, looser and cooler than anything of mine; nicer than any Mother Rogg had ever made for me.

I laughed, pleased by her comment. "How could it, Belle? We do look alike, after all."

Belle's fingers came up to explore her sun-roughened cheeks, patting the skin around her eyes as if to smooth the lines away. "Not exactly alike . . . not anymore." Her voice was uncertain; I sensed a plea for reassurance.

I paused. "Of course we do!" But I had waited too long, and my voice was too hearty. She turned abruptly away.

"Remember how we used to fool Mama and Pa, Belle? Mama giving us half a scolding each, because she could never tell which of us deserved it?"

"Belle, probably," Bazz said, offering his bowl for a second helping.

Belle's eyes narrowed. "What in hell do *you* know about it!"

Bazz smiled. "I know you, Sybelle Garraty."

Her mouth pouted, then flicked up at the corners. "I guess you do, Bazzy . . . 'bout as well as I know Basil Cooper." The look they exchanged, amused but wary, implied not affection so much as hard-won understanding.

I refilled both their bowls with pea soup. "Maybe if we'd been allowed to stay together, Belle. Maybe if after Mama died—"

"'If, if, if,'" she cut in, mocking my earnest tone. She counted them off on her fingers: "*If* Mama hadn't died. *If* you hadn't been sickly. *If* Paw had been King of England instead of a drunken, filthy old rooster."

"I'd exchange with you those two years you suffered with him if I could!"

"Would you, Reenie? Would you, really?" Her expression hardened. "A lot can happen in two years. More'n a good little girl like you can dream up in your worst nightmares."

Why did I feel as if she were accusing me of disloyalty? What could I have done? We were children! "I'm sorry, Belle," I heard myself whispering. "Truly sorry." And I was. Sorry for all our lost opportunities, past and future.

Belle put down her soup spoon, threw up her hands, and rolled her blue eyes at Bazz. "There she goes again, always sorry about something. But maybe we can fix that. What d'ya say to some of that port wine of your paw's with our coffee, Bazzy?"

"I'm afraid I didn't make a dessert," I blurted.

"Hallelujah!" Belle crowed. "For once she's not sorry, only afraid."

I lowered my head and began clearing the table.

"Oh, for heaven's sake, Reenie, no need to pull a

218

long face. I was only teasin'. 'Sides, we don't need a dessert—that old port wine's sweet as sugar candy."

"Then I'll get the coffee and the wineglasses for you," I offered.

"For us," Belle corrected. "Bazz already has the glasses . . . he put them out earlier, on a tray in the fireplace alcove. He don't need your help," she added as I moved automatically to do so. "This is our thank-you for the fine meal you gave us."

Since it was Ross Cooper's wine and Bazz doing the honors, I couldn't quite see what Belle had to do with it. "I appreciate the thought, but—"

"No buts. This is by way of bein' a celebration."

"What are we celebrating?" I asked. "Leaving Morning Star or going out to meet adventure?"

"I don't believe in looking back," Belle said.

Her defiant tone puzzled me. "You can't look back on something you haven't done yet," I said reasonably.

"As good as done," I heard her mutter as Bazz returned bearing a handsomely embossed, if tarnished, silver tray with three cut-glass goblets filled with a mahogany red liquid. She accepted the glass Bazz offered her. He took a glass for himself and extended the tray to me. I hesitated. I was already tired, and there was still much to do.

"C'mon, Reenie! This is fancy imported stuff, not like that homemade jackass brandy Jed sneaks into the bunkhouse."

I hadn't known about Jed's secret store of brandy, but I wasn't surprised. "He was all set to come back early and give us a good time," I said dryly. "I allowed as how we had better things to do."

"Jed's not such a bad sort . . . he always pays right up for what he wants."

I stared at her, speechless.

She laughed. "Not what you seem to be thinkin',

Reenie. It's that white poppy elixir of mine. He finds it real relaxin'."

"That's not the only relaxation he gets from you," Bazz muttered.

"You hush up, Bazz! Pay him no mind, Reenie," Belle commanded archly, as she refilled his glass. "Like I was sayin', this port wine slides down slick as silk."

Slick as silk? Maybe one glass . . . a toast to a farewell different from the one Belle had in mind. I took the remaining glass and clinked it to theirs. *Should I tell her I've decided to stay now?* Her mouth parted in a smile; her eyes were alight with anticipation. *No, tomorrow would be soon enough —after we found the gold.* I forced a confident smile. "Tomorrow at sunrise."

"At sunrise," they chorused.

The ruby liquid was as smooth as syrup on my tongue. Candy sweet, just as Belle had said, almost cloying, save for the hint of bitterness in the after-taste. Belle and Bazz looked at me anxiously.

"It's lovely," I said. "What did you say it was?"

"Port," Bazz said. "It's a special kind of wine from Portugal. Someone once told my father it was what gentlemen drank after dinner, so he ordered a few cases sent out from San Francisco. This is the last bottle. I wasn't about to leave it for Quinn to guzzle."

"Lovely," I murmured.

Belle poured coffee for us; Bazz kept our glasses filled. As darkness fell, we chatted of this and that, our voices hardly rising above a murmur. Presently Bazz got up to light the lamps. It should have been the signal to bid my companions good night; but I found the pulsing glow mesmerizing, and I felt too languid to give the chores awaiting me more than a passing thought. Before long, their urgency and specifics escaped me altogether.

"More wine, Serena?"

I peered up at Bazz. His face and the glass he held out to me wavered like reflections on water rippled by the wind. I tried to speak, but the words stuck to the end of my tongue. My arms slipped off the arms of my chair; my head lolled to one side. "Sorry," I whispered as I slid slowly to the floor. "I'm so sorry . . ."

I felt myself being lifted up, and I heard Belle's voice, very far away, saying something about chickens. "The hen, Bazz. Bring the hen." As I struggled to make sense of it, I felt liquid pouring over my head, trickling cooly down my arms and my back. Then the shadows closed in, and I felt nothing at all.

I woke in darkness relieved only by a flickering golden glow. Could it be sunrise? Why hadn't someone wakened me! I scrambled to my feet, only to knock my head a stunning blow. I instinctively hunched, then reached up cautiously. My hand traced along a rough wooden beam. I stepped back, and bumped into another, my shoes grating over finely graveled earth. Where could I be? My head began to throb, but when I gently explored the swelling bruise on the top of my head, the crimped texture of my hair was as unfamiliar to my searching fingers as the low-beamed place in which I found myself.

I turned toward the light. On the bottom plank of a steep flight of roughly cobbled steps, a tray had been placed. I thought I recognized it, but the goblets of ruby-red wine had been replaced by the stub of a candle, a water jug and two pottery cups. Above it, the steps disappeared into darkness.

"Belle!" I called. "Bazz! Where are you?" The low-ceilinged room smothered my cries, and behind me, off to my left, I heard a slithering sort of scurry that made my dry mouth go even drier. Was it a snake, seeking shelter from the heat, or a rat or— A child-like whimper reined in my runaway imagination. *Someone was in here with me.*

"Who's there?" I challenged.

Another scurry, hushed as leaves stirred by a passing breeze, then the mistakable clink of glass. I whirled to see a bare foot, barely perceptible in the gloom, being pulled behind a wooden rack on whose warped shelves I glimpsed a few wobbling jars through a grille of rusty ironwork. Suddenly, I knew where I was. Belle had said she stored her herbal elixirs in the storm cellar; there must not have been room in her hampers for these few remaining bottles. The ironwork must be the grille from Bazz's nursery window.

I stole closer. "Who are you?" I could hear breathing: quick, short, fearful gasps. "Please come out," I begged. "I won't hurt you, I promise. *Please.*"

The breathing slowed and evened. Presently, one foot, then the other, emerged from behind the rack. A slight, girlish figure slowly hitched itself out, and the pain evident in the dark eyes that gazed up at me caused me to sink to my knees. Her coarse, sacklike dress was torn and filthy, and as my eyes adjusted to the dim light, I could see new bruises swelling over the old.

"Poor little Fawn," I crooned, cupping her small, pointed chin in my hand, "what has he done to you? How did you get back to Morning Star?"

"Quinn . . . he say the journey too hard for me . . . he bring me back, very fast . . . he put me in his house and say I must hide."

I recalled the whirlwind I had seen, fancying it a horse and rider.

Hide? From whom? I was bewildered. "I would

222

have helped you, Fawn. I want to help you now, if you'll let me."

Fawn shook her head and retreated, crabwise. "I not know. You sound like the nice lady—S'rena?—but you look like the other one."

My hand sprang to my head to explore again my hair's unfamiliar texture. Its crimped strands reminded me of something . . . the dressmaker's form I had seen in Belle's room. *Of course! Belle's wig!* I must have had too much of the port wine, and Belle put it on my head as I slept. *It was a joke, just one of her silly jokes. . . .* I yanked one curly lock, but it remained firmly attached, the pain telling me the truth of it: this oddly textured hair was my own. If it were a joke, I failed to see the point, and I was moved more to tears than laughter.

"I *am* Serena, Fawn. I don't know what has happened or why we're here, but I know that much." My head ached, from the wine last night, the blow on my head, and the strain of trying to make sense of it all. Was I awake or was this a peculiarly vivid dream? That would explain why nothing fit together: me in this dark place with Fawn, my strangely changed hair, her new bruises.

"How did you get down here, Fawn?"

"The other lady brought me . . . after the red-haired man find me." A shudder wracked her thin frame. She paused and looked at me fearfully. "I hide away like Quinn say, but it so hot. . . ." She dropped her eyes, as if ashamed about feeling the heat. "I come out, only for a little; but I fall asleep, and he find me . . . he hurt me . . . he hurt me very bad." Her small hand crept toward her crotch. Her pathetic gesture spoke louder than anything she might have said.

Bazz. It must have been the day before yesterday, when he searched Quinn's quarters. I recalled the scratches on his face and neck, his torn shirt. *Barn cat, indeed.* "And after he . . . hurt you, what happened then?" I kept my voice low and even, so as not to frighten her.

"After, he hit me, here and here." She pointed to her stomach and small breasts. "I try to get away, but he keep hitting. I cried," she whispered, reluctant to admit what she saw as weakness. "Then other lady come."

As if on cue, the slanting door to the cellar crashed open above us.

"Reenie?"

"Belle!" I rushed to the stairs, almost knocking over the candle in my eagerness. The sky above was dark, starless. I could barely make out the outline of my sister's head.

"Awake, are you? There's water in that jug on the tray, and I'm putting a bowl of food here on the top step. It'll be dawn soon—you don't want to be leavin' on an empty stomach."

Why was her voice so matter-of-fact? "I don't understand. . . ." My head was awhirl. "For God's sake, Belle, why are we here? What's going on up there?"

"Lordy, Reenie, so many questions! It's kind of a long story . . . too long to tell right now, with sunrise coming."

"You and Bazz want the gold for yourselves, is that it? I don't mind, honestly I don't. I decided yesterday to stay here; I was going to tell you this morning."

Belle made a regretful clucking noise with her tongue. "'Fraid that wouldn't have changed anything, Reenie." She began to close the doors.

"Wait!"

She pulled the doors back open, her head now silhouetted against a gradually paling sky more green than gray.

"You can't leave us here! No one will hear us . . . Fawn is hurt, Belle; she could die down here. She knows nothing about the gold."

"Here, there, what difference does it make? How was Bazzy to know Quinn's skinny little squaw was still a virgin?" She laughed. "He never could keep his hands off the little dark ones. First he takes them, then he punishes them for not being good little girls anymore, just like his daddy punished his mama.

"I was there the day Ross caught 'em, her screamin' about his Injun whore, both of 'em bleedin' from the beatin' Ross gave 'em. As if it was Bazzy's fault his precious mama loved him so! The way she carried on with him was purely a scandal, 'most as bad as Pa with me, but d'ya think that bastard Quinn would understand any of that?

"Takin' the gold'd be enough to put him on our trail, I knew that from the beginning, but Bazz pokin' the little squaw Quinn was savin' for himself? Why, he'd whomp the life outta Bazz for that. See, we planned on layin' down a false trail for him. Naughty Belle was goin' to steal the gold, then get robbed and killed by a band of rovin' outlaws—that was Jed's idea. Now we're goin' to have to kill off Fawn, too. We'll make it look like she was forced to go along so she couldn't tell no one. With you lyin' dead in the dust lookin' like me, who'd ever think the silver-haired girl who run off with Bazz to git married was anyone but sweet Serena?"

"My God, Belle! You're not even sure you'll find the gold!"

"Maybe, maybe not. If not, we mighta left you here for Quinn to make use of; but the girl . . . well, she's sort of an extra complication, and to tell the truth, I'm not keen on spendin' the rest of my life listenin' to your conscience. Sorry, Reenie."

Her cruelly deliberate mockery was like a slap

225

across the face. I knew now that Belle had never been sorry for anything or anyone. A hot rage born of betrayal seized me. I lunged up the stairs, but Belle was too quick for me. The doors slammed down; the bolt slid home. I pounded until my knuckles were raw, then slumped exhausted on the steps, my breathing ragged, overcome by the desperateness of our predicament. She was right, of course: everyone *would* take my dead body for hers.

Neither Quinn nor Cobby nor any of the hands had seen Belle without her wig. No one but Bazz and me knew she had been wearing one while her hennaed hair grew out to silver. *The hen*, I'd heard Belle say. *Get the hen.* But it wasn't chickens she was talking about; it was henna. They had put something in my wine—one of Belle's concoctions, no doubt—then dyed my hair and curled it . . . even the dress I wore had been Belle's. She must have been planning this for a very long time. . . .

My senses swam. I took a deep rasping breath, and I reached for the water jug on the tray on the step below me. As I leaned forward, my ringleted reflection shone back dimly from the tarnished surface of the tray, courtesy of the lighted candle Belle had thoughtfully provided. *Thoughtful?* I drew back my hand. If our function in their scheme required that we die, why bring us food and water? Unless, like the wine the night before, they had been drugged to insure our relaxed cooperation. The only way, in fact, our removal up those steeply pitched steps could be efficiently accomplished. *No, not thoughtful . . . crafty was more like it.*

Deliberately, while Fawn watched in anguished disbelief, I poured the water from the pitcher, then took the bread from the basket and ground it under my heal into the earth floor, until its crumbs could no longer be distinguished from the grains of soil. I

226

knew if I had not, we could not have resisted for long the temptation to eat. This way we still had a chance to fight for our lives.

The candle flame flickered and dimmed, its waxy fuel nearly consumed. I skirted my way around the tray and nestled down beside Fawn. I slid my arm around her frail shoulders and tried to explain to her why I had discarded the bread and water, but I could tell her attention was elsewhere. She began to shiver.

"Wind coming," she whispered. "Very big wind."

I cocked my head. I heard nothing. If anything, the air was closer than ever; down here it was suffocating.

Fawn's slim hand clutched my arm. "We must ask Tirawa to keep us safe."

"Tirawa?"

"Yes, chief of all the heavens. Tirawa lights the moon and stars. He sends the wind and makes the rivers flow."

"And does he watch over the sailors on the sea, too?" I asked bitterly.

Fawn looked up at me. The puzzlement in her eyes shamed me. She knew nothing of the sea; why should she? Did that make her god any less worthy of respect than mine?

To keep us safe. Mother Rogg's favorite maxim once again came to mind: God helps those who help themselves. If we couldn't get out of the cellar, we could at least try to keep Belle and Basil from coming in. . . .

I knew there were handles on the inside of the doors; I had bruised my knuckles on them. If I could find a length of rope or twist of wire to tie them together. . . . I got to my feet, taking care not to hit my head again on the low beams, and turned slowly, feeling along the cobwebbed walls, straining to see into the gloom, silently entreating the dying flame to stay a little longer.

227

The shadows crept closer. The candle guttered, inviting the darkness, then flared high. A stub of polished straw caught the light. It looked like . . . yes, it looked as if an old broom had somehow gotten wedged behind the stairs and forgotten. *Brooms have handles.* . . . I reached up, grabbed the worn straw head and pulled it clatteringly free. I scurried up the canted planks and fed the stout pole through the handles—hoping it was long enough, praying it would withstand the strain—and rammed it home just as the candle flame sputtered out.

Step by cautious step I made my way back to Fawn. As I settled down beside her, I heard a low, threatening grumble like the growl of a large, angry beast. Fawn began to chant, a high, quavering singsong that made my skin prickle. The next rumble of thunder was longer and louder, a reverberating drum roll followed by the ripping sound of lightning so bright that my eyes, staring upward, were blinded by its searing flash through the cracks of the cellar doors.

Fawn's chant quickened as the wind began to blow, rattling the heavy doors as if they were sheets of paper, accompanied by rain so torrential I could only stare in appalled wonder as it flooded down upon us. It wasn't until the rain slackened and the wind began to drop that I had sense enough to try and catch the streaming rivulets in the jug I had emptied, but by then it was too late.

Suddenly, I heard the bolt securing the cellar entrance from above slide open, its loud metallic clack followed shortly by a furious rattling when the doors failed to open.

"Serena! Let us in!"

I could feel Fawn cringe at the sound of Bazz's voice. Together, we crawled away from the stairway, sure the old broom pole could not long withstand the battering by our captors. Somehow, they must have found the gold, I thought confusedly. They found it, and now the plan they concocted to cover their tracks was falling apart.

"Oh, God!" Bazz cried. "It's almost upon us."

"Damn you, Reenie! I wish I'd broken your neck instead of your leg, I wish—"

I clapped my hands over my ears to shut out my sister's enraged growl. Her visits to my infirmary bed, her tearful farewell before she left on the orphan train, had they all been sham? Had her loving letter been accompanied in her heart by a similar litany of hate?

I bowed my head in despair. Tasting the salt of my tears on my lips, I murmured a Christian prayer to the rhythm of Fawn's tribal chant. Blasphemy, some would say, but I knew the God I loved would enjoy the harmonies. *Our Father, who art in heaven. . . .*

The pounding stopped. I removed first one hand, then the other, from my ears, only to be assaulted by a scream of such terror my heart stuttered in my chest.

"Belle, oh, Belle," I cried, but my instinctive rush for the stairs stopped short as a roar like a thousand steam engines running amok exploded above us accompanied by a rattle of hail so violent as to make me cower, arms flung protectively over my head, should the huge icy stones the noise portended break through upon us. The deluge of rain that followed seemed gentle by comparison, and this time the downpour lasted long enough to allow me to fill the cups and jug to their brims.

The rain slackened. Fawn's chanting slowed, faltered, ceased. The thunder, far distant now, was hardly more than an intermittent purr. I stood listening, cup in hand, hardly daring to breathe, distrustful of the silence. Had the storm truly passed, or was it merely gathering strength for another onslaught? I handed Fawn the other cup, and we gulped the muddy water eagerly, heedless of the grit. If, as they say, we all eat a peck of dirt before we die, I imagine Fawn and I consumed our allotted share in the few minutes it took us to slake our thirst.

We waited. The terrible wind seemed to have gone with the rain; we heard only a gentle puffing, as if the earth itself was sighing in relief. Then, our sense of time distorted, and with no idea of what had happened above us, the creaking of the cellar doors lifted by the freshening breeze became a lullaby that nothing, not our empty stomachs nor our bruises, long allowed us to resist. Spooned together, hoarding our warmth against the rain-sodden earth beneath us, we slept.

FIFTEEN

Open the doors!

In my dreams I cowered behind a huge, iron-studded oak door that shuddered under the hammering of a giant fist. *Open the doors!* the voice roared again.

No, I whimpered, trying to hide myself among the gleaming bars of gold that surrounded me. *No-o-ooo . . .*

I woke with a start, my own wail echoing in my head. As I struggled to collect my sleep-scattered thoughts, the broom handle I had pushed through the handles of the cellar doors clattered to the earth floor, and the doors yawned wide. "*Quinn!*" I heard an excited voice say. Blinded by the light streaming down upon me, I saw only a head and shoulders silhouetted above against a bright rectangle of blue.

"Bless me, Fawn, we'd just about given you up." It was Quinn's voice all right, gentler than I'd ever heard it. "Here, take my hand . . . up you come. . . ." There was a long silence. "My God, what have they done to you!" The gentleness had gone. "Cobby? Take her down to my quarters. I'll see to this. . . ."

I shrank back as Quinn's booted feet pounded down the stairs, wishing it was still only a dream. His eyes darted furiously from corner to corner before

231

coming to rest on my huddled form. He looked down at me, his lips curling in disgust, arms hanging loose at his sides, fists clenched. I threw my hands up across my face, fearing he would act first and listen afterward—if at all. He reached down, grabbed one of my wrists and yanked me, stumbling, my knees and shins cruelly barked on the rough-edged steps, up into the sunlight.

I stood unsteadily before him, blinking tear-blurred eyes, trying to make sense of the devastation I saw around me. "Quinn, I—"

"I'll do the talking," he commanded. "Where's that no-good bastard brother of mine?"

"I don't know, I. . . ." I looked at the house. There were only black, empty holes where windows had once been. "What on earth has happened here? *Oh, dear Lord, my sister!*"

I started to run, but Quinn pulled me back. "Don't give me that, Belle, you damn well know what happened. You saw the twister comin' and left your sister up here to die. Mighty convenient, wasn't it? This way the gold only had to be split two ways. What were you plannin' to do with Fawn? Take her along to keep ol' Bazz warm on the trail?"

"I'm not Belle, Quinn!"

Quinn dropped my wrist and leaned toward me, long hands on his narrow hips. His dark eyes bored into mine; the twist of his mouth expressed disgust. "Well, if that don't beat all. You got Belle's hair and Belle's dress, and you certainly got her shifty ways. Who are you, then, the Queen of Egypt?"

"I'm Serena, I— *No, listen to me!*" I cried as he deliberately turned on his heel and stared out over the horizon. "Bazz and my sister, they wanted everybody to think I was Belle. They were going to make it seem as if Belle had run off with the gold and been robbed and killed by an outlaw band, while she, looking like me, eloped with Bazz. Belle drugged me, and they

232

dyed my hair and—"

"And I just been to the moon and back," he said, turning back with a contemptuous smile. "What d'ya take me for, Belle?" He grabbed my wrist again and dragged me after him. Across our path lay rain-scoured ditches deep enough to hide a jackrabbit. Quinn's long, muscular strides took him clean across them; I had no choice but to scramble through as best I could, praying I wouldn't turn my ankle or worse, but as we approached the front of the house, the scene that met my eyes drove all other considerations from my mind.

The roof was largely gone. The pillars, toppled like jackstraws, had crashed through the west wall, knocking the blocks of stone askew and demolishing the big front door. The central pair, cleft into huge shards, lay athwart Belle's garden, their carved slitted eyes blinded by muddy debris. Below the shattered windows a thousand fragmented suns glittered from the glassy bits spewed across the dooryard. It was as if a horde of malevolent imps had been loosed upon this place, the more so when I realized how narrow the erratic path of destructon had been.

Untouched were Rita's shack, the henhouse and the vegetable garden no more than fifty yards to the north. To the west, save for a curving swath swept clean of posts, the prairie grasses, revived by the rain, responded pliantly to the wind's bidding. The old windmill, its rusted vanes and tower spared, had resumed its grating complaint, and around its base, a patch of sunflowers nourished by the trough's slimy overflow flaunted gold-rayed heads.

In answer to the question in my eyes, Quinn pointed to the dooryard garden. At first, not seeing her, I thought perhaps she had suffered only a glancing blow from which she had recovered after Quinn saw her, and wandered off.

"Belle?" I called, "Belle? Where are you?" Quinn

233

kept his distance, watching in silence as I turned and turned again before glimpsing a familiar bit of sprigged cotton and glint of silver half-hidden among the broken stalks and mangled leaves. *Cradled by her babies.* The metaphor seemed apt until I moved closer, shouldering aside the oozing stems to reach her side. I feared no Lazarus-like resurrection awaited my poor sister.

It had not been an easy death. I looked down into staring eyes and a mouth frozen wide in a silent scream. Her bloodless fingers clutched at the vine drawn tight around her throat; her silver head hung suspended in its murderous grip. *That briony is a hardy critter,* Belle had said proudly. *I swear it'll outlive you and me.* Tears blurred my vision as I tried to pry her rigid fingers loose, but the wiry whiplike strands resisted my frantic efforts.

I looked up to see Quinn still standing outside the garden, still watching through hooded dark eyes.

"Have you a knife?"

His hand moved toward a leather scabbard on his belt, then hesitated. Although his face was expressionless, I sensed his wariness about my intentions.

"In the name of heaven, give me your knife so I can cut her free!"

He pulled it loose and flipped it toward me in a practised motion that sent it somersaulting to a quivering, point-down landing within my easy reach.

Once severed, the vine uncoiled from around Belle's throat in slithering loops soon lost in the torn and tangled undergrowth. I traced its stigmata in her swollen flesh; I smoothed back her silver hair and pressed my tear-stained cheek to hers. I no longer cared that she had betrayed me, had even been ready to kill me if it suited her purpose. She was my sister, my twin, and I grieved not so much for what I had lost, as for what might have been.

I rocked her in my arms, protecting her in death as no one had in life. Grateful my mother had been spared this, I hummed her favorite lullabye, wishing her dear little Belle sweet dreams into eternity. *Hush-you bye, don't you cry, go to sleepy little baby . . . when you wake you shall have all the pretty little horses . . .*

"If that don't beat all."

I looked up. Quinn stood over me, hat pushed back, one hand raking through his dark mop of hair. "I'll be damned for a horsethief, you *are* Serena!" It was the first time he'd bothered to give my name all three of its syllables.

"If you'd listened—"

"I listened well enough; the believin' was the hard part."

Understanding him, but not wanting to, I looked away. I was in no mood to spar with him.

"It was that tune of yours did it, 'bout the pretty horses. A donkey sings prettier than Belle ever could." He paused, took off his hat and ran the brim between his calloused fingers. "It was true, then, what you said about her? What she did? What she had in mind doin'?"

I nodded, not trusting myself to speak.

"Lordy, Lordy." I could barely hear him. "Sharo and me, we'll dig her a grave, if you want to get her ready."

He hunkered down beside me and effortlessly lifted her up into his arms. "Cobby's goin' into town for supplies and to roust out the boys; you want he should fetch back the preacher?"

If I had accepted Bazz's proposal of marriage, was this the preacher who would have done the honors? The one who could have testified to a wedding at Morning Star of Basil Cooper to a silver-haired girl, never mind which one he took away with him? I recoiled at the thought.

"No," I said firmly. "Belle wasn't much for religious observances. I'll say whatever needs saying."

"Suit yourself." He walked beside me up the path, bearing his burden lightly, slowing his stride to match mine. Belle's silver hair streamed down across his forearm, bannered by the breeze. "Where d' ya want her?"

I clenched my teeth, forcing back the angry words clamoring to be said. For all her sins, Belle was my sister, not some animal found dead out on the prairie.

"In Rita's shack. She left soon after you did," I added stiffly, "just as you predicted."

We walked on in silence.

"I sure wish she'd stuck around," he muttered.

"If wishes were horses—"

"Yeah, I'd be outta the horse business."

"None of them were hurt, were they?" I blurted, ashamed for not having spared a thought for the horses sooner. "Is Bingo all right?"

"All of 'em safe as a bet on five of a kind, 'cept for the horses we rode to hell and gone gettin' back here. That twister was a ripper, but it ran on a narrow gauge track."

"We weren't expecting you back so soon," I admitted.

He smiled knowingly. "I reckon not. If it wasn't for Sharo, you and Fawn—" He broke off, looking sheepish. "He had this . . . hunch."

"Hunch? You mean what women call intuition?"

Sensing a jeer, Quinn bridled. "Cobby's knowed him longer'n me. Says Sharo can sniff out weather better'n anybody he ever saw. Interestin' kid, Sharo. Lot like me, only more . . . more—"

"Dignified?"

He slanted a look at me. "Yeah, you could say that."

Quinn preceded me into the simple shack, ducking

236

in sideways under the low door frame. The only illumination was the light filtering through the cracks. My eyes, straining against the gloom, picked out a couple of blankets stacked up against the plank wall. I hastily unfolded them and spread them out, one on top of the other, both of them old and torn and none too clean. Quinn knelt with his sad burden. I sank to my knees across from him, and together we arranged her as best we could. In that dim light, with her eyes and mouth now closed, I could almost convince myself she looked at peace. Quinn got to one knee, then hesitated, finding it hard to say what he felt he must.

"I'll get Cobby up to stay with her while you get whatever you need for the laying out."

"I can manage," I said, hoping I sounded braver than I felt. "There's no need to delay his trip to town on my account."

Quinn shifted uncomfortably. "This hut's got no foundation; the floor boards is broken . . . the little critters. . . ."

I turned away, pressing the heels of my palms to my temples, trying not to shudder as images of bright, beady eyes and small, sharp teeth skittered through my mind's eye. I forced myself to speak. "I hadn't considered the . . . hazards. If you can spare Cobby . . ."

He nodded. "It has to be done fast, S'rena, but it'll be done proper; I promise you that."

He left too quickly to hear my whispered thank you.

True to his word, Cobby arrived sooner than I would have thought possible, his bowed legs forcing a rolling gait that set to sloshing the fuel in the lamp he carried. I hurried out to take it from him.

He looked at me for a long moment, his rheumy

237

eyes satisfying him that what Quinn had said about my transformation was true. "A sad business, missy."

He followed me into the hut, hunkered down next to Belle and lit the lamp. The wash of light over her livid face and foam-flecked lips destroyed the illusion of serenity. My nostrils detected the cloying smell of death.

"Sad business," Cobby repeated in a mutter, shaking his grizzled head. "Go along now, missy. I'll see she comes to no harm."

I dreaded returning to the big stone house. The kitchen, however, had suffered little damage aside from its windows. Sitting untouched on the big work table were the four baskets I had packed with food for a journey that would never be taken. It was like entering the galley of one of the deserted ghost ships sailors spin hushed tales about. I took some soft, clean clothes for the washing, filled a bucket of water at the kitchen pump, and for Belle's shroud cut off a length of the homespun she had used for straining her herbal concoctions. If her hampers had survived the destruction, perhaps they contained something sweet-scented I could use to disguise the tell-tale odor of decay.

The hall had borne the brunt of the pillars' collapse. Now open to the sunlight, the uncompromising illumination revealed Bazz's beautiful piano, shattered beyond repair. The boxes containing his books and music and Belle's bags and trunk had been first battered by fragments of stone, then sodden by the driving rain. Leaves torn from the plants in Belle's garden plastered the tumbled blocks and slithered wetly under my feet. Only the hampers, stacked at the far end as I had last seen them, seemed to have weathered the storm virtually undamaged.

Fragments of glass clinked off the lids as I lifted them, revealing rows of bottles and jars inexplicably intact amidst the carnage wrought by a wind powerful enough to wrench stone pillars from their foundations and whip a vine around a fragile neck. Packed between the exotically labeled elixirs and the humbler ointments Cobby set such store on, I found some rose geranium toilet water that would suit my purpose.

As I picked my way back through the muddy, glass-strewn debris I paused to cock my head, thinking I heard footsteps stealing softly, slowly, across the floor above. A door slammed. I could feel my heart stutter.

"Who's there?" I cried.

The door slammed again and yet again, accompanied by a long, creaking sigh. Caught by the wind, I told myself. Mortally wounded, the house had already become prey to the elements. I hurried back to the kitchen, where, set at ease by its homely ordinariness, my heartbeat slowed to its normal rate. Then, after packing a basket with the things I had assembled, I returned to the hut and the difficult duty awaiting me.

At best a man of few words, in this case Cobby's lack of them proved a blessing. He held the lamp as I did what had to be done, lending a hand when the need arose. Working together thus, in silence, the task was soon accomplished. I sat back on my heels, unable to look away from the waxen mannequin wrapped in plain ivory homespun, her silver hair its only ornament. This wasn't my sister; it couldn't be! Belle could never be this pale, this still. Tears flooded my eyes, and I cried out in anguish, a long, keening wail of grief that I smothered in Cobby's shoulder.

"There, there, missy," he muttered, patting my head clumsily, more at home with fillies than human females. "There, there."

Minutes later, Quinn appeared in the doorway to lead us to the grave site Sharo had dug at the far edge of a small fenced plot in a grove of cottonwoods. He

239

must have read the question in my eyes.

"I reckon Belle is due a place with the family that took her in. Judgin' what she done, well, that's been took out of our hands. No point punishin' the dead for it." He cleared his throat, as if embarrassed to be found wanting in harshness. "There wasn't time to make a box, but we put some planks down."

Sharo stood beside the grave he had dug, its sides as cleanly cut as the youth's high-cheekboned features. He sprang lithely down into the pit as Quinn approached, solemnly extended his arms to receive my sister's body, and set it down gently on the planks that served as her final resting place. He then joined us at the graveside as I recited the passage from Ecclesiastes that Belle had misquoted to me only yesterday, neither of us dreaming how tragically apt its sentiment would shortly become.

"To everything there is a season and a time to every purpose under heaven: a time to be born, and a time to die; a time to plant, and a time to pluck up that which is planted; a time to kill and a time to heal. . . ."

It was soon over. Quinn led me away quickly, and we were almost out of earshot before the rhythmic thudding of shoveled earth began.

"Cobby'll soon be leaving for town. He'll be stoppin' by the station to buy you a ticket on the next train east. Anythin' you want from Rita's hut?"

I shook my head. "That's where I'll be staying."

"Not much of a place. Cobby can move in with Sharo for a coupla days—"

"It'll do," I cut in. "I'm handier than you give me credit for."

He gave me a sidelong glance. "Oh, I give you a whole lot of credit, S'rena, but what's bein' handy got to do with where you lay your head 'til your

240

train pulls out?"

I swallowed hard. *Convince him he needs you*, I told myself. *You'll never achieve your purpose unless you make yourself an essential part of his.*

"I'm not leaving, Quinn."

He stopped dead. He turned to stare at me for a long incredulous moment, then threw back his head and laughed. "You didn't find the gold, did you? You didn't find it, and now you want to hang around 'til you do, and you and your sidekick Basil." He wasn't laughing anymore; his frowning eyebrows formed black bars above his eyes. "Well, let me tell you—"

"No!" I blurted. "I mean I don't *know* if Bazz and Belle found the gold or not, and with the pillars smashed and the posts gone, maybe no one will ever find it. Yes, I'll admit I told them how they might find it, but I had already decided to stay. Before . . . before all this happened." I raised my hands to indicate my hennaed hair.

"'No . . . yes . . . maybe . . . might. . . .'" He gave a clod of earth in our path a powerful kick; I suspect he wished it were me. "You already got me to believe one impossible thing today, S'rena, how many times you plannin' on ropin' me in? If, like you say, there's nothin' to keep you here—nothin' I know about, anyway—why you thinkin' on stayin'?"

I looked directly into his eyes, braving his disbelief. "I've got nowhere else to go. There's no reason you should care what happens to me, but tell me this: If you send me packing, who's going to look after Fawn? Do the cleaning? Tend the garden and the hens? Like it or not, Quinn Cooper, the fact is you need me here at Morning Star. I'm not asking you to like me; I'm just asking to be given a chance to prove I'm worth my keep."

"Oh, I like you well enough, S'rena, trouble is I don't trust you farther'n I can throw a bull calf. Cobby'll find someone in town . . . there must be somebody who—'' His confident tone faltered.

"Somebody who *what*, Quinn?" I didn't know what the Kansas version of the grapevine was, but I was willing to bet every woman in the territory, red-skinned and white, had heard unsettling rumors about Morning Star; and Quinn, belatedly realizing it, ignored my defiant question.

We walked on in charged silence, but as we neared Rita's shack I was beset by doubts. *That sagging roof probably leaked . . . that single narrow window offered little in the way of ventilation. . . .* My steps slowed. The list had hardly begun, yet I knew at the head of it should be my fear of never being able to rid my nostrils of the smell of Belle's mortality.

Quinn paused beside me, eyeing first the shack, then me. "The roof overhang needs shoring up."

"It offers more shade the way it is," I said evenly, sensing a chink in his armor.

"And the cracks in that wall are near big enough to see through."

"Only if someone's standing closer to them than they ought," I countered. "Besides," I added off-handedly, "by the time the cold winds blow, you'll have made up your mind one way or the other."

"How 'bout *your* mind, S'rena?"

"Mine's already made up," I replied, and all at once, realizing this was true, my misgivings melted away like late-April snow. I held my breath.

His dark eyes challenged mine. "I can't pay you much."

"I'll settle for bed and board until you can," I said. "And help bringing a few things from the house. Some bedding, if any survived the storm, a table, a chair or two. . . ." I hesitated. "In the kitchen there's food packed in baskets. Enough to tide us over until Cobby returns."

Quinn grinned. I'd almost forgotten how appealing the dancing lights in his dark eyes could be.

242

"Food all ready for you to skedaddle, huh? Guess maybe there's some truth in that old saying about an ill wind."

I opened my mouth to deny his mistaken assumption, but what was the use? I could hardly blame him for not believing my decision to stay had been made before I had been dragged and dumped into the cyclone cellar. To convince him otherwise would take more time than either of us had just then.

"Sharo'll give you a hand with the essentials. The rest'll have to wait 'til the men get back, but don't you be forgettin' me and Cobby give the orders. I don't want you swishin' your skirts down around the bunkhouse like your sister used to do. And if you want to ride that little pony of yours, you just saddle up and git. No flutterin' or ankle flauntin', savvy?"

Holding my tongue so hard I could taste blood, I nodded. "Anything else?"

"I'm not keen on havin' to ride herd on folks every minute of the livelong day. Got better things to do. If you see somethin' needs doin', I expect you to grab holt and do it."

He turned away, then looked back over his shoulder, a grin of pure devilment splitting his craggy face. "Oh, yeah, almost forgot. Leave the henna be. If I'd wanted a fancy woman, I'd've left Cobby here and taken the wagon to town myself."

He raised one finger to the rolled brim of his hat, winked, and strolled away with a lazy, hip-swiveling gait. He hadn't an ounce of lazy flesh on him. All bone and sinew, he was, and a lot quicker-witted than it suited him to let on. I fumed as I watched his progress down the hill, down to his quarters where Fawn awaited him. *Was there ever a man more self-satisfied?* Then I caught myself. He had been kind to me in his way and, at the time of our rescue, almost fatherly toward poor little Fawn. . . . I clapped my hand to my mouth. *How could I have forgotten her?*

"Quinn?"

He turned and stared up at me.

"Fawn was . . . she's hurt, in ways best seen to by another female. . . ."

"You hintin' at askin' to come down to see about it?"

"I guess I . . ." I drew myself up. "Yes, I am."

He planted his fists on his hips. "Hell's roarings, S'rena, was I talkin' to myself just now?" I could see his frown from where I was standing. "Grab holt, girl! If you swing too wide a loop you'll be told soon enough."

I turned away with a sigh. *What have you gotten yourself into, Serena?* I trudged wearily back toward the ruined house for a jar of Belle's heal-all salve. *Grab holt, and let the devil take the hindmost.*

I knew who the devil was well enough . . . I wondered how often I could expect him to come nipping at my heels?

SIXTEEN

True to his promise, Quinn sent Sharo up from the barn to help me. Few words passed between us, but for a bright lad like Sharo few were needed, and he was quick to do my bidding, although plainly ill at ease in my company. Whether this was because he was unused to being alone with a woman or because I didn't look like the woman he remembered, I could not tell.

"I'll need a chair, and something I can use for a bed. I already have a lamp and bucket, but upstairs, at the end of a corridor, you'll see a black bag standing outside the door to my room . . . at least it was. . . ." I thought of the sodden condition of Bazz and Belle's things. "Wet or dry, just bring it along. I can always hang my clothes out in the sun, and at least I'll have my hair brush."

Sharo looked at me anxiously. "Your hair, Miss S'rena. You have Miss Belle's hair; she has yours. How this happen?"

Sensing he wasn't asking *how* so much as *why*, I was at a loss for an answer. It was too recent, too raw a hurt. "I know, it's hard to understand, Sharo. Hard for everyone, even me. But it's too long a story for now, maybe some day."

"And Spotted Fawn? She try not to cry, but the

245

tears, they leak through." He closed his eyes, and drew the tips of his slender fingers down his cheeks.

"That's even harder to explain, Sharo, but I'll do everything I can to help her heal."

"Make her good as new?"

His earnest use of the white man's lingo made me smile. "Good as ever, anyway." I picked up the bucket and the wet cloths I had used for washing Belle; scrubbed and rinsed, they would serve as well for Fawn, an irony that did not escape me.

"There are baskets of food on the table in the kitchen," I added. "You can take them to Mr. Cooper's quarters after you've brought my things. They'll tide us over until Cobby comes back from town tomorrow. Oh, and Sharo, at the very end of the downstairs hallway you'll see a pile of wicker hampers. In the top one are jars of that healing salve my sister prepared. Look for the label with the star on it. Bring two, please . . . and mind the broken glass!"

I knocked at Quinn's door, but when there was no answer, I let myself in. The large room in which I found myself was surprisingly homey. A row of windows had been punched through the stone walls along each side, flooding with sunlight a comfortable arrangement of wide, high-backed plank chairs centered on a huge stone fireplace. The chairs were cushioned with thick, curly sheepskins; a buffalo hide lay sprawled in front of the hearth. Quinn's Indian heritage was well represented by an assortment of baskets and clay pots figured with curious geometric patterns and a long, beaded leather shirt lying across the end of the long, low couch under the windows. I picked it up. It was much too small for Quinn.

"Fawn?"

246

A faint groan, hardly more than a sigh, came to me from behind a door, slightly ajar, opening from the far side of the room. Water-filled bucket and cloths in hand, I pushed it open with my shoulder. The room was dim, lit only by a narrow window set high in the wall, the furnishings simple: a chair, a small table, a lamp and a bed of the same simple plank construction as the chairs in the parlor. I lit the lamp. Its light revealed Fawn's girlish form lying curled upon the bed. "Oh, Fawn. . . ."

I knew at a glance that she could not be made good as ever, let alone good as new. Her legs, streaked with the dark mahogany of dried blood, were drawn up protectively against her stomach; the new crop of bruises on her face and arms had ripened to the color of plums. She grimaced as I gently straightened her legs, the better to ease from her body the ragged tube of soiled burlap that served as a garment. The pain of its rough-fibered passage over her abraded flesh caused her to draw in her breath, and her exposed thighs bore the blue-black imprints of fingers, testimony to the force it had taken to rob her of her innocence. It was easier to think Quinn capable of such brutality than it was Bazz, but Fawn's own words on the subject, few and halting as they had been, left no room for doubt: the only red-haired man on Morning Star was Basil Cooper.

Why Fawn, I wondered as I sponged the dried blood from her ravished thighs. Her breasts were hardly more than rounded bumps on her narrow, ribby chest; her hips still had the angularity of a child. I flattered myself I was prettier in the conventional sense than this dark-haired, dark-skinned little wilding of Quinn's: given a more enthusiastic wooing, I might well have succumbed to Bazz's well-spoken charm; at the end, wooed or not, I was too drugged to resist. Had Belle been telling the

247

truth about the reason for his preferences? I had thought it more likely my sister's vision of others, especially men, had been fatally skewed by our father's drunken depravity, yet hadn't Cobby hinted at it, too? Looking now at poor Fawn . . . it was as if Bazz had *wanted* to hurt her.

I washed her from head to toe, from behind her delicate little ears to the hardened, very dirty, soles of her long, slender feet. She seemed to take comfort from my cosseting, so while I waited for Sharo to return with the salve I decided to wash her hair as well, having noticed a rain barrel close by the entrance to Quinn's quarters. The combination of well-lathered soap and sun-warmed rain water soon dissolved the greasy dirt away, and by the third rinsing I could hear the long, dark strands squeak between my fingers.

I left her, head wrapped in striped toweling like a Hindoo grandee, to answer Sharo's rap at the front door.

"I bring chair and your bag and quilt for sleeping," he said as he handed me the jars of salve.

"No mattress?"

"No. House no good . . . your mattress no good."

"Better than quilt," I muttered to myself, distressed at the thought of nothing but a thin layer of quilted cloth between me and the damp, cracked plank flooring in Rita's shack. We stood in silence for a long moment. His eyes looked beyond me, searching, I suspected, for Fawn.

"The baskets, Sharo?"

His eyes sped back to mine. I sensed a reluctance to return to the house, but in the end the need for food overcame it. "Yes. I go bring them now," he said.

After he left, I led Fawn out into the front room where the light was better. She winced as I applied the ointment to the tender places—dear Lord, there

248

were so many of them!—but uttered not a single word of complaint. I picked up the beaded shirt from the end of the couch, unwound the cloth from her head and slipped the soft leather garment over it, tugging it gently into place on her narrow shoulders, then tied the rawhide strings at the neck. I combed her damp hair with my fingers into a long, straight fall that glistened in the lamplight like a raven's wing. When I stood back to inspect what I had wrought, she looked up at me gratefully, the shy smile curving her mouth giving promise of the beauty she would soon become.

From Sharo's expression as he entered minutes later with three baskets, it was clear that in his eyes the promise had already been fulfilled. I glanced from one to the other. His longing gaze kindled a becoming glow of color in Fawn's cheeks; her long-lashed eyelids swept down. Quinn would not be pleased.

"Take one of the baskets with you to the barn, Sharo. I'm sure you've had an exhausting day."

Sharo regarded me solemnly, considering my words. *Exhausting?* The concept of fatigue, much less exhaustion, was all but meaningless to this untiring youth, but he recognized my tone of warning well enough. He turned on his heel and left without a word, allowing his proud bearing to speak for him. As I watched him go, I wondered how long his forebearance could be expected to last. One day soon, Quinn might find his lithe, young rival's challenge more than he had bargained for.

Quinn's performance upon his arrival home added to the pleasure I felt at the thought of his eventual comeuppance. Treating Fawn like a pretty new toy, he poked into the food baskets, taking what looked

249

best to him, and from them choosing for Fawn the choicest tidbits. Between them, they consumed the meat pies I had made from dried beef to the last gravy-soaked crumb; I made do with cold beans and bread.

I brought over the pot of coffee I had brewed in the fireplace and filled the cup he held up. To reach it I was forced to negotiate the log jam created by his long legs, stretched out and crossed at the ankles.

"Mighty fine chuck, S'rena. If you could get shed of those airs of yours, you might make some rancher a good wife."

"Are they all like you, these ranchers?"

He looked up at me, his expression bland, but I sensed amusement in his dark eyes. "Mostly. Dumber, maybe . . . uglier for a fact."

"Oh, my. Dumber *and* uglier, you say? Not much of a bargain . . . I think I'd rather earn my own keep, thank you very much."

He peered at me over the rim of his cup. "Well, now, one tasty meal don't make a summer's worth. I don't keep on anythin' don't earn a place here, folks and critters alike."

"And how are you expecting Fawn to earn hers? I'm not sure I did her a favor by cleaning her up!"

Quinn's eyebrows rose. He began to laugh. "By God, if that ain't just like a woman. Fawn's what, fifteen? Sixteen? And you must be pushin' thirty. You're jealous, pure and simple."

Thirty! Deciding a correction would serve only to encourage more insults at my expense, I looked down my nose at him. "It's your expectations of Fawn that are simple; purity has nothing to do with them."

"And bein' righteous don't have much to do with bein' right."

We glared at each other. Out of the corner of my eye, I became aware of Fawn's mounting distress as she looked from me to Quinn, aware our anger was

250

because of her, but not understanding why. Quinn, alerted by my distracted gaze, got up and leaned down to scoop her up like a kitten out of the chair next to his.

"Off you go, little one," he said as he carried her back to her little room. "I reckon you'll know better'n me what needs doin'," he added as I followed him through the door.

"I reckon so," I said cooly.

"Quinn?" Fawn murmured from the cot where he'd laid her down. "You stay?"

"I'll look in on you later," he said, smiling down into her anxious face, "after S'rena leaves."

Disgusted by the implication I inferred, I closed the door firmly behind him, wishing it had a lock and I the key. I helped Fawn off with her shirt and applied more salve to her bruises. I was newly shocked by the extent of them, but relieved to see no signs of inflammation. She had no nightdress; but the old wool blanket was soft and warm, and before I had finished tucking her in she had fallen asleep.

"It won't be necessary for you to disturb her," I announced as I joined Quinn in the front room. He was seated in front of the fire, a lamp at his elbow on the roughly cobbled table beside his chair.

"I said you needn't disturb her." My tone was louder, testier.

He looked up, startled, the glow from the ruddy embers tracing out the craggy contours of his face. There was an open book in his lap.

"You're reading?"

"Godalmighty, is that a sin, too?"

"No . . . no, of course not. I didn't mean . . ." I faltered. If my voice had expressed but a fraction of the astonishment I felt, it was no wonder he took exception.

"Course you did. The likes of me, readin' . . . it

251

riles you, don't it?"

"Surprises, not riles. What are you reading?"

He turned the leather spine for me to see the title stamped on it in ornate gold letters.

"*Ivanhoe?*" I clapped my hand to my mouth.

Quinn turned the tables of astonishment on me by laughing out loud. "Can't bluff worth a damn, can you, S'rena? I'd surely like to play poker with you— why, I'd strip you clean in no time."

I could feel the heat rise in my cheeks. "It's just that *Ivanhoe* isn't the type of book . . . it doesn't have much to do with cows and ranching, the kind of life you know."

He shrugged and tapped the cover with his finger. "Different place, different time, maybe, but folks is folks, even if these in here talk prettier'n we do . . . me, anyway. A bullet doesn't kill a man any deader than a sword through the belly did in olden times, and his family mourned him and laid him to rest just like . . . well, just like you did Belle today."

To hide my confusion, I turned back to the dishes I'd left to soak in the big washtub Quinn used for a sink. Quinn Cooper, a reader of romantic adventure? It hardly seemed credible.

"Brian Niven, the English feller I worked for up Nebraska way? He had a whole shelf full of books. He said I'd have to learn to read if I ever hoped to run a ranch on my own. Started me off on schoolroom stuff, and kept me at it 'til I worked up to something I didn't want to stop readin'."

The mental picture of Quinn puzzling out the pious preachments of a child's primer was too much for me. I giggled.

"What's so funny?" Quinn demanded.

"I was just thinking of that old saying: You can lead a horse to water, but you can't make him drink. Your Brian Niven seems to have done just that."

"Good man," he said. "Good rancher, too, for all his highfalutin talk. Shows his neighbors proper respect. Fer instance, he always boards line riders from other spreads without expectin' payment, but thinks twice 'bout askin' favors from one-hoss oufits. Spaces 'em out far's he can, and if he can figure out a way of payin' without them knowin' it, he does. A bolt of calico for the missus, maybe, or playthings for the kids."

"Generous as well as good—a rare combination."

"That's for sure," Quinn agreed, "'cept in the case of anyone overseppin' property lines. Grass pirates we call 'em. He reads the scriptures to anyone does *that* fast enough, friend or foe."

I wiped the last of the dishes and put them back in the baskets. "Why did you come back, Quinn? It appears to me if Mr. Niven went to all that trouble preparing you to run a ranch, he was hoping the ranch you'd one day run was his."

"Reckon you're right about that, S'rena, but it'd never be mine, not like Morning Star. Ranch work's hard, no matter what job you got, but *runnin'* one— well, the way I see it, that's nothin' I'd want to hire out for. All that sweatin' for something you can never call your own?" He shook his head slowly, emphatically, from side to side. "Besides, those English fellers, they got their fancy names and schoolin' and more money back of 'em than I'll ever see, but they don't know the country, never will. They ship their blooded stock over here for feedin', many as they can, fast as they can, in and out, with no thought for tomorrow. A grass factory, that's how they see it— just like the factories they came here to get shed of, only a whole lot bigger."

"How can you say that? All I see are the differences: the clean air and the big sky and the spaces—why, there's enough space here for the whole world to grow and prosper in!"

"That's 'cause you growed up lookin' at those little rain-watered pastures you got back East, where a herd of cows can be grown on the ten acres it takes to feed one measly cut-back maverick out here. You figger what we got here just goes on and on, no end in sight, like when they started shootin' buffalo for sport from railroad cars, leavin' 'em to rot where they fell. Why, when my paw was a boy, the herds were so big he said the sound of 'em put the thunder to shame. . . ."

Quinn got to his feet and began to pace, dark eyes flashing, hands waving. "Mark my words, S'rena, the grass'll go, too, just like the buffalo. Fact is, it's already happenin'. The newcomers just keep crowdin' in with too many cows on too little grass, never seen a bad winter or a two-year dry spell. . . ." He shook his shaggy head. "When the grass factory shuts down, those poor gaunt critters'll never make it through the first big blizzard, and come spring the stink of 'em will hang over this land as heavy as coal smoke ever did over those milltowns in England I heard tell about."

He turned to confront me, expecting an argument, unprepared for my openmouthed stare of wonderment at this unexpected flow of eloquence. For the first time since I met him he looked discomfited. He cleared his throat, hooked one thumb behind his tooled-leather belt and combed through his thatch of unruly hair with the other. "Listen to my yammering," he muttered, looking away.

"Why, I do believe you've got a plan. . . . You do, don't you? A way of keeping Morning Star going in the face of this disaster you see coming?"

"Not much of a plan, S'rena, more like common sense." His voice was gruff, but he looked more his cocky self again. I doubted if a woman had ever paid

254

him attention of this sort before, and I sensed he found it pleasing. I tried to ignore the flex of his muscles as he lazily stretched, intertwining his fingers as he reached high above his head.

"Tell me about it," I said, walking over to sit in one of the chairs in front of the fireplace.

"You're not too tired?"

This simple courtesy, awkwardly delivered, surprised me, touched me even, but I had no intention of showing it. "Yes, I am, but why don't you tell me anyway?"

He looked at me, wary of my teasing tone, not knowing quite what to make of me. Set adrift by the events that had turned my world upside down, I didn't know what to make of myself. *Grab holt,* he had commanded, but as yet, unable to define the shape of my new life—unwilling to have it kneaded into one that bore his fingerprints—I could only grope. Given time, my point of balance would make itself known. Until then, I decided, I would be best served by inviting him up now and again to teeter along the tightrope with me. But for that I needed my wits about me, and at the moment they were fogged by fatigue.

He backed up to the fireplace, hooked his elbows up onto the wide stone mantel, and looked down at me. "It's simple enough. I'm not a greedy man: while the others are forcin' quantity, I'll be raisin' quality. There'll always be a need for good stock, cattle and horses both, no sense puttin' all my eggs into—you listenin', S'rena?"

My eyelids snapped open. "Quality not quantity," I recited, "and something about eggs. I'm afraid I missed that part . . . did you mention baskets?" I stood, suddenly wide awake. "Baskets! There are only two here; there should have been three. Surely Sharo would have taken only one for himself. . . ."

"What in *hell* are you talkin' 'bout?"

I waved my hands. "Nothing . . . it's not important. Just something that's been niggling in the back of my mind. No need to bother you with household details." The day had finally caught up with me; I wondered if I looked as confused as I felt.

Quinn ambled over to stand close, too close. My breath caught in my throat as he smoothed flyaway strands of crinkly, henna-dyed hair off my brow. I could see flecks of amber in his dark eyes as he studied my face; I felt his warm breath on my cheek. I tried to turn away, but he caught my chin in his long fingers. "Look at you! Pink and white as a prairie rose. Pushin' thirty? I musta had sand in my eyes. More like twenty."

"Twenty-one," I whispered. I felt a sort of . . . singing inside; and as he drew his calloused thumb softly across my cheek my vision blurred, and I felt my mouth go slack.

"Twenty-one. Old enough, I guess."

"Old enough?" I backed away. "Belle warned me, about you being like your father, but I thought maybe if I worked hard enough, proved my worth—"

"Old enough to be on your own, s'all I meant. Old enough to be fightin' drought and bad winters." His expression hardened; he lifted and squared his work-muscled shoulders. "I never forced myself on a woman—never had to—and I'm not about to start with you."

"With Fawn, then? That's what you bought her for, isn't it?"

"Godalmighty, S'rena, Fawn's not even grown yet!"

"Aren't you forgetting? She is now. Bazz saved you the trouble."

Quinn stiffened. "Bazz doesn't know what trouble is yet."

256

I stared at him. "But surely he's dead!"

"Nothin' sure about it, any more than what Belle told you about me and my paw, unless you're plum set on thinkin' the worst."

"I believe what my eyes tell me."

"Is that a fact?" He gave a harsh bark of laughter. "Then, tell me this, who do you think the hands'll believe they're seein' when they look at your curly, hennaed hair tomorrow?"

I shook my head and twisted my hands together, lowering my eyes to avoid his accusing gaze. I was tired, too tired, to know what to think any longer. "It must be very late," I murmured, turning toward the door. I picked up the bucket to take with me up to the shack, but Quinn barred my exit.

"I'll sleep up at the shack tonight; you can have my room."

"But—"

"You need a proper night's sleep. Like I said, Cobby and the hands'll be back tomorrow. You'll have a lot to do . . . can't have you draggin' around all day lookin' for a shady spot to rest."

I nodded, too fatigued to dispute the point. As I entered Quinn's room, I heard Fawn's door open, then a moment later close, and his footsteps crossed the parlor. He had looked in on her as promised . . . looked in and left. At least I'd accomplished that much.

Sleep was slow in coming. I felt lonelier than I could ever remember. Before, whenever Belle and I were separated—before she came to the orphanage; after she left on the orphan train, even when she locked me in the cyclone cellar—I was aware of her presence in my heart and soul. In fact, in early childhood I wasn't altogether sure where I left off and

257

Belle began. Later, the sense of her presence within me dimmed, growing fainter with the passing years, yet taken as much for granted as the silent coursing of blood through my veins. It wasn't until today, as I heard the distant, dull thump of clods of earth on her body, that my heart, seized with anguish, at last allowed me to let her go.

Allowed me to let her go. . . . Lying there in the summer dark, stunned by my realization that Belle would never have suffered this aching sense of relinquishment, I felt tears slide down my cheeks. Had her presence, always thought a loving one, been an illusion all along? I recalled Belle's words, drawled with murderous indifference, about not wishing to spend her life listening to my conscience. *Loving?* She hadn't even cared enough to hate me.

I shivered. I was wholly dependent now on the kindness of strangers, which, unlike love, was rarely given without the expectation of something in return. I pulled Quinn's blanket close around me. It smelled of smoke and horses and the warm saltiness of the man himself. Had he meant to reveal himself as he had to me tonight? He wasn't given to idle chatter. I could not, for example, imagine him discussing Morning Star's future with Cobby—or with Fawn, for that matter—as he had with me. *What did he want from me?*

Drifting on the edge of sleep, a picture of Quinn and Fawn disporting playfully together, cowboy sultan and his raven-haired harem girl—a picture more fanciful than my conscious mind would have allowed—blossomed in my head. Had Fawn's blushing response to Sharo's longing look made her seem less a victim in my eyes? Had Quinn's indulgent treatment of her tonight blurred my perception of his villainy?

Try as I might, my weary brain persisted in mixing

258

black and white to gray, until finally, resisting any further attempt to sort out my confusions, it took refuge in dreams. In them, Quinn's work-roughened Levi's were transformed into silken robes, and jeweled rings glittered on the long fingers that stroked a long fall of silver hair back from eyes as blue as cornflowers, warm fingers that strayed to my naked shoulders, cupped my breasts. . . .

Heat pulsed through me, jagged as lightning. I pushed Quinn's blanket from my taut body, gasping as the ebbing tremors smoothed my blood to syrup. Stunned by sensation, I closed my eyes, unable to think; unwilling if I could. My breathing slowed, and a tremulous faraway sigh—could it have been mine?—released me to dreamless darkness.

SEVENTEEN

The next day, alerted by a distant rumbling, I paused in the pegging up of my damp clothes from the rain-sodden bag Sharo had delivered to me the afternoon before. I shaded my eyes with my hands the better to see below me a straggle of riders hazed by the dust billowing in the wake of the heavily loaded ranch wagon's wheels. Slouched in their saddles, their departing yips of anticipation silenced by five days of drinking, gambling and womanizing, the hands' return to Morning Star bore little resemblance to their exodus. Even their horses seemed woebegone.

What a sorry bunch they were, I thought as I shook out another of my creased garments. I doubted if they had more than a dollar left between them; I knew they had nothing to look forward to but hard work and winter. Yet were my pockets any less empty or my prospects less bleak? They at least had the memories of their coarse pleasures to exchange while patroling the ranch boundaries and bringing breeding stock in ahead of a storm.

My well-worn workaday dresses snapped on the jury-rigged line as the gusting breeze caught them, gray and brown sails above a landlocked sea of grass. I lifted my face to the sun-lit, white-puffed bowl of summer blue. The havoc wreaked by the terrible twisting wind could have seemed nightmare-dreamt were it not for the broken house and the newly dug grave down in the hollow. I secured a second batch of wooden pins to the wind-tugged garments, wishing my spirits could be bolstered as easily, reminding myself that storms were as much a part of life as the fair-weather clouds above, that winter was many months away.

Voices floated up from the barnyard. *Grab holt,* Quinn had said. I shoved a last pin onto the line, sighed, and prepared to enter the fray. There was a wagon load of supplies to be stored. Thanks to the damage wrought by the storm, adjustments to the usual schedule of chores would be required, and Cookie would probably need an extra pair of hands to help with the meals for the men. Whether he would welcome mine remained to be seen.

I needn't have worried. When I asked Cookie if he had enjoyed his holiday, he grabbed off his hat and peered at me out of bloodshot eyes so mournful I hadn't the heart to pursue it. Instead I offered my help, which he immediately and gratefully accepted. This was after Quinn called the hands together to acquaint them with the new circumstances, telling them Belle and his brother were no longer living at Morning Star—he omitted details—and that Rita had left, too.

"That Rita, she comes and goes. Miss S'rena's agreed to stay on as housekeeper, for the time bein', anyways. The house ain't for livin' in; so you'll be seein' her up at Rita's shack—her choice, boys—and unless she asks for somethin', you stay clear, savvy?"

"You sure which one of them girls took off, Boss?" a brash voice called out.

"I won't ask who said that," Quinn said. "You all heard of henna, I reckon," he drawled. A couple of the men snickered. Fresh from town, henna-haired ladies were no doubt very familiar to them. "Well, sometimes exper'ments like that turn out how you least expect. Let's just say she's real sorry about it," he said in a tone clearly meant to discourage further comment. "Isn't that so, S'rena?"

I nodded, not trusting myself to speak. All red-gold ringlets like I was, who could blame them for doubting? It wasn't until a few moments later, when I felt an unwelcome arm slide around my waist, that I fully realized how misleading the truth could be when not all of it is told.

"I'm thinkin' you're Belle," Jed muttered in my ear, "and Cooper's got your silver-haired sister hid away somewheres, along with that scrawny little breed of his."

The foulness of his breath made my stomach turn. I struggled in silence against his tightening arm, not wishing to draw attention to my predicament. His roving free hand moved lower to squeeze my bottom. He gave a grunt of surprise.

"No way Belle could've shed so much so fast—"

I whirled on him. "Belle is dead," I said in a harsh whisper. "She died in the storm . . . we buried her yesterday."

He nodded his satisfaction. "I figured Belle wouldn't take herself off without tellin' me somehow, not with the plans we had."

Jed rubbed his hand over his unshaven chin and peered at me, slyly, fearfully, wondering, no doubt, if I knew of the scheme to take the gold and leave me dead on the prairie. He didn't care that Belle was dead, only that she hadn't crossed him.

"You look younger'n her," he breathed. His dirty calloused hand reached toward my face. "Those worn-out hags in town left me wantin' for a bit of fresh—*Jesus!*"

I swung my fisted hand hard, aiming for the fork of his greasy Levi's. His grip loosened abruptly, and as I walked away, very fast, to join Cobby at the wagon, I

262

saw him doubled over, hands cupping his groin, out of the corner of my eye.

"Jed givin' you trouble, missy?"

"Nothing I can't handle, Cobby."

He peered at me. "You all right? I ain't much of a hand with a cook pot, but I'm thinkin' a rest'd do you good."

Cookie must have told him of my offer to help, I thought. "Keeping busy will do me even better, Cobby. I'll be fine. I have a place to lay my head, and I've got you as a friend."

Cobby colored. "Not much of a friend, not helpin' you find a better place for that pretty head of yours."

I hastened to head off Cobby's implied criticism of Quinn. "The shack really was my choice, Cobby. All it needs is a little fixing up . . . well, maybe a lot," I admitted as he looked at me askance, "but there's plenty of time before cold weather sets in."

"Anythin' you need, you ask me," he said in a conspiratorial whisper, although there was no one near enough to hear. "'Cept for Jed and a couple of his mangy pals, this is a right useful bunch of boys. If we can't find it, we'll make it."

"And if you can't?" I teased.

Cobby knitted his grizzled eyebrows, plucked his pipe from the pocket of his stained, ragged leather shirt and stuck it upside down his mouth. "Then, I reckon you don't need it. Hey, Woody," he called, "go give Cookie a hand with peelin' the taters! As fer you, missy, you'd best be heatin' up your cook pot. We ain't et nothin' since early mornin'."

I traversed the yard between the barn and corrals as primly as a preacher's wife—no fluttering or ankle-flaunting—sidestepping the crisscrossing paths of hands hastening from one chore or another, avoiding their curious sidelong looks. I failed to notice Jed's deliberately timed approach, entering the bunk-house door a moment ahead of him only to be shouldered out of his way. I shrank back as he sidled by me, unable to avoid contact with him or the heavy sack he allowed to clank painfully across my bosom. "I'll be paying you a visit sometime soon," he muttered. His mean little eyes were unforgiving. "We got a little settlin' up to do."

Jed's threat would have worried me more if I'd had less to do, but no sooner had I sliced and cooked the potatoes Cookie needed for the hash he was preparing from canned corned beef brought back from town—there wasn't time to bring in fresh meat—than I had to run up to Quinn's quarters and start all over again for him and Fawn, this time with fresh eggs, vegetables from the garden, and biscuits with milk gravy made from the scrapings from the meat pie pans. It would have been easier if we'd all eaten together, at least until the ranch settled back into a routine, but Quinn was reluctant to expose Fawn to the hands' curious eyes.

"Seein' how Bazz treated her, they might get to thinkin' she's fair game. It was bad enough before."

In other words, private property, no trespassing allowed. Thinking of Jed's unwanted attentions, I wondered how far his protective impulse extended. "And I am? Fair game, that is?"

He looked at me appraisingly. "You're free, white, twenty-one and healthy as a—well, mighty healthy-looking. 'Sides, without some encouragement, I reckon none of the cowpokes here's man enough to brave those schoolmarmish looks you give—yep, just like that," he said, laughing as I looked down my nose at him.

We ate in silence. This evening, I was glad to see, Fawn's appetite was worthy of a trencherman. At this rate, we'd soon see roses in her dusky cheeks. Quinn's thoughts were elsewhere.

"Would you care for another helping?" I asked as he mopped gravy from his tin plate with a bit of biscuit. He held his plate up wordlessly.

"A penny," I offered as I spooned out the last of the vegetables.

"Hmm? A penny for what?"

"For your thoughts. Assuming they're for sale to the likes of me," I added dryly.

His eyes snapped into focus. I could sense his weighing of the pros and cons as he silently, methodically, forked the vegetables into his mouth. At length, he tilted back his chair and hooked his thumbs into his belt. "Fawn, honey, fetch the coffee, will ya?" he drawled.

Pleased to be of service, Fawn's eyes brightened as she scurried to do his bidding. I observed this little scene of subservient domesticity with distaste.

"I sure hope St. Peter ain't no kin of yours," Quinn said.

"What are you talking about?" I demanded.

"Judgments, S'rena. You sure do have a way of stampedin' into 'em."

"Why, I never said—"

He waved an impatient hand. "I know well enough what you never said. You're forgettin', I've spent my life with critters what never say anythin', but that don't mean I don't know what's goin' on inside their fool heads."

Fawn returned with the coffee. I waved the pot away. "Forget the penny!" I scraped my chair back. "What's going on inside *your* head's not worth it."

My snappish tone made Fawn round her eyes, but Quinn just grinned and wagged his finger. "Temper, temper. You keep on like this and I'll start thinkin' we buried S'rena 'stead of Belle. Fact is, it's her and Bazz I was broodin' on. I 'spect you know they was owed money by the terms of my paw's will. I was thinkin' of puttin her share in the bank in Ellsworth for you."

I stared at him. My penny was buying more than I

bargained for . . . or was it? "In my name or yours?"

He chuckled. "In yours, S'rena. Vamoosin money, case you got a mind to take it on the lope."

"We made a bargain. Are you suggesting I break it?"

He threw up both hands, palms out. "Whoa, there. I'm not much for suggestin'. If that's what I meant, I'd tell you, flat and out."

I nodded, mollified. "Then, I thank you for it. I never thought. . . ." I could tell by the look in his eyes there was no need to finish. He knew I hadn't expected him to honor any right I might have to Belle's inheritance. The funny thing was, knowing I would have money in the bank, in my own name, even if only enough to buy a ticket elsewhere, made me all the more determined to prove my worth to him and to Morning Star. I wondered if he knew that, too.

"My half-brother's share—how'd that lawyer talk put it?—*re*verts to me," Quinn continued. "That's what I was thinkin' on just now. About puttin' it back into the horse-breedin' end of the business. A clever, gentle-broke cow pony's worth a lot more'n some rough-busted range mustang. There's this fine Appaloosa mare I got my eye on—"

"You're talking as if Bazz were dead!" I cried.

The amber lights in Quinn's dark eyes went out. "If he's not, when I find him he'll wish he was. Soon's I get the boys started breakin' the horses I got me an order for, I'll be on his trail. He ain't got a horse; he's too soft to get far without one. The tree's already picked out."

"That's murder," I whispered.

His eyes were as cold as marbles. "You seen what he done to Fawn, and if that's not enough for you, how 'bout those two orphans him and Belle took in?"

"Now who's rushing to judgment! I hate him for what he did to Fawn, but those other girls . . . rumors, Quinn, nothing more." Belle had talked of

266

Bazz "punishing" them, whatever that meant. Like Fawn, I supposed. But cruel as he'd been, surely that wasn't call to *hang* him. . . . "You can't hang a man because of rumors!"

His mouth thinned and tightened. "Haven't you anythin' better to do than point out the error in my ways?"

After insisting I stay another night in his quarters, saying it might improve my disposition, Quinn left. Fawn and I made short work of the cleaning up, and after I smoothed more salve on her bruises and saw her off to bed, I decided to go up to the big house with the baskets I had brought down the day before. This would be as good a time as any to put away the supplies Cobby had the men deliver to the kitchen. The evening was lovely—warm and still, with insect choirs humming in the grass—but I was too distracted to take proper note of it. Would I ever find the time to ride the prairie on Bingo again? How I had loved our excursions! I had accepted without question my role as pampered guest, exploring the brushy slopes and chalky outcrops, lazing by the pond, heedless of the passage of time. I had never thought Belle would prove a piper to be paid, much less what the cost of her tune would be.

The ruined house loomed above me, a dark blot against a sky still luminously blue, pricked here and there with starshine. My footsteps slowed as I recalled Quinn's telling of the Pawnee sacrifice to the morning star. How many times had the gruesome ritual been celebrated here? I wondered. How much innocent blood needed to be shed to insure its eternal consecration? I thought of the young captives, fears allayed by months of kindness, encouraged to hope for union with a chief's son, dragged to a scaffold, their naked bodies pierced by a score of flaming arrows, their young flesh torn and scattered together with seed on the spring-awakened earth. *Pampered guests betrayed. . . .*

The ugly parallel struck me with a force that made me gasp aloud. The house in which I had spent so many happy hours seemed doubly cursed now, and as I opened the door to the kitchen, even the homely complaint of its hinges struck a sinister note.

I entered and lit the lamp suspended above the work table. My nervous fingers set it swaying, the shadows advancing and retreating from the erratic circle of light, now here, now there, coming to rest upon a pair of empty baskets on the knife-scarred tabletop. I placed the two I had brought with me beside them.

Yes, I thought, just as I remembered. Four baskets, not three. I had offered one to Sharo; might he have taken two? It seemed unlikely, but who else. . . . Just then, my shoe crunched on a rivulet of sugar trailing from the chewed corner of one of the sacks Cobby had brought from town. Dismissing further conjecture as profitless, I concentrated instead on storing away the supplies in the pantry's tin-lined, rodent-proof bins and barrels.

As I moved back and forth from kitchen to pantry, I became aware of distant creakings and groanings, very like those I had heard in the night when I first arrived at Morning Star. Mice and squirrels I had thought them then, and thought they must be now, for Belle was dead, and Bazz. . . . I pushed the possibility away. *Mice and squirrels, or the warping of rain-soaked floor boards in the rooms above, or . . .* Cornmeal spilled from the scoop in my hand. *Or Bazz.*

I slumped against the pantry shelves. If Bazz were here, I did not want to know. I would not allow my mind to dwell on the little irregularities I had noticed: two cans of beans instead of five; a slick of moisture in a sink that had ample time to dry since my last use of it. The affection Bazz had kindled in my heart might now be as cold as winter's ashes, but that did not, could not, warrant my betraying him to Quinn. I had no proof of his willing complicity in Belle's schemes—a weak man was no match for a determined woman—and how could rumors of murder be woven into a rope strong enough to serve as a hangman's noose? *Vengeance is mine . . . saith the Lord.* I would not serve as a handmaiden to blasphemy.

I gathered up the emptied sacks, folded them, and walked around the table to place them on shelves reserved for such uses. As I did so, I noticed a smallish dark rectangle at the table's far end, just beyond the circle of light. I picked it up. The feel of pebbled leather between my fingers instantly identified it as Belle's herbal, forgotten in the aftermath of the quarrel she and Bazz had had about it. The sight of the worn covers brought vividly to mind the hours she had spent here concocting her herbal salves and elixirs. They were the only times I could recall seeing her forgetful of self, seeing her . . . content. I couldn't help thinking how upset she would have been to find she had left it behind. . . .

I riffled stained pages densely written in a childish hand. The phrasing was awkward and marred with misspellings, but her observations were keen and the descriptions of process carefully and intelligently detailed. If only Belle had had a Malcolm Wilcox to guide her! *"If, if, if, Reenie. . . ."* Regretful tears blurred my eyes as her mocking chant rang again in my head.

Even though I might never wish to use Belle's herbal myself, I knew it must be saved. I slid it into my pocket. As I did so, I recalled her slipping Lottie Cooper's fine red leather-bound herbal into her own, the morning of our last day together. I could see her fingers buttoning the flap, her eyes daring Bazz to further dispute her right to it. Where was it now? In the hampers packed with her concoctions? More likely in her room, to be carried with her in a hand satchel. I stood, irresolute, unable to bring myself to climb the stairs, terrified of what I might find.

It was true. Haunted by its bloody legacy, my early delight in the golden stone house had wholly surrendered to fear. Its inhabitants, save for me, were either dead, in flight, or in hiding, and June had not yet run its course. I would ask the men Cobby had promised to send for furnishings for the shack to keep an eye out for the little red book. For now, I wished only to return to Quinn's quarters and the uncomplicated affection Fawn had developed for me in the course of my ministrations, simple acts complicated only in my own mind by the knowledge that their success owed as much to Belle's salve as my nursing skill.

I sighed, reached up to turn out the lamp above the table, then paused to light my lantern first. There was no need to invite darkness to Morning Star.

The next evening Quinn again pooh-poohed my intention to take up residence in the hut.

"I'd say it's more a line-campin' sort of place than a res-i-dence," he said, poking fun at what he obviously considered a la-di-da choice of words.

When I told him of Cobby's offer to help set me up, he frowned. "I can't spare any of the boys to give you a hand right now; 'sides, it's good for Fawn to have you here."

"But the men, what must they be thinking?"

"'Bout a pretty woman like you stayin' here?" He pulled at his ear. "Just what you're thinkin' they're thinkin', S'rena . . . and wishin' they was me," he added with a grin.

270

I could feel warmth rise in my cheeks. "Then, all the more reason—"

"They'd be thinkin' it no matter where you lay your head at night." He looked down at Fawn sitting cross-legged at his feet. "Fact is, I got me two pretty women," he said, placing a hand on her dark head. "You're lookin' a whole lot better, little one."

Fawn smiled up at him. "Miss S'rena, she very good to me."

I couldn't take my eyes from Quinn's gently stroking, proprietory hand. *Good to her?* I looked away, shamefaced, as Quinn's hand moved lower to squeeze Fawn's shoulder. It was not my place to lodge a protest, yet by not doing so I felt implicated in her . . . whatever her relationship was with him.

"Time for me to bed down." He rose and stretched. "Hard day tomorrow."

"Good!" I pronounced. "Hard enough, I hope, to keep the men too tired to think of things that don't concern them."

A smile curved his mouth. "Never heard tell of a man too tired for thinkin' on it." He flexed his arms and slowly lowered them. "But we got a cavvy of horses waitin' to make 'em too tired to do anythin' else."

"Cavvy?"

"Yep, cavvy . . . caviada, some say." He paused consideringly. "Funny soundin' word, ain't it? Brung up from old Mexico, most likely . . . means a bunch of range horses needin' to be broke to saddle."

I nodded. "Mustangs," I supplied smugly.

He grinned. "We'll make a sage hen outta you yet, S'rena. But these ain't no ordinary broomtail mustangs. You recall that Appaloosa stallion of mine?"

"Bucket, you mean?"

Quinn nodded. "Finest breed of horse I ever rode. Smart, brave, strong as rawhide—I'd like to see a

271

camel outlast 'em. The Nez Perce bred 'em, and the United States Army killed most of 'em. Got fed up with bein' outrode and outfought, so they crippled the savages by killin' their horses." Quinn's mouth twisted in disgust. "*Savages* . . . why, their horses was better bred'n most people." He shook his head.

"But you say some did survive."

"A few of us, who know the breed and value it, are doin' what we can. Brian Niven had a small herd—I bought Bucket and a couple of mares from him when I left."

I raised my eyebrows. "That was certainly decent of him."

Quinn's jaw set hard. "I paid his price. No favors asked; none given. Niven knows he don't have time to do right by them—backers of a big spread like that put their money in cows, not spotty-rump Injun ponies."

"How do *you* find the time?"

"I don't find it, S'rena, I make it, 'cause I'm the only backer I got. I don't need no others; don't want none, neither."

His lips tightened; his eyes hardened with purpose. I was beginning to understand why he'd been so set on paying Bazz off.

"I don't rough-break my horses—not my Appaloosas, anyway. They got spirit and heart enough to take you clear over the moon, and any man tries quirtin' and steelin' it out of 'em ain't welcome at Morning Star." He frowned. "I sure hate to see critters suffer for men's cussedness."

I wondered if he, too, was thinking of Jed. "How do you find buyers for them? I imagine with all the time you put into them, they must command premium prices."

He laughed. "They surely do, S'rena, but this string's already spoken for. Rich slicker back East fancies havin' a barn full of genu-wine cow ponies so

272

he can play at wild west with his pals. Saw an Appaloosa in some show somewhere, sent the word out to find him some, and old Brian, he passed it on. 'Spirited enough for the men, gentle enough for the ladies.' That's what the feller ordered; that's what he'll be gettin'." He paused. "Can't have all of 'em he wants, though."

"Holding out for more money?"

Quinn looked startled. "What d'ya take me for? I got my breedin' stock to think of!"

Fawn, who had dozed off, woke with a cry, frightened by Quinn's suddenly raised voice.

"Godalmighty, girl!" Quinn exclaimed, almost stepping on her as, sleep-dazed, she shrank away from the tall figure looming above her. "How long'll it take you to get some starch back in your spine?"

I choked back the angry words that clamored to be said. "I don't like to see a child suffer for a man's cussedness, either," I finally managed.

Quinn blinked. Then, as the import of my altered version of his earlier words registered, his eyes narrowed. "Child? I recall you tellin' me this poor little critter ain't been a child since—" He broke off. "Fawn? Best go to your room now. You still ain't up to snuff—I reckon none of us is tonight," he added, drawing a weary hand across his brow.

Fawn got to her feet, squared her slim shoulders and glared at him defiantly, clearly unwilling to miss the rest of this interesting exchange.

"The starch seems to be returning," I observed.

"Git now," Quinn muttered gruffly, shooing her with his hands. "Show's over. Miss S'rena'll be in to see you directly."

He waited until the door clicked behind her. "Your mind's all made up 'bout me, ain't it? Always has been, never mind what you're feelin'." He stepped toward me.

"Nonsense!" I protested. I moved back, only to

273

stumble over the edge of the buffalo-skin rug. I reached out to regain my balance, grabbed at his extended hand and as quickly pulled away, as if from a flame. "I think you're good at your job . . . I think you're better than most, probably." Why couldn't I control the tremor in my voice?

"I'm not talkin' about what I do, S'rena, I'm talkin' about me. And I don't care what you think . . . thinkin's not feelin'. . . ." His voice was low and soft and deep. "That day at the pond, remember?"

I stepped back again, and came up against the table. I could go no farther.

He lifted my chin. "You ain't no child," he murmured, looking deep into my eyes. A long, work-roughened finger traced the fullness of my lips; his other hand slipped around my waist. "No child was ever this soft . . ." My breath quickened, betraying my stirred senses. "Or this willing. . . ."

His mouth covered mine, capturing the moan I had never meant to escape. As before, at the pond, his warm lips and persuasive tongue worked their rough magic; as before, he was the first to break their spell.

I stood there, not knowing where to look, what to say, my hands fluttering about my head, smoothing errant strands of my crinkly, hennaed hair. Quinn walked to the door, took his wide-brimmed hat from a peg and set it on his head, its rakish slant testifying to his satisfaction. He paused in the opened door. "Maybe you got a little bit more thinkin' to do, S'rena."

I stared after him for a long moment. Then, after I was sure he was well away, I stepped outside and plunged my face in the rain bucket. I came up gasping and spluttering like a landed fish, my swirling emotions shocked into subsidence, my mind clearing. Once inside, I patted my face dry and went straightaway to Fawn.

"It rain?" she said, looking at my moisture-dewed hair.

"No, it not rain," I said testily. She dropped her gaze, and I sighed, knowing I had hurt her feelings. I sat down beside her and reached for the jar of salve on the table next to her bed. "I just . . . washed my face a bit too enthusiastically. I must look a fright."

"Not you," she returned gravely. "Only hair. Silver nicer."

"Yes, it is," I agreed, "and it will grow in again one of these days—just about the time all of these bruises of yours are gone," I said as I began applying the ointment. "These new ones, I know how you got them," I began cautiously, "but the ones you had when you arrived . . . did Quinn . . . I mean, how—"

"Yes, Quinn!" Fawn cried. She sat up, her gleaming hair falling like a shawl across her face. She parted it with her fingers and peered out at me. I found her smile perverse. I sighed. The jar of salve rolled out of my lap; I kneeled down to fetch it from beneath Fawn's bed.

"Quinn very brave."

I flung my head up. Fawn was on her stomach, looking down at me. I raised myself into a sitting postion on the floor. "Brave?" I repeated stupidly.

"And . . . and . . ." She pointed to her head, then laid a finger alongside her nose.

I guessed wildly. "Two-faced?" She frowned and shook her head. "Thoughtful? Clever?"

She clapped her little hands together. "Yes, yes, very clever, very brave." She sat up, crossed her legs and gave a satisfied little nod. I waited for her to continue, but it soon became clear she had said all she thought needed to be said. I, on the other hand, needed more. Much more.

"Fawn, why don't you begin at the beginning? Where did you meet?"

"Quinn or bad men?"

275

Be patient, I told myself. "Quinn first."

"At hotel. I sweep, make beds, clean . . . clean . . ." She described a bowl in the air with her hands and pretended to spit into it.

"Spittoons?"

"Yes! You clever, too!" She laughed with delight. "Quinn come. I sweep his room, make bed, he give tip, he go away. Then bad men come." She held up three fingers. "Want me go with them. I say no. They come to me at night. I fight, but they hit me very hard. They make me walk, walk, walk, and then we make camp. My feet very bad. They tie my hands . . . I too tired to fight."

Her voice fell and her body slumped. I could almost feel myself in that trailside camp with her, alone with those brutal men.

"Then Quinn come by. He see me"—her eyes flew wide with exaggerated recognition—"but he not know me." She laid her finger alongside her nose again. "Quinn have cards, whiskey. They play and drink, and Quinn lose and lose and lose. Quinn say he want to see me dance. They laugh, untie me, make me dance. My feet . . . I hop like crow. Everybody laugh, drink, play more cards, but," she lowered her voice, "forget to tie me." She paused.

I was impressed by Fawn's natural sense of drama. "And?" I prompted.

"Quinn turn pockets out, say he broke. So he bet Palousie horse . . . not for money, for me. Bad men laugh. But he win!" Fawn stood on the bed and mimed someone shouting, then reeling drunkenly and falling down. "They go loco!" She frowned fiercely and pointed her finger at me. "Quinn point gun. I tie them up, take guns. We leave very fast. Two days we come Morning Star."

In my mind's eye I again saw her slight form, abused and exhausted, scuttling from Quinn's wagon to his quarters. "Couldn't he at least have

276

stopped long enough for you to eat?"

Fawn stared at me, then shook her head deliberately from side to side. "Bad men very angry," she explained in a kindly tone, as if to a slow-witted child.

I nodded. "Of course they were. I understand, Fawn." *I won her in a poker game*, Quinn had said. And so he had. Won her and saved her life. The evidence of my eyes and ears had again been proven wrong, and yet. . . .

As brave and clever as Fawn's account had proven Quinn to be, this very steadfastness of purpose in the face of unfavorable odds made me doubt his ability to see life in anything but stark terms of white and black. Shades of gray had no place in his spectrum of values, I feared. In Fawn's case, thank God for it; but if Bazz were hiding at Morning Star, Quinn would not hear it from me: too much innocent blood had been spilled already at Morning Star; I did not want Basil Cooper's on my hands.

EIGHTEEN

When I arrived at the bunkhouse the next morning to help Cookie with the morning meal, I found him elbow-deep in dishwater and the room empty save for one figure sprawled facedown on one of the bunks.

"I saved out some biscuits and sowbelly," he said, peering at me over a beefy shoulder. "Coffee, too, if you got the stomach for it."

"Good heavens! Where is everybody?" I asked. "The sun's only just up."

"The boss routed us out 'fore light this mornin', missy. Him'n Cobby and the saddle stiffs're already out runnin' up those 'Paloosey mustangs of his. Morning Star got a big order for 'em, and the boss's ridin' close herd on all of us. Beats me what the all-fired hurry is," he added in a mutter.

I could have told him. Bazz was the hurry, for all his being "too soft" to go far on foot.

"They'll be back midday, mebbe sooner. If you want to watch those bucky horses get broke, best get your chores done early."

I thrust Quinn's threatened cat-and-mouse pursuit of Bazz out of my mind. "Are you recommending it as an entertainment, Cookie?"

"It surely is sumpin' to see—next best to a town blowout, I reckon."

I nodded to the figure on the bunk. "Looks as if one of you is still recovering from the one you just came back from."

Cookie wiped his hands on his big soiled apron and folded his arms. "That Jed," he said with a disgusted shake of his head. "Calls himself a bronco buster, a real flash rider. Mebbe he was once, 'fore the drink took him. The boss is powerful set against drinkin' in the bunkhouse, ever'body knows that, but Jed, he thinks he can just keep coastin' on those fancy spurs of his."

Jed groaned, and one leg slid to the floor; but he showed no sign of waking. I turned my back on him. "The men'll be wanting a hearty dinner come noon," I said. "A couple of Rita's hens have seen better days; why don't I pull some onions and carrots from the vegetable patch for a chicken potpie?"

Cookie looked doubtful. "The boys'd like that fine, but I ain't much of one for pluckin' chicken feathers."

"I'll see to that," I promised rashly. "All you have to do is mix up another batch of biscuit dough for the topping; that way we'll both have time to watch the show in the corrals."

Cookie's broad face lighted up. "Missy, I sure hope you're plannin' to drop your traces and stay awhile."

Inferring a question in his words, I hesitated. At length, I settled for a noncommital smile and a brisk departure.

Spotted Fawn was up when I returned to Quinn's quarters, and as she ate the food I had brought back for her, I repeated what Cookie had told me.

"I go with you?" she asked. "Paloosey horses very fine . . . Quinn and Sharo very good riders."

I looked away from her intense gaze. Her pleading dark eyes, the prayerful clasp of her small hands and her hopeful, dancelike circling of me combined to make it all but impossible to reach an objective decision. Clearly, she was physically much improved. Maybe, if she stayed close to me. . . .

"Please?"

Her tremulous whisper did the trick. "All right, Fawn, I'll take you; but we have chores to do first, and if Quinn says no, you must promise to come back—"

"Oh, Miss S'rena!" she cried, her eyes lighting with pleasure. "I do what you and Quinn say. Cross heart," she added solemnly.

"Well, the first thing is to stop jumping about like a grasshopper . . . you're making me dizzy. The next thing is, how are you at plucking chickens . . . ?"

Fawn was, it turned out, very good at plucking chickens. When the cleaning and laundry chores were done, Fawn dispatched the pair of elderly hens with an expert twist of her small hands, plucking them so furiously she was soon cloaked in floating feathers.

I put down my basket of onions and carrots and brushed the white down from her long black hair and the shoulders of her doeskin garment. "You look as if you'd been out in a snowstorm," I said, laughing.

Fawn proudly held the chickens up for my inspection.

"Clean as a whistle," I said. "Now, take them and the vegetables down to Cookie. I'm going up to the big house to see what can be salvaged when the men have the time to take a wagon up."

Fawn's eyes widened. "No! You not go there, Miss S'rena. Very bad place . . . please, you not go."

She stuffed the hens under one arm and clutched my sleeve with the other. I gently detached myself. "I can't stay with you in Quinn's house forever, Fawn. I must see how much of the furniture is fit for use in

Rita's hut, and . . . ," I hesitated, "and my sister's ointments should be returned to the cyclone cellar for storage," I amended, knowing my speculations about Bazz's whereabouts would only distress her further.

Although the big order Quinn had received for his Appaloosas was too important to Morning Star's future to delay, once the breaking of them was under way I had no doubt the search for Bazz would begin in earnest. But suppose I found him first? Wouldn't I be morally obligated to warn him of his brother's terrible intention? If I did, Quinn might never forgive me; if I didn't, I doubted I could ever forgive myself.

Fawn tugged again at my sleeve. "Miss S'rena? You hear? Horses come!"

At first, my mind still tossing on the horns of my dilemma, I was conscious of little more than a sound like wind blowing through the tasseled grasses. But as it grew louder, an ever increasing din comprised of hoofbeats, whinnies and the piercing yips and whistles of the cowboy wranglers, I felt excitement rising within me, that rare and marvelous sense of anticipation a child feels when the circus comes to town. I thought of Quinn, centaurlike on his big black stallion, driving the band of horses before him like leaves before a storm. The house could wait, I decided.

"Take the hens down to Cookie, Fawn . . . but remember, work before play!" I called after her as she scampered headlong down the slope to the bunkhouse, a plump, plucked carcass dangling from each joyously upraised hand.

I descended after her at a more sedate pace with my basket of vegetables, entering the bunkhouse just as Jed stumbled out. His gait was unsteady, and although his bloodshot eyes recognized me well enough, he was clearly intent on getting to the corral before Quinn sent someone after him. His hair was unkept, his hip-slung pants filthy, but he'd taken the time to polish up the silver spurs that jingled on his boots. The gleaming rowels, a couple of inches in length and filed sharp as knife points, seemed to me more instruments of torture than correction, an impression reinforced by the stout quirt with a yard-long lash dangling from his wrist. Quinn would have something to say about that, I thought.

Cookie, Fawn and I needed no more incentive than the spectacle awaiting us in the corrals to spur us into action. Without a word we sorted out the tasks among us: I sliced the vegetables while Fawn cut up the hens; then I browned the pieces in Cookie's big iron pot as he rolled out and wrapped in a damp cloth the pie crust to be added later. We grinned at each other as a mighty whooping reached our ears through the open door. Cookie shoved the pot on the back of the stove, slammed on its lid and pulled off his apron.

"Better git a move on, ladies," he said, "less'n you want your heels stepped on."

One look at his huge boot-shod feet persuaded me to grab Fawn's hand and step out smartly. "You stay close, Fawn," I admonished her. "I don't think Quinn's going to be happy to see you here, but maybe, if I act as your chaperone, he'll—" I broke off, realizing "chaperone" was unlikely to be included in Fawn's vocabulary. *Guardian? No, that sounded too much like a jailer.* "Think of me as a bossy big sister," I said.

Fawn smiled up at me shyly. "Yes, Miss S'rena. Sisters." She squeezed my hand.

I swallowed hard. The Lord surely did work in mysterious ways. "In that case, Fawn," I said, squeezing her hand in return, "just Serena will do."

On seeing our approach, Cobby plucked his pipe from his mouth, spat sidewise into the dust from his perch on the topmost rail of the near corral, and beckoned with his pipestem. He reached down to pull us up beside him. In the far corral, twenty-five to thirty Appaloosas milled: bay and chestnut, blue and strawberry roans, all with dot-splotched blankets of white splayed across their well-muscled rumps. They whirled and reared, protesting their confinement, their agile hooves spinning up clouds of dust transmuted to gold by the early-morning sun. The middle corral was empty; below us in the third, his neck through the loop of Sharo's reata, a striking blue roan pranced.

Quinn, lounging across from us, arms folded on the top rail, confined his acknowledgement of our arrival to a pause in his words of instruction to the hands and a long, level stare that made my toes tingle.

". . . As I was sayin'," he continued, "Sharo here'll show you how its done."

A low mutter arose from the men who, wranglers or not, had been pressed into horse-breaking duty. Clustered in twos and threes along the rails or straddling them, they shifted uneasily, exchanging comments and sharing complaints.

"Don't need no breed pup showin' me nothin'," I heard someone say. It was Jed, of course. He was sitting, cocky as a bantam rooster, on the top rail only a few feet from Quinn. Considering his condition, I figured only sheer willpower was keeping him from toppling off.

"This breed says you do," Quinn said calmly, stepping away from the fence, daring Jed to dispute his authority.

"I forgot more'n he'll ever know." Although his words were defiant, this time Jed's voice was barely loud enough to hear, and he kept to his place on the rail as if glued.

"I seen you ride, mister," Quinn said, "and it 'pears to me what you forgot prob'ly wasn't worth knowin' in the first place." A few of the hands chuckled knowingly. "Like those spurs of yours. If I was you, I'd take 'em off now."

Jed pulled his head into his shoulders and snubbed his toes behind a lower rail. He wasn't about to give up his fancy silver ornaments.

"Dern fool," Cobby grumped. "Just keeps diggin' his grave deeper. Won't be many mourners at *that* funeral."

All attention returned to Sharo as the young wrangler, alert to every nuance of his captive's movements, gradually pulled the horse toward him, talking quietly all the while, until the trembling roan was within handling distance. Then, with the Appaloosa's distinctive white-rimmed eyes following his every move, Sharo glided his hand gently down the horse's neck and flanks, still talking, never raising his voice.

At length, the horse bent his proud neck and began to explore the youth's head and clothes with his velvety muzzle. Sharo captured it in his hands and exhaled gently into the flaring nostrils, causing the startled horse to throw up his head. Sharo's hand resumed its rhythmic stroking. Quieted, the horse snuffled again at Sharo's face, then tossed his head, snorted, and stood four-square, ears pricked forward, gazing at Sharo as if to say, "Well, what now?"

The answer was soon forthcoming. Sharo picked up the hackamore bridle lying at his feet and held it up for a thorough sniffing and eye-rolling inspection before slipping it on. Then, after allowing ample time for the animal to accustom himself to the feel of this strange, new contrivance on his head, Sharo eased the saddle brought over by one of the hands onto the roan's twitching back.

284

"He keeps on like this, these here cayuses won't get broke afore the snow flies," Jed sneered. "Hell's fire, I seen molasses move faster!"

"I don't understand," I whispered to Cobby. "What other way is there?"

"Jed was a contract buster 'fore he come to Morning Star, missy. Hired out to outfits too small to keep a bronc rider on the reg'lar payroll. Got paid so much a head."

"I see . . . the quicker the breaking, the more money he made."

Cobby nodded. "Quick and dirty."

"I shouldn't think a horse broken like that could be very reliable."

"Well, they ain't, and that's a fact. What you get is half a ton of ornery critter that turns plumb inside out every time he sees a jackrabbit's shadow, throws you into a thorn bush, then stomps your sorry hide to death."

Just then, Sharo lightly tossed the reins over the roan's ears, gathered them in his left hand and vaulted into the saddle as light and quick as a cat. The horse grunted as he felt the unaccustomed weight on his back, then, with arched back and stiffened knees, crow-hopped across the corral.

Cobby chuckled. "See the way Sharo keeps that cayuse's head up? A horse gotta tuck his head between his knees to do much in the way of fancy buckin'." He cupped his hands around his mouth. "Waltz him 'round again, Sharo!"

The onlookers laughed appreciatively and added a few earthier comments of their own.

"Will you be riding today?" I asked.

Cobby shook his grizzled head regretfully. "My buckarooin' days are over, missy. Most of my bones been busted by now." He pulled his pipe from his mouth and used the stem as a pointer. "My horse kicked out both my knees a little while back . . . nice, gentle horse, too."

Bemused by his matter-of-fact acceptance—Cobby made less of a to-do about his crippling injuries than I would a splinter—I could think of nothing to say. I suspected an expression of sympathy would only offend him.

Fawn pulled at my sleeve. "Sharo, he ride very fine."

Her dark eyes were fixed on the tall, slim figure that sat the pitching mustang as easily as a rocking horse in a child's nursery. Fawn's mesmerized expression made me wonder if my bringing her here was wise. That Sharo was aware of her interest was obvious, to me at least, from the way he edged his mount ever closer so as to display his skills to their best advantage. Youth called to youth, blood to blood. He was courting her, plain and simple, regardless of what Quinn or I or anyone else thought about it.

"Fawn, I think maybe . . ." My words trailed off as I looked from this Pawnee Juliet to her Romeo. Their beauty just about broke my heart. One foot each in the red world and white, betwixt and between a century of hard feelings and misunderstandings, what hope of tenderness did they have except with one another?

"Yes, S'rena?"

The trust in Fawn's huge eyes tugged at my heart. *To hell with what Quinn Cooper thought.* "I think maybe Sharo's the finest rider I ever saw!"

As if to prove the truth of my statement, the roan's hopping, pitching motion gradually smoothed to a broken trot. Sharo circled along the rail once, twice, three times before bringing his snorting mount, its sides heaving, its steel blue coat almost black with sweat, to a halt. Sharo then threw his leg over the saddle horn, slid forward to the ground and, with the reins still gathered in his hand, bestowed a light approving slap on the horse's neck.

"And that, gents, is how it's done here at Morning Star," Quinn said, climbing up to sit astride and easy on the top rail. His deep voice, although pitched low, carried to my place across from him. "We don't break horses here; we gentle 'em." He paused, tipped his hat back on his black shag of hair, and tugged at his ear. "Don't know as I'd recommend puttin' your ol' grandma on that roan just yet, though," he said gravely. "Might take another few days fer that." The men laughed.

He sat up straighter; his dark eyes searched through the shifting knots of men. "Anybody taking exception," he added in a louder, more deliberate tone, "is free to find another outfit to ride for. You'll get what's owed you, a horse to ride, and no hard feelings."

Fair warning, I thought. I glanced over to where Jed slouched, his long-lashed quirt tapping an angry tattoo on his boot.

"All right, then," Quinn continued. "Four at a time, two in each corral, pick your own horses. Sharo, Woody, Billy, Jed. Cobby'll turn your critters out into the holding corral when you're through, startin' with the blue roan."

As Quinn vaulted off the rail and ambled over toward us, Cobby scrambled down to take the roan's reins from Sharo. Fawn and I waited. I crossed my fingers behind my back.

"You're sure lookin' perky, young'un," he said to Fawn.

She smiled. "S'rena take good care of me."

"I'm thinkin' the pink in your cheeks comes from somethin' other'n S'rena's good care."

I drew myself up, bridling, as Fawn lowered her eyes. "She wanted to see the horses . . . I don't see the harm in it."

Quinn raised his eyebrows. "No harm," he said

287

mildly. "But it got Sharo's attention wanderin', and if that roan'd been less of a gentleman. . . ." He sighed heavily in a parody of despair.

Fawn's mouth curved down in dismay. "I go home now. No want Sharo hurt."

"Or you neither," Quinn said gently. "Can't tell what those wild 'Paloosas'll do. Little thing like you, I'd as soon drop a mouse in a herd of elephants."

Fawn scampered off, her long, dark hair gleaming like satin in the sun.

"She's right about the good you done her, S'rena."

"I've become very fond of her." I took a deep breath. "Don't you think it's about time you stopped mother henning her? She may still look like a child, but she's a grown woman now, with a woman's feelings."

Quinn leaned back against the rails of the corral and peered at me from under the wide brim of his hat. "Me? Mother henning?" He sounded incredulous. "Well, if that don't beat all." He took off his hat and flicked the dust from its creased crown. "Tell me, S'rena," he drawled, "when did I leave off bein' the devil incarnate?" He looked down at me. His eyes danced with teasing lights; his slow, wide grin shallowed my breath.

"Fawn trusts me . . . she tells me things." I fingered the tucks in my bodice, needlessly adjusted the fit of my skirt, then folded my restless fingers inside my palms. "For instance, she told me all about that poker game you won her in, and I'm wondering, how much does Sharo know? About you and Fawn, I mean?"

Quinn's grin faded. It was like turning down a lamp in a dark room.

"I thought you liked him!" I exclaimed.

"Liking's got nothing to do with it," he said stiffly. "My mother was a Comanche. A Comanche's got no call to explain anything to a Pawnee." His

288

jutting jaw was as unyielding as the spine of rock looming above us.

"Oh, for pity's sake, Quinn! Both of you are half-white, too, aren't you? Then, let your white blood do the explaining! Us white folks are good at that."

"Too good by half," he muttered. His chin raised up another notch. "You do it, then. I ain't no matchmaker . . . I got better things to do with my time."

We glared at each other. Just then, a blood-chilling scream of pain sent our attention winging toward the center corral. It sounded like an animal.

Quinn jammed his hat down on his head. "It's that no-good Jed," he muttered. He strode off, shouldering startled cowboys out of his path. I didn't think to wonder how he knew it was Jed. We all knew something was bound to happen; it just happened sooner rather than later.

I pressed forward with the men. Jed, astride a beautiful chestnut that looked like a firecracker about to explode, laughed down into Quinn's angry face. "You said no quirtin' or steelin' . . . show 'im, Cookie!"

Cookie, looking shamefaced, held up Jed's quirt and spurs. "Told me to hold 'em for 'im, Boss."

Quinn stroked the quivering horse with one hand, and slid his other up under its mane as if feeling for something. His head jerked up. "Usin' a ghost cord, Jed?"

"You didn't say nothin' about that."

"Didn't think I had to."

"What's a ghost cord?" I asked the cowboy next to me.

"Bit of string tied to a mustang's tongue and gums. You feed it 'round his jaw, hold it in your hand along with the reins, and if he does somethin' you don't want 'im to . . . *whumpf!*" He jerked an imaginary string tight. "Hurts like double hell . . . pardon

289

m'language, ma'am."

Quinn removed the offending device and turned it slowly in his long hands. "See you added a few 'improvements' of your own." Murmurs of disgust arose from the men close enough to inspect it. Quinn suddenly reached up, grabbed Jed by his sweaty shirtfront and hauled him out of the saddle. Sharo darted in to lead the wheeling, jittering horse away.

"You better hope you didn't do that critter any lasting damage," Quinn rasped, his face no more than six inches from Jed's. He abruptly released him. "Whew! Not only are you meaner'n a snake, you smell worse'n a saloon on Sunday mornin'." His eyes searched the crowd, and came to rest on me. "Serena? Go on up to the bunkhouse. See if Jed's hidin' whiskey in his bunk."

I stared at him open-mouthed. *Why me?*

Cookie lumbered up. "I'll go up with you, Miss S'rena. Time I got that chicken pie put together." He grabbed my arm and yanked me along.

"Why me?" I repeated aloud.

"The men can't be 'spected to round on a bunkmate, even one they ain't got no use for."

Grab holt, S'rena. I felt as if I'd plunged my hand into a patch of nettles.

Jed hadn't put much effort into concealing his jug. I found it in one of the two gunny sacks stuffed under his bunk, along with two jars labeled White Poppy Elixir, one empty, one still sealed. At first I assumed he had stolen them from the hampers in the ruined house, but a closer examination revealed the labels as less elaborate than those on the jars Belle had intended to sell. *These must have come from an older batch.* Belle, mentioning this elixir by name, had said Jed always paid for what he wanted. Jed—and Bazz, too, I recalled—had hinted at a relationship of an amorous as well as business nature. I had been forced by events to accept many unwelcome differences between my twin and me, but I sincerely hoped an attraction to Jed was not one of them. Just the thought of it made me shudder.

I slipped the sealed jar into my pocket and returned to the corrals. I handed the jug to Quinn without a word. He uncorked it, sniffed, and unpended it. It was hard to read the expressions on the faces of the men, but I'm sure it pained more than just Jed to see that liquor puddling in the dust.

I stepped back into the crowd; Cobby edged up beside me, carrying a saddle.

"Sorry business," he said. "Quinn'll set him down for sure."

". . . I don't owe you a red cent," Quinn was saying. "You asked to borrow against your pay to go to town, and like a fool I let you. Fact is, you owe me, but I'm willin' to call it quits." Jed began to protest, but Quinn cut him short. "Listen up and listen up good," he said, jabbing a finger at Jed's pointy nose, "you and your lead-head quirt and filed-down spurs ain't welcome here at Morning Star, never was for that matter, so pack up your plunder and git." He turned on his heel.

"Which horse you givin' me?" Jed yelled after him.

"Lordy, Lordy," I heard Cobby mutter beside me. "I allus knew that Jed for a damn fool."

Quinn turned back. "You already got one," he drawled, "known as shanks' mare."

The men fell silent. In the center of the ragged ring they formed, Jed swayed on unsteady legs, his sagging shoulders at last admitting defeat. It was a tableau I would not soon forget. Then Quinn strode off, and the men soberly dispersed to their tasks. Cobby stepped forward to give Jed his saddle, taken from the mistreated chestnut.

"You'll be wantin' this."

Jed took it without a word and slung it over his shoulder. He cornered bloodshot eyes at me as he passed by. "You best keep a lookout over your pretty shoulder. We got some reckonin' to do."

His voice was low, his tone mild, but I was jolted by the hate that radiated from his sidewise glance.

"Pay him no mind, missy," Cobby said. "I'm bettin' this ain't the first outfit Jed's been throwed out of. Even walkin', he'll be in Ellsworth by tomorrow nightfall, and too liquored up by midnight to even think 'bout comin' back."

I gave Cobby a grateful smile, but my uneasiness remained. I recalled his description of Jed's way of breaking horses. Quick and dirty, like the man himself. I knew I would not rest easy for a long time to come.

NINETEEN

By the time the men came up from the corrals for dinner they were too hungry to waste words on Jed's fate. The chicken pie was judged "good grub" by everyone whose mouth wasn't too full to talk. I exchanged a pleased smile with Cookie over the heads of the men and told them they had earned it with the morning's work they'd put in. Unused to compliments, they shifted uneasily on the long plank benches, although I caught here and there a sheepish grin of acknowledgement.

When the washing up was done, I was too tired to do anything more than trudge up to Quinn's quarters to lie down for a bit before it was time to start supper. "Beans and sowbelly," Cookie had confided as he shaped a batch of sourdough into loaves, "and as much bread as it'll take to fill in the cracks."

I awoke to a quiet house. I peered out the parlor windows to see Fawn, edged with gold by the light slanting in from the west, sitting at the top of the slope. Arms hugged around her knees, she was staring down into the corrals, no doubt hoping for a glimpse of Sharo. The work wouldn't stop much before dusk, so I had a couple of hours to spare before lending Cookie a hand. Should I go up to the big house? I wondered. I knew I couldn't put it off forever. I thought of telling Fawn, but it would only upset her, and if she followed me . . . suppose Bazz *was* hiding there, and suppose he saw her. . . .

Deciding it wasn't a risk worth taking, I closed the door quietly behind me, edged around to the side and walked swiftly, keeping first Quinn's quarters, then Rita's hut and the henhouse interposed between us. As I passed the garden, I noticed leaning against the gate the hoe I had used that morning to pry carrots and onions from their earthen beds. I picked it up, intending to return it to its proper place in the henhouse, but suppose . . . just suppose Bazz was even half as villainous as Quinn thought him? I decided to take it with me, reluctantly, not liking myself for it, but Bazz had, after all, been ready enough to see me dead, even if not by his own hand.

I did not dally in the kitchen; decisions about the choice of utensils and remaining stores to be transported to the bunkhouse awaited Cookie's inspection and advice. I crossed the wide front hall, leaned the hoe against what remained of the wall and knelt to open Belle's hampers. I compared the jars to the one I had found under Jed's bunk. The difference in the labels proved what I had suspected: Jed's had come from an earlier batch, confirming him as an opium eater in addition to being a drunk and a mistreater of animals. I prayed Morning Star had seen the last of him.

I slipped the jar back into my pocket and moved cautiously into the parlor. Although the cushions were too rain-soaked to salvage, the stout, pegged wooden furniture needed little more than a sanding down of storm-inflicted gouges and scratches and a dressing of oil to restore them to usefulness. The long, wide couch could serve as a bed for me, and if the Indian rugs were hung out in a shady spot to dry, perhaps they could be folded to use as a mattress. . . .

The sour smell of wet ashes filled my nostrils as I

walked slowly through the large room, poking at this, discarding that, putting off going upstairs until I could no longer justify further delay. Debris littered the stairs and the long corridor above. Rain, wind-driven through the shattered windows in my and Belle's rooms, had, as Sharo had said, reduced the contents to soggy junk, now fuzzed with mildew. Belle's dressmaker's dummy lay crushed under dislodged blocks of stone, the strawberry locks of her wig curling out from beneath them as if by the mocking intent of some malevolent spirit.

I climbed to the third floor. The roof was entirely gone; the whirling tunnel of wind had scoured Ross Cooper's room of its furnishings, including the long, coffinlike chest and whatever gruesome mementos it contained. They would not be missed. All that remained were the pale deerskins I had seen upon his bed, torn and tumbled in a corner, damaged beyond repair.

I descended again to the second floor. Wishing I had not left the hoe in the downstairs hall, I paused to take a deep breath before easing open the door to Bazz's room. I need not have worried; the room was quite empty. Empty of any human occupant, that is. I stepped in and looked around me wonderingly. The water-stained, heavy red velour drapes drawn across the shattered windows had apparently shielded the contents of the room from the storm-driven rain. What debris there might have been had been cleared away, and the signs of recent human habitation were evident: empty cans of beans and milk, broken egg shells, even the feathery tops of carrots. The pretty lace-inset coverlet on the bed had been neatly folded at its foot; but the pillowcase was bloodstained, and bloody rags littered the floor below.

As I stared at them, wondering how badly Bazz had been hurt, the smell of hot wax reached my nose. I whirled and gasped at the sight of the distorted

295

reflection of my alarmed self in a large, cracked, gilt-framed mirror above an elaborately carved and painted dressing table. On its crowded top the stub of a fat candle guttered in a puddle of hardening wax. I hurried to extinguish it. Half-hidden in the litter of perfume bottles and jars of salves, I spied a pair of fancy silver combs—the ones Belle had said one of the orphan girls had taken? This could be a different pair, but somehow I doubted it. Beside them lay a small red book. Lottie Wohlfort's herbal. . . .

Of course! Her herbal, her dressing table, her mirror, her lacy coverlet—Bazz had gathered about him the belongings dearest to the person he had loved best in the world. Had he crept up here expecting to die in the shrine he created? Where was he now? How long had that candle been burning? A day? An hour?

As I pondered, I absently picked up the finely bound little book and began riffling the gilt-edged pages. The paper was of the finest quality; the faded handwriting, in an old-fashioned German script, various. Toward the back, however, the writing was in English, a fine copperplate script that near the end became interspersed with a rounded childish hand I recognized. As I leafed slowly through the remaining pages I realized Belle had not only contributed to Lottie's herbal, but in the end her observations dominated it. I pushed open the drapes, sat down on the edge of the bed and began to read.

I have no idea how long I remained there after closing the covers on those final damning words, staring down at the red book in my lap as if at a viper curled to strike. But its venom had already leaked into the pages; the harm had long since been done. Belle had described in meticulous detail the medications she had prepared and administered to Lottie Cooper, dutifully recording the dosages increased in strength and frequency. Lacking in conscience in every other respect, in this she had been conscientious to a fault: *monkshood, Jimsonweed, belladonna, castor bean, henbane, briony, poppy* . . . her babies, Belle had called them; spawn of the devil was more like it. At the very end, beneath her notation of the date of the death she had so attentively ensured, she had signed her name with prideful flourish.

The band of light admitted grudgingly by the parted drapes had lost its earlier brilliance. I thrust the herbal into my pocket and sprang to my feet; there was little time left to do what I must. I clattered down the stairs, stopping only long enough to snatch up the hoe I had left in the downstairs hall before plunging out onto the long veranda littered with the battered remnants of the pillars that once lent it a certain majesty.

The sun had paused, blood-orange, just above the horizon, as if unwilling to relinquish the vibrant hue it had taken twenty-four hours to acquire. In the dooryard, the leaves on Belle's herbs, black in the fading light, rustled importantly; vines torn from the fallen pillars reached up blindly, sinuously searching for new support. I could no longer distinguish the crushed patch where my sister's body had fallen, so lush was the growth in the wake of a storm that had sown such lasting devastation elsewhere.

I took a deep breath and stepped boldly into the garden. Beneath my feet, swollen stalks burst audibly; vine tendrils, slender and supple as silken threads, whipped up the handle of the hoe, around my wrist. I tore them off, raised the hoe high above my head and brought it down hard, again and again, deeper and deeper, until my rage was spent. At my feet the long, pale, many-branched root of the briony vine lay exposed, along with a number of other rootlike, harder fragments.

As I bent to inspect them, the fetid odor of the root's split, white flesh rose to gag me. I nudged one of the objects with my foot, exposing knobs first at one end, then the other. *Could it be. . . .* I closed my eyes, recalling to mind the minutely detailed engravings in the anatomy text Father Rogg kept in his pharmacy. *Yes, it was a bone.* I gingerly teased the rest out of the soil with the toe of my shoe, two . . . five . . . seven . . . all of them bones. An animal, I told myself. Something a coyote had killed and eaten here. I tugged at a rounded edge protruding from beneath the broken root. The dark earth relinquished it reluctantly, and no wonder. It was a skull. A human skull. *Those orphans?* But which one? Who would know . . . or care?

I straightened up, sick with apprehension. The ruined facade of the great stone house, stained red by the setting sun, gaped eyeless ahead of me. It was as if the skull at my feet, bloodied and bloated to enormous size, had by some monstrous agency been transported there. "Dear God!" I cried, my hands closing into fists as I fought down the panic that threatened to seize me. "Haven't I had horrors enough?"

"Thinkin' on doin' some gardening?"

I dropped the hoe, startled by the voice that issued out of the dusk. My head whipped first to one side, then the other. Nothing. I felt suddenly dizzy . . . *was I hearing things now?* Just then a figure emerged upon the veranda from the darkened square where the shattered oak door once stood.

"I never figgered on catchin' you so easy."

The voice, rasping and mean, brought my heart into my throat, but it was the jangling of the spurs that identified with certainty the man approaching me through the dusk.

"What are you doing here, Jed?" I slowly bent my knees; my hand searched for the hoe. "I expected you'd be long gone by now."

"Don't allus do what folks expect," Jed drawled as he slammed his boot down on the handle of the hoe. "Too dark to do any more hoein', S'rena." The rowels on his spur sliced through my sleeve; I cried out as he hauled me up by my arm. "Cut ya, did I?" He tsk-tsked slowly, mocking my distress.

Although shorter than I, years of bronc busting had made him as wiry as an old root. Sober now, his steady grip on my arm was too strong to even think of breaking. "Horses are out back," he said, yanking me along. "We got a little travelin' to do."

"Traveling? Where? You can't—"

"Oh, I guess I can. You see, after Cooper set me down, I moseyed up to the big house, see what the storm had left in the way of pickin's, and guess what I find: ol' Bazz-eel, his head wrapped up, lyin in a bed all lace and fluffs, wild-eyed, like he'd been grazin' on loco weed."

"You're saying Bazz is alive?"

"Last time I seen him. He knows Quinn'll be lookin' fer 'im, so seein's how our little plan got bent clean outta shape by that twister, we struck a bargain. I hauled him down to that old line rider's shack in the draw out yonder. Time he got there he was lookin' like he been hit with a pack saddle, so there's no tellin'. . . ." Jed shrugged. "Thing is, he wants me to bring you to 'im, and that's what I'm gonna do."

"But *why?*"

"Well, you see he spied on you from upstairs t'other day, and he got it in his head you're Belle. Now, I know Belle well as anybody, an he knows that, but he's past listenin' to anythin' he don't want to hear. Kept talkin' about some red book he got and 'bout how you gotta be punished, like those little orphan gals Belle buried for him. Can you figger that? Havin' the stomach for killin' but not the buryin?"

Oh, sweet Jesus.

"So, like I say, we made us a bargain, Bazz and me. He gets you and I get the gold." He paused, and although it was too dark now to see his face, I guessed he was grinning. "Hey, mebbe I can have you first. Don't think he much cares one way t'other long as he gets you in the end."

"What gold are you talking about?"

He jerked me forward to face him. "What'd'ya take me for, Serena? I know all about the gold. How you was lookin' fer it, an' how Belle and Bazz found it an' then she got killed. He wants you more'n the gold now, and I ain't about to turn you over 'til I get it."

I kept my silence. Maybe Bazz *had* found the gold. I doubted it, but as long as Jed believed it and needed me to bargain with, I had a chance of staying alive.

We had crossed around the far end of the big stone house. Ahead of us, standing near the east wall of the kitchen, two horses patiently waited. On the smaller, white blotches shone like beacons in the thickening shadows.

"Bingo!" I cried.

The little horse threw up her head and whickered a welcome.

"There'll be no more of that!" Jed said, roughly pulling my arms behind my back. He tied my wrists tightly together with a thong cut from the long lash of his quirt. Hoping I might find a chance to escape when mounted, I allowed him to boost me up into the saddle and suffered his intimate caress of my bottom without protest.

"You treat me nice and maybe I can change Bazz's mind about you," Jed suggested. "Your sister never had no complaints."

I choked back angry words and lowered my head submissively.

Jed mounted and gathered up Bingo's reins along with his own. "On horses good as these we could go mighty far, mighty fast."

"I don't imagine Quinn'll be too happy when he finds them stolen."

"Stolen?" Jed laughed. "That little paint's your horse, ain't she? And who's to say ol' Bazz-eel didn't give me his chestnut in return for favors I done 'im? Takin' 'em was easy as that chicken pie you made . . . why, those cowpokes never saw 'em go!" He laughed again, full of himself. "Quinn wore 'em out, ev'ry last one of 'em, even ol' Cobby. I saw 'em stragglin' up to the bunkhouse, too set on settin' and eatin' to look back."

My hope that his renewed confidence might lead to a relaxation of his guard was soon dashed. The prairie grasses muffled our slow, cautious passage along a rarely trodden route that sloped out of sight below the rim of the bluffy rise above the bunkhouse and corrals. Quinn might be annoyed by my absence—*where the devil has the woman got to!*—but the extra duties awaiting everyone at the end of this very busy day made it unlikely anyone would seriously wonder where I'd gotten to for some hours yet.

We rode for some time in silence. As the dusk deepened, a mournful coyote dirge rose and fell along the ridgeline pencilled on the darkening horizon. I was aware of Jed's head turning at frequent intervals to check on me. Presently, our path began to angle obliquely down a slope that descended into a brushy bottomland. The odor of the willow wands crushed by our passage rose to my nostrils, fresh and moist and tangy, an odor I always think of as green. Freshly cut grass; watercress plucked from a rushing brook; new-mown hay. It was an aroma uncommon in this wide, dry prairie-land, and I knew at once where we were.

We emerged into a small clearing. Ahead of us, half-hidden in the undergrowth, stood the old line rider's shack I had first seen in Bazz's company earlier in the spring.

"Hey there, Bazz-eel?" Jed called. "I brung you sumpin."

After a long silence, a door scuffed open. Candlelight, flickering from within, outlined a figure sagging against the jamb. A white rag was wound around his head.

"Bazz!" I cried. "Let me help—"

"Daughter of Satan!" The figure shrank back. "Don't let her wicked fingers touch my flesh. . . ." It was Bazz's voice, but weakness and madness had tuned it to a high, unsteady pitch.

"I'm Serena, Bazz," I began in as calm a voice as I could muster. "The first time I came here was with you . . . we had a lovely picnic by the stream . . . you told me about the forget-me-nots, remember?"

"Serena's dead!" he said, pointing an unsteady finger at me. "You called up the whirlwind and killed her. You killed my mama, too. You must answer for your sins." He gestured with his bandaged head to Jed. "Bring her here." He pushed the door wide. Candles flickered on the low table. Jed dismounted and stepped closer, pulling Bingo behind him. Next to the candles were two flat wads, thickly covered with long black hair. They looked like . . . had Bazz rifled his father's store of grisly mementos?

Jed turned, grinning, at my horrified gasp of recognition. "Ol' Bazz, here, he don't fool around. Those little orphan girls? They had a powerful lot of hard answerin' to do, too, but they ain't doin' much of anythin' anymore."

I felt sick. They were scalps, yes, but not old, not Pawnee.

"I told you to bring her—"

"I heard you," Jed cut in. "Seems to me I brung you a whole lot already: first I brung you the horses,

302

then I brung you here, and now the woman you wanted—even if she ain't the one you think she is," he added in a mutter. "So when you bringin' me somethin'? You promised me gold, mister. If you don't show me quick where it's at, I guess I'll just take her and the horses away."

Jed began backing slowly, leading me and Bingo along with him, talking all the while. "Quinn'll be after us, y'know. I reckon this little lady'll kinda mount up the score he's lookin' to settle, but the way I figger it, I ain't got near as much to lose as you— why, when it comes to love lost, you two could teach Cain and Abel a thing or two, and that's a fact."

Clinging with one hand to the door, Bazz leaned out after us, his protest a labored gasp, as futile as the buzz of a fly disputing the swatter descending upon him. He sagged, his body admitting the defeat he resisted putting into words, then laboriously pulled himself up. "Come in," he said at last, his voice hardly louder than a whisper. "The gold's hidden back at the house . . . I'll draw you a map."

Jed chuckled. "See? That wasn't so hard, was it? I'll be along soon's I see to the lady." Jed cut more thongs from his quirt to tie my ankles to the stirrup leathers and to hobble Bingo. "There you go," he said, grinning up at me, "that'll keep you from roamin' off the range." He leaned close. "This won't take long, sweet thing," he whispered. "Soon's I put him out of his misery, we'll hightail it outta here. . . ." His hand kneaded my thigh. "You can thank me proper later."

I watched Jed strut across to the shack and duck inside. I saw his hands reach out to grip the edges of the table; his wiry form blotted out the flickering candlelight. As I waited I wondered which of the two fates awaiting me was the worse?

From inside the shack there arose the muffled but unmistakable sound of argument punctuated by a shout loud and sharp enough to cause Dancer to shy and Bingo's head to fly up. Before my heartbeat had a chance to settle, I heard two shots, fired in rapid succession, and saw a figure stagger out, hands upraised toward me as if in supplication, only to collapse, twitching, in the dust just outside the door. *Poor Bazz*, I thought, not in regret for his death, but of the waste he had made of his life.

A second figure emerged. He prodded the now still body with his boot. "He thought I'd be too weak to resist," Bazz muttered, "but I showed the cocky little bastard . . . never understood what you saw in him, Belle," he added as he wedged a small pearl-handled gun under his belt.

I shrank back as he approached, step by shuffling step. I tugged futilely against the thongs that bound my wrists; Bingo, restrained by her hobble, snorted and shifted restively beneath me. At last he stopped, and although I could not see his expression as he reached up to stroke my hair, I suspect he saw it as another souvenir to add to his macabre collection.

"My punishment is just and sure . . . no one can escape it. Especially not you, Belle."

TWENTY

Bazz led Bingo and me over to the door of the shack. The pale wash of flickering light issuing from inside was enough to show dark blotches on the white rag wound around his head.

"Bazz, you're bleeding!"

His fingers reached up to explore the soiled and ragged bandage. He groaned.

"I have a jar of Belle's white poppy elixir in my pocket . . . it will ease the pain."

He shrank back. "You've done devil's work enough with your elixirs!"

"Not mine, Bazz! Belle is dead. Look at me! I'm Serena . . . can't you tell?"

He giggled, his pain for the moment forgotten. "Oh, my, of course I can tell!" He reached up again to stroke a lock of my dyed hair, allowing it to slide through his fingers. "I bought you the henna, remember? I helped you make my father see a desirable woman instead of a little orphan girl. What fun we had fixing you up like the stage actresses in the magazines I brought you!"

Bazz's smile faded; his hand clutched my knee. "Your lip rouge and low-cut dresses kept Paw out of Mama's bed well enough, but I never meant you to make sure she never left it! What a fool I was, not seeing you as you really are."

"I'm not Belle," I whispered hopelessly. "I'm innocent of what you say."

"Innocent?" he rasped. "You were cursed from the day you were born. You'll see."

My heartbeat stuttered. What new horror was brewing in that hurt, fevered mind?

Bazz moaned and raised his hands to his head. "I must rest now. Just for a little. We must get to the pond before sunrise. . . ." He shook his head slowly. "No, star rise. Something happens at first sight of the morning star . . . something. . . . *The pond!* If you're still afloat at sunrise I'll tie you to a stake and heap branches all around and the next morning at star rise . . . *whoosh!*" He flung his hands up to indicate the leap of flame.

I listened in mounting despair as Bazz's sick mind spun a bizarre new fabric from the threads of a hodge-podge of old beliefs and myths. "And if I drown?"

"You won't, Belle, because I know you for a witch, but if you did . . ." He paused to pinch the bridge of his nose with his fingers. "If you did," he repeated slowly, "then I'd bury your bones in the garden, with the others. . . . This time I'll do it myself."

He looked up at me as if hoping to be complimented. I did not ask what would become of my hair; I already knew.

As he turned to go inside, Bingo's reins trailed from his fingers *Please, God, let him release them,* I prayed. Hobbled though she was, I hoped Bingo would respond to the pressure of my legs well enough to give me a chance at escape. Behind my back, I crossed aching fingers.

Bingo, sensing the release of pressure on the reins, pulled back, ever so slightly, against them. To me her motion was barely perceptible, but it was enough to focus Bazz's wandering attention. He jerked her forward, looped the reins through the notch where a door latch had once been set, and tied them securely. I uncrossed my fingers; I wouldn't be going anywhere soon.

I don't know how long I sat there shivering, fighting my fears. Jed's body lay no more than three feet away, close enough for the rusty smell of his blood to reach my nostrils. Had I been cowardly not to try harder to escape? Pride usually checks the impulse to surrender to fate, but courage isn't as simple a thing as we usually imagine. Although sometimes rashly brave, more often it assumes a variety of guises. Our daily lives see a score of small measures taken, confirmations of our moral strength and integrity, of our nerve and physical endurance. Bazz's weakness had made him cautious and crafty; I would need cunning to best him and patience to wait for the right opportunity.

I must have nodded off in my saddle, for gray was beginning to rim the eastern edge of the night sky when Bazz emerged again from the shack. He had changed his clothes. I felt my eyes widen at the sight of a tweed suit and vest more appropriate for a wedding than a witch hunt. On his head, which was wrapped in the same grubby, bloodstained cloth I had seen earlier, a black derby hat balanced precariously. He looked ridiculous, but my impulse to laugh was checked by the hectic look in his eyes and the pearl-handled gun in his hand.

"The time has come to meet your judgment, Belle," Bazz proclaimed. He transferred the gun to the holster protruding beneath the skirt of his jacket, undid Bingo's hobbles, gathered up both her and Dancer's reins and pulled himself, gasping, into his saddle. I held my breath as he swayed there, head

307

lolling, but I waited too long. He soon recovered himself, and when he wrapped the reins around his wrist, securing them in case of another spell of weakness, I knew it was too late.

We rode in silence. The slow pace allowed my senses full and greedy reign of whatever time remained to me: the scent of the night-dewed grasses seemed uncommonly sweet; the fresh morning air, quickened by the expectation of a new day, brushed a cool caress across my cheeks. As the spreading blush of dawn dimmed the stars, it became apparent Bazz had already forgotten the place of the morning star in his motley mythic fabric. I had no intention of reminding him; I could only hope its weave was too unbalanced to long endure.

Once rooted, hope is a stubborn plant: I could sense its leaves unfurling in my heart, its buds about to open. I must have been missed by now, I mused. Would Fawn think to tell Quinn of my intent to visit the ruined house? If he searched there would he realize, as I had, that Bazz had survived the storm? Had Cobby or Sharo noticed Dancer and Bingo's disappearance from the pasture? My buds of hope burst into gaudy bloom. Even if I could not escape the inevitable, I could at least attempt to delay it.

The rising sun's red crescent peeped above a crumbling outcropping of rock on the rise above us. Behind it, sheltered from the wind, was a luxuriant tangle of prairie roses where Bingo and I had often seen young rabbits playing hide-and-seek amid its thorny protection. It was, I recalled, no more than an hour's ride from the pond. *An hour.* . . . I decided to try to engage Bazz in conversation.

"Do you intend to travel far?" I called.

Bazz straightened in his saddle and turned cautiously to look at me. "Travel?"

"Yes. I was admiring your smart new suit. A

308

traveling suit . . . for trains and busy big cities."

He pulled up on Dancer and allowed me to ride closer. "You think so? It's not new. I bought it . . . I don't remember . . . some time ago . . ." His words trailed off as he looked down at himself. "Not much use for ranching. . . ."

"Denver perhaps?" I prompted, "or San Francisco?"

His face lighted up. "Yes, San Francisco! Do you think they'd like our songs there?"

He looked at me hopefully, clear-eyed, for a moment remembering who I was. Then the light went out, and his brow creased in puzzlement. "Why am I asking you? A rooster crows a prettier tune than you, Belle."

In desperation I began to sing, hoping my voice would strike the same chord of recognition it had with Quinn, but it served only to agitate him further.

"Stop!" he cried, pressing his ears with his hands, pulling taut the two pairs of reins he held. Unable to make sense of the conflicting signals being given them, the horses sidled nervously. *Could I chance jabbing Bingo with my heels?* "What filthy devil's pact gave you an angel's voice?" he shouted as he lengthened the distance between us. His rage had revived his caution; I dared not test it.

"Bazz, *please listen—*"

"No! No, no, no, no. . . ." As he tossed his head from side to side, the derby toppled from his head, freeing the tattered end of the rag around his head to strike his eyes, his cheeks, his neck. "Enough of your wicked tricks and words!"

I saw him fumble for his gun beneath his jacket. "The pond," I whispered urgently. "It can't be far now."

His hand stilled, then emerged empty. "The pond, of course. Water is the cure for witches."

Deciding silence was safer than plunging into another conversational abyss, I now welcomed the space that again opened up between us. At length, we topped the rise above the pond. I had never seen the sky so blue. The coralline shadings of dawn had faded, leaving it pure as a robin's egg, unsullied by the clouds the afternoon would bring. It was, I thought, the very vault of heaven; a perfect day on which to die. A soft-blowing breeze fingered my hair; a moment later the pond's shimmering surface shivered below us, as if in ecstatic gratitude for the azure perfection it reflected. How could anything so beautiful cause me harm?

Bazz led us down the gentle slope to the grassy ledge above the water, where he pulled up in consternation. The thick fringe of cattails, their smooth, green tubes now ripened to coffee brown, barred easy access to the little dock Cobby and Quinn had buit so many years ago. He began to back Dancer out of the narrow, level passage, paying out Bingo's reins in the process. Threatened both by Dancer's hindquarters crowding her from the front and the short but steep drop-off on her right, Bingo scrambled up the slope to gain turning space, then plunged down and around the willow at the shallow end of the pond. The loosened reins, pulled from Bazz's hand, danced after us, accompanied by his rasping shout of rage. Sunlight glinted off the barrel of the little gun he pulled from beneath his coat.

My elation was short-lived. Hearing a shot, I instinctively bent low, my cheek brushing Bingo's wiry mane. A second bullet tunneled into her outstretched neck, a scarlet gash on white. I felt Bingo's stride falter. She crumpled beneath me, trapping me between her heaving sides and the ground. I cried out, more in frustration than pain, falling silent as Dancer's hoofbeats slowed, then stopped, only inches from my prickling scalp.

"Water would have been better." Bazz's voice was murmurous with regret. I closed my eyes.

"Sere-e-e-na!"

My name, bellowed from above, sounded like a war cry. Hoofbeats, thunderously approaching, trembled the ground beneath me.

I could see very little. My legs were crushed by Bingo's weight, and my tied arms afforded me no leverage. I managed, however, to turn my head by sliding my face along the smooth, slick grass. I became aware of Dancer moving off in front of me, his long chestnut legs curving around the end of the pond to stand beneath the willow that had so often sheltered Bingo and me. A moment later, I heard Quinn's voice.

"Serena." I had never heard my name said so tenderly. "Thank God you're alive."

"Bazz. . . ." I gasped.

"I see him. He's not going anywhere; I can promise you that."

"But he has a gun—"

My warning came too late. Before Quinn had time to reach for his own gun, a shot rang out. Bucket snorted, reared, and plunged away as Quinn toppled from his saddle, clutching his leg. Bazz emerged on Dancer from under the willow to stare down at us. He aimed his little gun at my head. I stared back defiantly.

Without looking at Quinn, he ordered him to throw his revolver into the pond. "This little beauty of mine belonged to my mama," he said as Quinn's big Colt arched up and into the water. "Our paw bought it for her." He laughed at the irony of it. "She taught me how to load it and clean it . . . used to take me out to the trash dump to practice. That was after you tried to drown me, Quinn. She said a gentleman was obliged to protect himself from varmints. I started out plinking cans and bottles; moved up to picking off rats. Human varmints are easier targets . . . especially when they can't run."

I felt Quinn lift himself up slowly beside me. Bucket, alerted by his groan, gave a high, excited whinny. Hearing it, something began to slide up out of my memory . . . something from another day at the pond, with Quinn.

"Ah, ah, ah," Bazz cautioned, transferring his aim to Quinn's dark, shaggy head. " 'Ladies first,' Mama always told me, but in this case . . ."

The memory snapped into focus. "Call Bucket," I whispered.

Bazz rambled on, savoring the unfamiliar, seductive taste of power. "Did you know Belle here poisoned my mama, Quinn? Do you think that's something a lady would do? My mama always said . . ."

"Now!" I urged.

I heard Quinn take a deep, ragged breath. *"Bucka-Bucka-Bucket!"*

Behind me, I heard Bucket whinny again, followed by the sound of his hoofbeats. Above me, Dancer lurched forward, and I saw Bazz's mouth fall open, his arms flying up to flail the air, the gun dropping from his hand as the big, black horse rocketed toward him, intent on reaching his master. Quinn told me later that Dancer's reaction was just what one would expect of a well-trained peg pony: faced with another animal cutting directly in front of him, and expectting the throw of a lariat from his rider, Dancer stopped in his tracks and squatted back on his haunches. Bazz, shaken loose from his insecure seat, catapulted over his head and into the pond.

Taking swift advantage of what he anticipated as merely a delay in Bazz's pursuit of his murderous

312

intent, Quinn dragged himself, one hand clutching his bleeding wound, toward the little pearl-handled gun. By the time he returned to my side, the splashing in the pond had become frantic, and we soon realized that despite the shallowness of the water where Bazz had landed, his fear of it had overridden what little reason remained to him.

"For God's sake, man," Quinn yelled, "you're no more than waist deep!"

"Try to stand up, Bazz!" I called.

It was too late. He was beyond hearing or thinking. We listened helplessly as he thrashed his way into deeper water, his cries growing ever weaker.

"Mama!" He sounded like a lost child. "Oh, Mama. . . ." And then there was silence.

Quinn pulled himself nearer to me. I felt his shaking fingers fumble with the thong on my wrists. "I meant him no harm," I heard him mutter, "I was only trying to teach him to swim . . . he was my *brother*. . . ."

At first, intent on freeing my wrists, I could make no sense of what he was saying, but then, after the thong fell away, I recalled Lottie Wohlfort's accusations.

"It wasn't your fault, Quinn," I said, rubbing my painfully cramped fingers. "His mother saw you only as a rival for Morning Star . . . in the end, it was her love that killed him, not the hate she imagined in your heart."

He groaned. "I swear, S'rena, with all that's happened, if I hadn't worked so hard to keep Morning Star, it'd sure be easy to turn my back on it."

"You?" I scoffed. "You've never given up on anything in your life, Quinn Cooper!"

"You think so? Well, maybe you're right at that." His tone lightened. "Fer instance, I got no intention of givin' up on *you*, 'spite of us bein' in a fix I don't

313

see no easy way of gettin' ourselves out of." His fingers gently rubbed my cheeks. "I bet your pretty face ain't been this dirty since you was a tadpole."

I tried to smile in return, but new worries rushed in to fill the place vacated by Bazz's drowning.

"Your leg?" I asked, looking anxiously up into Quinn's dark eyes.

He grinned. "Nothin' the sawbones in town and a jolt of whiskey can't fix."

"And Bingo?"

He hesitated. His eyes gazed down into mine, tender as flowers. "From the look of it, her leg's broke, S'rena."

"Nonsense!" I protested. "She's as sure-footed as a mountain goat . . . besides, the bullet struck her neck—"

"Taking her attention, most likely. She must have stumbled into a gopher hole."

I stroked Bingo's strong, warm neck, recalling the feel of her collapsing beneath me; her hide felt like satin under my fingers. She whickered softly. "Good girl," I crooned. "Such a good girl."

Quinn struggled to a sitting position and reached over to untie the thong securing my ankle to the stirrup. "Can't do much about the other one until—" He broke off. "Sharo'll be along soon," he said. "Fawn was some worried about you, S'rena. Roused me out in the middle of the night. I went on up to the house, and when I saw Bazz's room . . . That's when I rousted Sharo. We wondered if you'd gone off on Bingo, but when we found Dancer gone, too . . ." He shook his head. "I thought morning'd never come. Sharo spied your tracks first—he's off followin' 'em—but this time *I* had a hunch. Seein' that room Bazz was living in, his dead mama's room . . . it didn't seem natural, know what I mean?"

I nodded. I did indeed.

"And then I got this queer feelin' he'd end up here at the pond, where everything started going wrong all those years ago. . . ." He paused; the rest could wait. "Sharo'll be along soon," he repeated.

I looked up at the sky. As I watched, little puffs of white slowly unfurled first here, then there, into cottony sails adrift on a wide blue sea, harbingers of an afternoon I thought I would never live to see. Quinn eased down beside me. Shoulders touching, our hands intertwined, we waited in silence together.

EPILOGUE

Quinn's leg healed rapidly; by August, his limp was barely perceptible. The wounds to my spirit lingered longer.

I was aware of his dark eyes upon me more often than he knew; loving him, I was always aware of his presence. Proud as an Indian one minute, stubborn as a whole team of mules the next, soft as thistledown the moment after, I knew he would never bore me. But every time I looked in the mirror my fears revived.

"Hell's roarings, woman!" he growled at me one day, impatient of pussyfooting. "Are you goin' to make me wait 'til your hair turns all the way back to silver? That henna got poured over your head, not into your heart—why, you're the same sweet Serena you always was, always will be."

But my doubts continued to fester, yielding neither to reason nor his embraces. Even Fawn's expressions of marital bliss left me unmoved for all the tears of joy I had shed when Quinn gravely placed her little hand in Sharo's. Our relationship seemed to have reached a dead center. Then Rita returned.

Her arrival that late-August morning was observed by no one. She stolidly set about taking up residence, and by the time Quinn plodded up from the corrals to wash up for supper, her hens were scratching in the dooryard. As he strode in grim-faced to the quarters he had relinquished to me, his arms heaped with his belongings, I was forced to admit the scales of fate had finally been tipped, albeit by a most unlikely hand.

Shortly after daybreak the next day, Quinn took the wagon to town, arriving back with it full of supplies and a preacher on the seat beside him. He announced it wasn't fitting for a maiden lady to be sharing space with a roughneck like him, and he aimed to do the right thing.

"Besides," he added later, to the delight of the hands who had gathered to wish us well, "it'll be a whole lot cheaper havin' her as a wife than payin' a housekeeper's wages."

My wedding bouquet was a bunch of prairie flowers; my wedding night . . . I never dreamed wildness could be so sweet.

The stone mansion has been razed. The new, smaller, cozier house being built for us from its weathered blocks is almost finished. Belle's garden was burned and plowed under, and the pathetic bones unearthed there were buried along with Belle and Bazz in the graveyard in the cottonwood grove. Belle's herbal—and Lottie Wohlfort's—have been shelved with Quinn's novels. Perhaps, in time, I will put in a herb garden of my own.

I don't visit the pond much these days, except to put a bunch of tender grasses on Bingo's grave under the willow. I'm riding Dancer now. He's not as playful as dear Bingo, but Cobby says he's the cleverest cow pony he ever saw—except for his own sorrel, of course. Fawn confided that seeing me work him puts Sharo's nose quite out of joint.

What I most want to tell you happened early this

summer, after the round-up of the calves born during the preceding winter. Fawn and I were expecting babies of our own. I suspected, from the sly, speculative looks given our swelling bellies by the hands, that bets were being laid in the bunkhouse, but I did not share my suspicion with Quinn, whose awestruck view of impending fatherhood allowed little room for levity.

It had been a good year. The Appaloosas shipped to Virginia had generated additional orders; the money set aside for Bazz's holdings, having reverted to Quinn, allowed him to chart the future of the ranch along the lines of quality he had spoken of with a fervor I had come to share.

But the mild winters of recent years had encouraged an influx of ignorant newcomers, and in the cold winters that Sharo saw coming, the over-grazed prairie could not sustain the swelling herds loosed upon it. Short of "shootin' the dern fools!", which was Cobby's oft-expressed solution, we needed to store up every cent we could against the hard times.

It was very hot that last week in June. I was in my eighth month, with a yen for a fresh-pulled carrot to crunch between my teeth. I looked out from Rita's vegetable patch to see a pair of scrawny calves bawling near the old wooden trough. I could hear their cries above the creaking of the windmill's rusty vanes; I could see something greenly iridescent glisten across the surface of the dark, stagnant water.

They were ugly cut-back scrubs, canning quality at best, but they were alone, either lost or motherless, and as I felt my unborn baby shift within me I was moved to foolish tears by their thirsty plight.

How long had it been since anyone thought to clean out that slimy old horror? Not since I'd come to Morning Star. Cradling my belly in my hands, I made my way down to the barn as fast as I could waddle, and demanded the kit Ross Cooper had kept for cleaning the trough.

Quinn, leaning against an Appaloosa none to happy about his inspection of its hoof, looked up at me. "What the hell you talkin' about, woman?" The horse slyly bent its neck to nip him. "Ouch! Can't you see I'm busy?"

"That can wait, Quinn!" I said sternly.

Cobby, who, from the excessive care with which he treated Fawn and me, seemed to think our wombs harbored nitroglycerine, darted forward to take the horse from Quinn. "The kit's stored above the feed bins. Painted red. Can't miss it."

"There are calves out there about to die of thirst! I understand your father kept that old trough to remind him of his beginnings. Cleaning it was supposed to help keep him humble—something you haven't been much of lately."

He glared at me. "Hell's roarings, S'rena!"

I ran my hands over my belly and looked up at him through my lashes.

"Oh, shoot. . . ."

It didn't take long. He cleaned out the clogged intake, then knocked out the two plugs with the mallet he found in the box, and as the stinking water ran out, I scrubbed the slimed sides as best I could. For all its neglect, the wood seemed sound. I hitched the hem of my skirt into my waist band, climbed in, and began to scour the bottom.

"Godalmighty! You oughtn't be doin' that!"

"Do me good. Besides, considering the heat this week, I wouldn't mind if the baby came a little sooner than expected."

Just then the rag I was using caught on the edge of one of the planks. I tugged at it, and a two-foot square, nailed together like a lid, edged up above the others. Quinn climbed in beside me and lifted it aside, revealing a dark hole. He reached in, grimacing as he groped through the muck.

"Feels like stone at the bottom," he muttered. "Yep, a slab of stone. . . ."

Quinn began feeling for a handhold, and all at once I knew. Belle had said Ross Cooper asked her where her heart was: *Is it hidden in stone, like my gold?* And Quinn's gold ring. *A token of what'd be mine if I kept my wits about me.*

Quinn lifted up the slab, which was thinner than expected, and tossed it outside. Heads jostling, we peered down into the revealed cavity. One thing was for sure, there were too many gold bars down there for us to carry in one trip.

I plunked down on my bottom, heedless of the water pumping in. Quinn's face was streaked with slime. I lifted a corner of my wet skirt to clean it. "Like your father said, my darling, it does a man good to be reminded of his beginnings."

The calves rolled anxious eyes at us over the edge of the trough, bewildered by our presence there. "It'll be your turn soon," I promised. I closed my eyes and raised my face to the June sun. *June. . . .*

I glanced up at the windmill's blades rotating gently, rustily, above me. Squinting against the glare, my eyes traced an imaginary line back from the tail vane to where the arc of great stone pillars once stood. "Quinn? What's the date today?"

"Hmm-mmmm-mm?" he murmured, happily lost in heaving our insurance against hard times out into the dust.

"Doesn't matter, dear heart . . . just wondering."

For the first time in many years, June was bringing good things to Morning Star. I shook back my silver hair, worn loose as he liked it, and smiled. What did the date matter indeed?